AN UNOFFICIAL GRAPHIC NOVEL
FOR MINECRAFTERS

The ENDER EYE PROPHECY

CARA J. STEVENS
ART BY DAVID NORGREN
AND ELIAS NORGREN

Sky Pony Press
New York

This book is not authorized or sponsored by Microsoft Corporation, Mojang AB, Notch Development AB, or Scholastic Corporation, or any other person or entity owning or controlling rights in the Minecraft name, trademark, or copyrights.

Copyright © 2016 by Hollan Publishing, Inc.

All rights reserved. No part of this book may be reproduced in any manner without the express written consent of the publisher, except in the case of brief excerpts in critical reviews or articles. All inquiries should be addressed to Sky Pony Press, 307 West 36th Street, 11th Floor, New York, NY 10018.

Sky Pony Press books may be purchased in bulk at special discounts for sales promotion, corporate gifts, fund-raising, or educational purposes. Special editions can also be created to specifications. For details, contact the Special Sales Department, Sky Pony Press, 307 West 36th Street, 11th Floor, New York, NY 10018 or info@skyhorsepublishing.com.

Sky Pony® is a registered trademark of Skyhorse Publishing, Inc.®, a Delaware corporation.

Visit our website at www.skyponypress.com.

10 9 8 7 6 5 4 3 2 1

Library of Congress Cataloging-in-Publication Data is available on file.

Special thanks to Cara J. Stevens, David Norgren, and Elias Norgren.

Cover design by Brian Peterson
Cover illustration credit Bethany Straker

Print ISBN: 978-1-5107-1483-0
Ebook ISBN: 978-1-5107-1485-4

Printed in the United States of America

Editor: Rachel Stark
Designer and Production Manager: Joshua Barnaby

INTRODUCTION

If you have played Minecraft, then you know all about Minecraft worlds. They're made of blocks you can mine: coal, dirt, and sand. In the game, you'll find many different creatures, lands, and villages inhabited by strange villagers with bald heads. The villagers who live there have their own special, magical worlds that are protected by a string of border worlds to stop outsiders from finding them.

When we last left off on the small border world of Xenos, Phoenix was looking for a way to safely return home to her parents and brother. Unfortunately, the dangers she and T.H. had faced when curing the zombie monks still loomed large. What's more, the village in which Phoenix grew up still refused to allow her, a miner, inside its walls.

Our story resumes as T.H. and Phoenix are getting restless, waiting for their next adventure to begin.

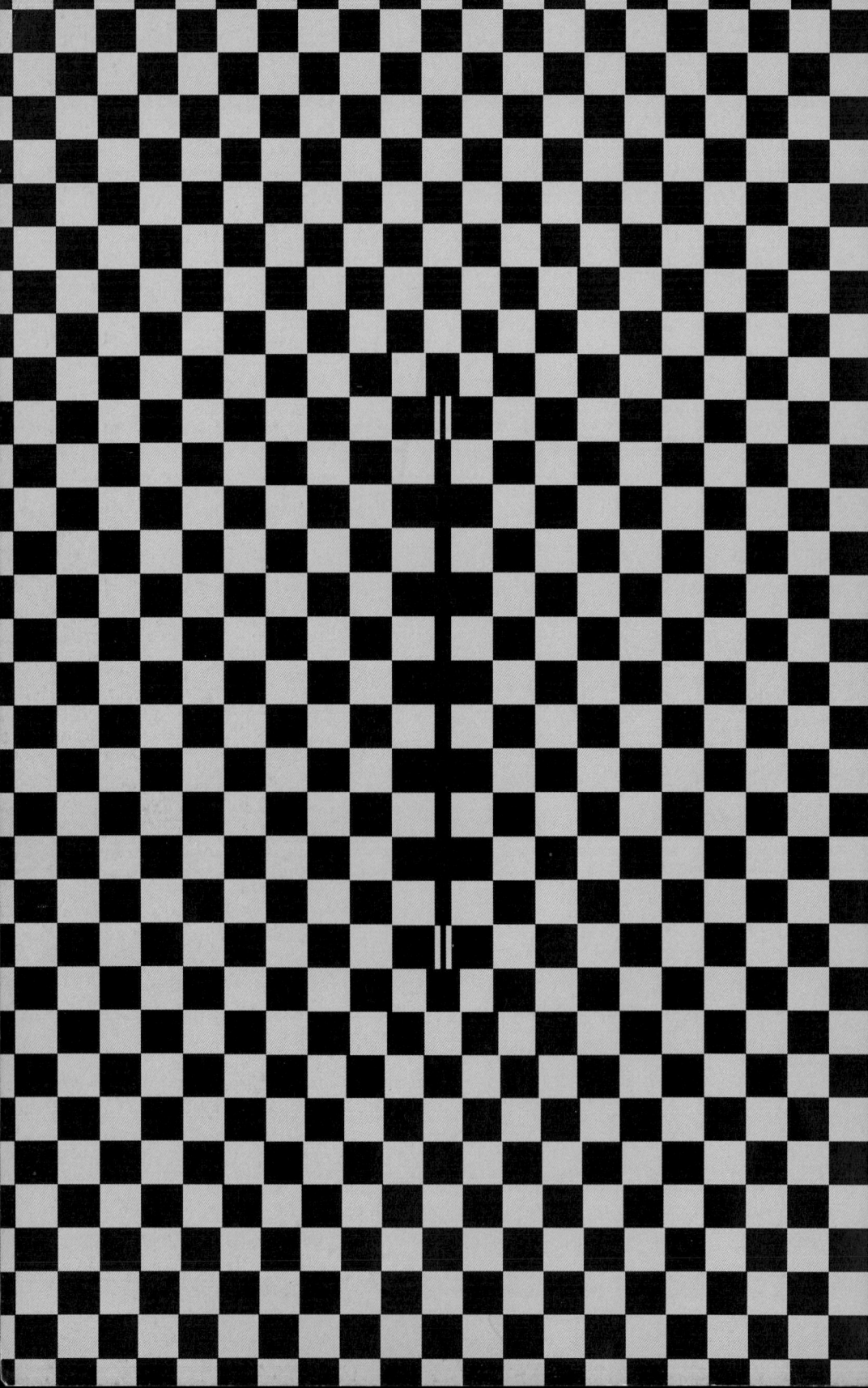

CHAPTER 1

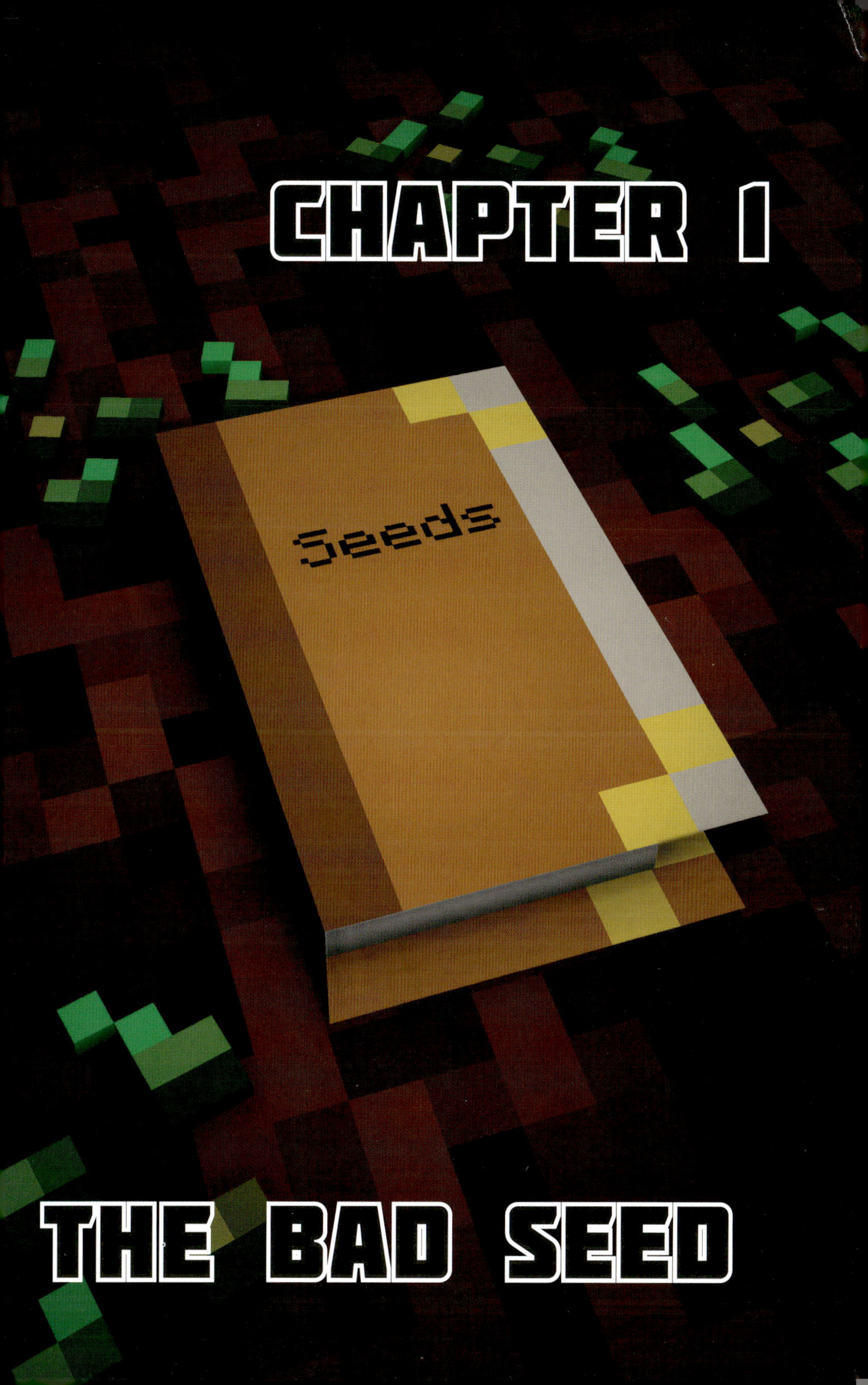
Seeds

THE BAD SEED

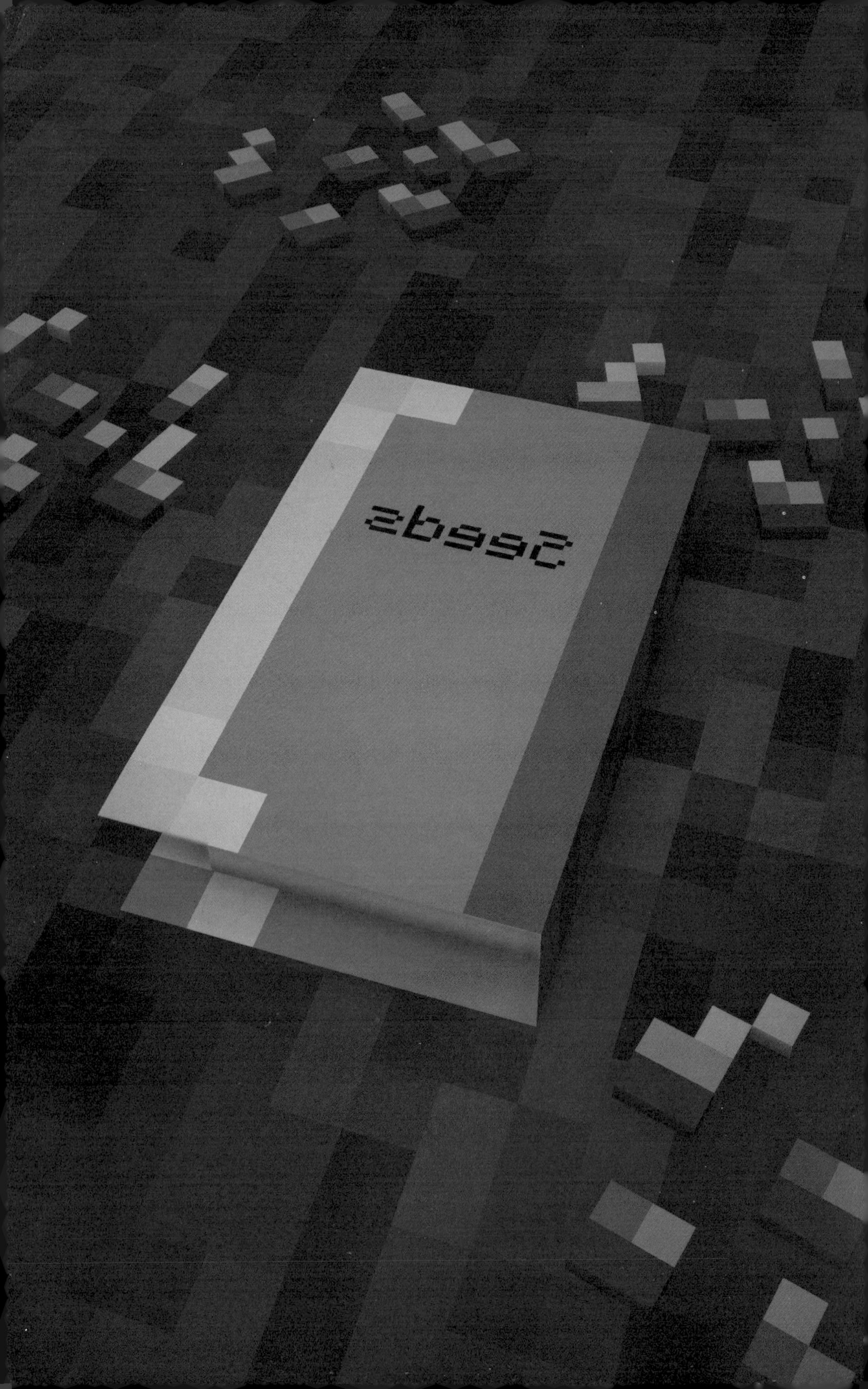
Seeds

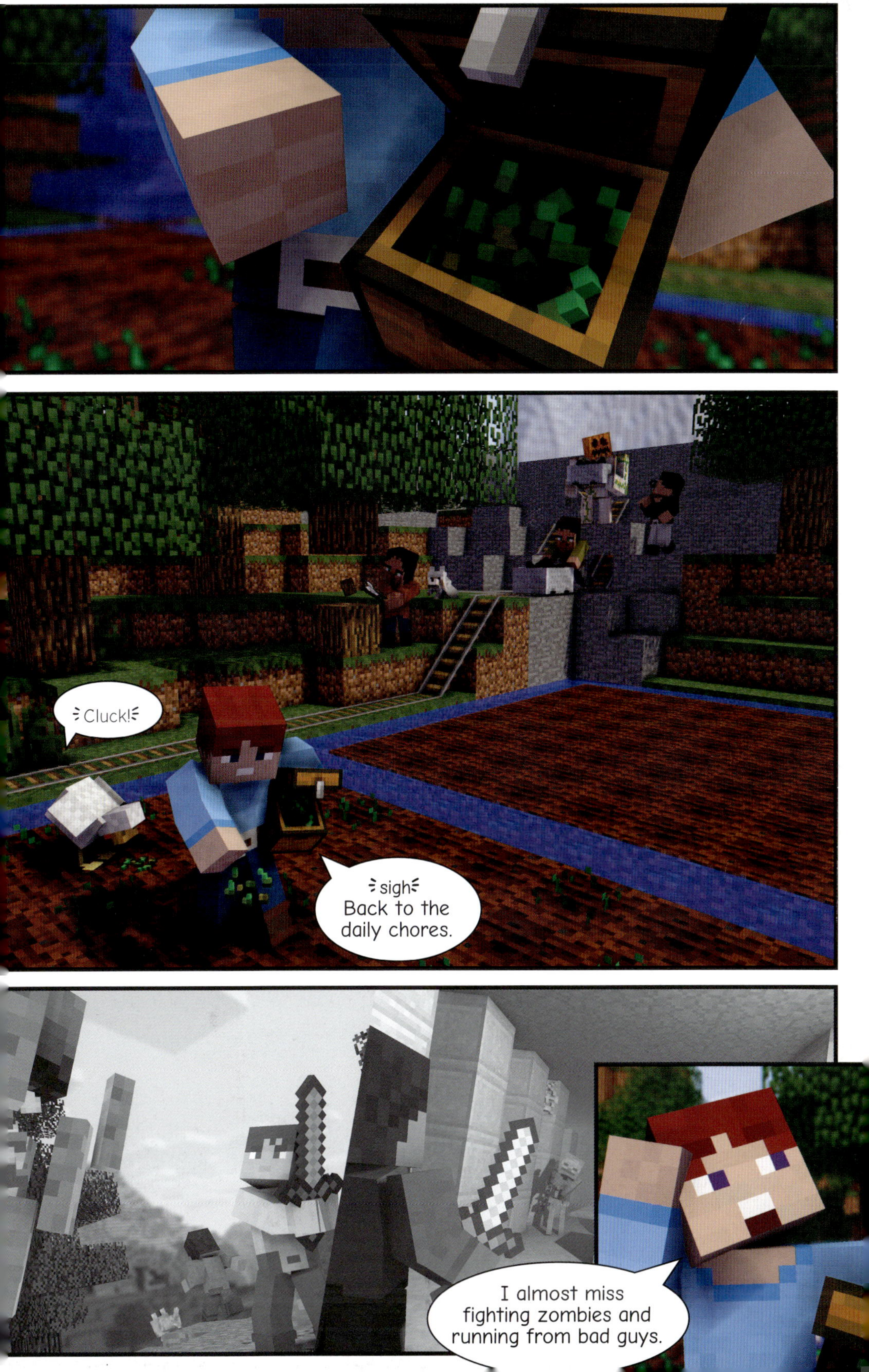
Cluck!
sigh
Back to the daily chores.
I almost miss fighting zombies and running from bad guys.

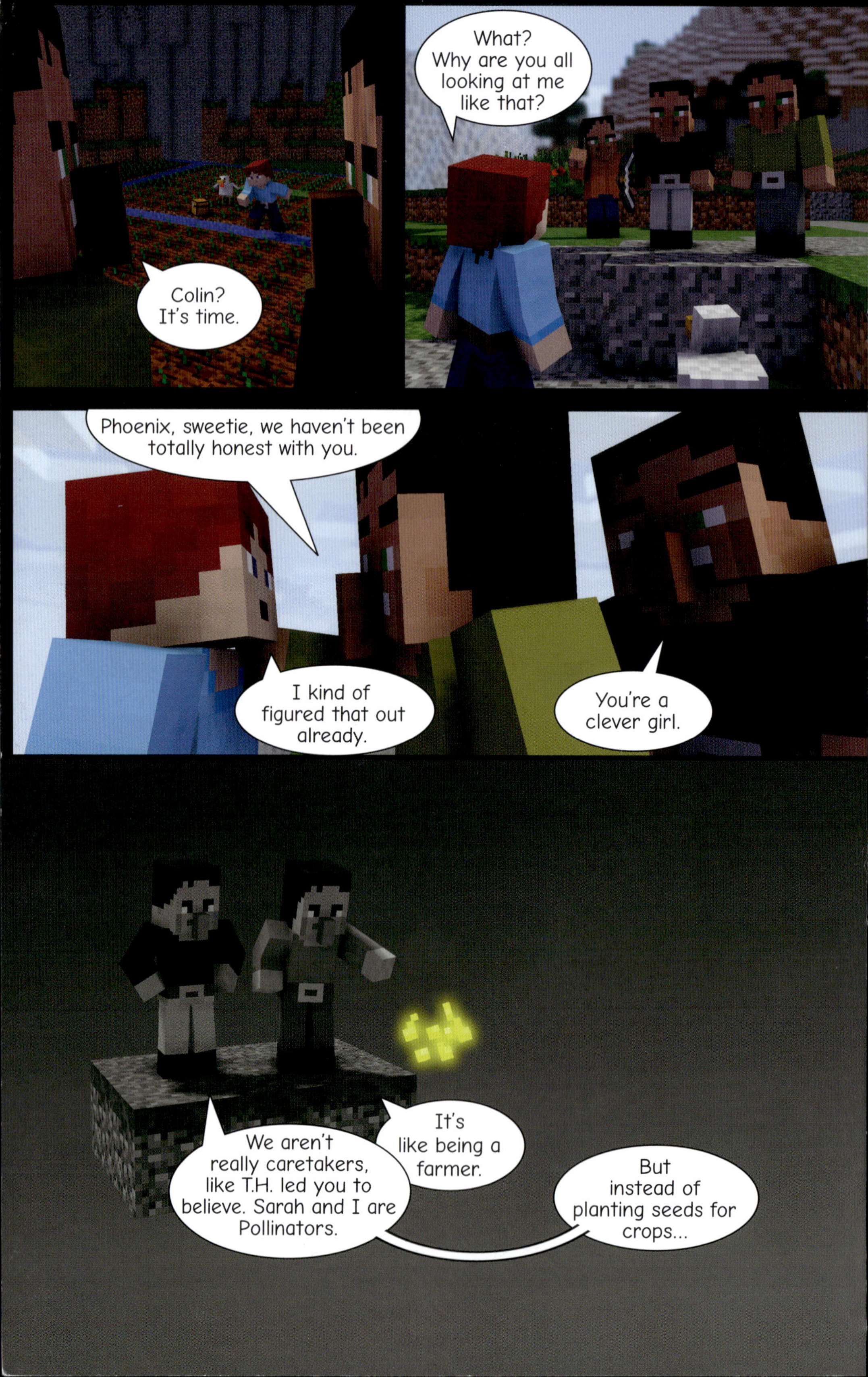
Colin? It's time.
What? Why are you all looking at me like that?
Phoenix, sweetie, we haven't been totally honest with you.
I kind of figured that out already.
You're a clever girl.
We aren't really caretakers, like T.H. led you to believe. Sarah and I are Pollinators.
It's like being a farmer.
But instead of planting seeds for crops...

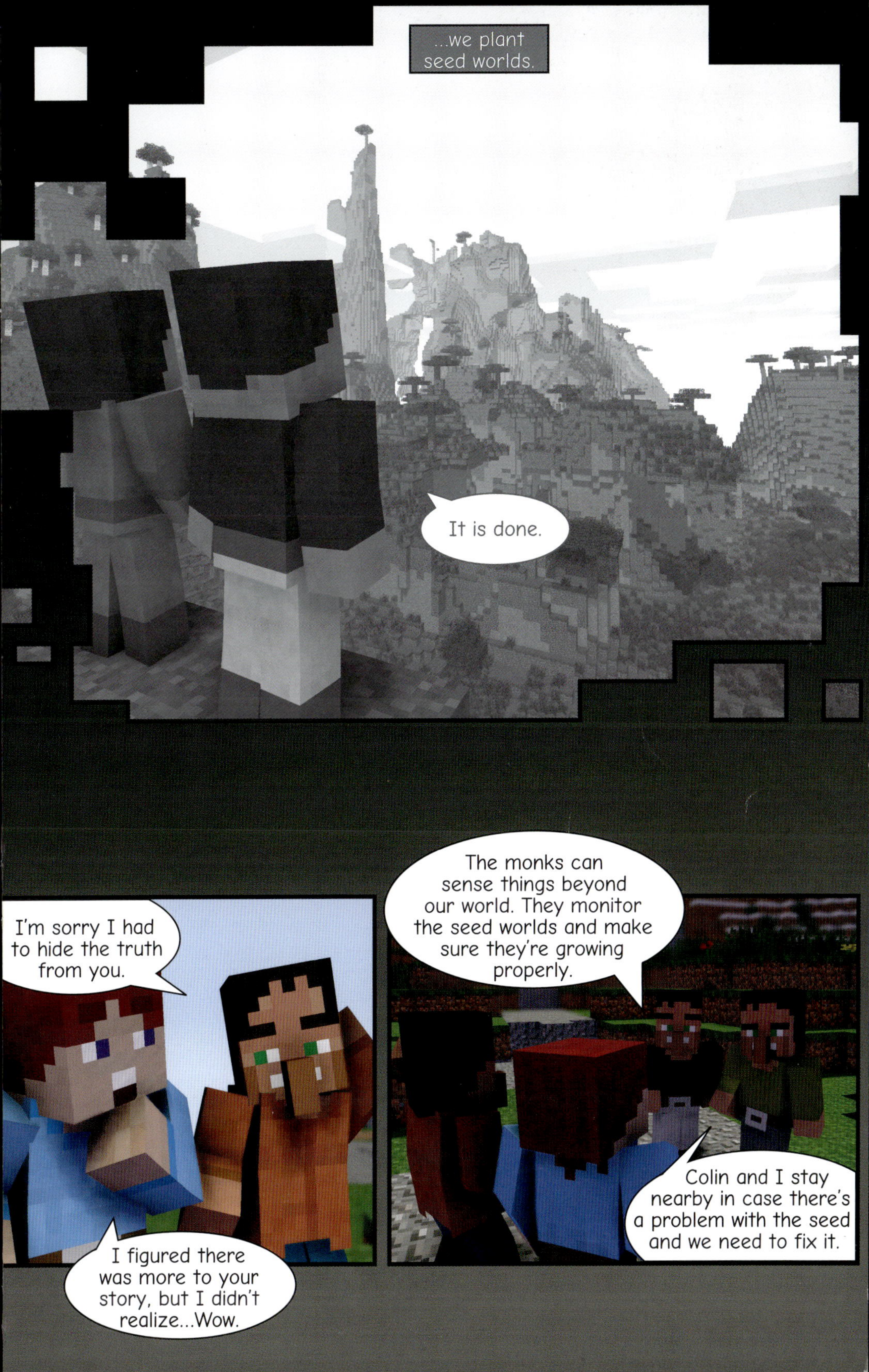
...we plant seed worlds.
It is done.
I'm sorry I had to hide the truth from you.
I figured there was more to your story, but I didn't realize...Wow.
The monks can sense things beyond our world. They monitor the seed worlds and make sure they're growing properly.
Colin and I stay nearby in case there's a problem with the seed and we need to fix it.

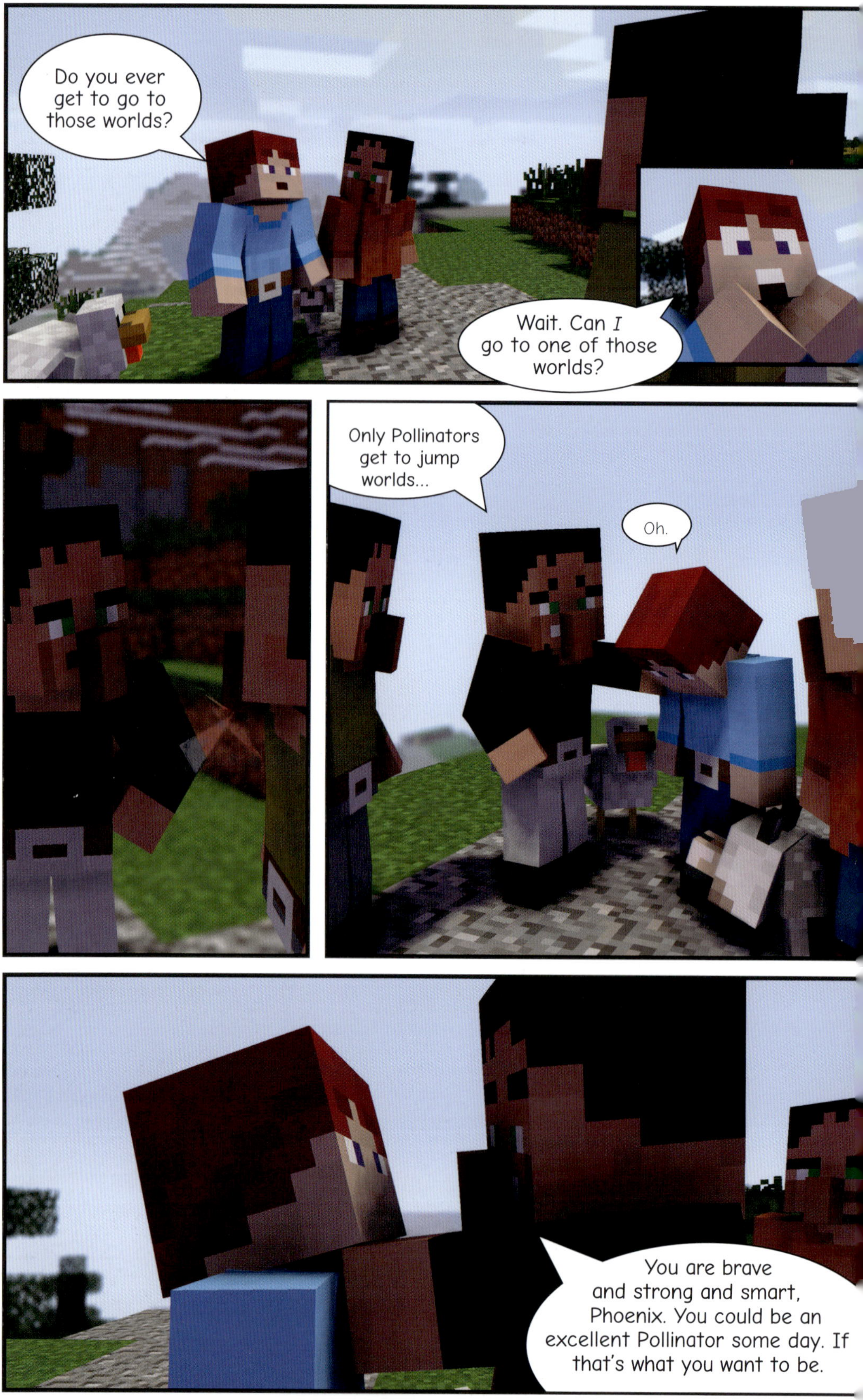
Do you ever get to go to those worlds?
Wait. Can *I* go to one of those worlds?
Only Pollinators get to jump worlds...
Oh.
You are brave and strong and smart, Phoenix. You could be an excellent Pollinator some day. If that's what you want to be.

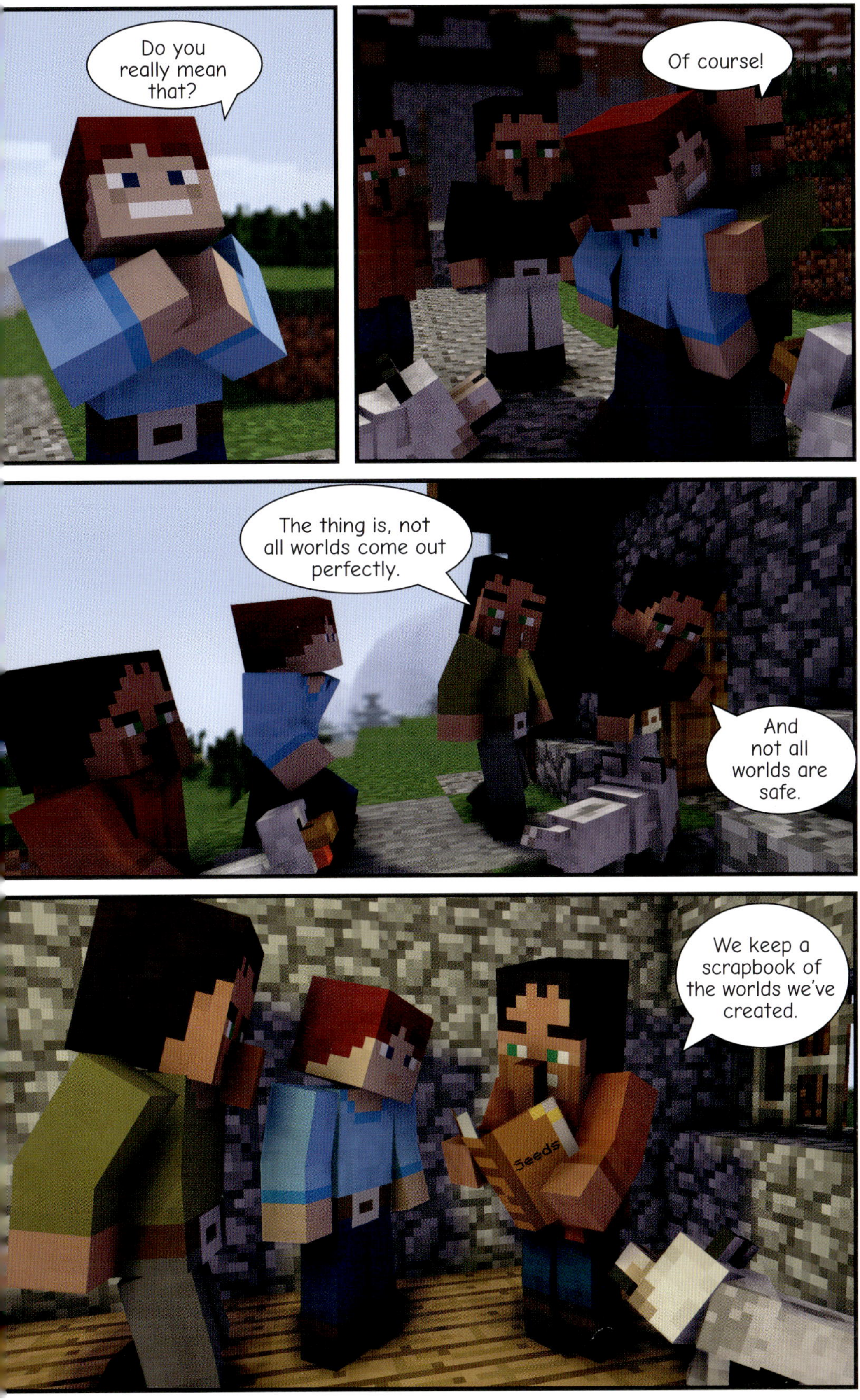
Do you really mean that?
Of course!
The thing is, not all worlds come out perfectly.
And not all worlds are safe.
We keep a scrapbook of the worlds we've created.
Seeds

Some are really neat.

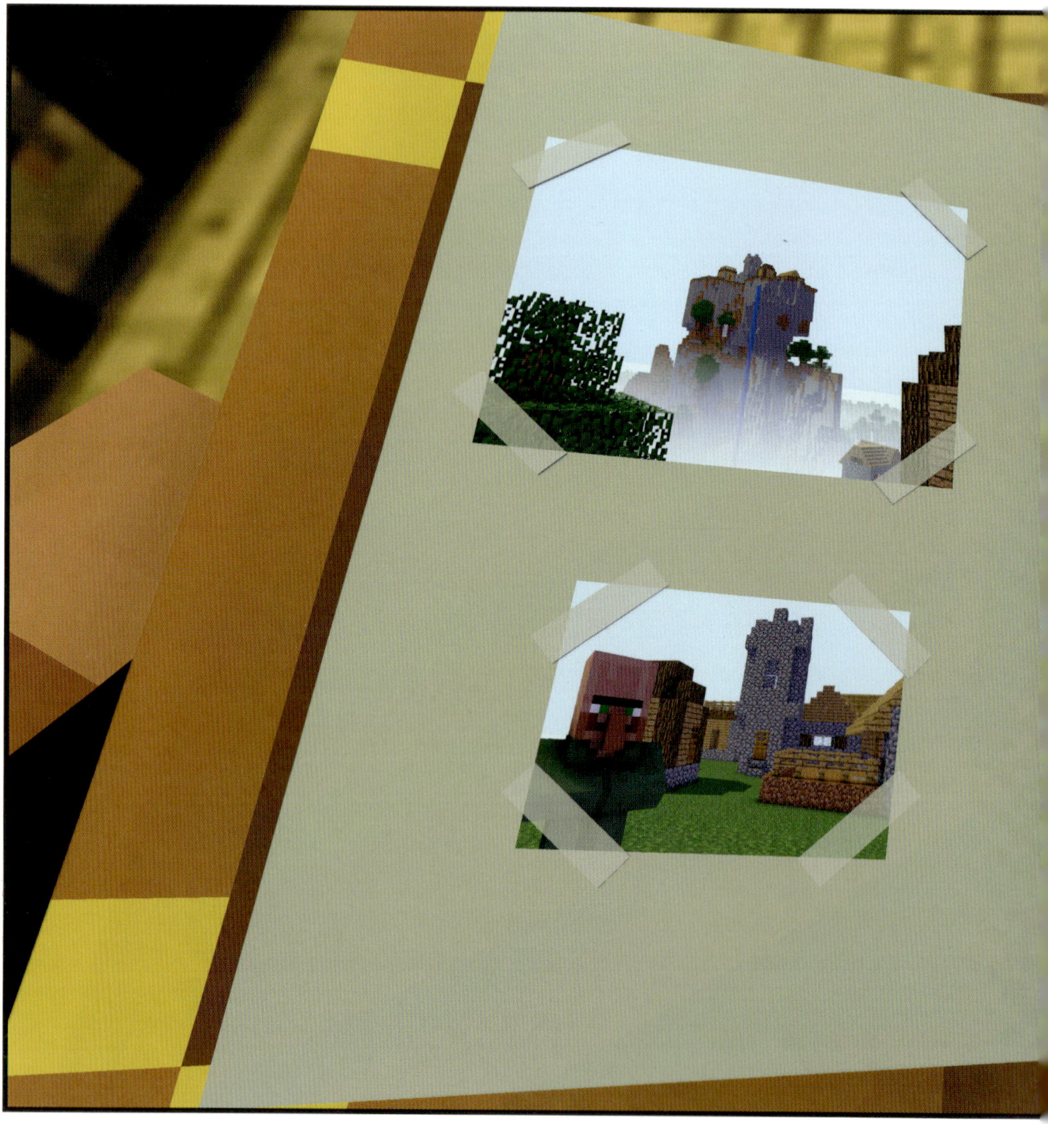

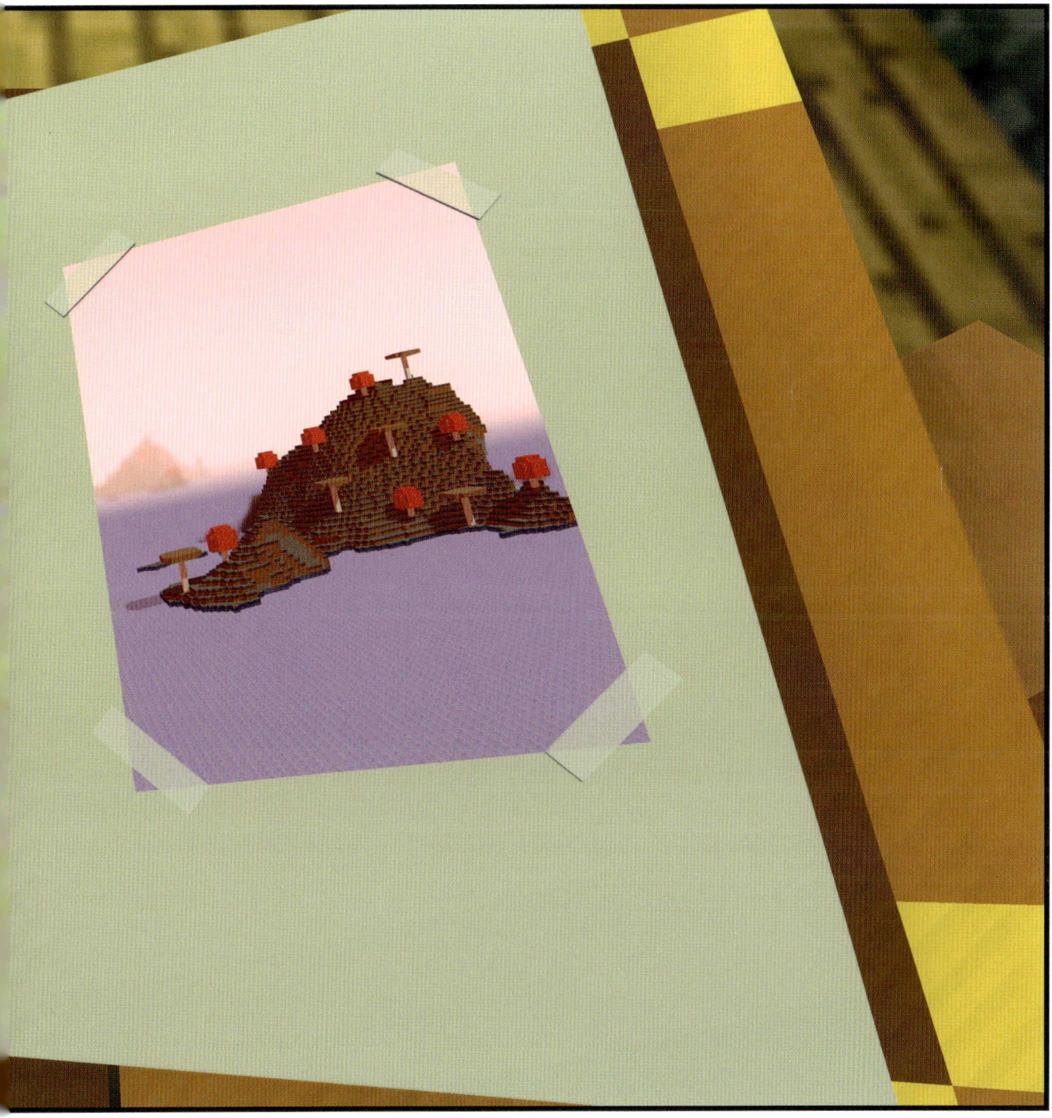

Some are epic fails...

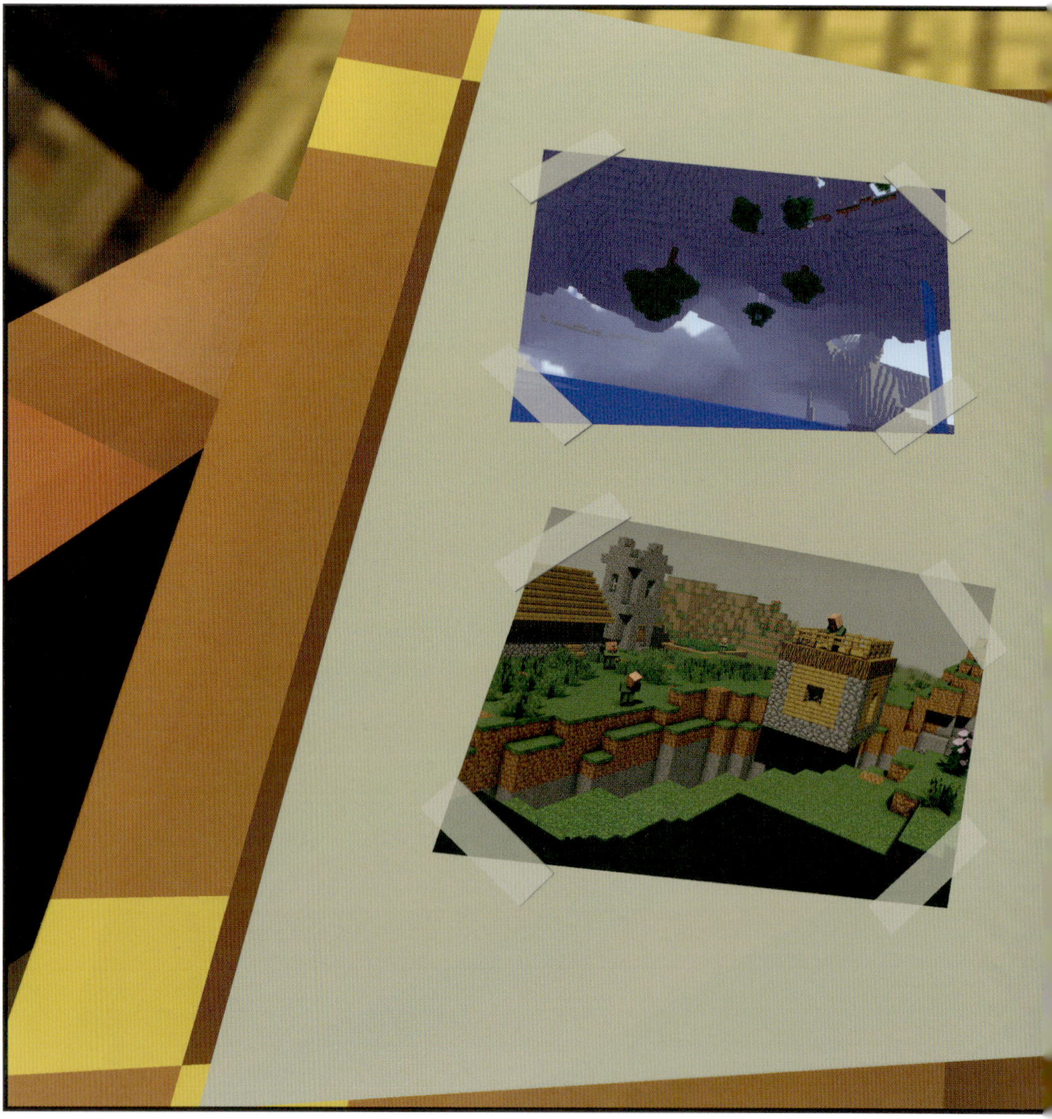

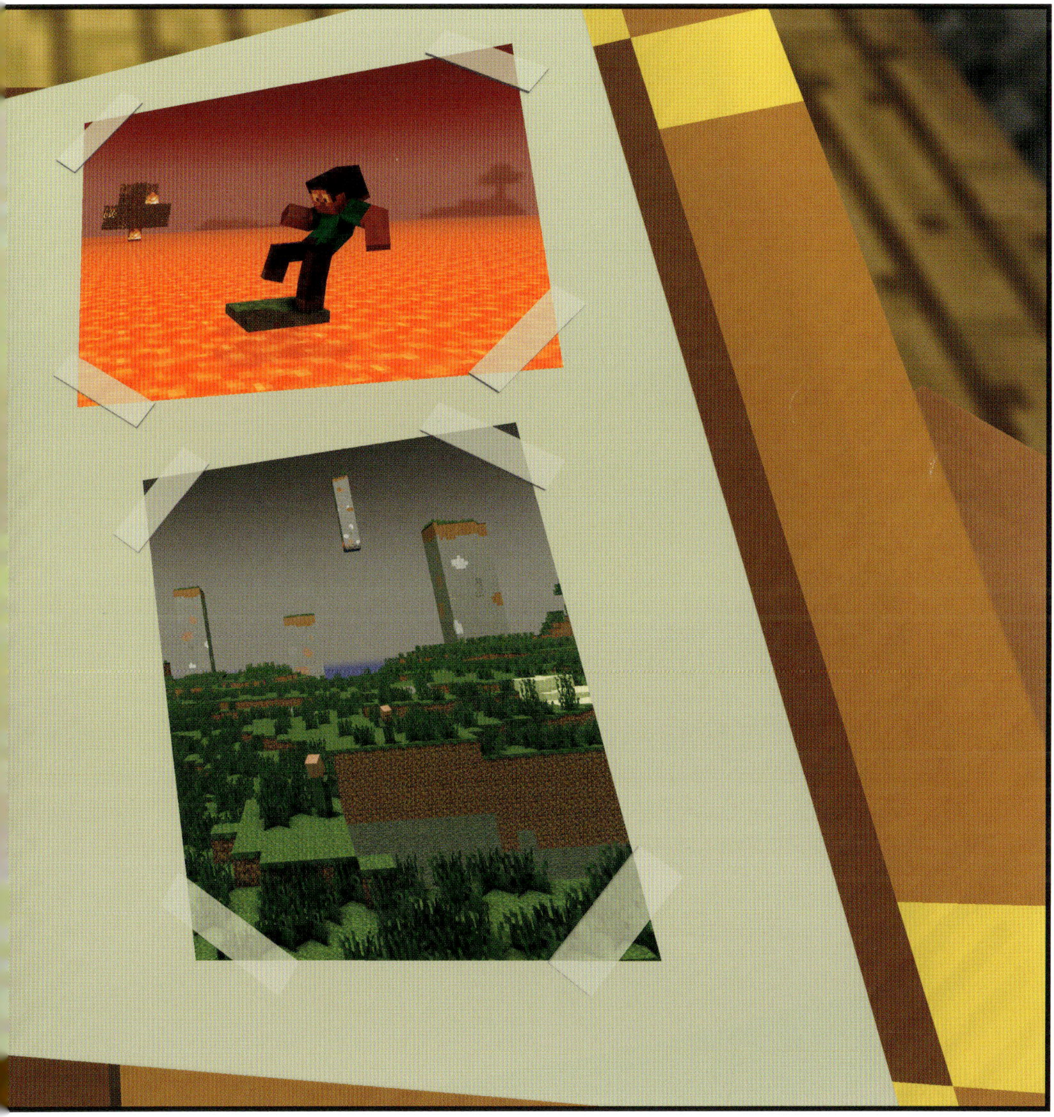

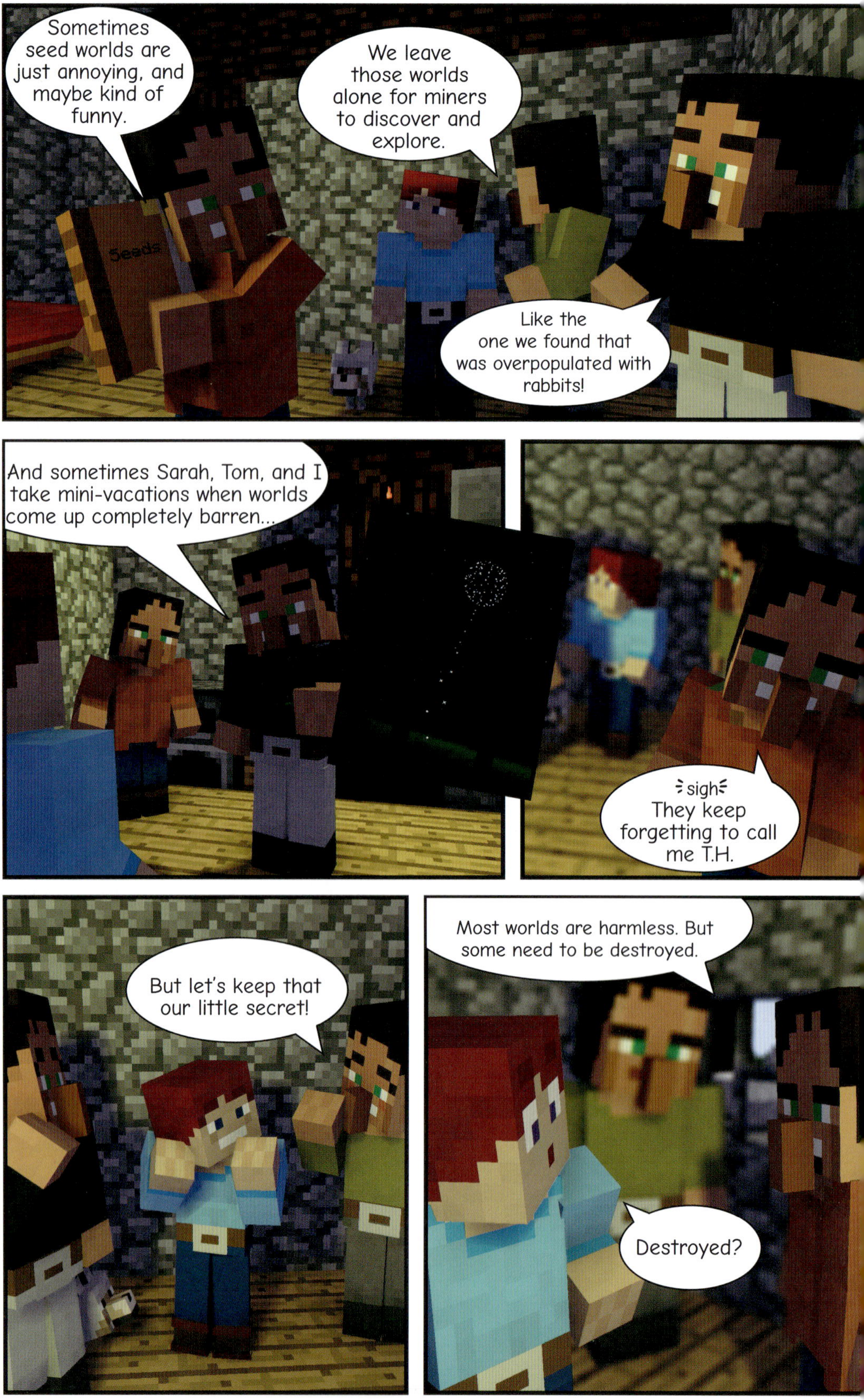
Sometimes seed worlds are just annoying, and maybe kind of funny.
Seeds
We leave those worlds alone for miners to discover and explore.
Like the one we found that was overpopulated with rabbits!
And sometimes Sarah, Tom, and I take mini-vacations when worlds come up completely barren...
sigh
They keep forgetting to call me T.H.
But let's keep that our little secret!
Most worlds are harmless. But some need to be destroyed.
Destroyed?

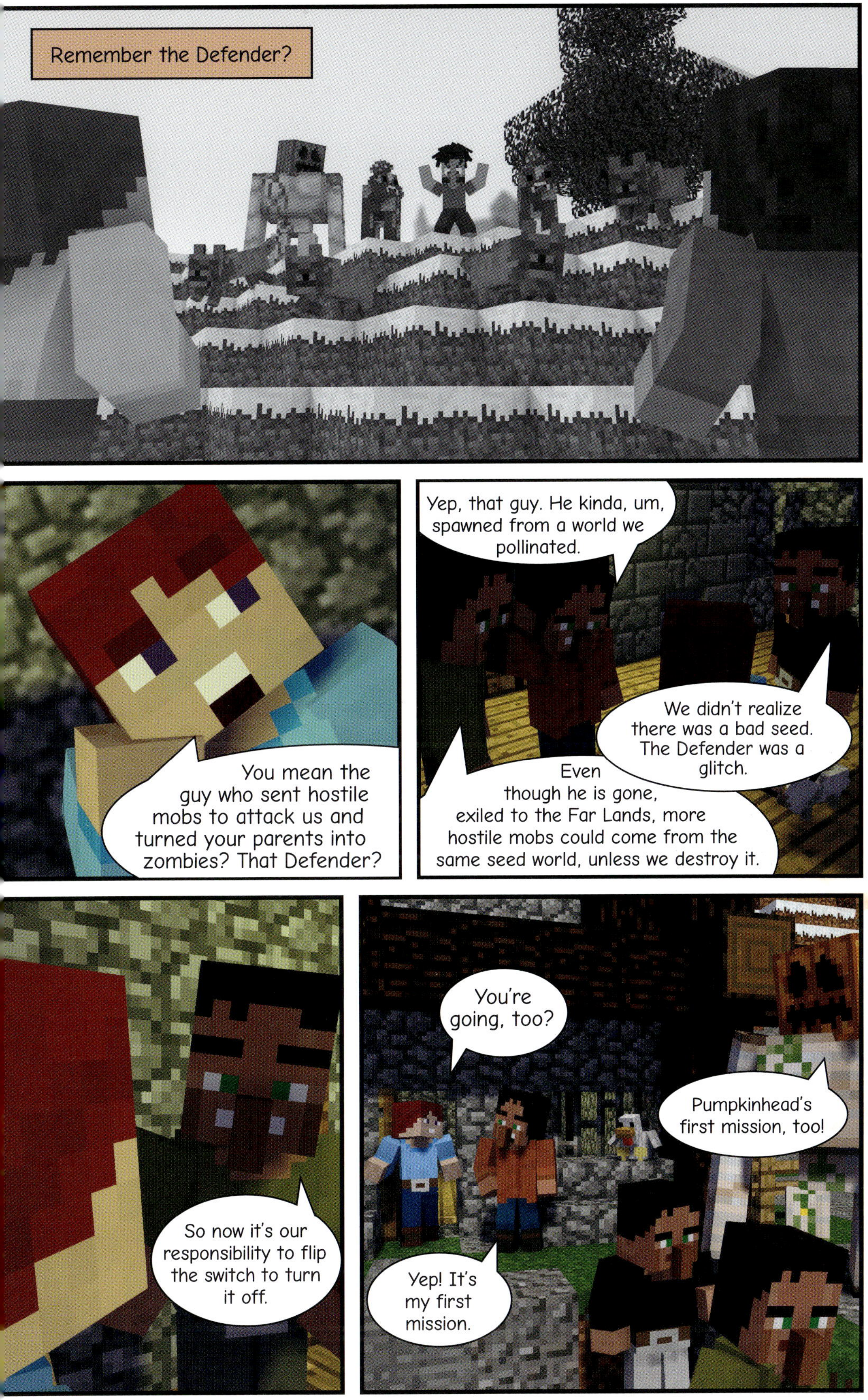
Remember the Defender?
You mean the guy who sent hostile mobs to attack us and turned your parents into zombies? That Defender?
Yep, that guy. He kinda, um, spawned from a world we pollinated.
We didn't realize there was a bad seed. The Defender was a glitch.
Even though he is gone, exiled to the Far Lands, more hostile mobs could come from the same seed world, unless we destroy it.
So now it's our responsibility to flip the switch to turn it off.
You're going, too?
Pumpkinhead's first mission, too!
Yep! It's my first mission.

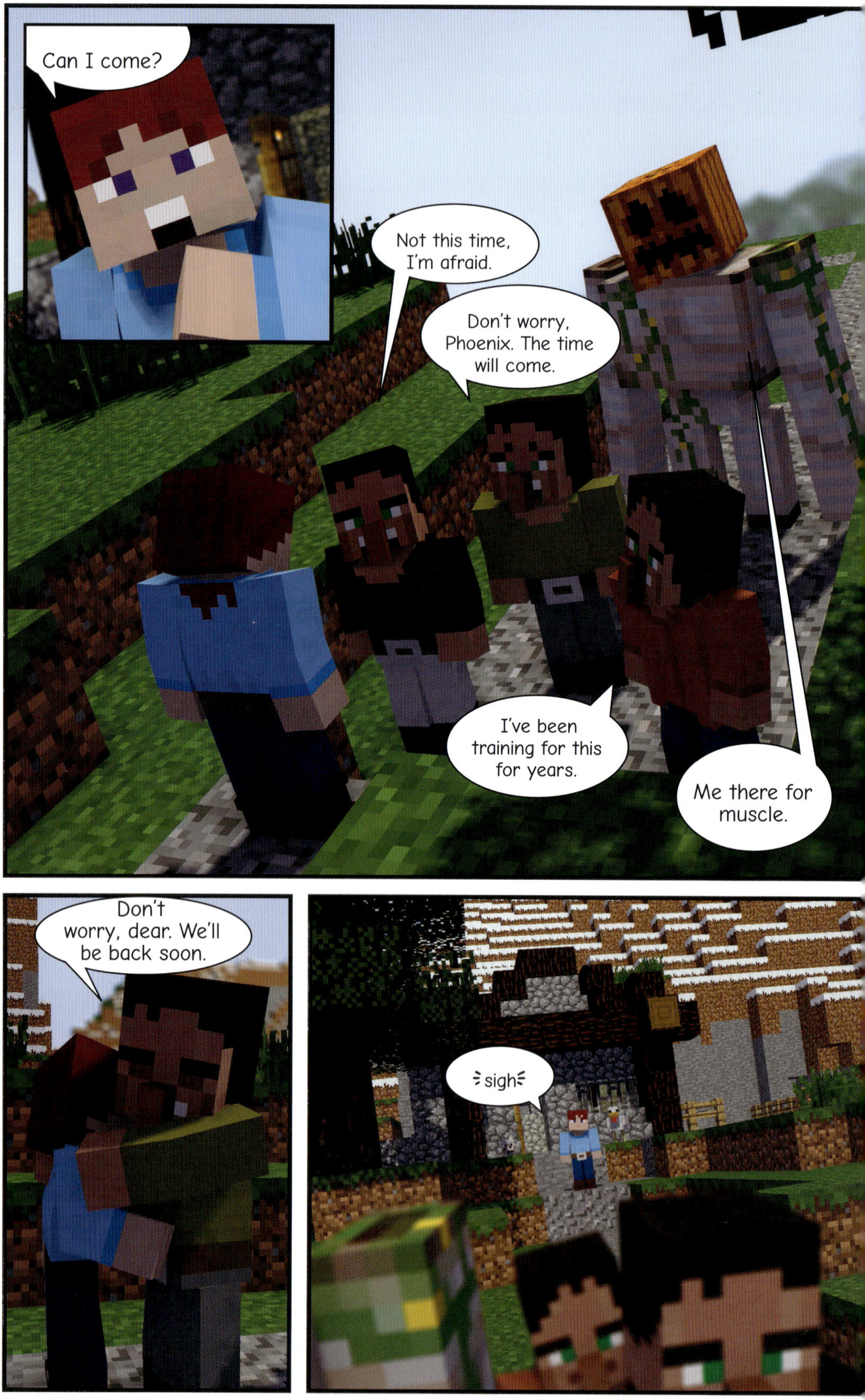
Can I come?
Not this time, I'm afraid.
Don't worry, Phoenix. The time will come.
I've been training for this for years.
Me there for muscle.
Don't worry, dear. We'll be back soon.
sigh

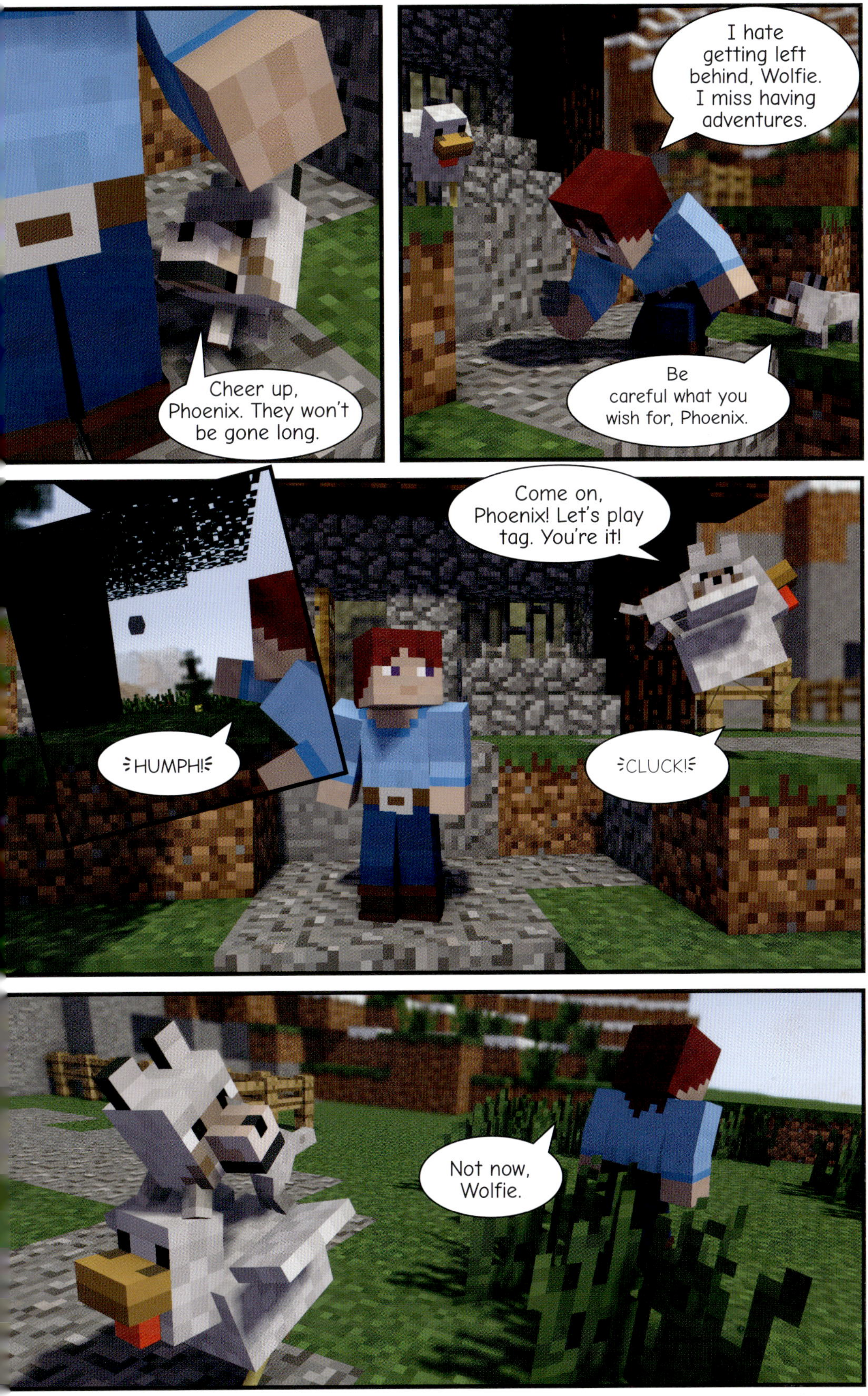
Cheer up, Phoenix. They won't be gone long.
I hate getting left behind, Wolfie. I miss having adventures.
Be careful what you wish for, Phoenix.
HUMPH!
Come on, Phoenix! Let's play tag. You're it!
CLUCK!
Not now, Wolfie.

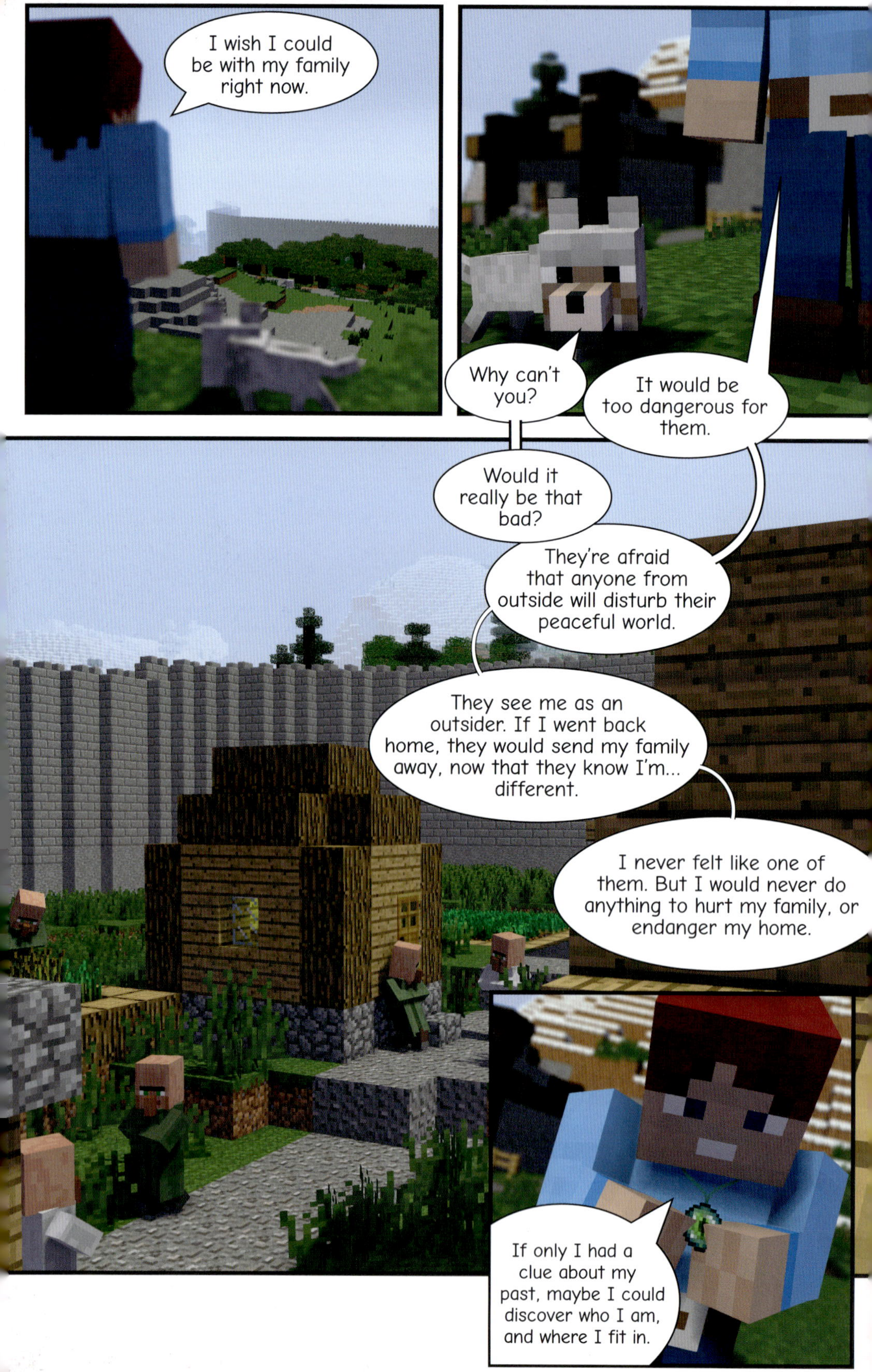
I wish I could be with my family right now.
Why can't you?
It would be too dangerous for them.
Would it really be that bad?
They're afraid that anyone from outside will disturb their peaceful world.
They see me as an outsider. If I went back home, they would send my family away, now that they know I'm... different.
I never felt like one of them. But I would never do anything to hurt my family, or endanger my home.
If only I had a clue about my past, maybe I could discover who I am, and where I fit in.

CHAPTER 2

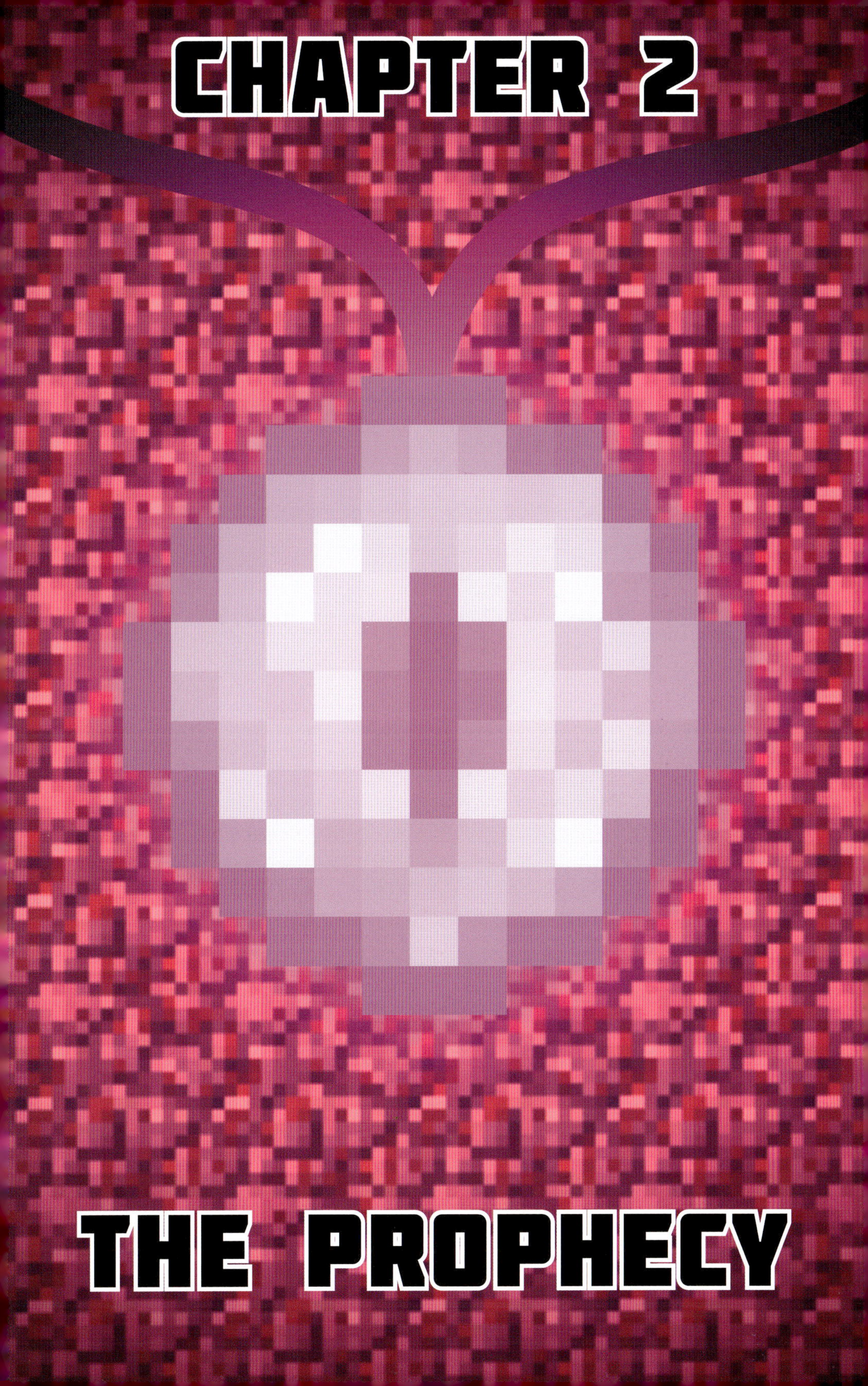

THE PROPHECY

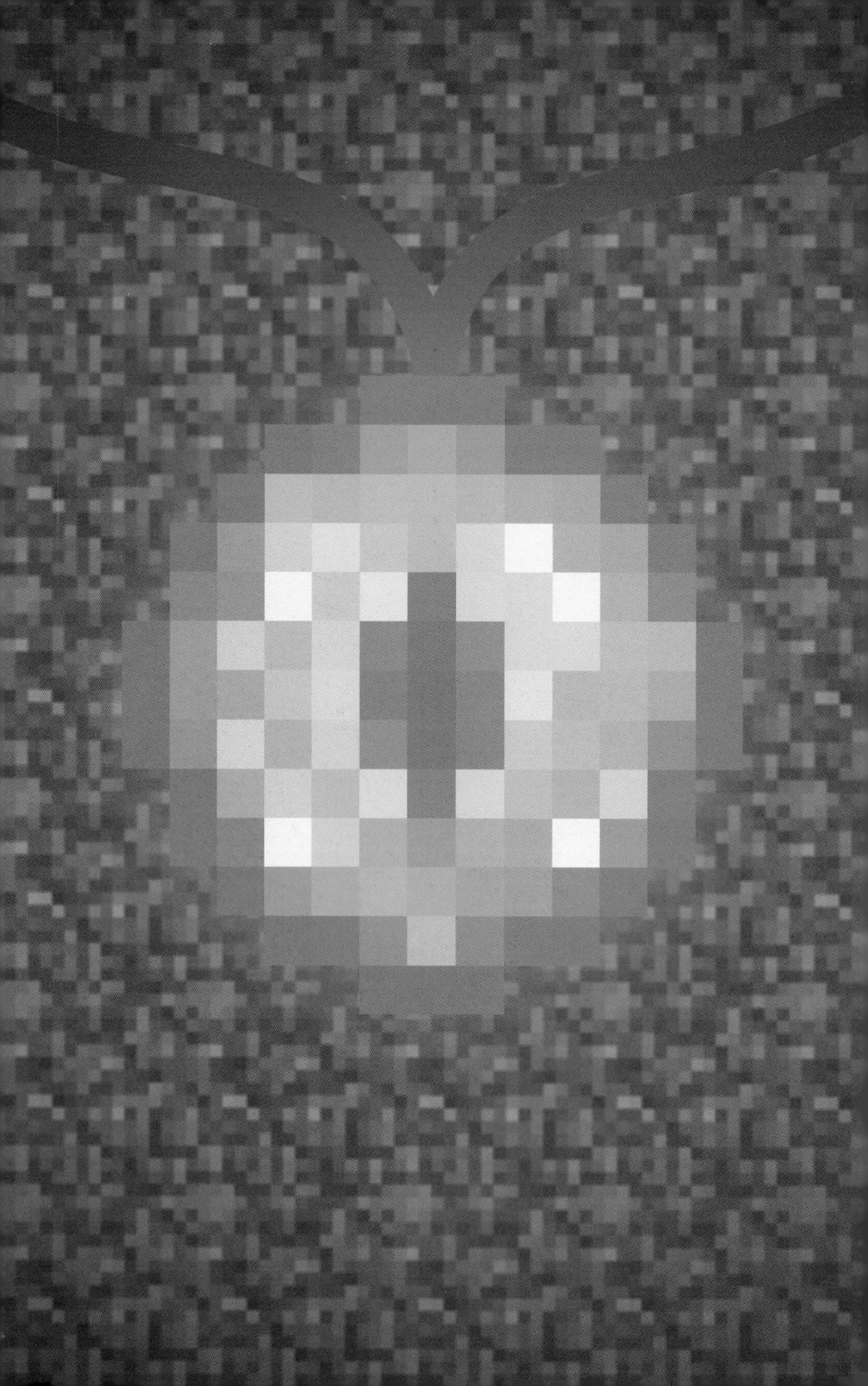

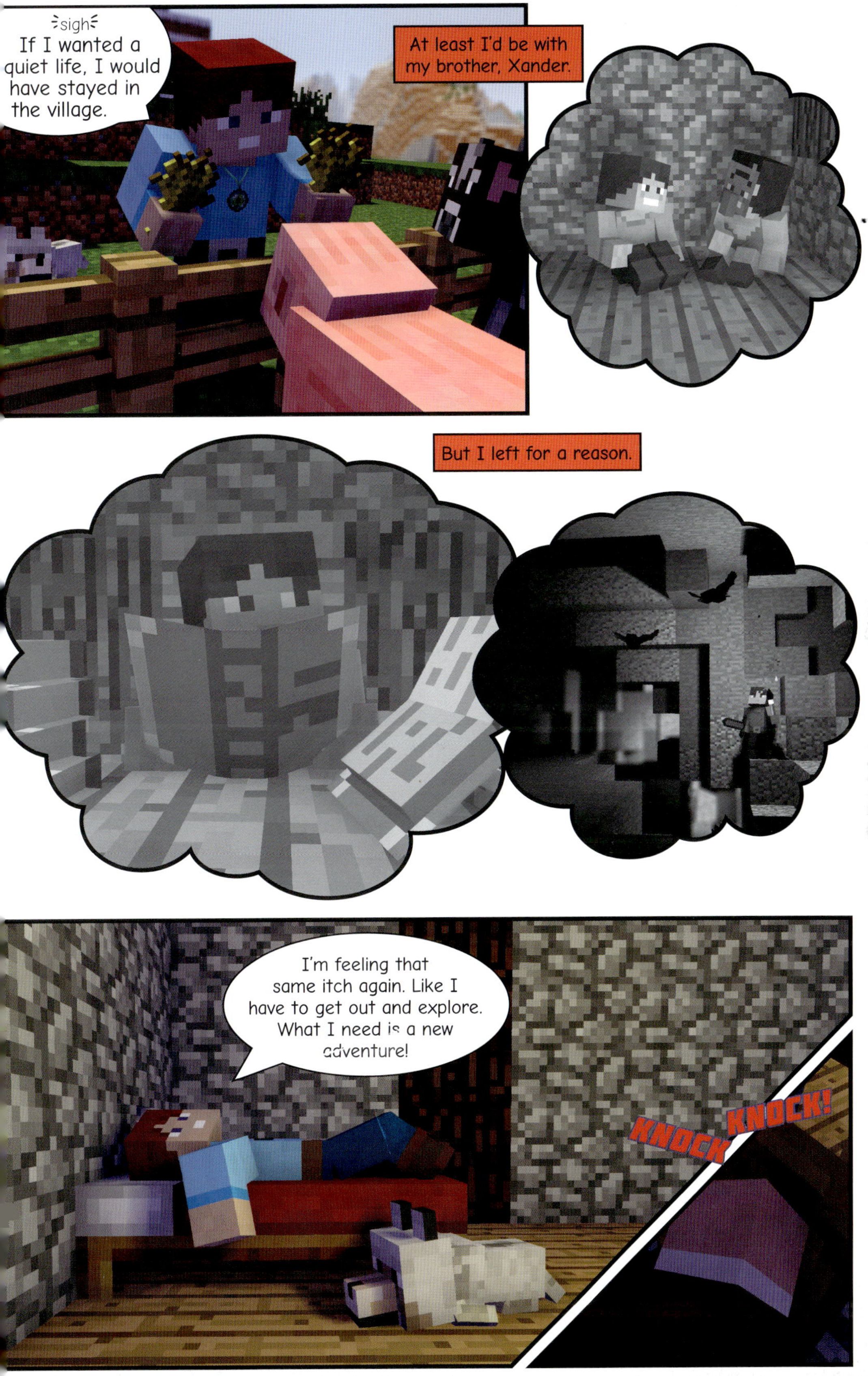
sigh
If I wanted a quiet life, I would have stayed in the village.
At least I'd be with my brother, Xander.
But I left for a reason.
I'm feeling that same itch again. Like I have to get out and explore. What I need is a new adventure!
KNOCK KNOCK!

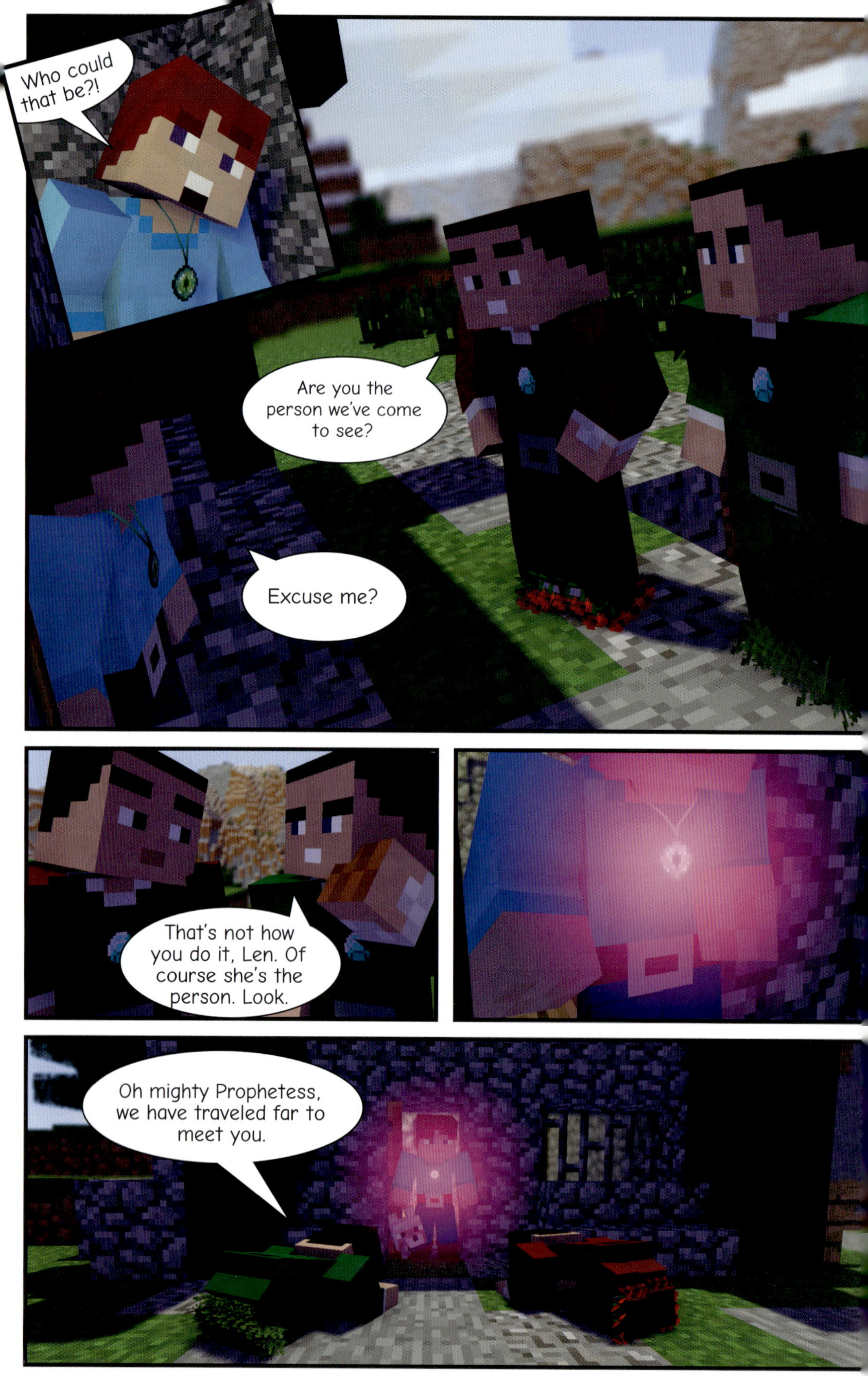
Who could that be?!
Are you the person we've come to see?
Excuse me?
That's not how you do it, Len. Of course she's the person. Look.
Oh mighty Prophetess, we have traveled far to meet you.

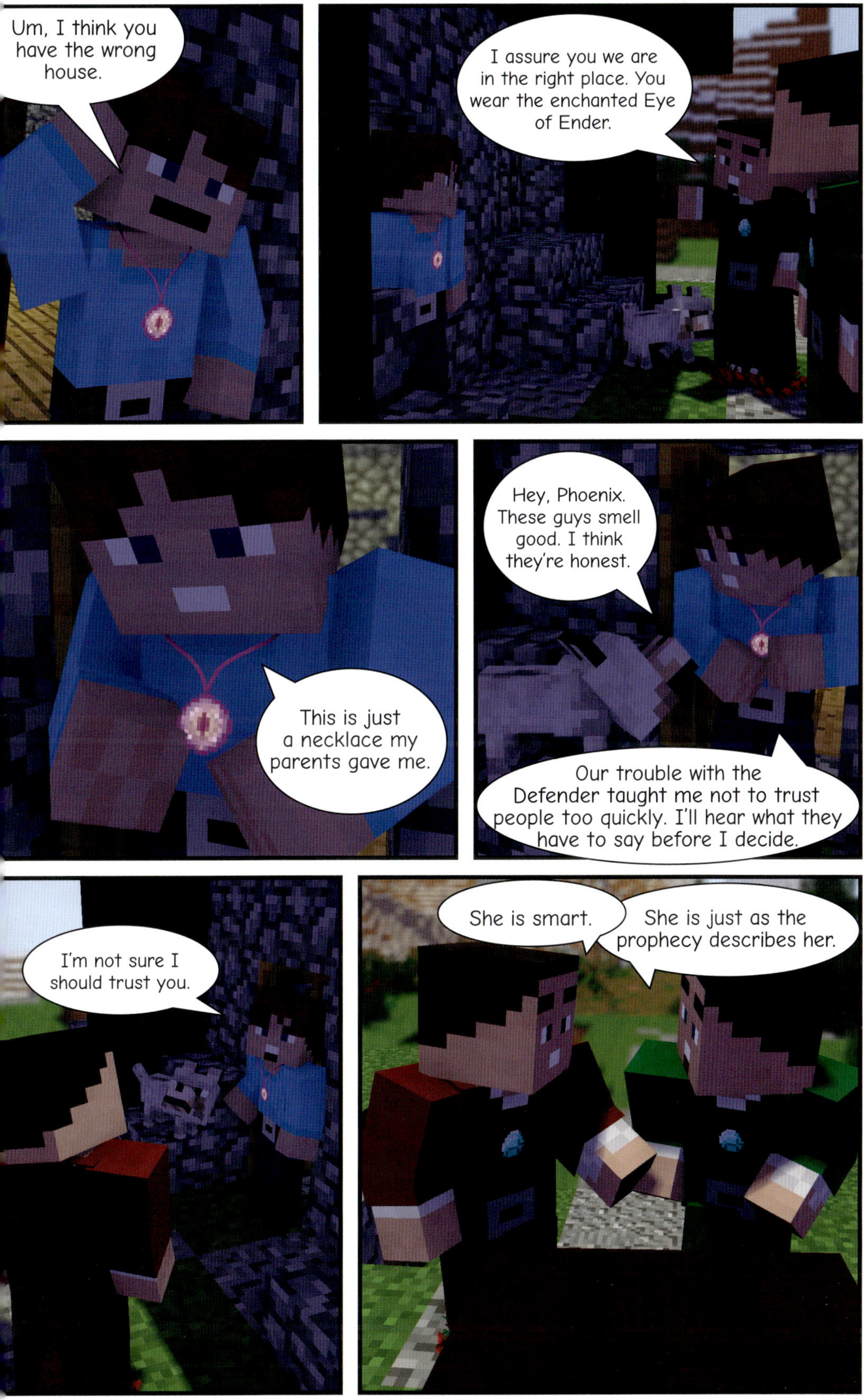

Um, I think you have the wrong house.
I assure you we are in the right place. You wear the enchanted Eye of Ender.
This is just a necklace my parents gave me.
Hey, Phoenix. These guys smell good. I think they're honest.
Our trouble with the Defender taught me not to trust people too quickly. I'll hear what they have to say before I decide.
I'm not sure I should trust you.
She is smart.
She is just as the prophecy describes her.

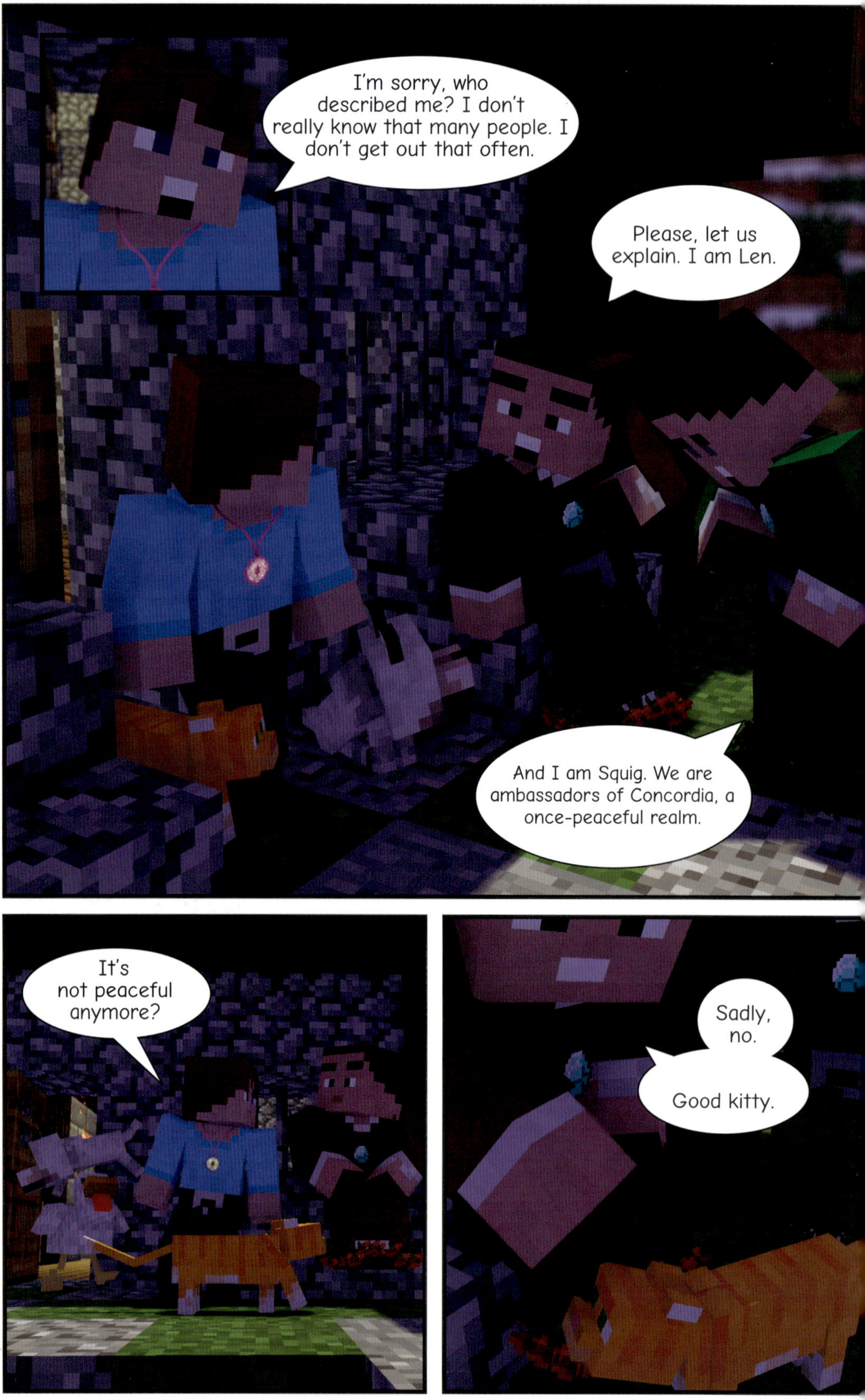
I'm sorry, who described me? I don't really know that many people. I don't get out that often.
Please, let us explain. I am Len.
And I am Squig. We are ambassadors of Concordia, a once-peaceful realm.
It's not peaceful anymore?
Sadly, no.
Good kitty.

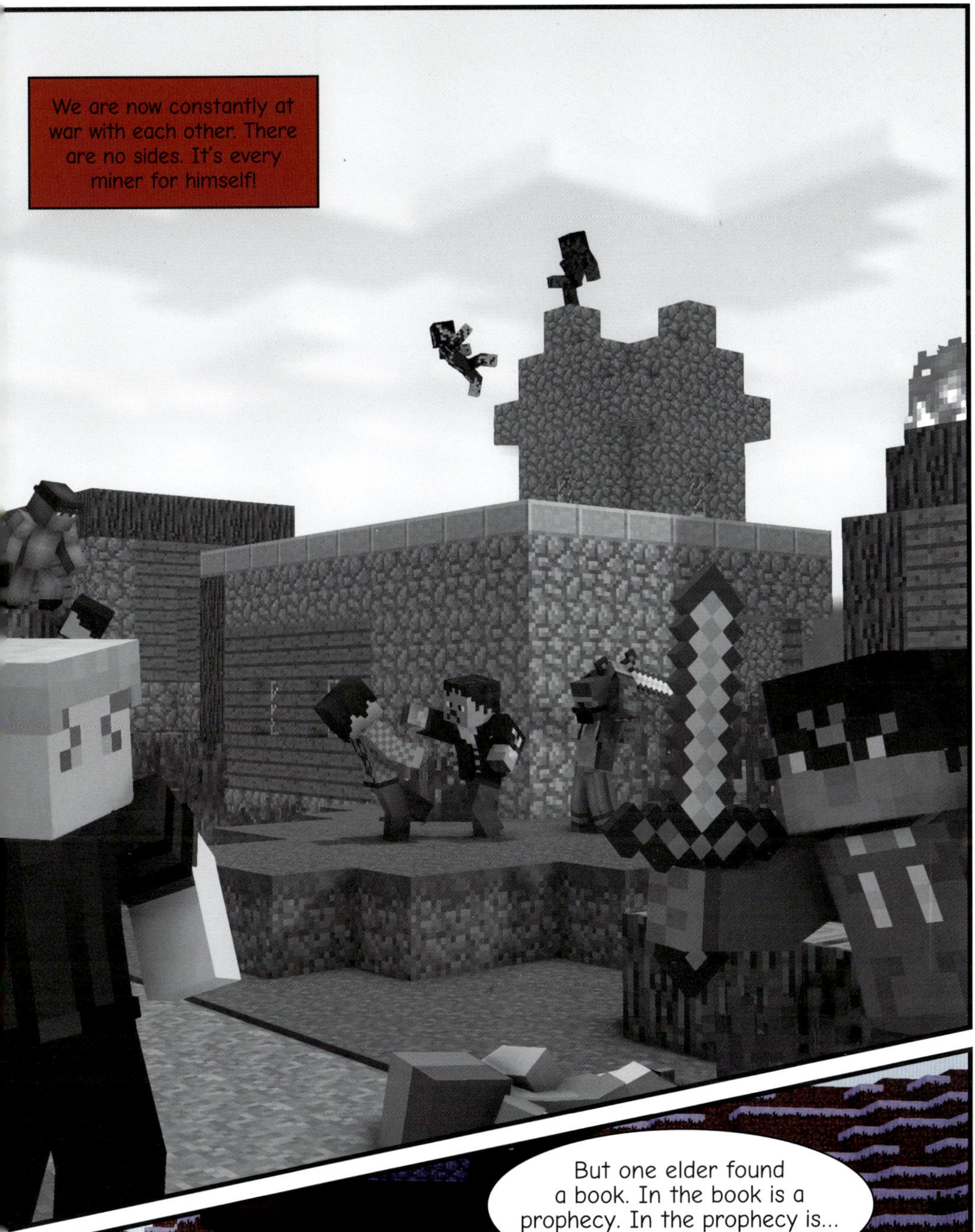
We are now constantly at war with each other. There are no sides. It's every miner for himself!

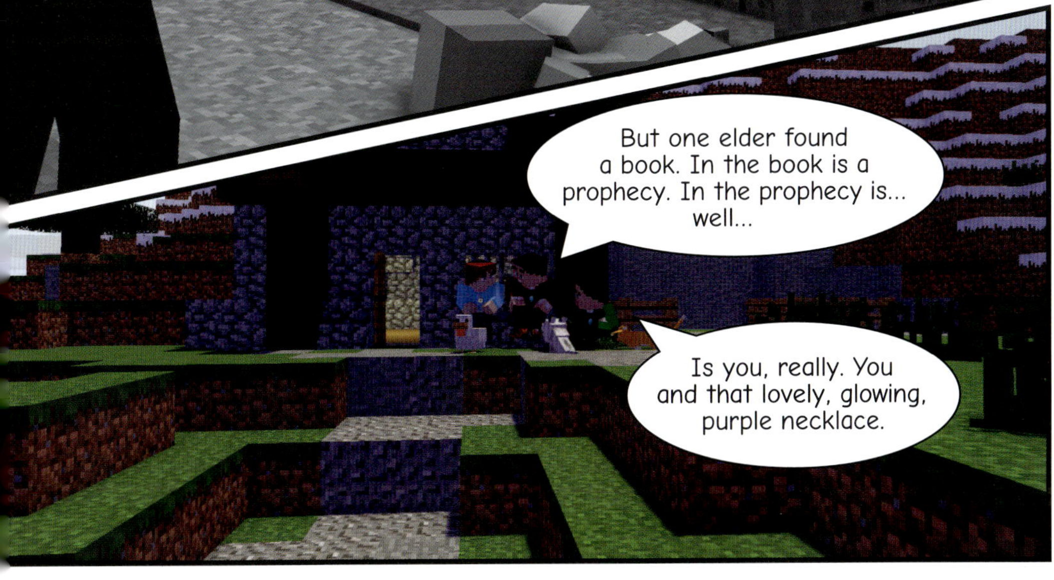
But one elder found a book. In the book is a prophecy. In the prophecy is... well...
Is you, really. You and that lovely, glowing, purple necklace.

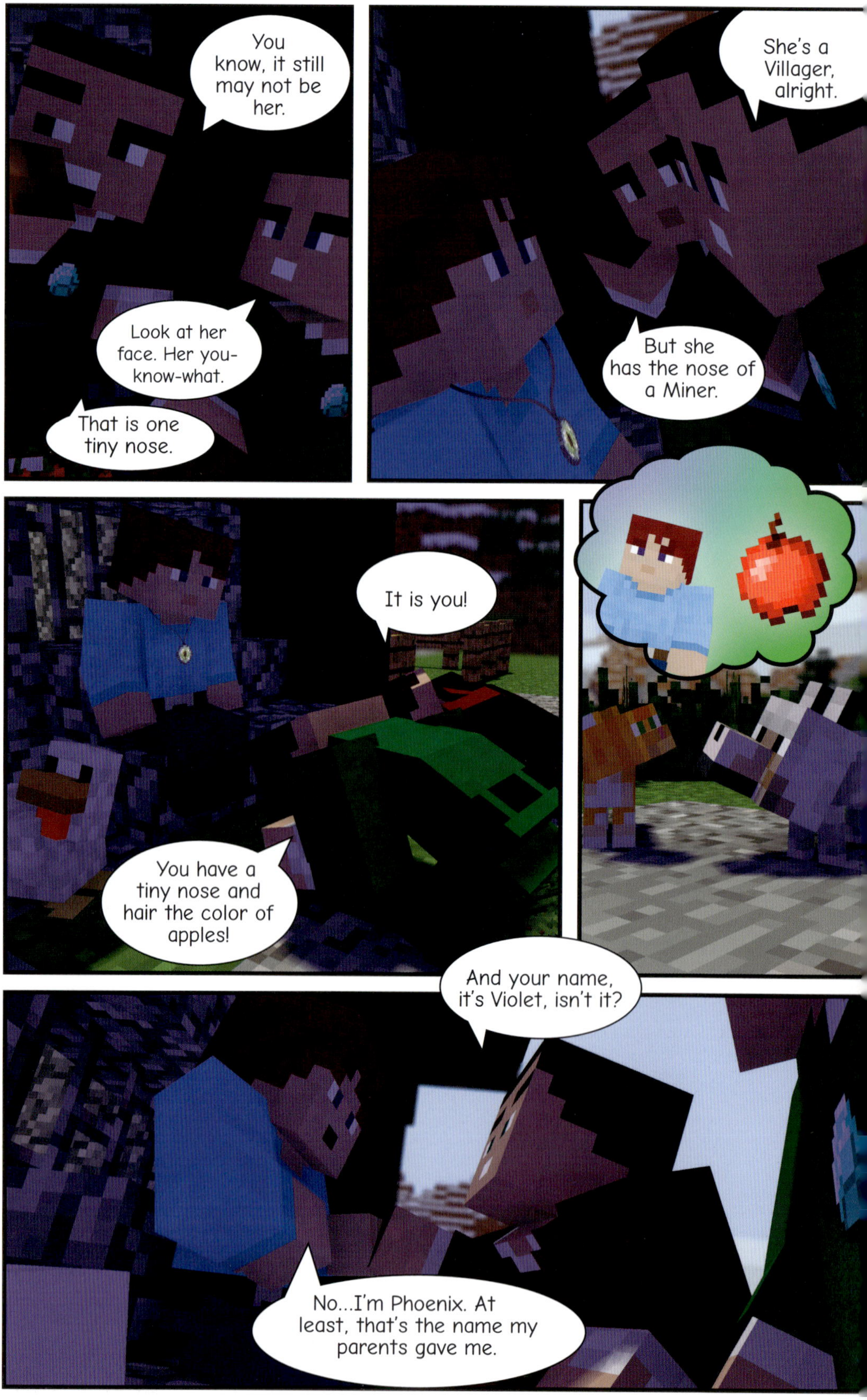
You know, it still may not be her.
Look at her face. Her you-know-what.
That is one tiny nose.
She's a Villager, alright.
But she has the nose of a Miner.
It is you!
You have a tiny nose and hair the color of apples!
And your name, it's Violet, isn't it?
No...I'm Phoenix. At least, that's the name my parents gave me.

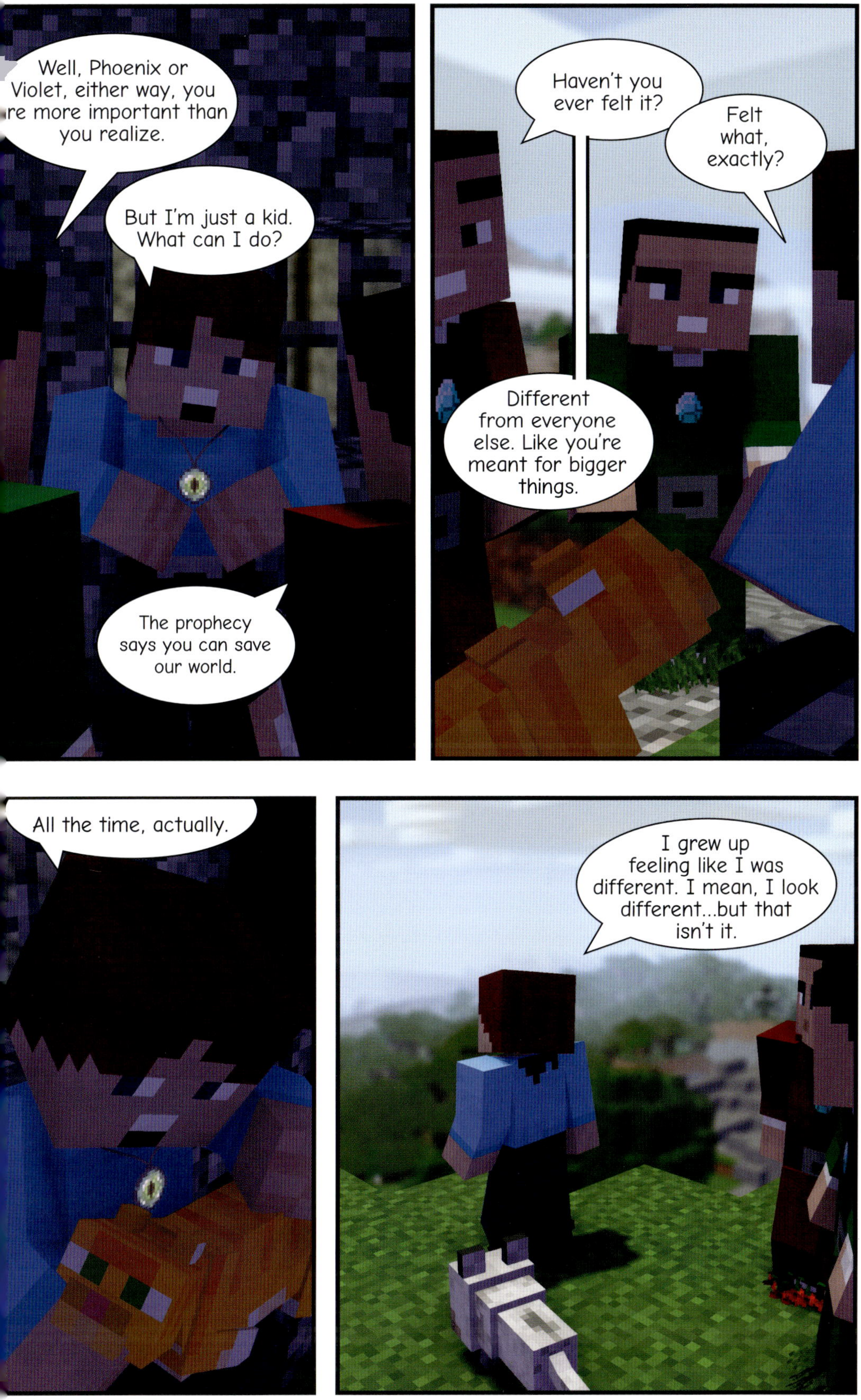
Well, Phoenix or Violet, either way, you're more important than you realize.
But I'm just a kid. What can I do?
The prophecy says you can save our world.
Haven't you ever felt it?
Felt what, exactly?
Different from everyone else. Like you're meant for bigger things.
All the time, actually.
I grew up feeling like I was different. I mean, I look different...but that isn't it.

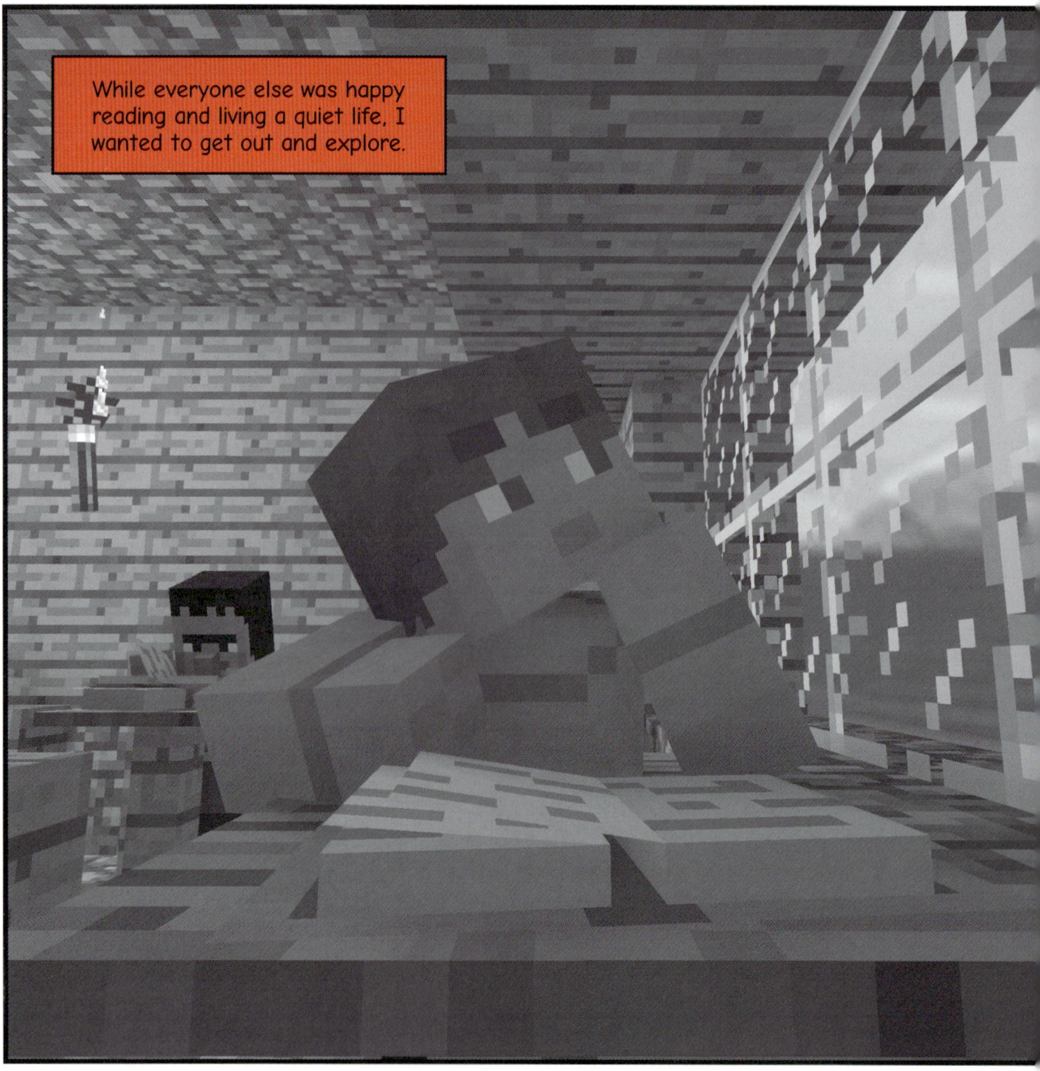
While everyone else was happy reading and living a quiet life, I wanted to get out and explore.

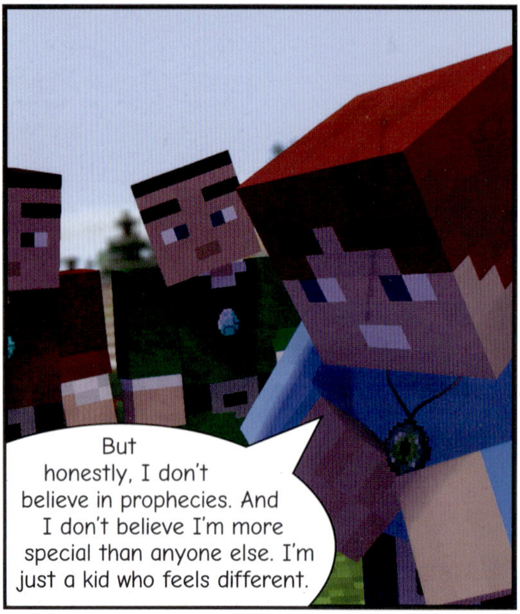
But honestly, I don't believe in prophecies. And I don't believe I'm more special than anyone else. I'm just a kid who feels different.

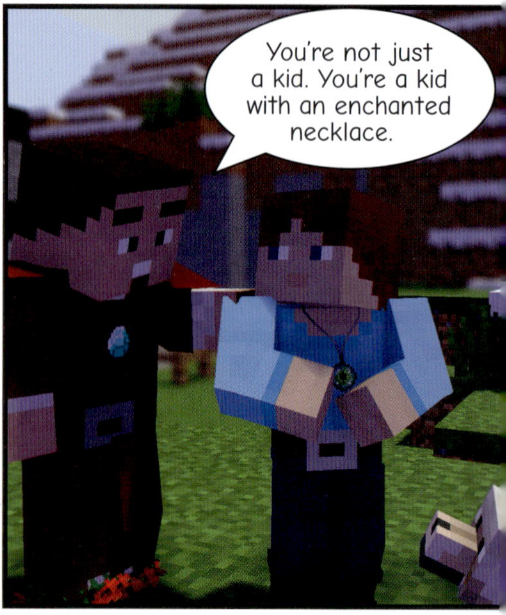
You're not just a kid. You're a kid with an enchanted necklace.

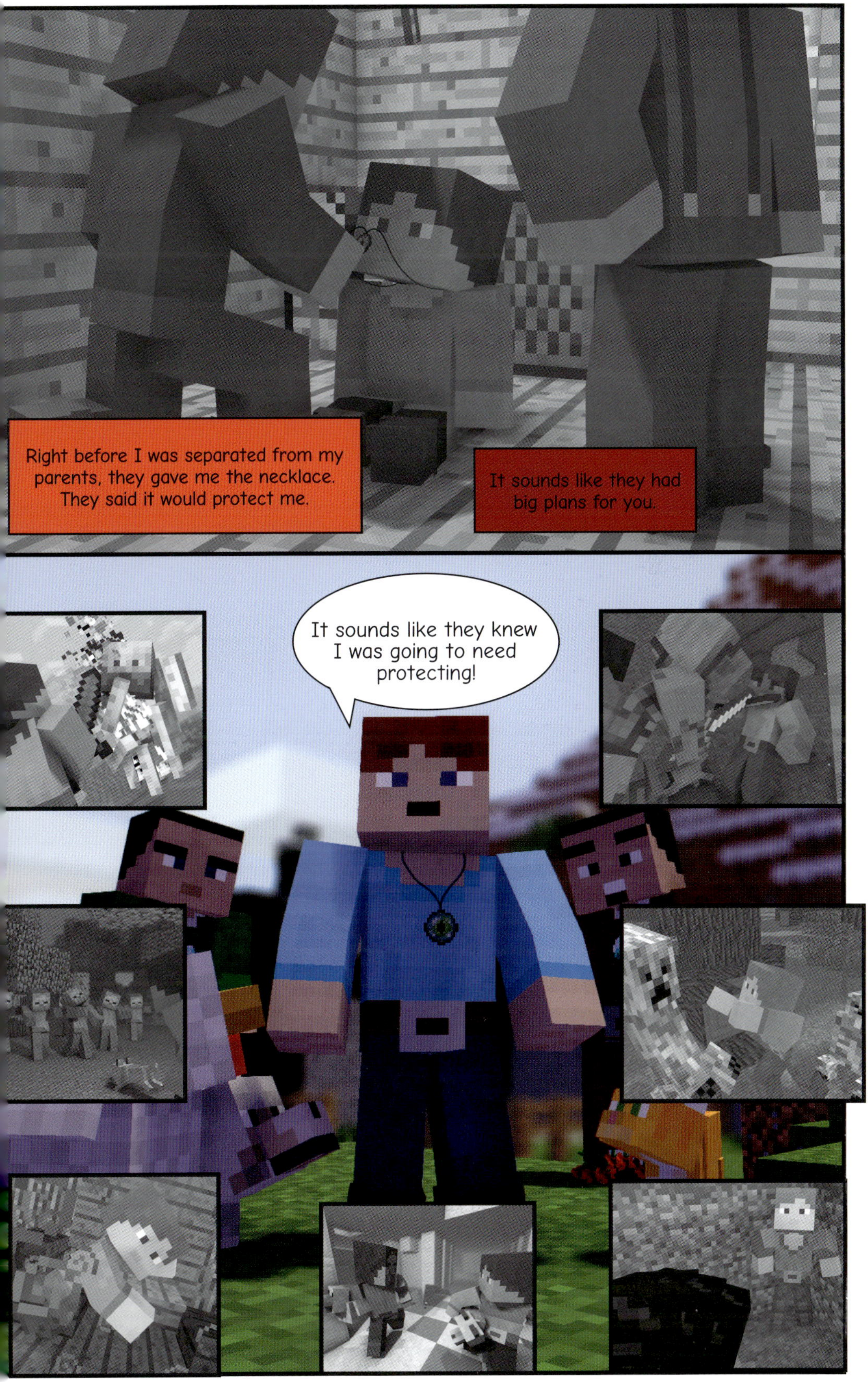
Right before I was separated from my parents, they gave me the necklace. They said it would protect me.
It sounds like they had big plans for you.
It sounds like they knew I was going to need protecting!

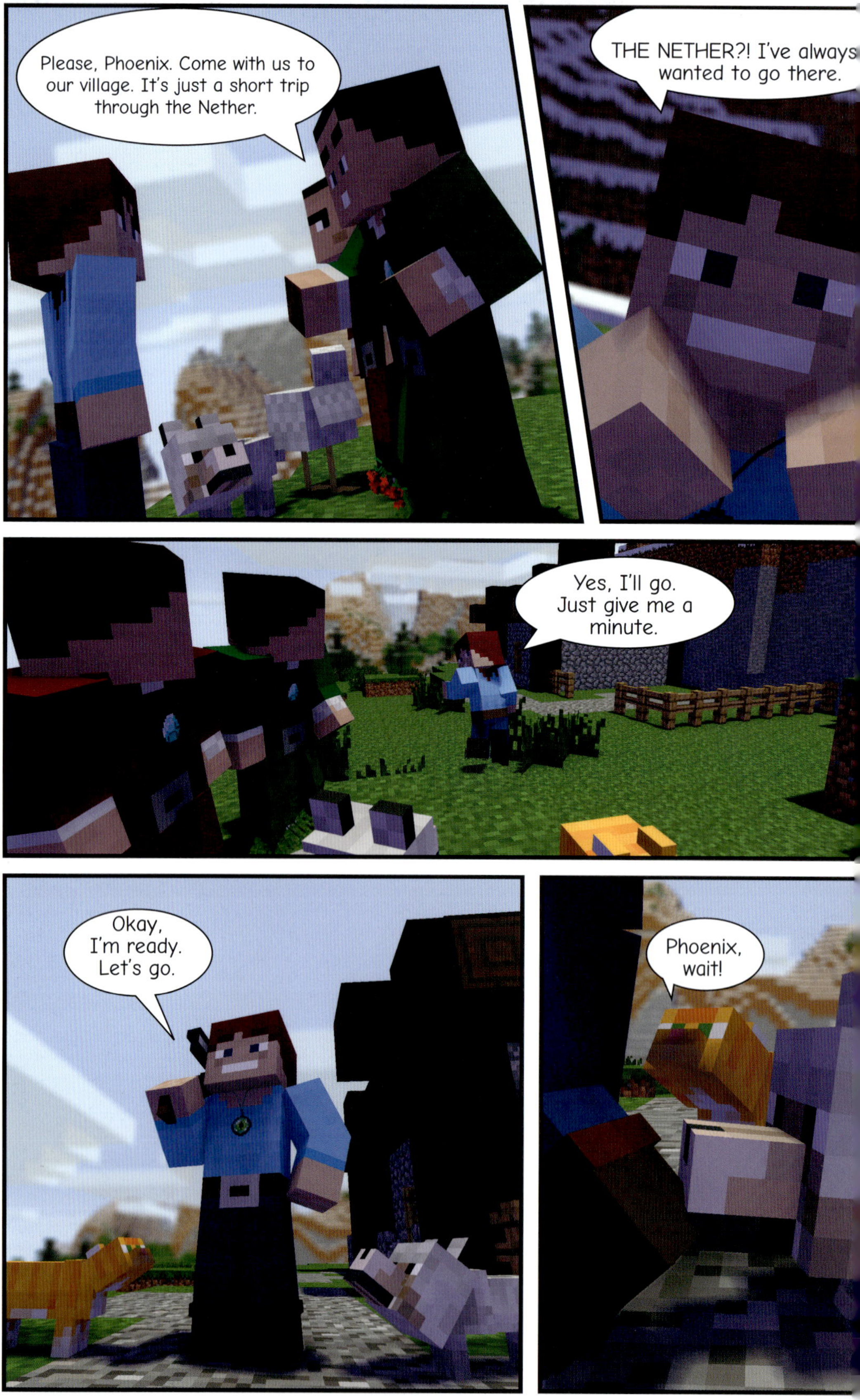
Please, Phoenix. Come with us to our village. It's just a short trip through the Nether.
THE NETHER?! I've always wanted to go there.
Yes, I'll go. Just give me a minute.
Okay, I'm ready. Let's go.
Phoenix, wait!

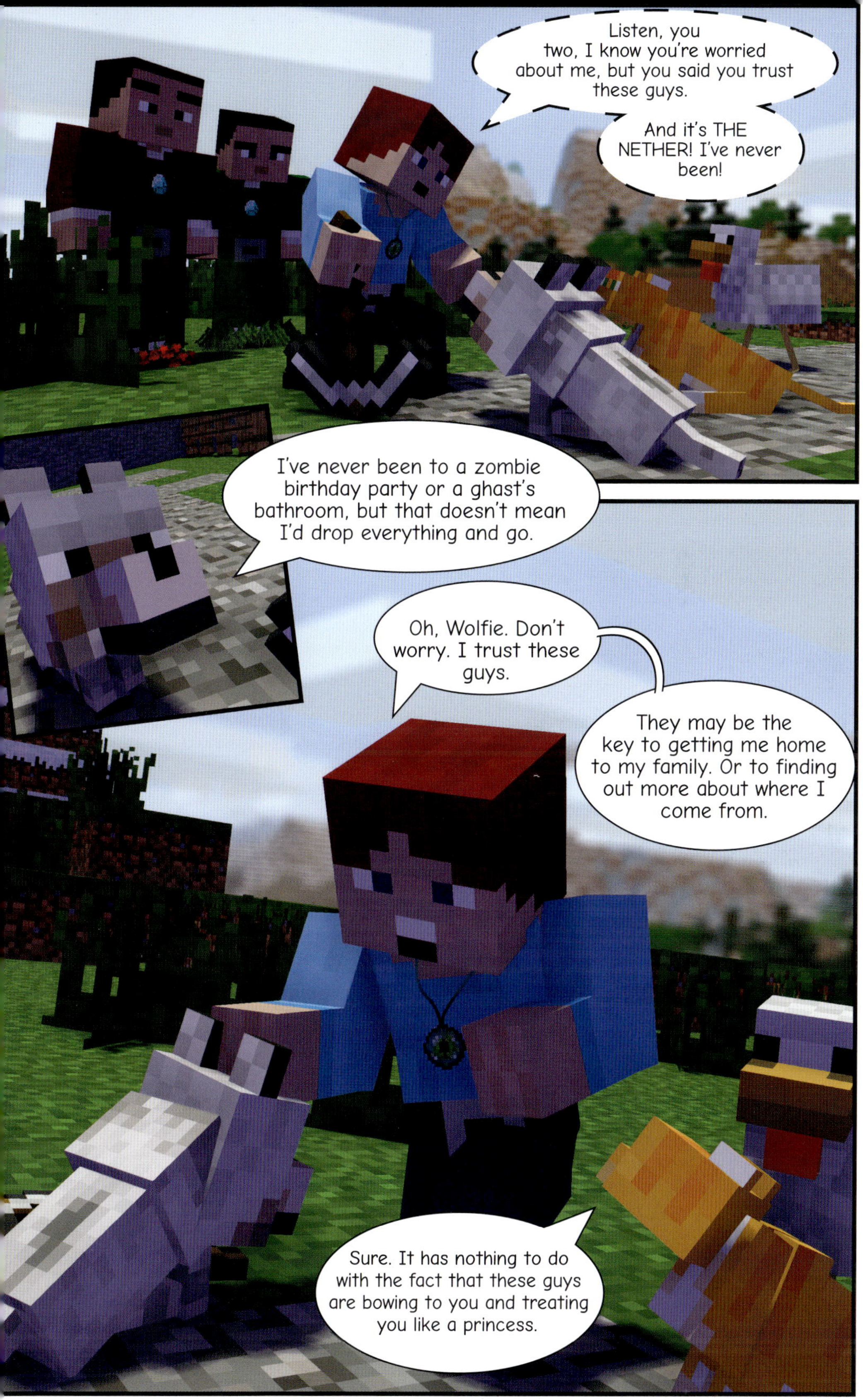
Listen, you two, I know you're worried about me, but you said you trust these guys.
And it's THE NETHER! I've never been!
I've never been to a zombie birthday party or a ghast's bathroom, but that doesn't mean I'd drop everything and go.
Oh, Wolfie. Don't worry. I trust these guys.
They may be the key to getting me home to my family. Or to finding out more about where I come from.
Sure. It has nothing to do with the fact that these guys are bowing to you and treating you like a princess.

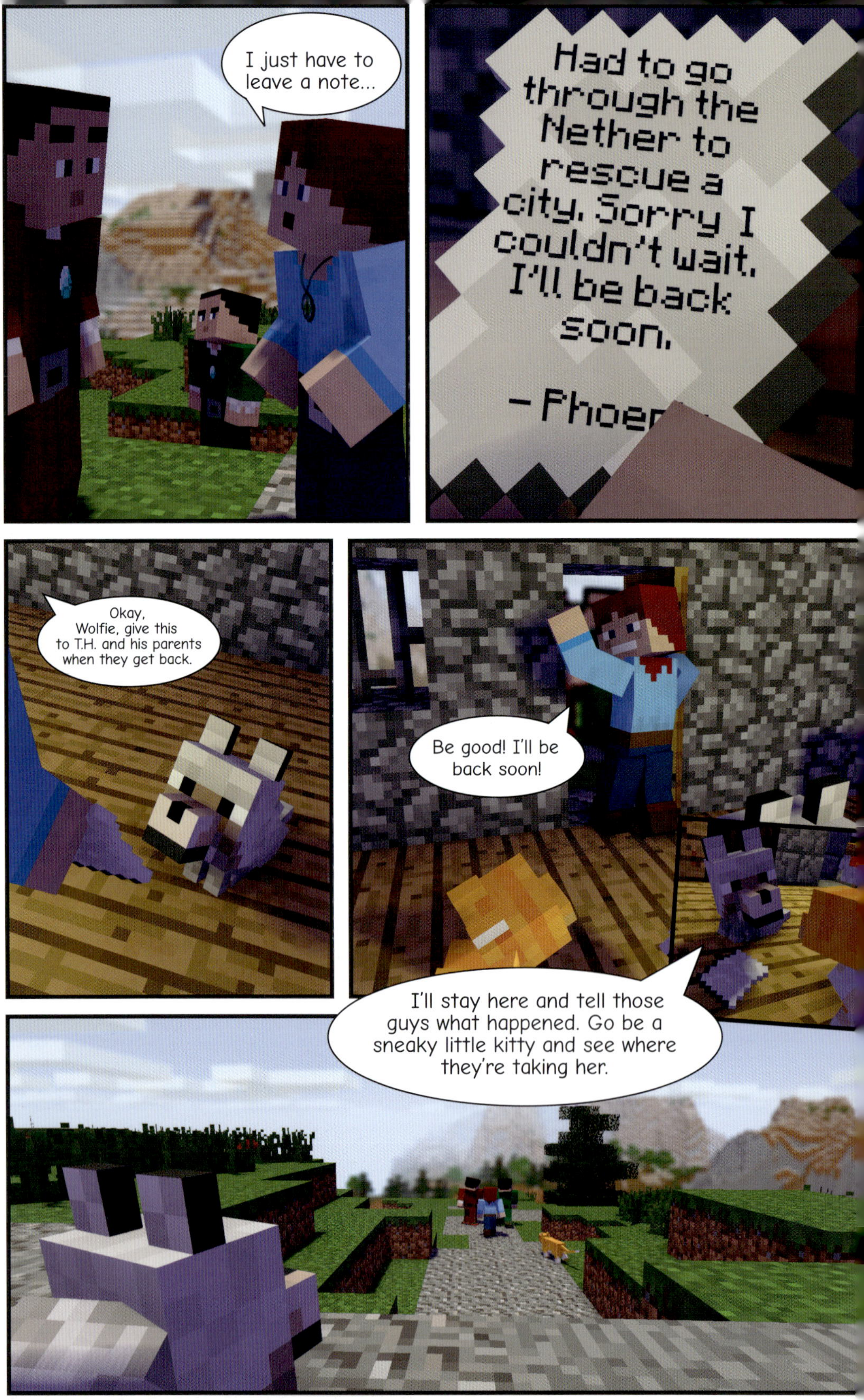
I just have to leave a note...
Had to go through the Nether to rescue a city. Sorry I couldn't wait. I'll be back soon.
- Phoe
Okay, Wolfie, give this to T.H. and his parents when they get back.
Be good! I'll be back soon!
I'll stay here and tell those guys what happened. Go be a sneaky little kitty and see where they're taking her.

CHAPTER 3

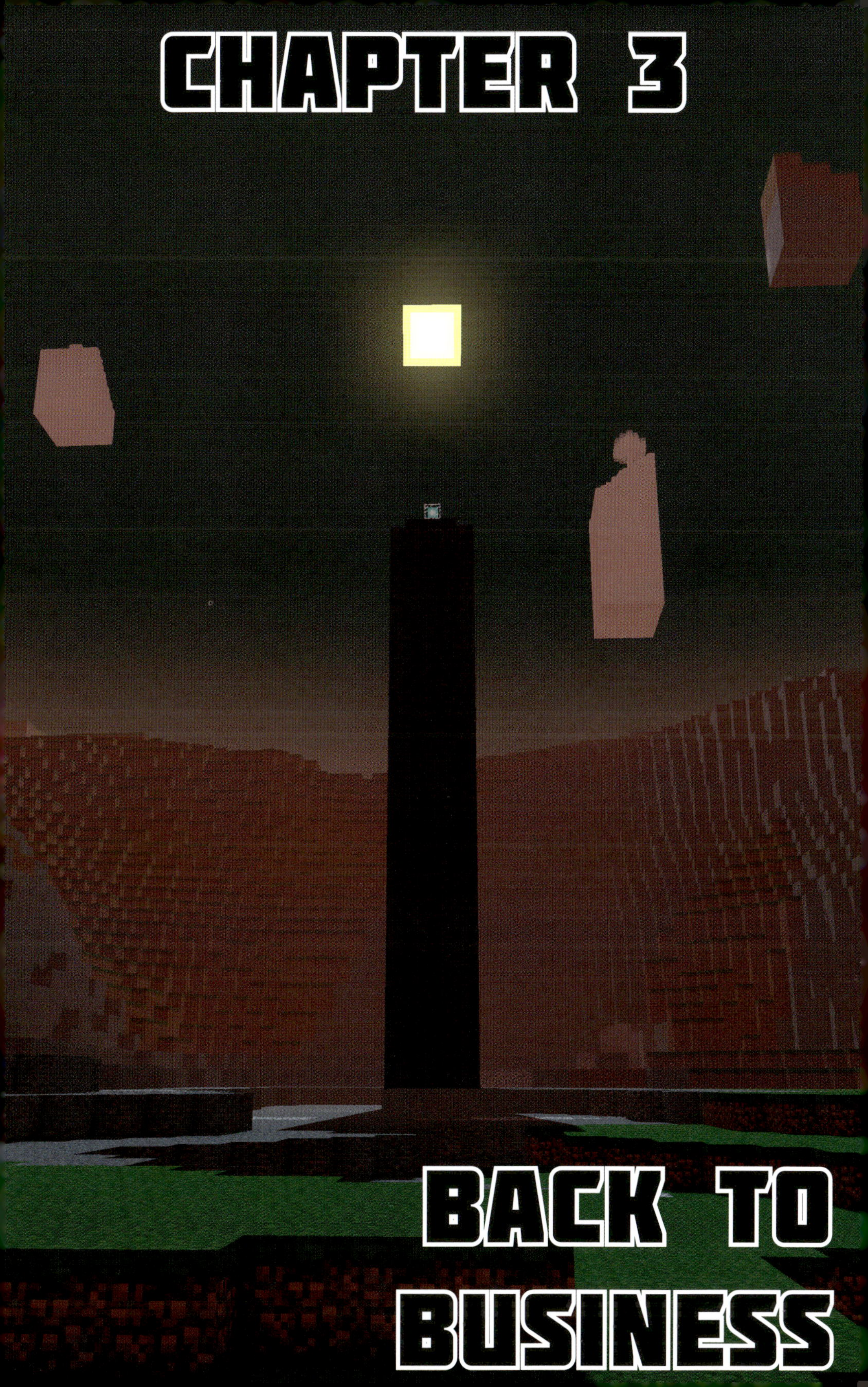

BACK TO BUSINESS

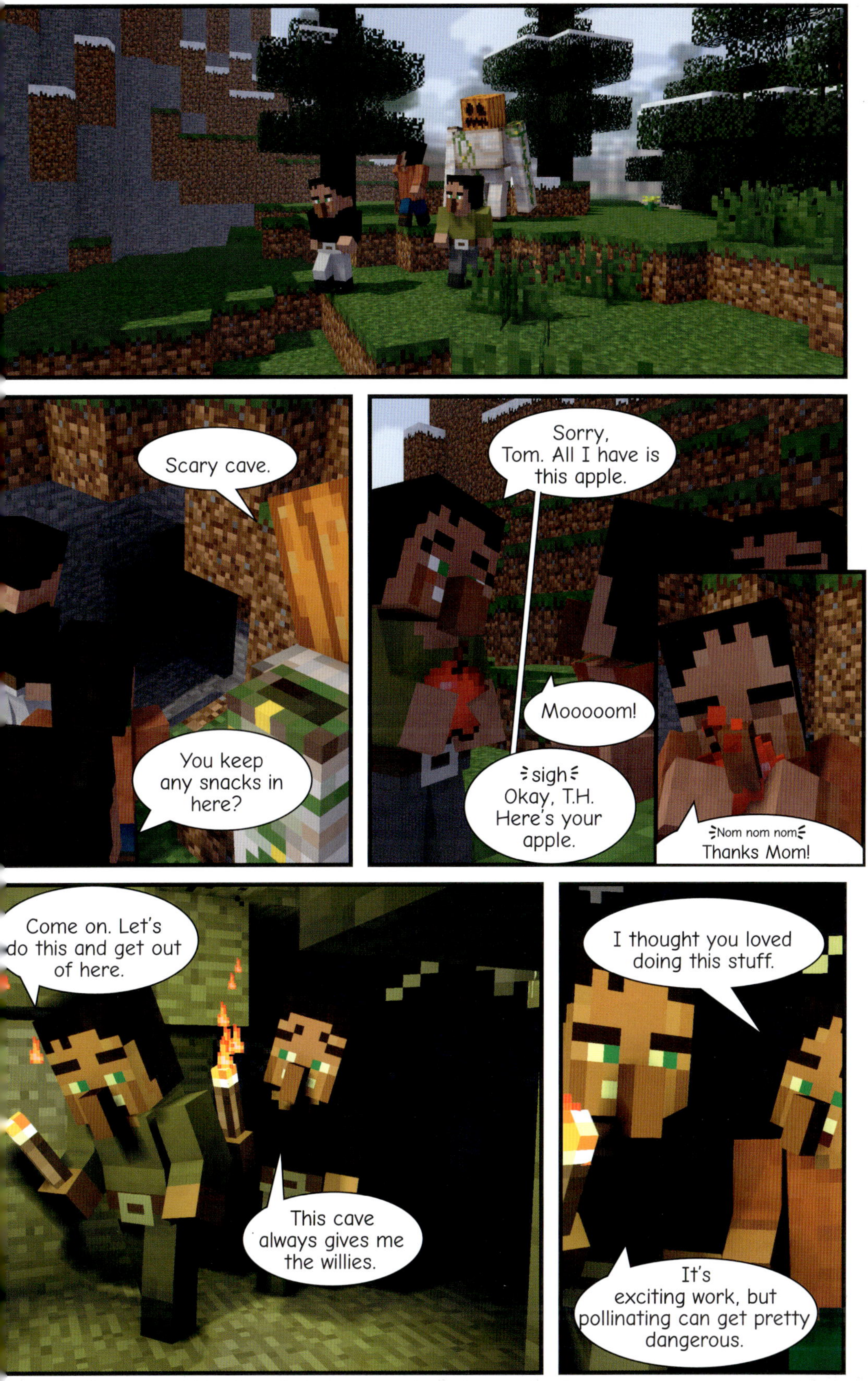
Scary cave.
You keep any snacks in here?
Sorry, Tom. All I have is this apple.
Moooooom!
sigh
Okay, T.H. Here's your apple.
Nom nom nom
Thanks Mom!
Come on. Let's do this and get out of here.
This cave always gives me the willies.
I thought you loved doing this stuff.
It's exciting work, but pollinating can get pretty dangerous.

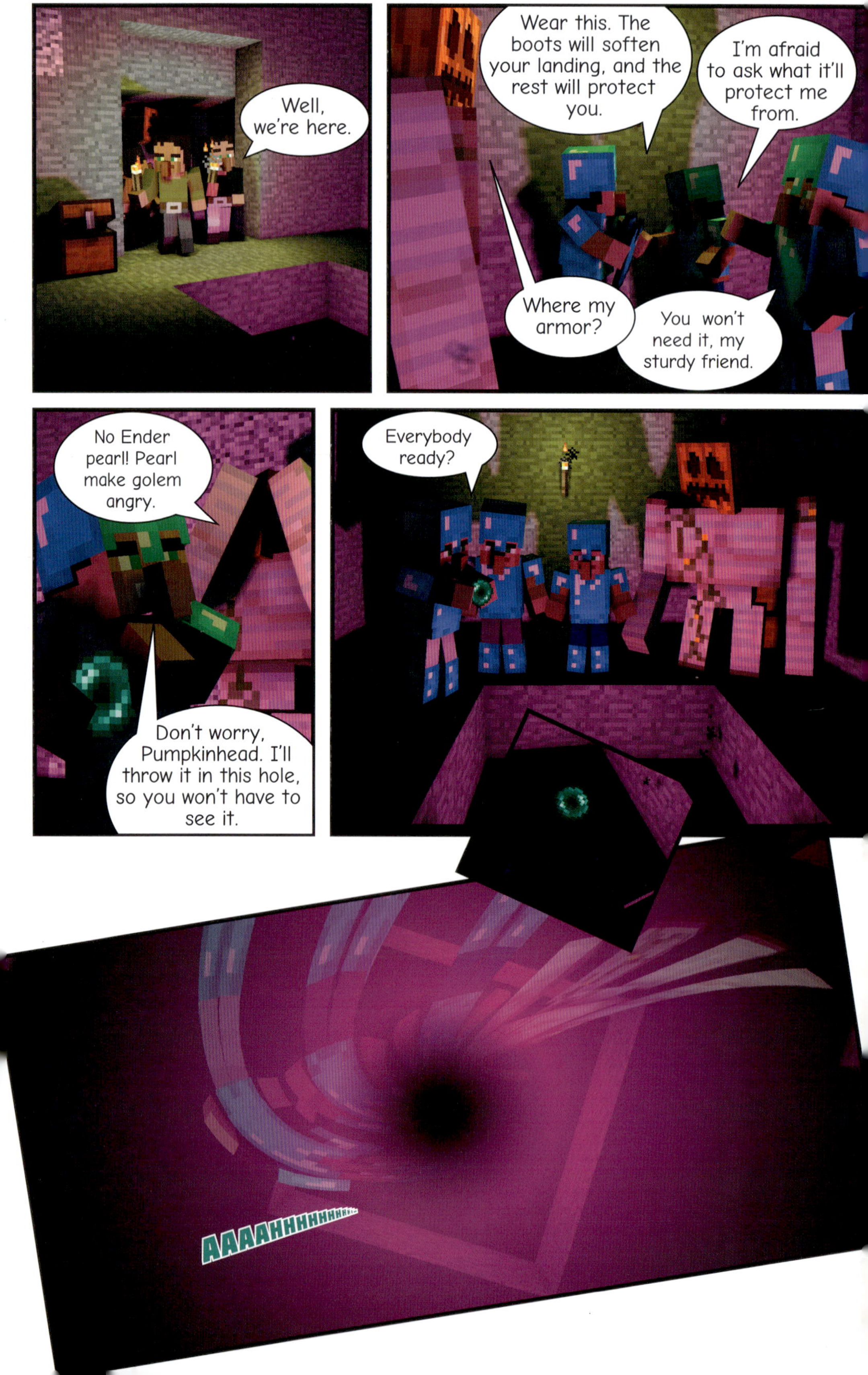

Well, we're here.
Wear this. The boots will soften your landing, and the rest will protect you.
I'm afraid to ask what it'll protect me from.
Where my armor?
You won't need it, my sturdy friend.
No Ender pearl! Pearl make golem angry.
Don't worry, Pumpkinhead. I'll throw it in this hole, so you won't have to see it.
Everybody ready?
AAAAHHHHHHHH

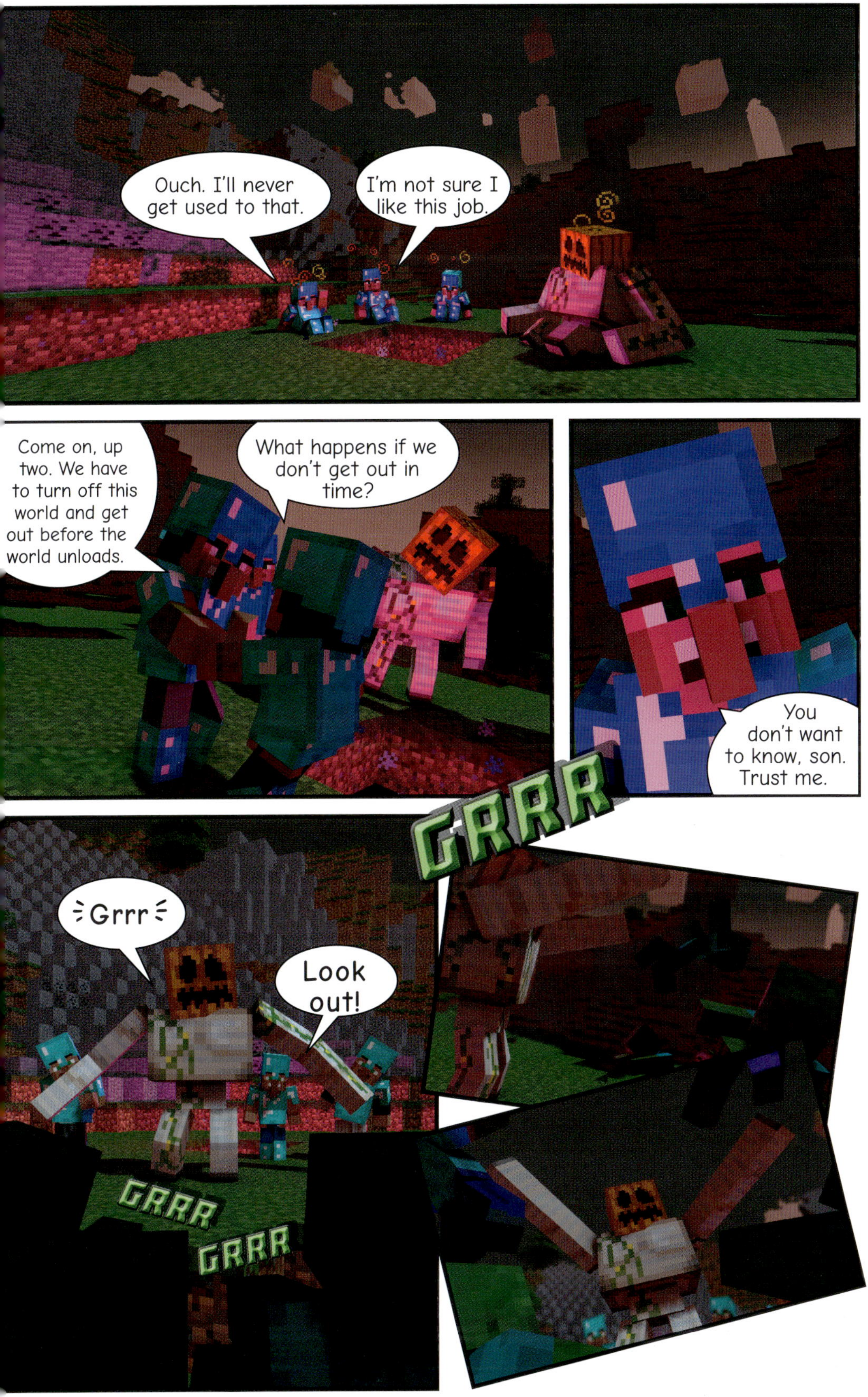
Ouch. I'll never get used to that.
I'm not sure I like this job.
Come on, up two. We have to turn off this world and get out before the world unloads.
What happens if we don't get out in time?
You don't want to know, son. Trust me.
Grrr
Look out!
GRRR
GRRR
GRRR

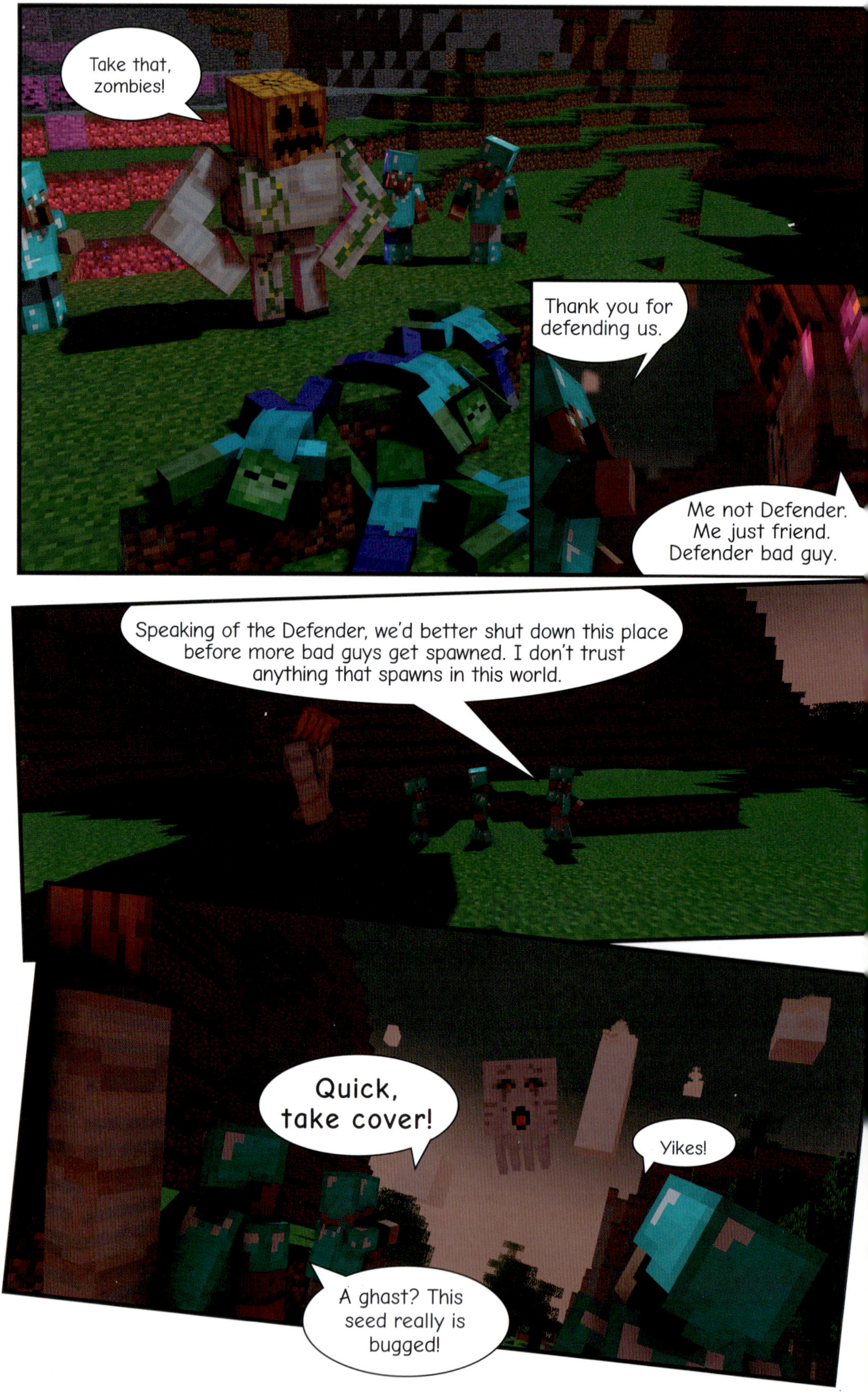
Take that, zombies!
Thank you for defending us.
Me not Defender. Me just friend. Defender bad guy.
Speaking of the Defender, we'd better shut down this place before more bad guys get spawned. I don't trust anything that spawns in this world.
Quick, take cover!
Yikes!
A ghast? This seed really is bugged!

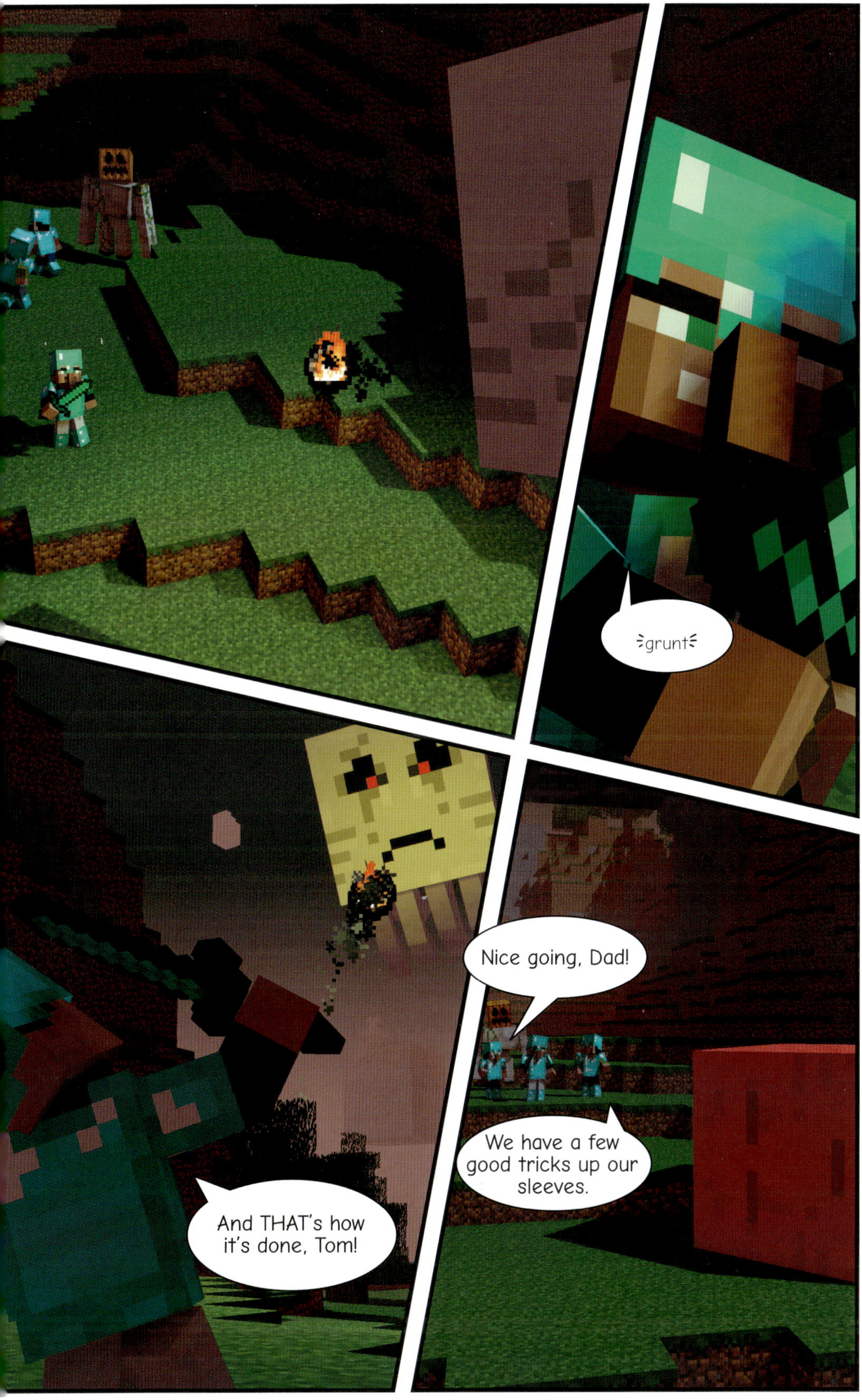
grunt
And THAT's how it's done, Tom!
Nice going, Dad!
We have a few good tricks up our sleeves.

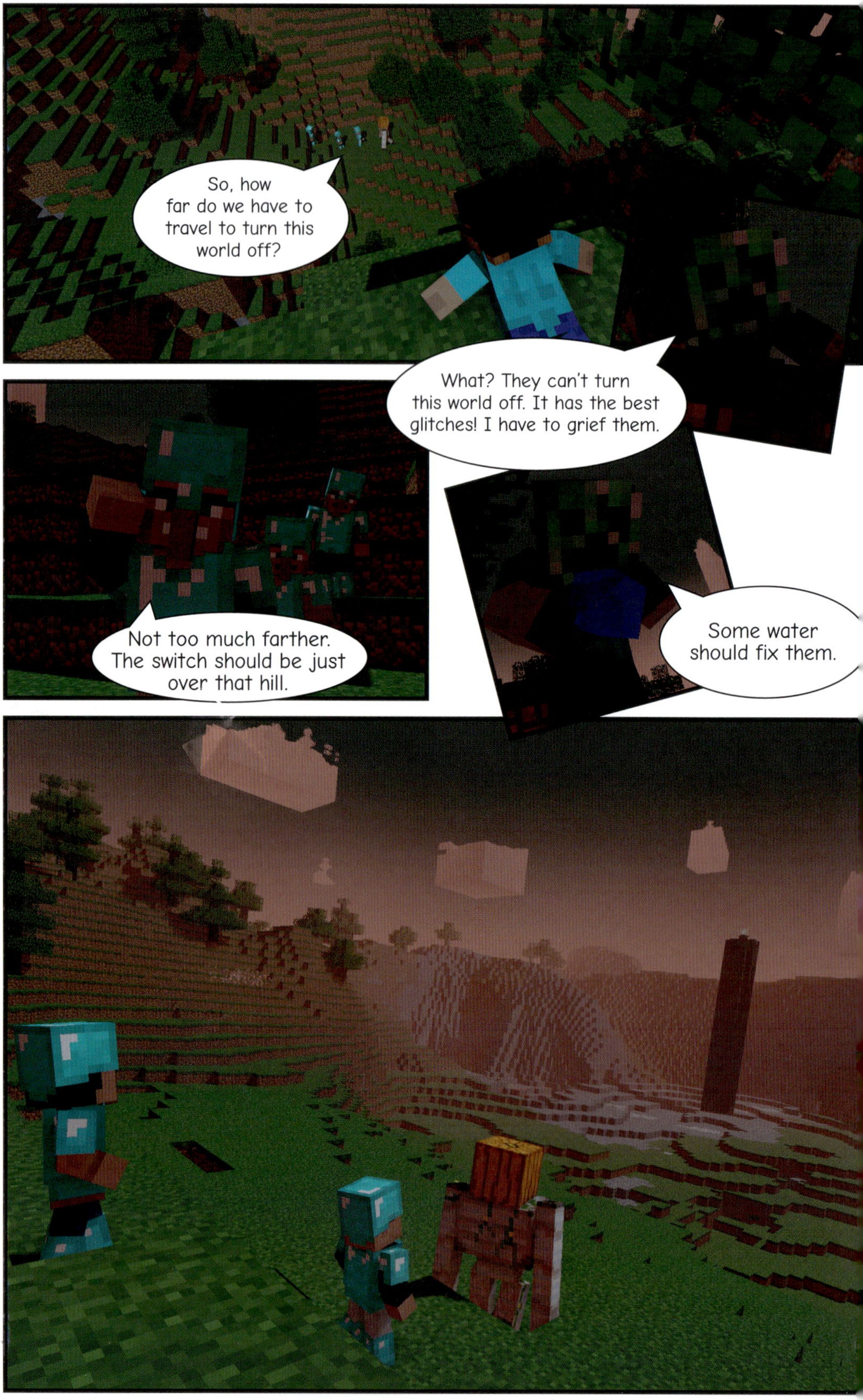
So, how far do we have to travel to turn this world off?
What? They can't turn this world off. It has the best glitches! I have to grief them.
Not too much farther. The switch should be just over that hill.
Some water should fix them.

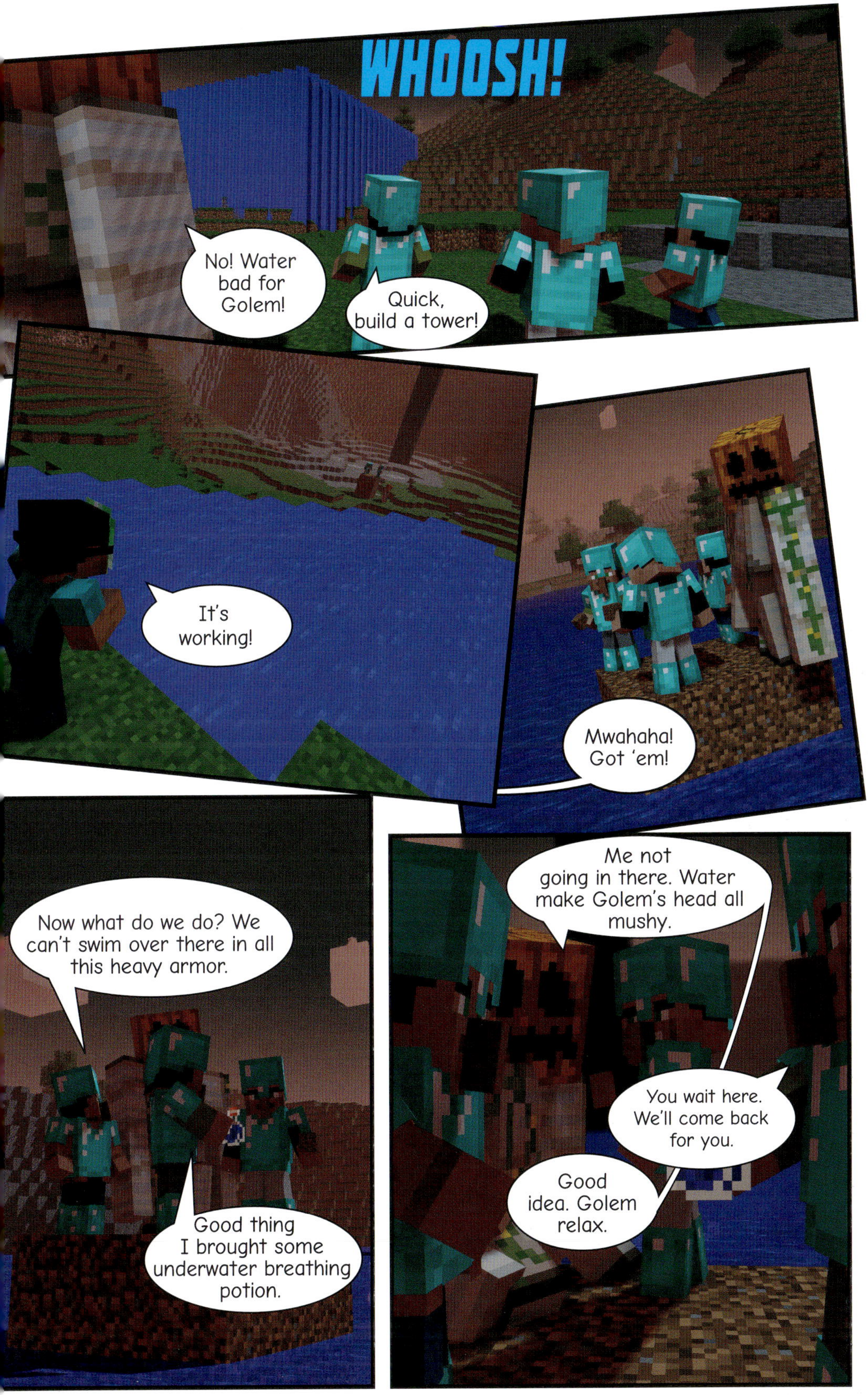
WHOOSH!
No! Water bad for Golem!
Quick, build a tower!
It's working!
Mwahaha! Got 'em!
Now what do we do? We can't swim over there in all this heavy armor.
Good thing I brought some underwater breathing potion.
Me not going in there. Water make Golem's head all mushy.
You wait here. We'll come back for you.
Good idea. Golem relax.

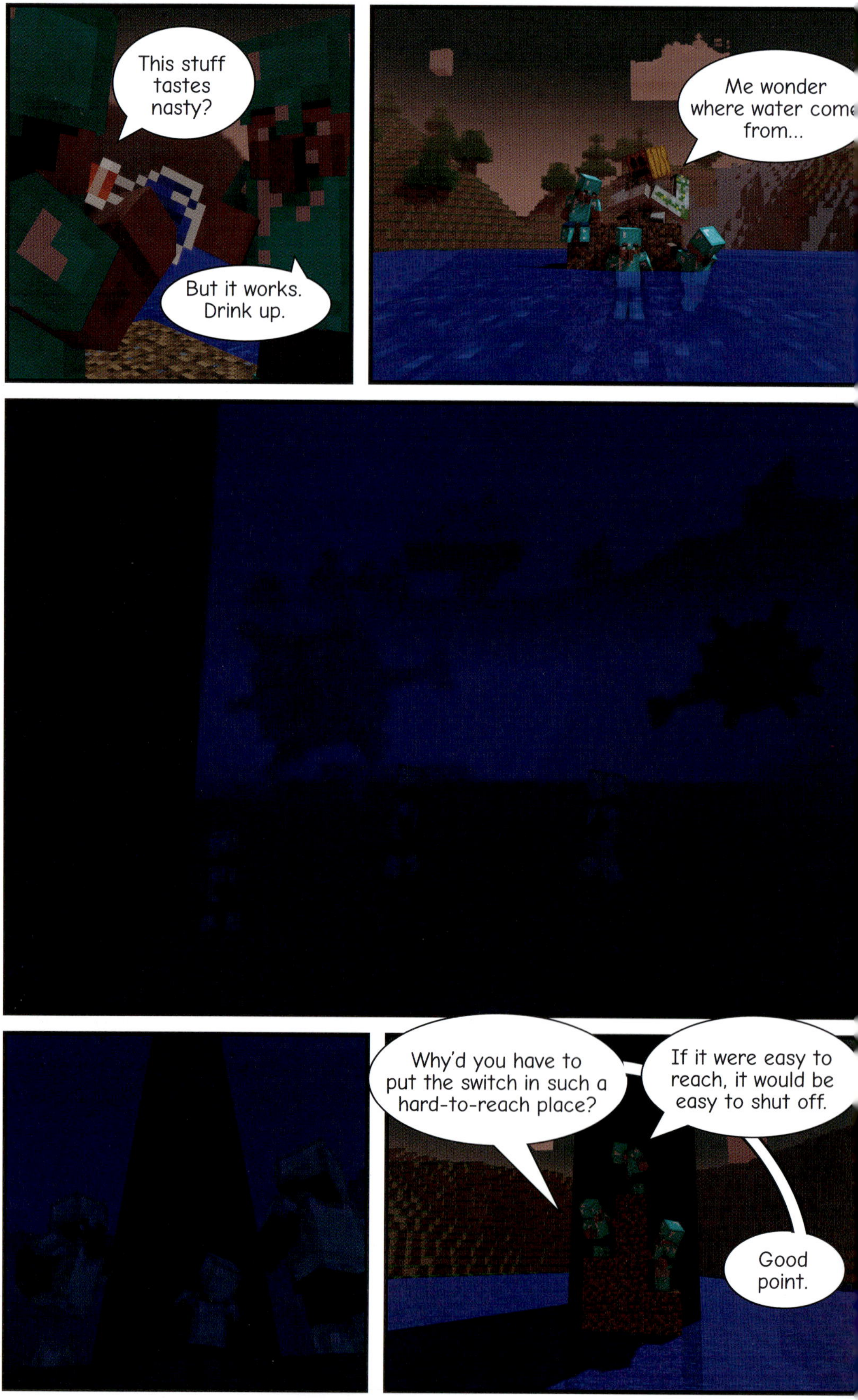
This stuff tastes nasty?
But it works. Drink up.
Me wonder where water come from...
Why'd you have to put the switch in such a hard-to-reach place?
If it were easy to reach, it would be easy to shut off.
Good point.

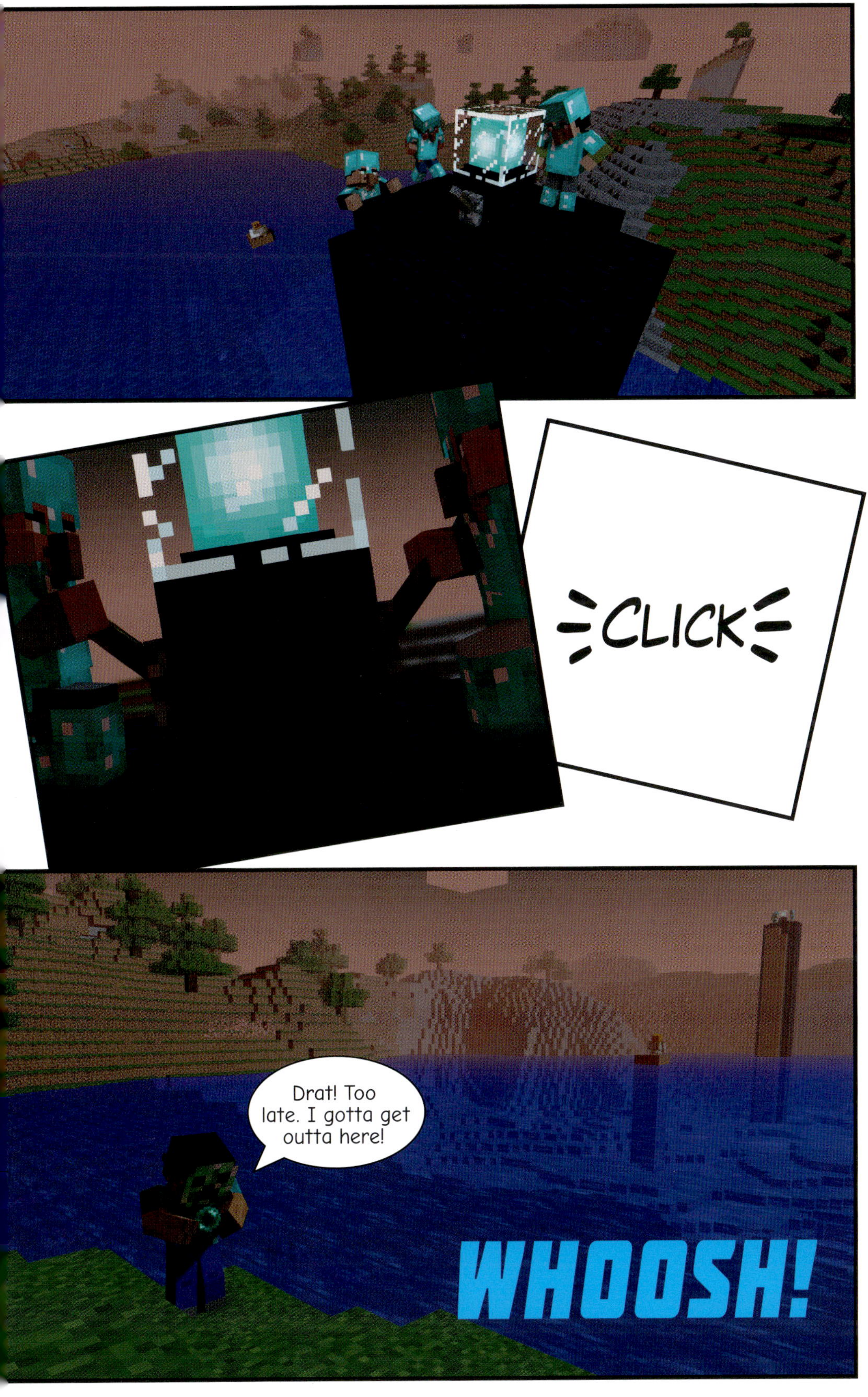
CLICK
Drat! Too late. I gotta get outta here!
WHOOSH!

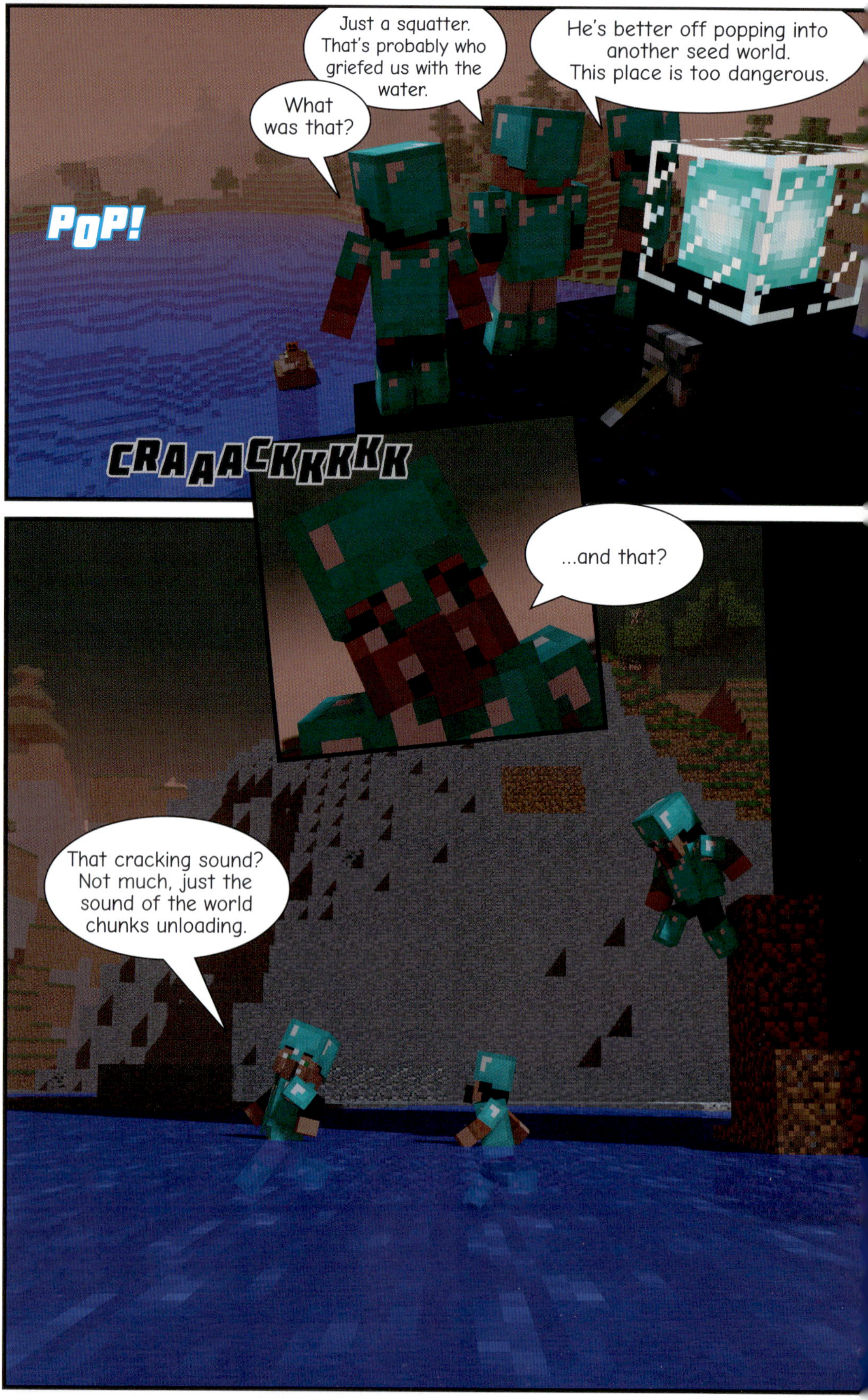
POP!
What was that?
Just a squatter. That's probably who griefed us with the water.
He's better off popping into another seed world. This place is too dangerous.
CRAAACKKKKK
...and that?
That cracking sound? Not much, just the sound of the world chunks unloading.

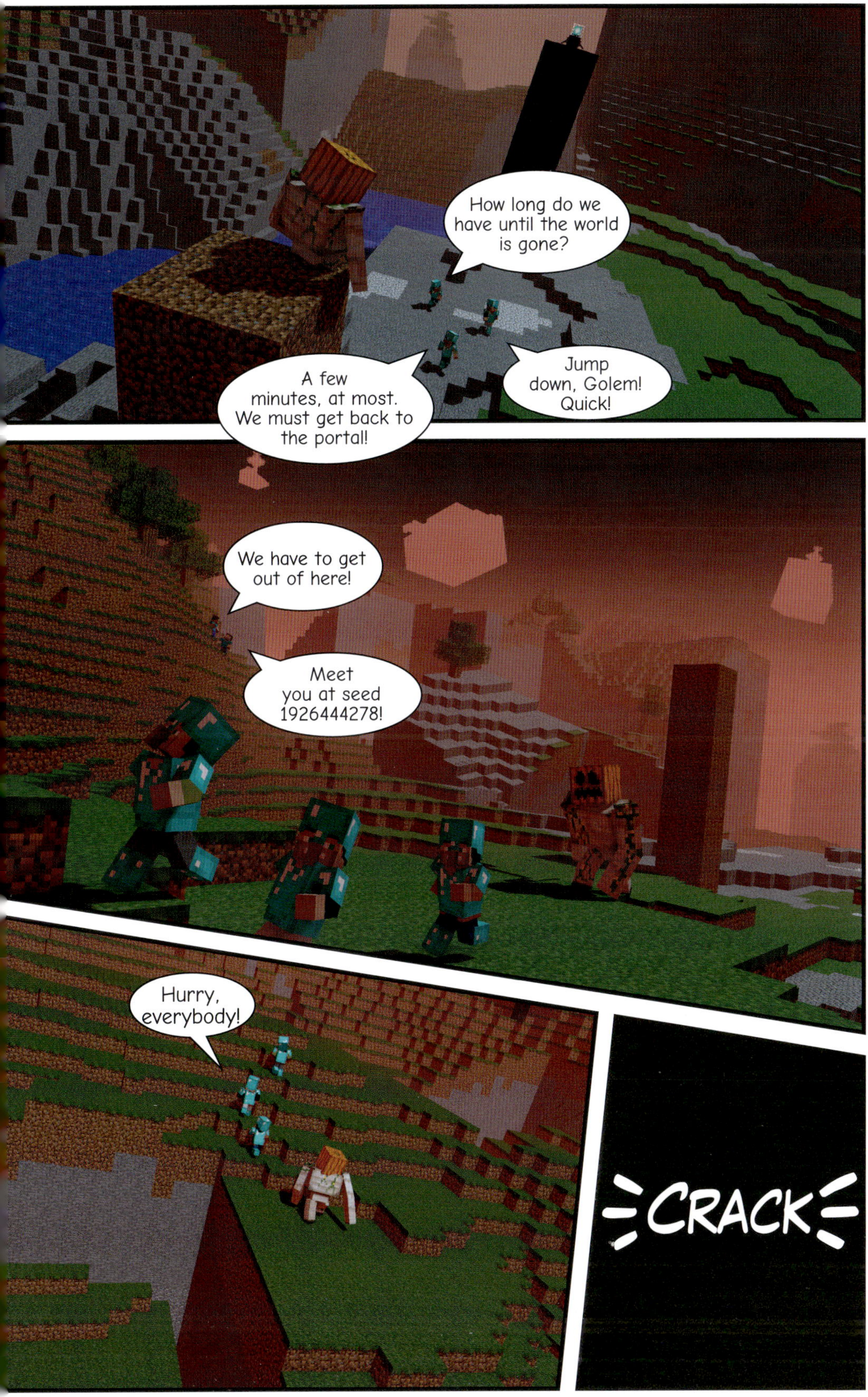
How long do we have until the world is gone?
A few minutes, at most. We must get back to the portal!
Jump down, Golem! Quick!
We have to get out of here!
Meet you at seed 1926444278!
Hurry, everybody!
CRACK

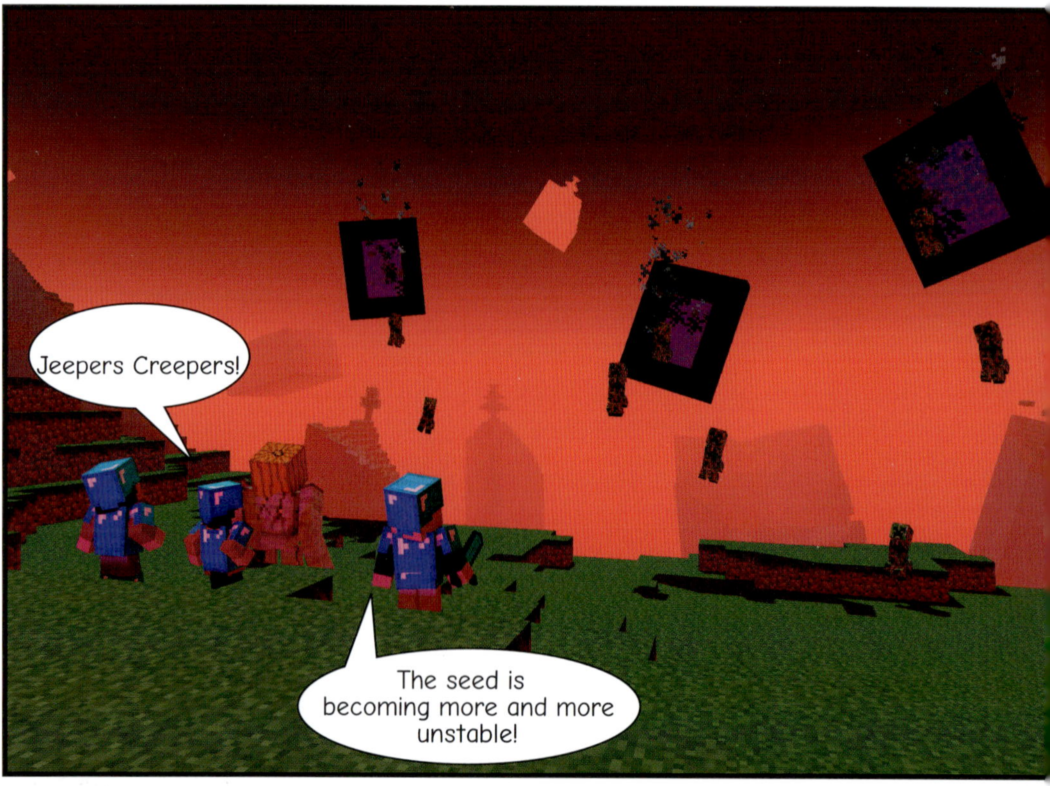
Jeepers Creepers!
The seed is becoming more and more unstable!

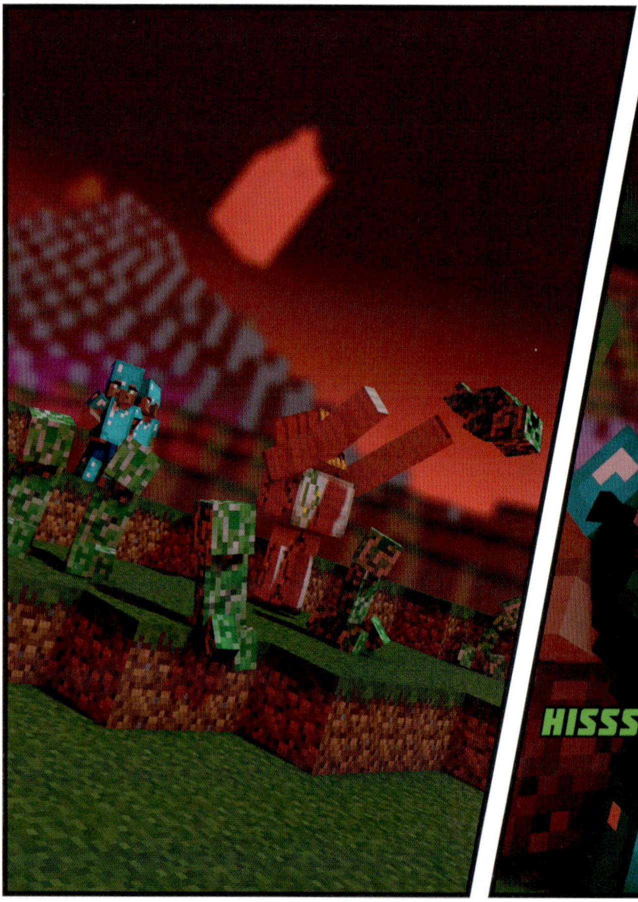

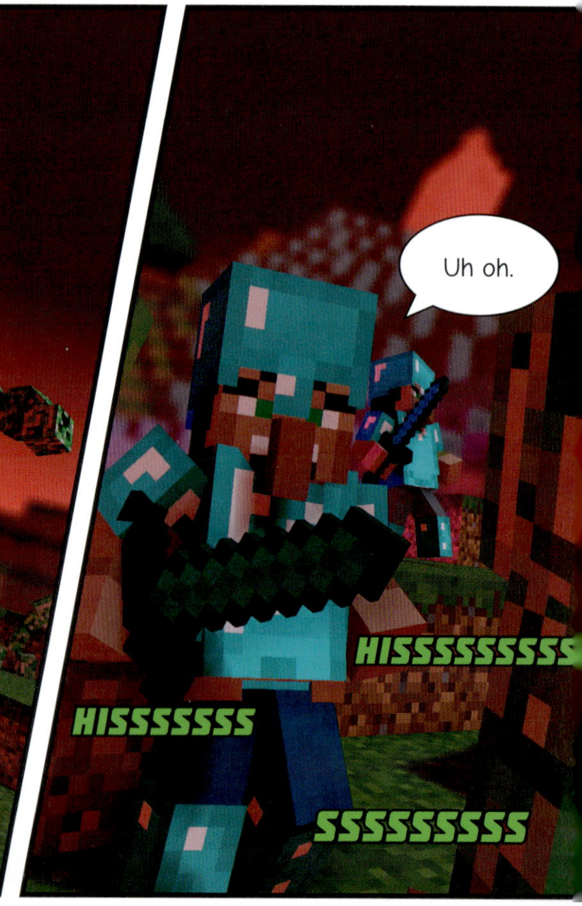
Uh oh.
HISSSSSSSSS
HISSSSSSS
SSSSSSSSS

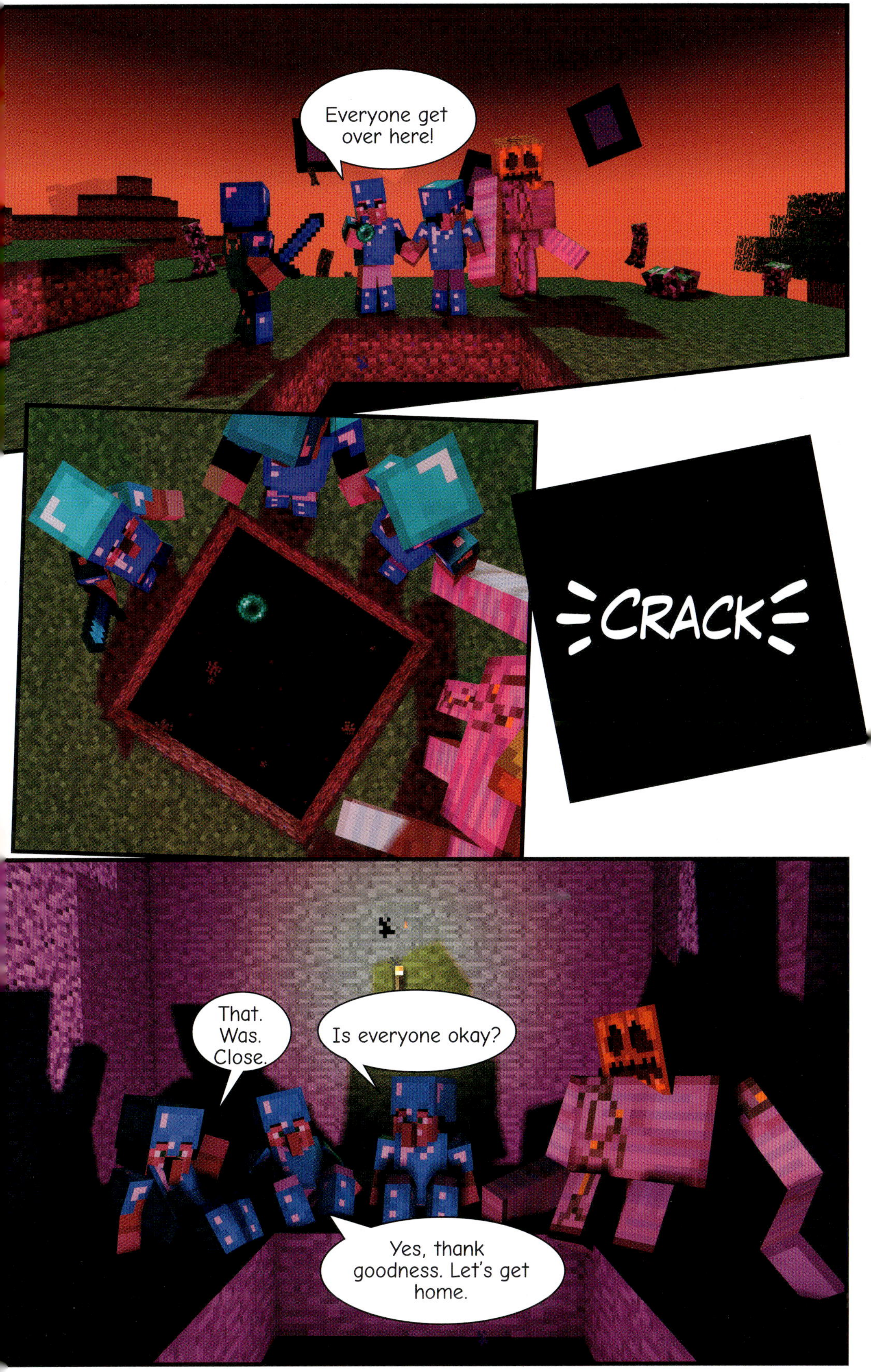
Everyone get over here!
CRACK
That. Was. Close.
Is everyone okay?
Yes, thank goodness. Let's get home.

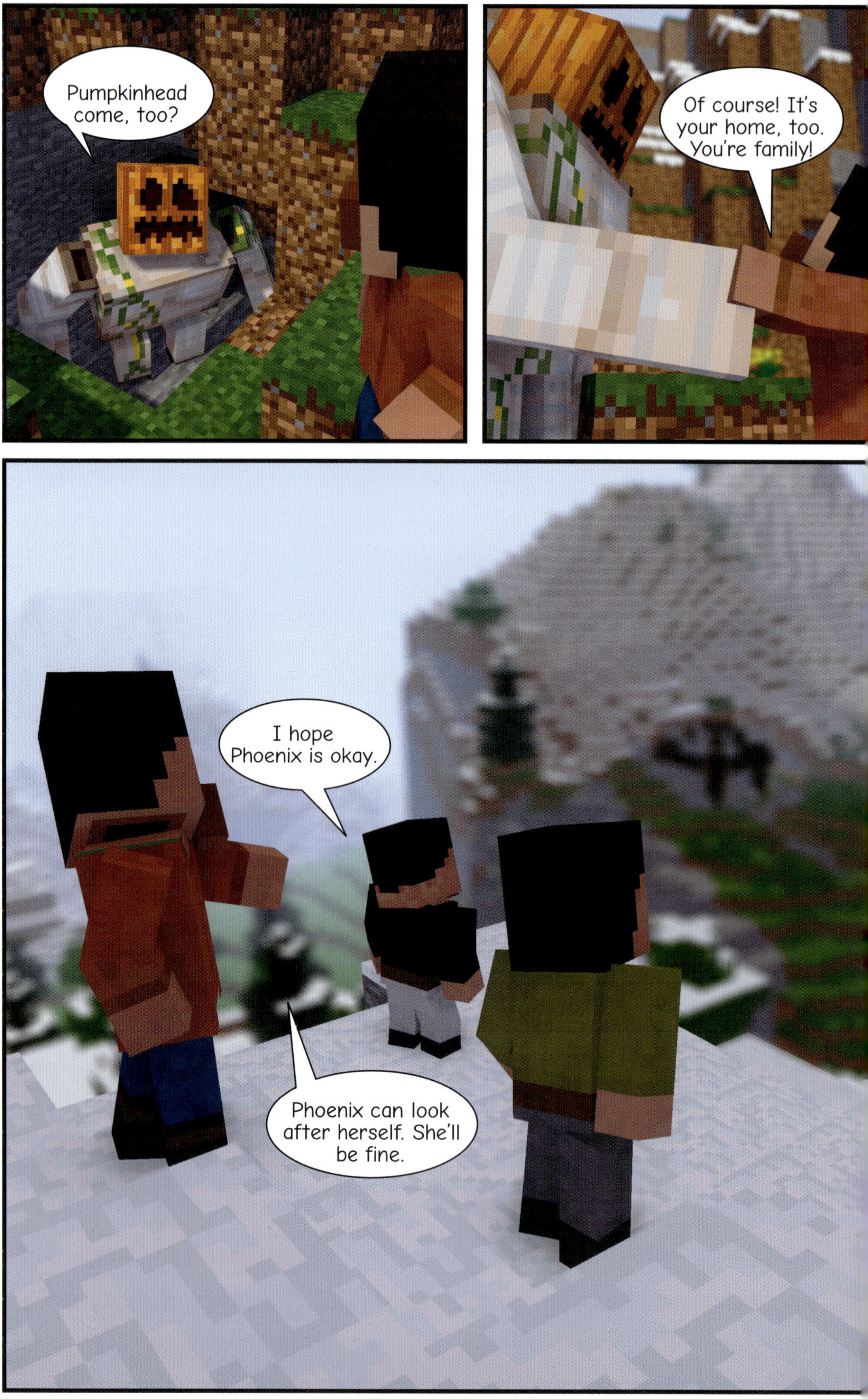
Pumpkinhead come, too?
Of course! It's your home, too. You're family!
I hope Phoenix is okay.
Phoenix can look after herself. She'll be fine.

CHAPTER 4

INTO THE NETHER

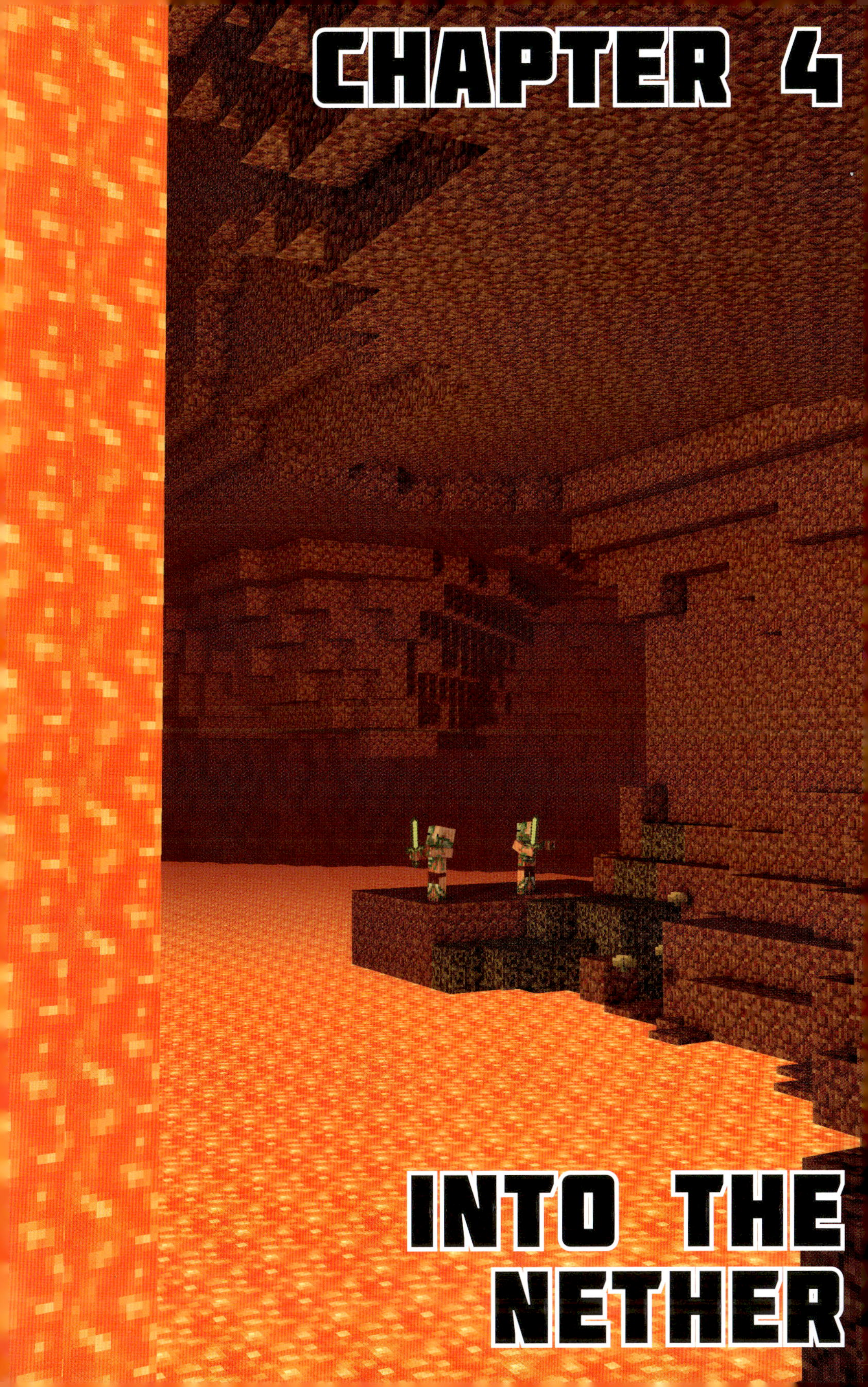

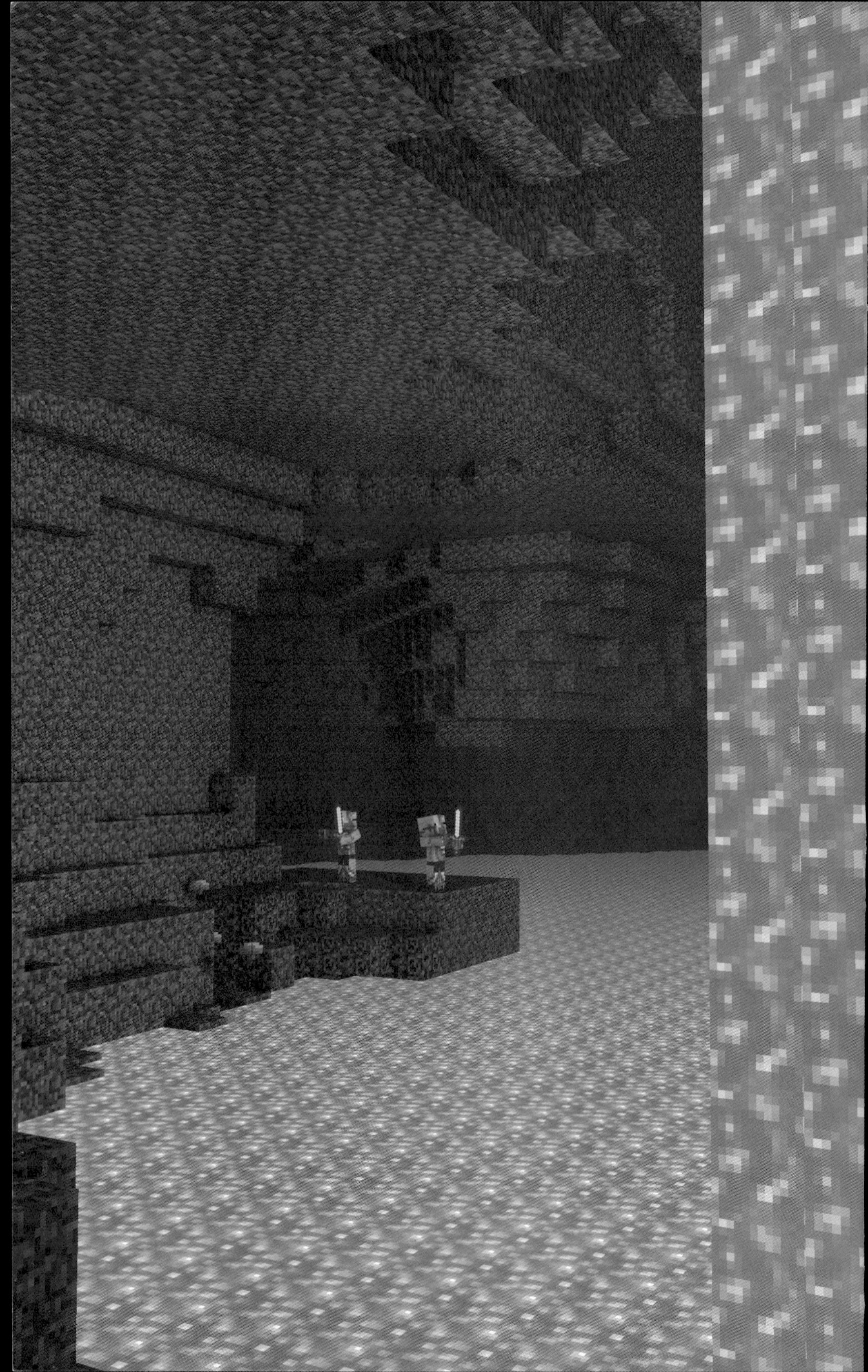

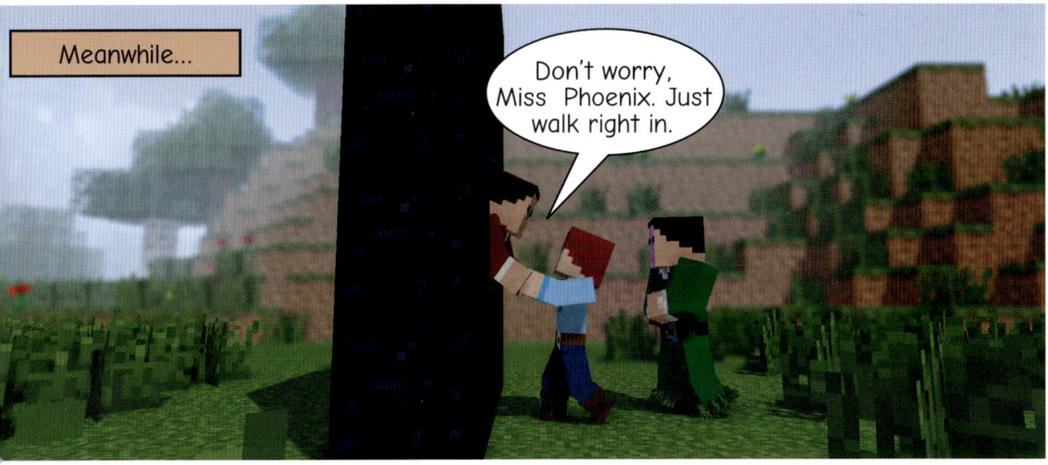
Meanwhile...
Don't worry, Miss Phoenix. Just walk right in.

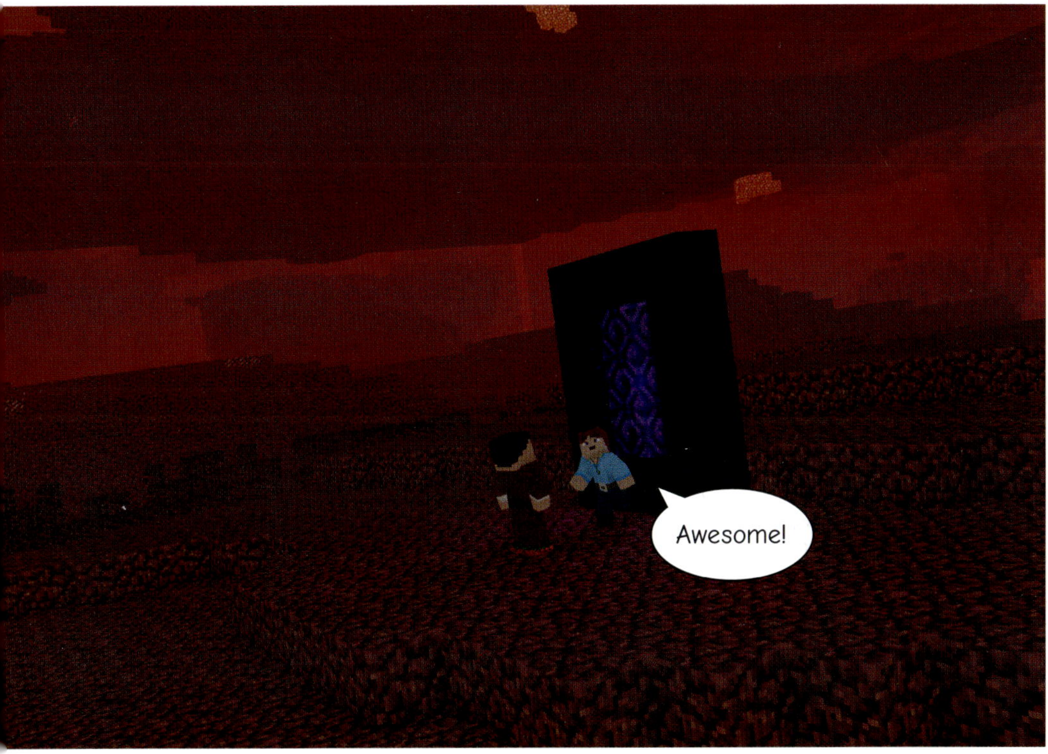
Awesome!

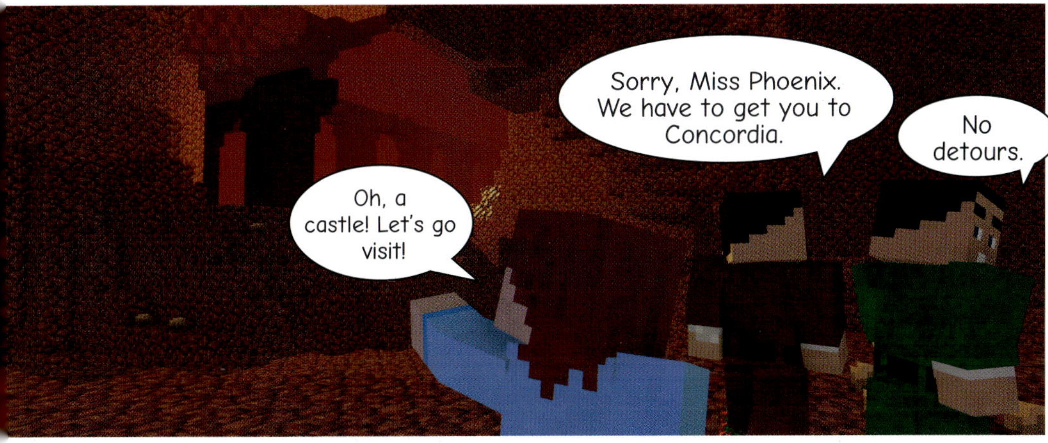
Oh, a castle! Let's go visit!
Sorry, Miss Phoenix. We have to get you to Concordia.
No detours.

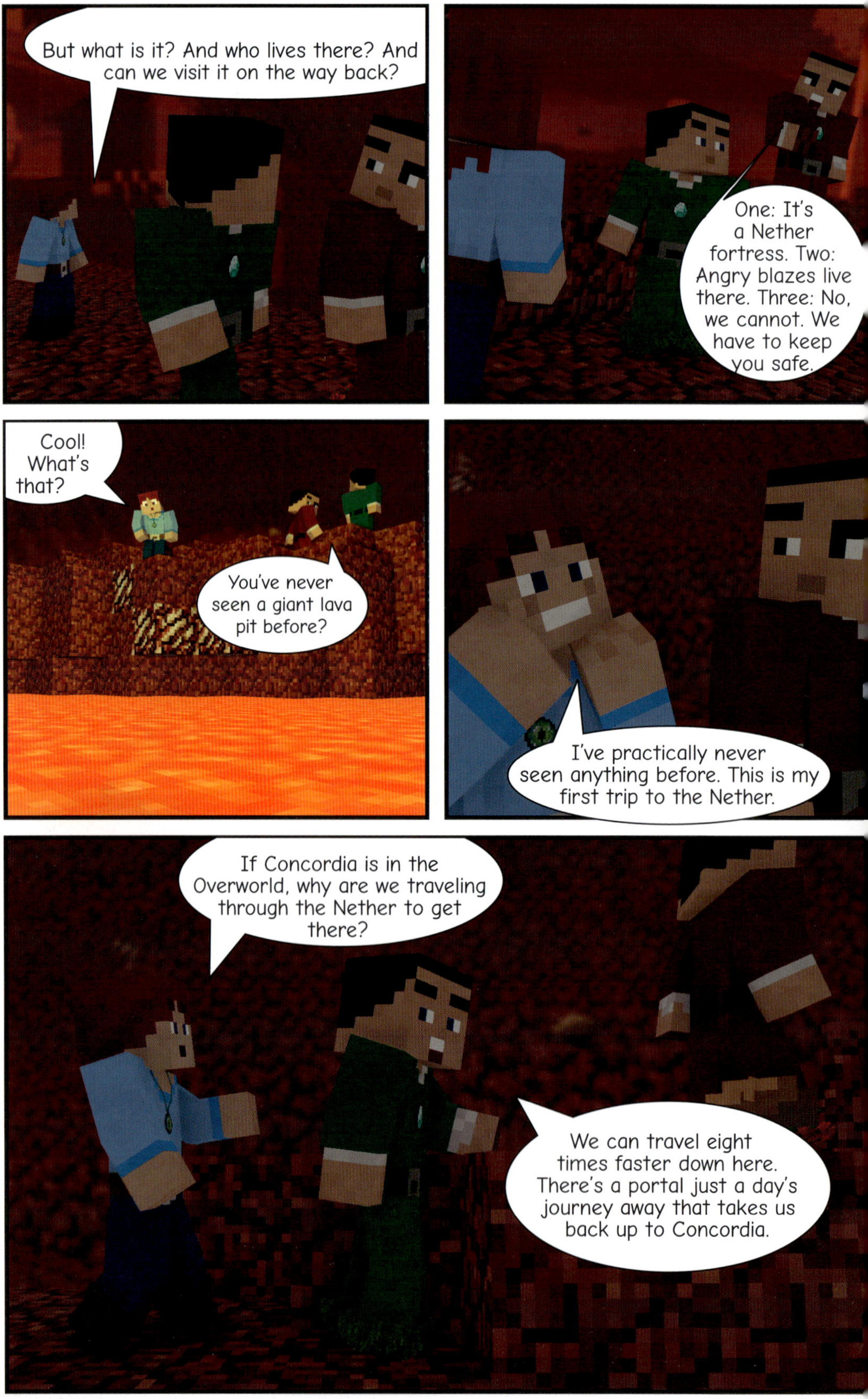
But what is it? And who lives there? And can we visit it on the way back?
One: It's a Nether fortress. Two: Angry blazes live there. Three: No, we cannot. We have to keep you safe.
Cool! What's that?
You've never seen a giant lava pit before?
I've practically never seen anything before. This is my first trip to the Nether.
If Concordia is in the Overworld, why are we traveling through the Nether to get there?
We can travel eight times faster down here. There's a portal just a day's journey away that takes us back up to Concordia.

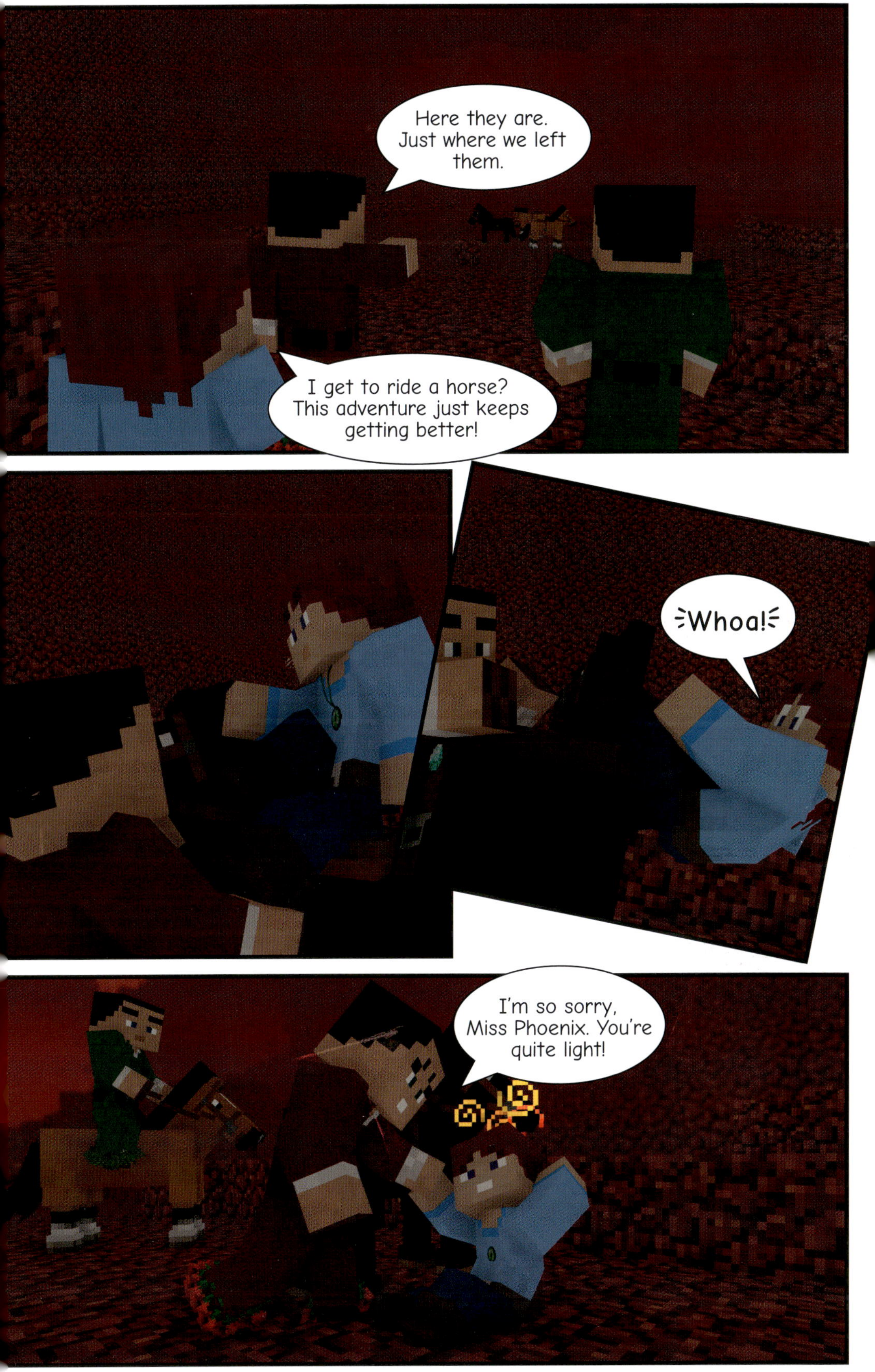
Here they are. Just where we left them.
I get to ride a horse? This adventure just keeps getting better!
Whoa!
I'm so sorry, Miss Phoenix. You're quite light!

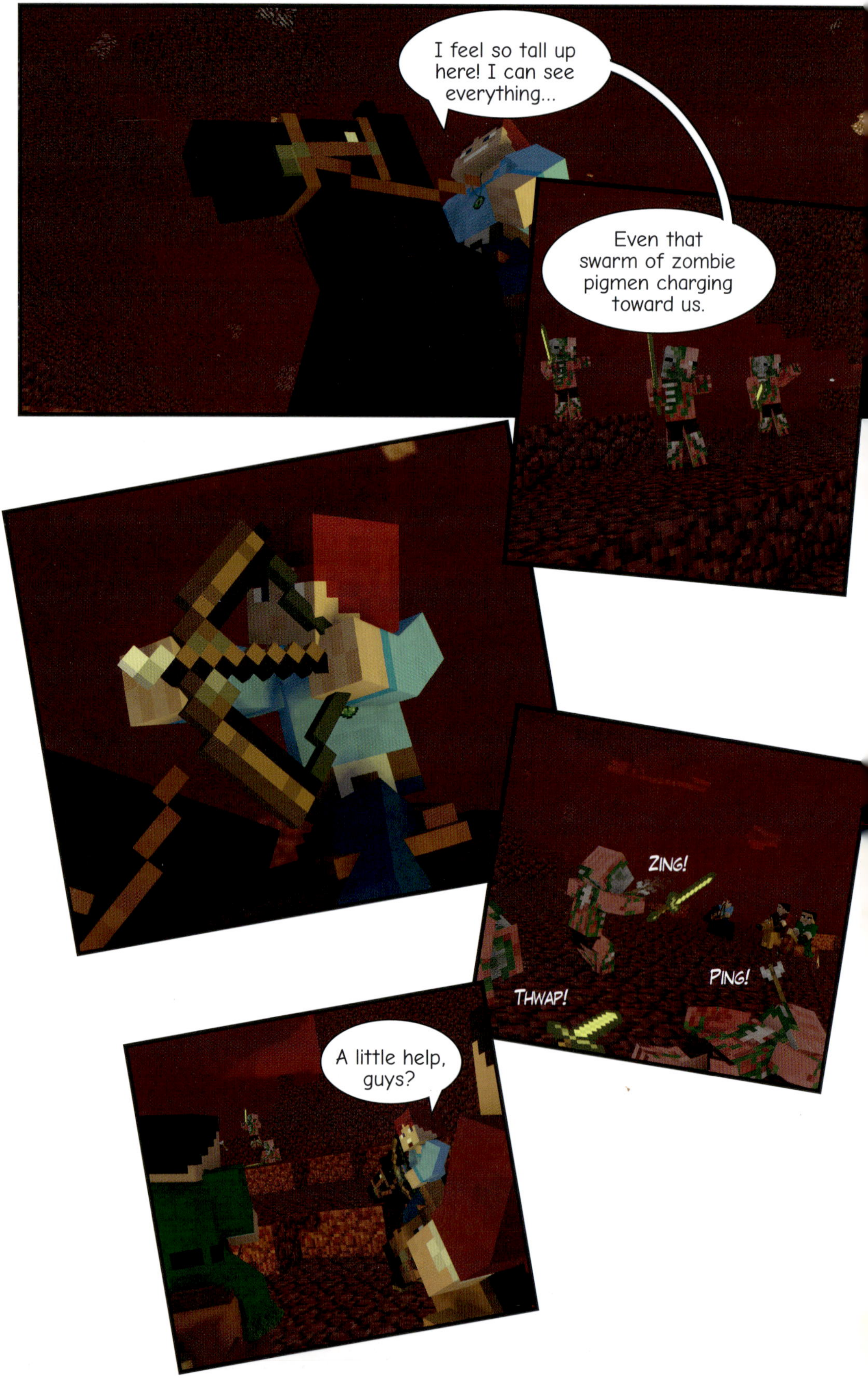
I feel so tall up here! I can see everything...
Even that swarm of zombie pigmen charging toward us.
ZING!
PING!
THWAP!
A little help, guys?

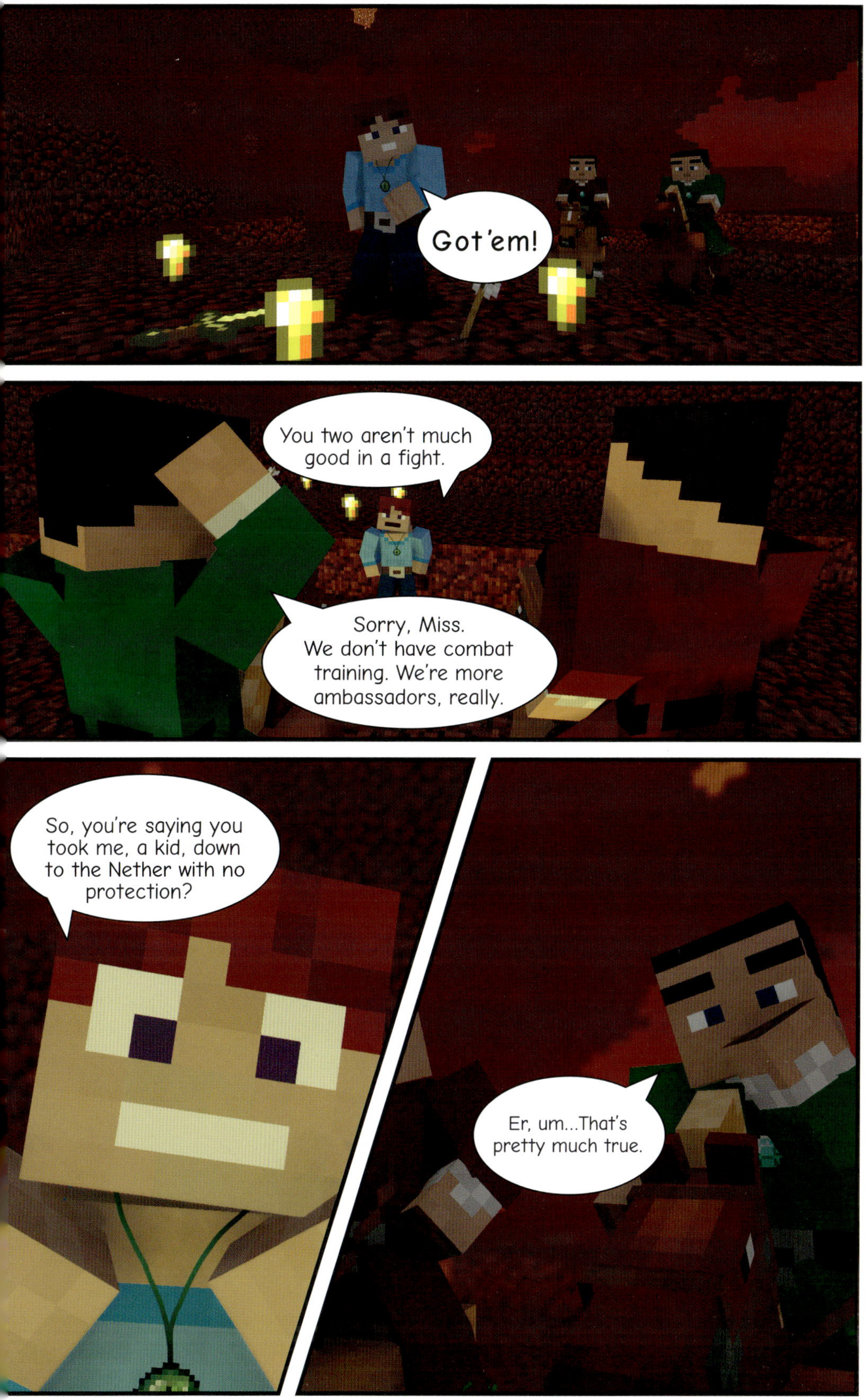
Got'em!
You two aren't much good in a fight.
Sorry, Miss. We don't have combat training. We're more ambassadors, really.
So, you're saying you took me, a kid, down to the Nether with no protection?
Er, um...That's pretty much true.

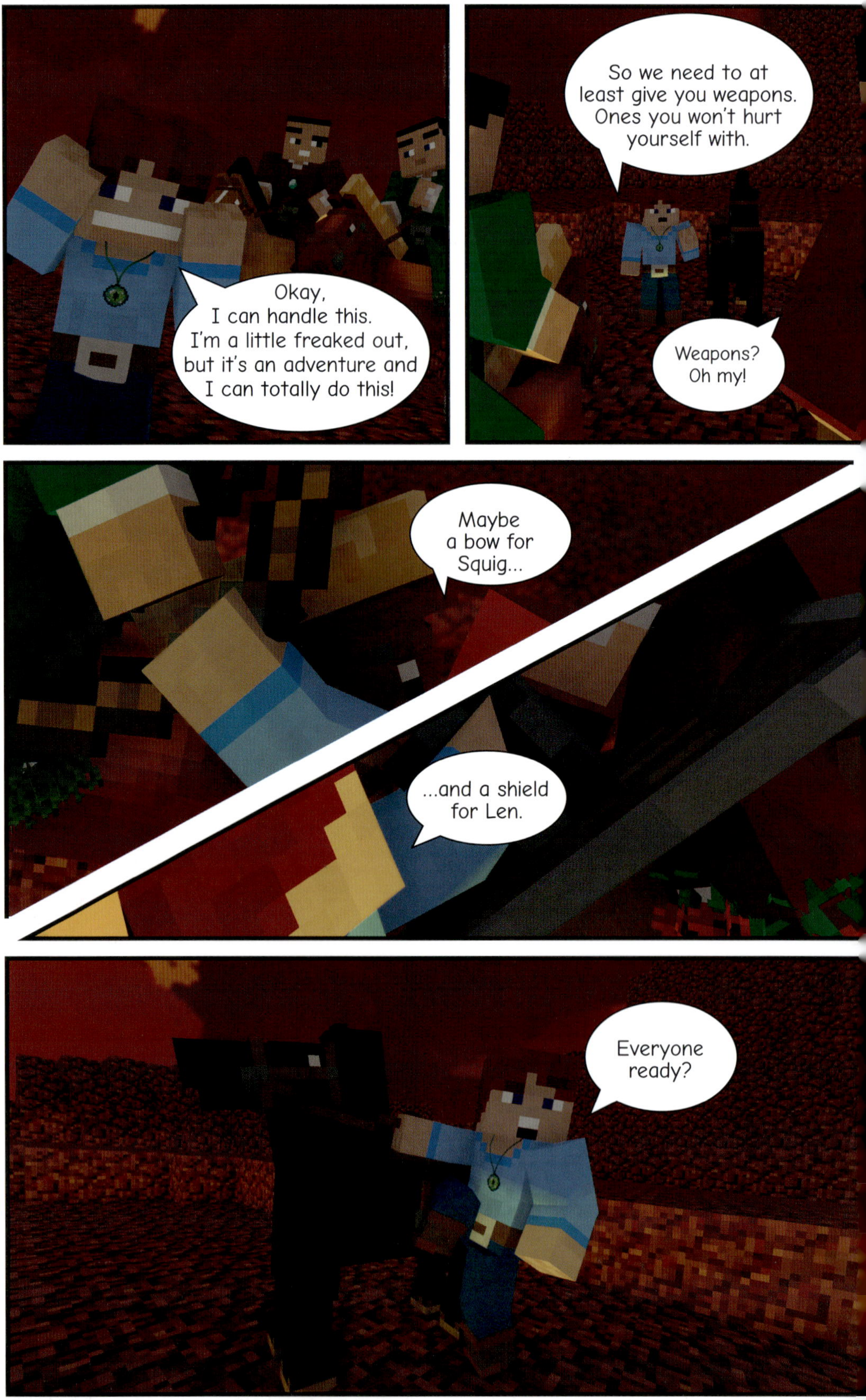
Okay, I can handle this. I'm a little freaked out, but it's an adventure and I can totally do this!
So we need to at least give you weapons. Ones you won't hurt yourself with.
Weapons? Oh my!
Maybe a bow for Squig...
...and a shield for Len.
Everyone ready?

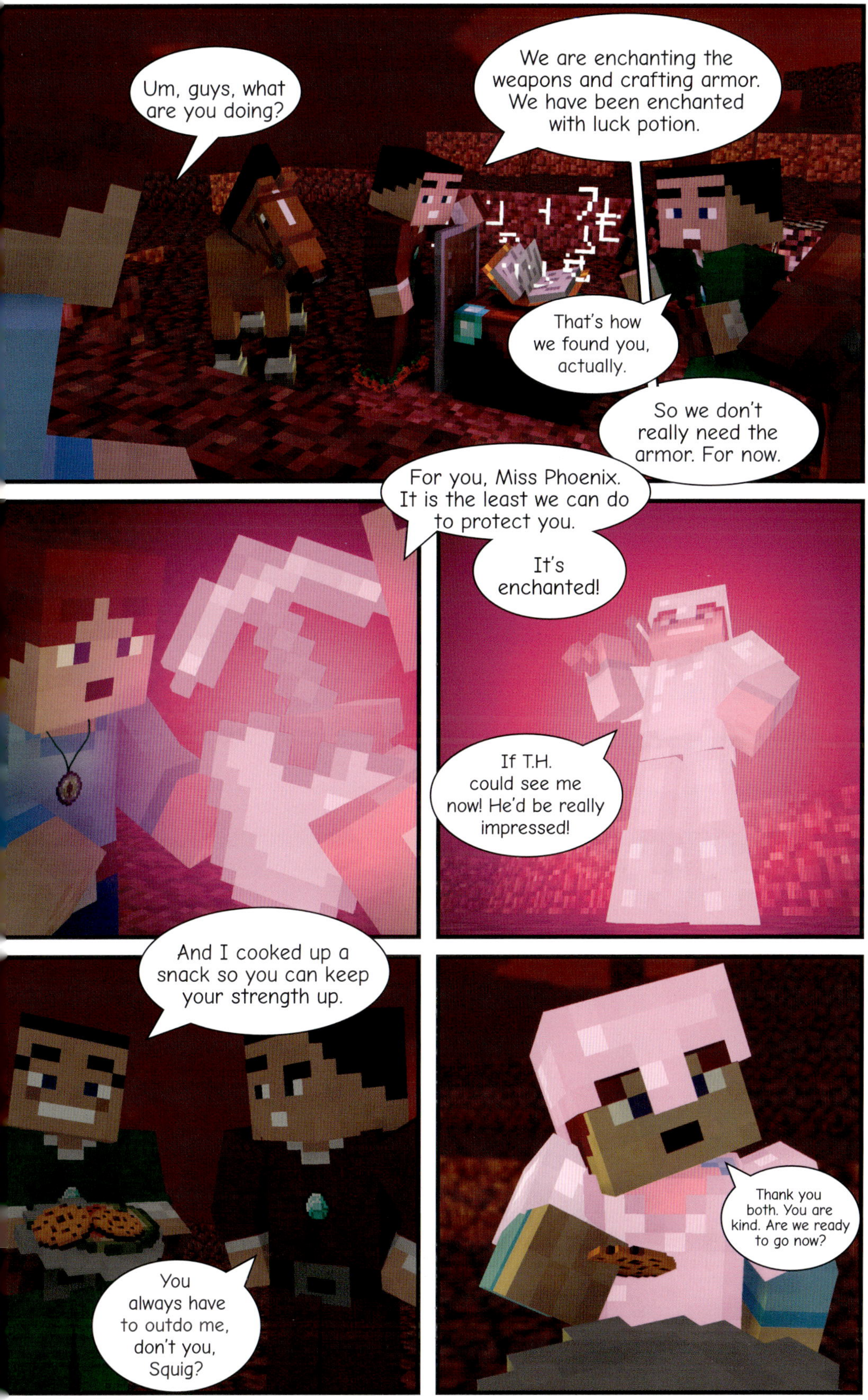
Um, guys, what are you doing?
We are enchanting the weapons and crafting armor. We have been enchanted with luck potion.
That's how we found you, actually.
So we don't really need the armor. For now.
For you, Miss Phoenix. It is the least we can do to protect you.
It's enchanted!
If T.H. could see me now! He'd be really impressed!
And I cooked up a snack so you can keep your strength up.
You always have to outdo me, don't you, Squig?
Thank you both. You are kind. Are we ready to go now?

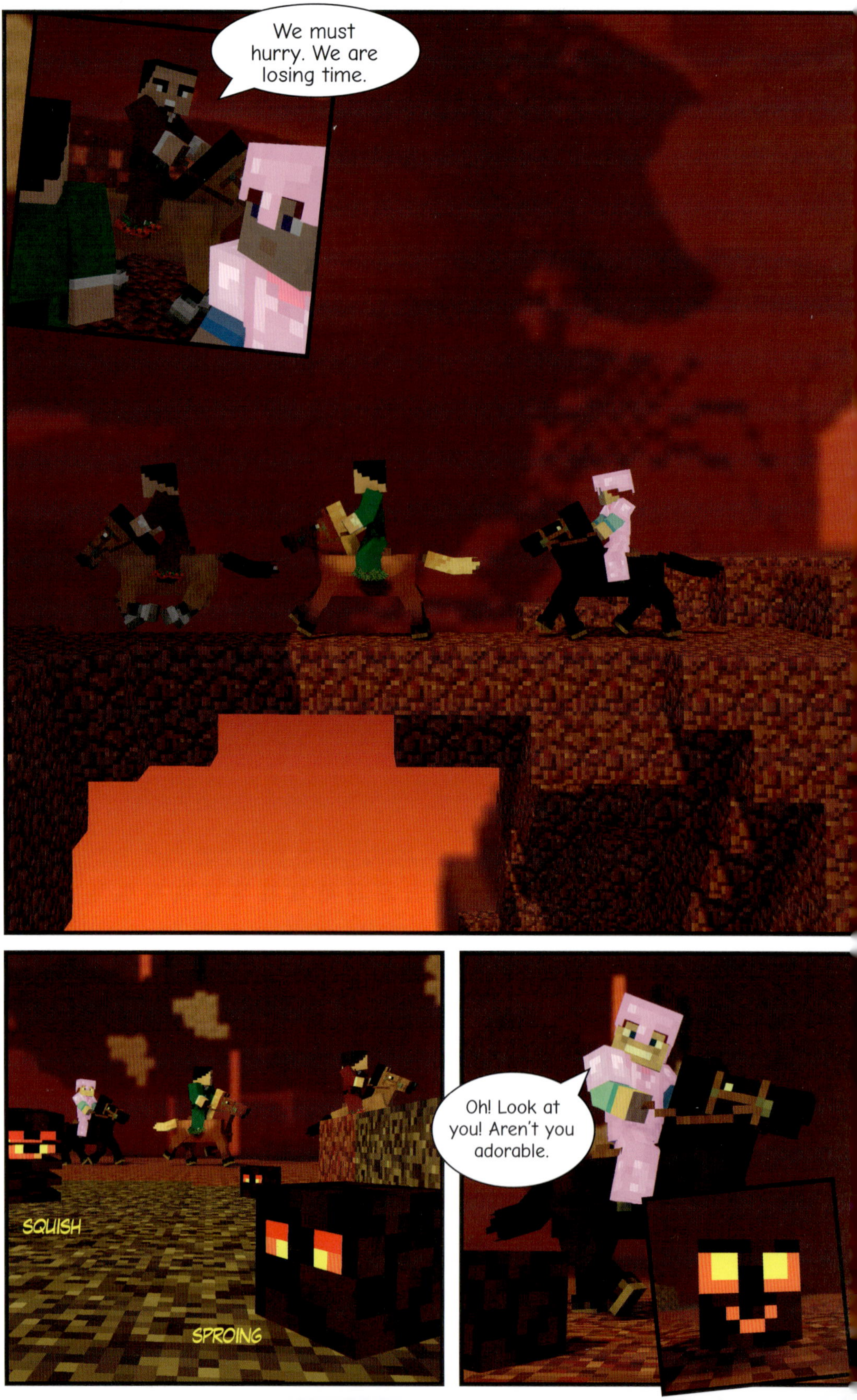
We must hurry. We are losing time.
SQUISH
SPROING
Oh! Look at you! Aren't you adorable.

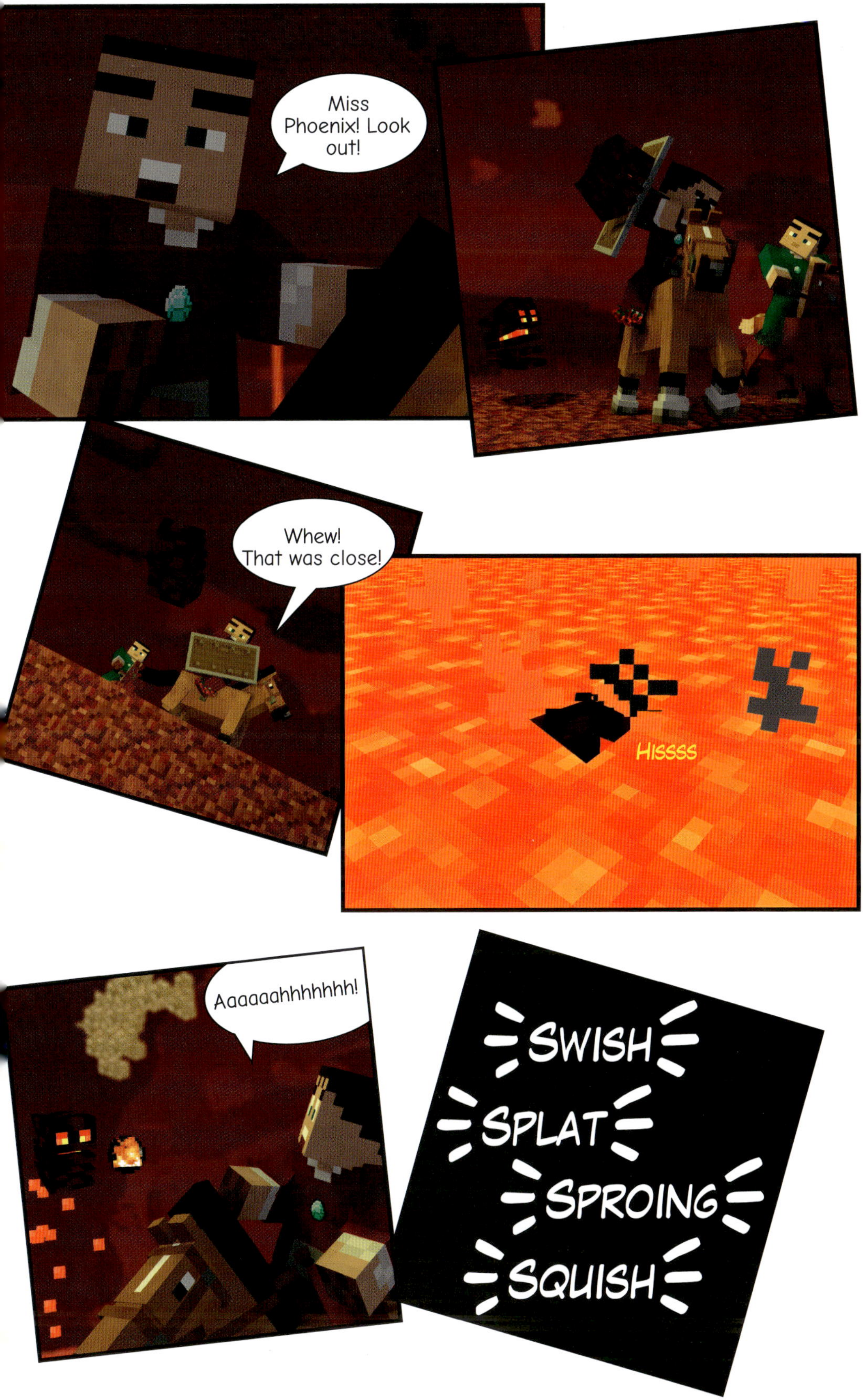
Miss Phoenix! Look out!
Whew! That was close!
Hissss
Aaaaaahhhhhhh!
SWISH
SPLAT
SPROING
SQUISH

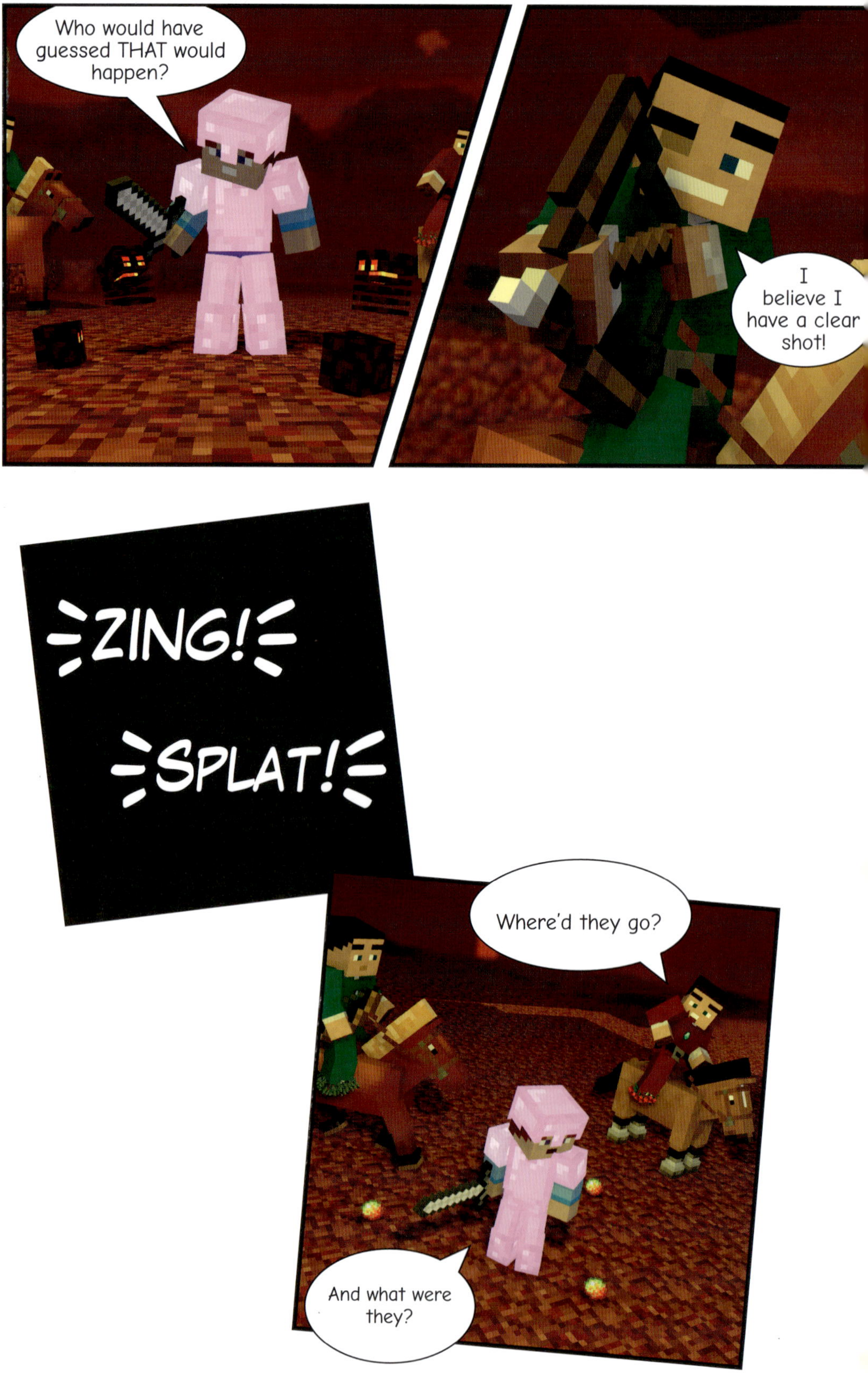
Who would have guessed THAT would happen?
I believe I have a clear shot!
ZING!
SPLAT!
Where'd they go?
And what were they?

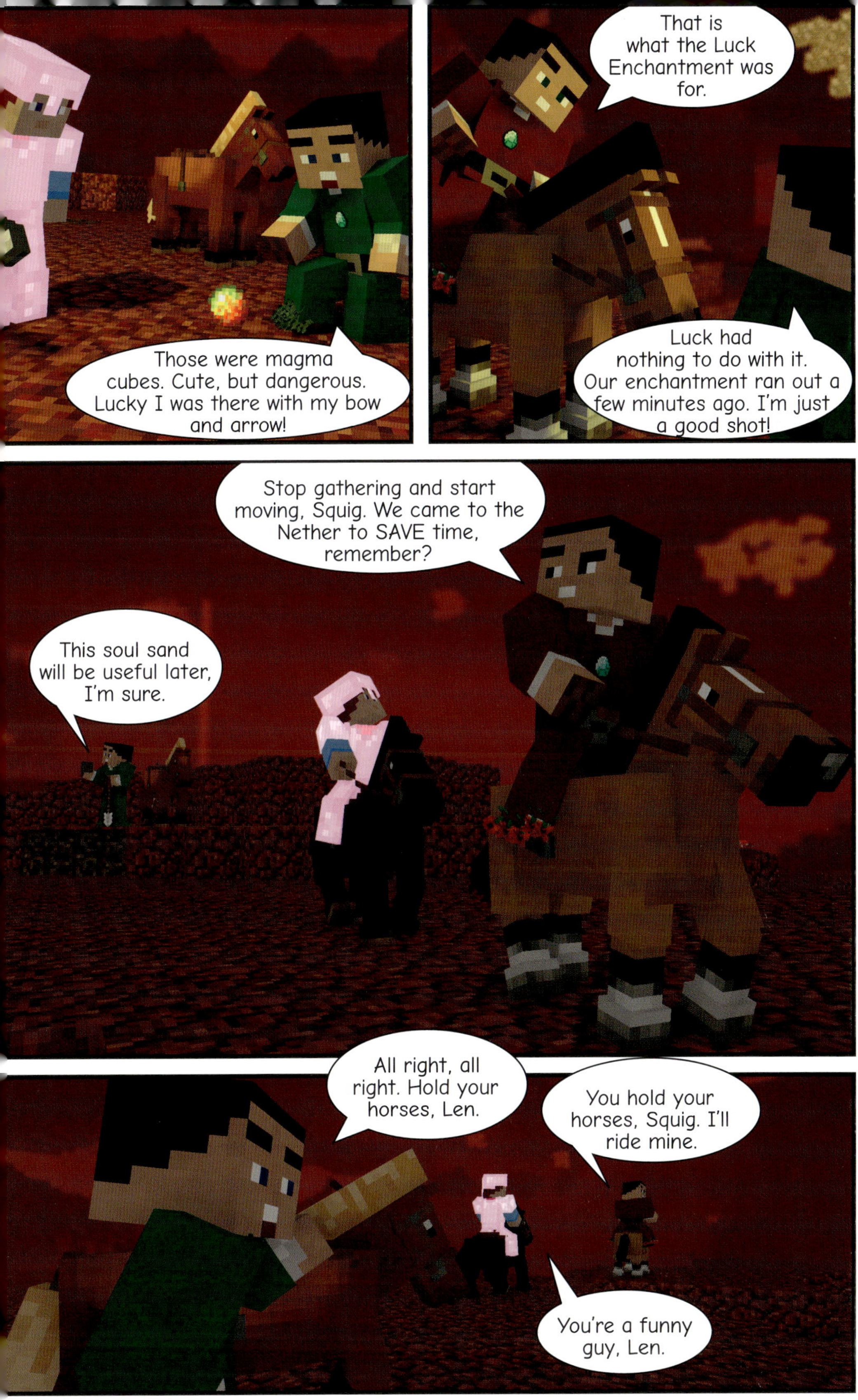
Those were magma cubes. Cute, but dangerous. Lucky I was there with my bow and arrow!
That is what the Luck Enchantment was for.
Luck had nothing to do with it. Our enchantment ran out a few minutes ago. I'm just a good shot!
Stop gathering and start moving, Squig. We came to the Nether to SAVE time, remember?
This soul sand will be useful later, I'm sure.
All right, all right. Hold your horses, Len.
You hold your horses, Squig. I'll ride mine.
You're a funny guy, Len.

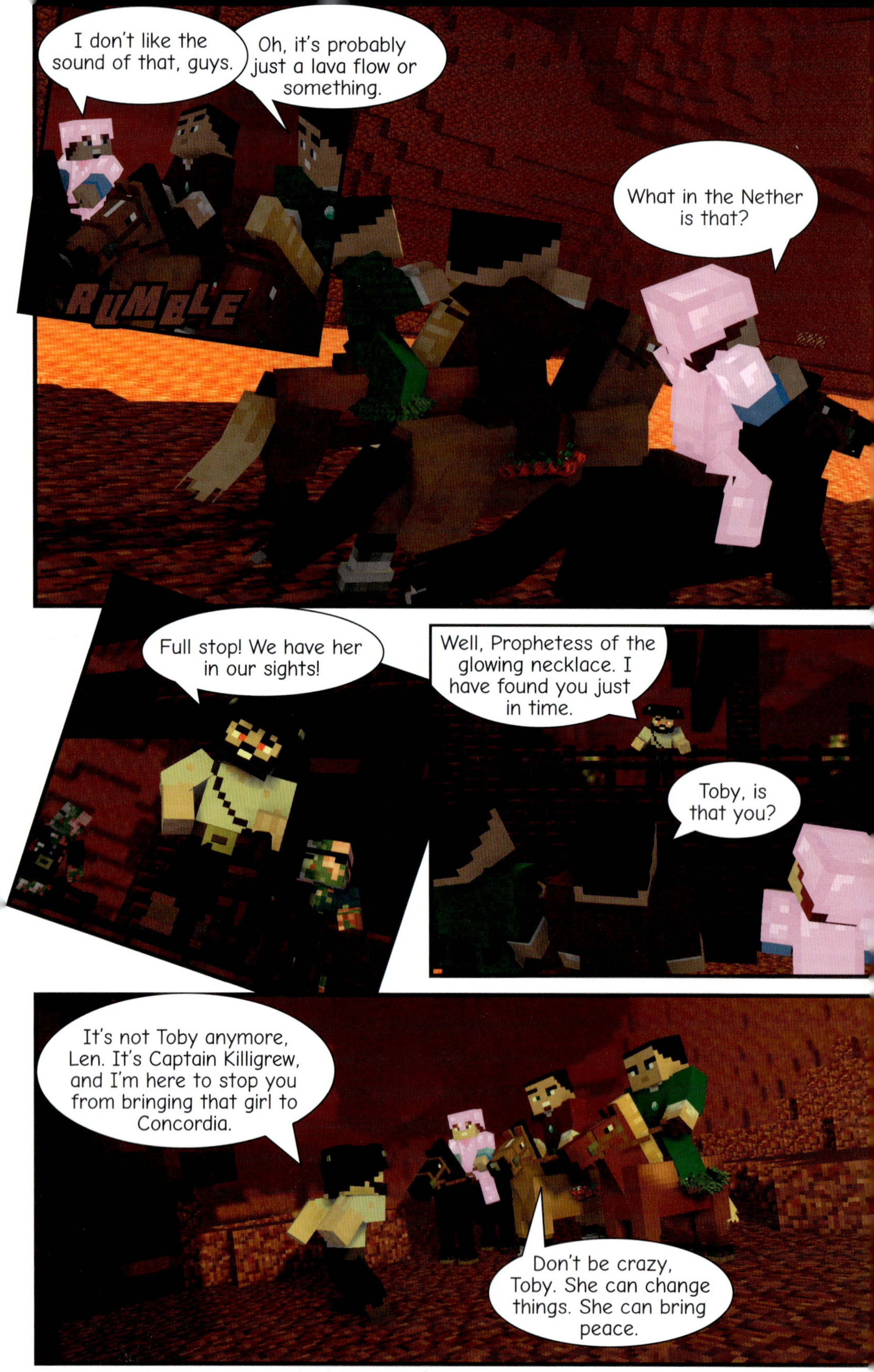
I don't like the sound of that, guys.
Oh, it's probably just a lava flow or something.
RUMBLE
What in the Nether is that?
Full stop! We have her in our sights!
Well, Prophetess of the glowing necklace. I have found you just in time.
Toby, is that you?
It's not Toby anymore, Len. It's Captain Killigrew, and I'm here to stop you from bringing that girl to Concordia.
Don't be crazy, Toby. She can change things. She can bring peace.

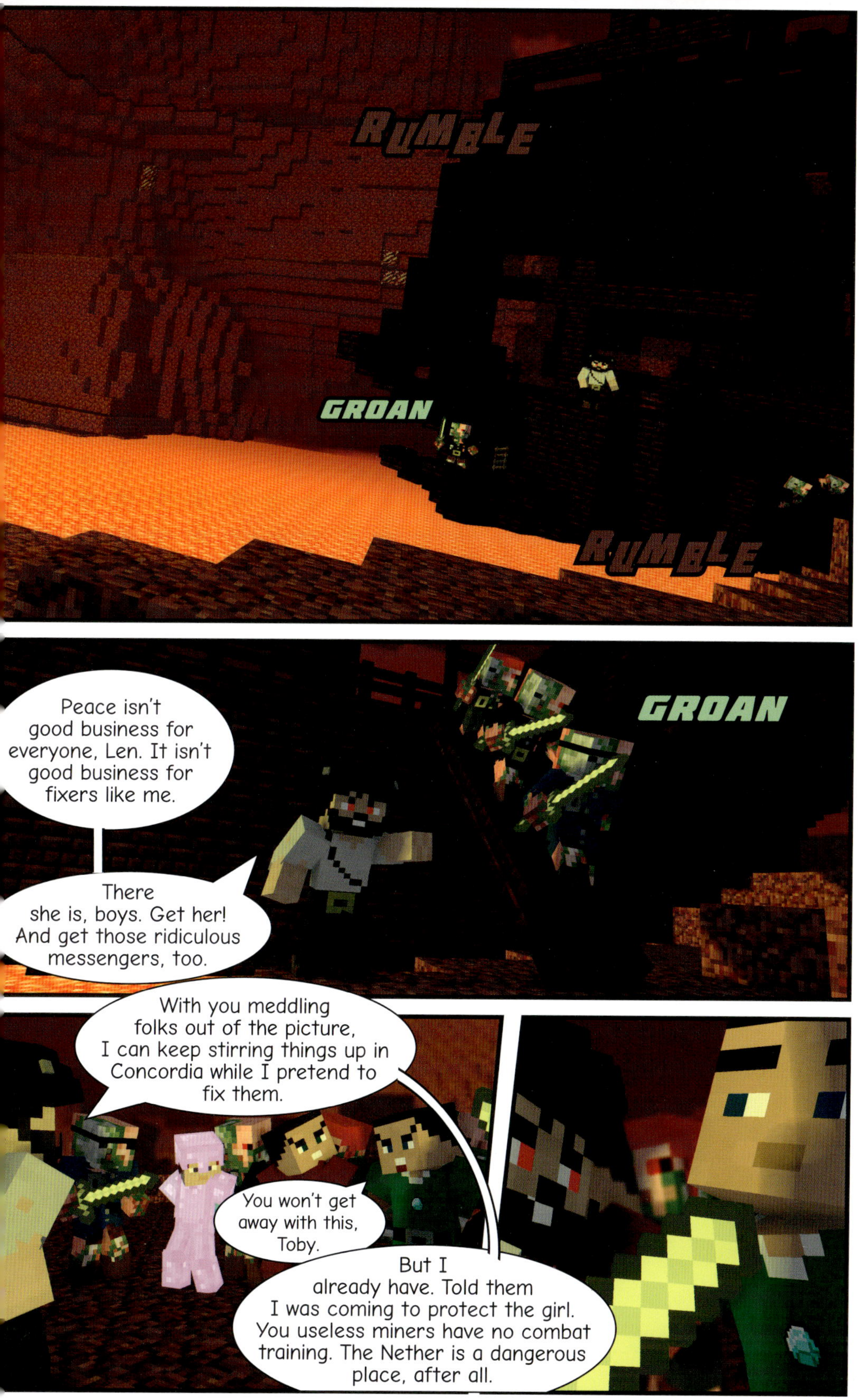
RUMBLE
GROAN
RUMBLE
GROAN
Peace isn't good business for everyone, Len. It isn't good business for fixers like me.
There she is, boys. Get her! And get those ridiculous messengers, too.
With you meddling folks out of the picture, I can keep stirring things up in Concordia while I pretend to fix them.
You won't get away with this, Toby.
But I already have. Told them I was coming to protect the girl. You useless miners have no combat training. The Nether is a dangerous place, after all.

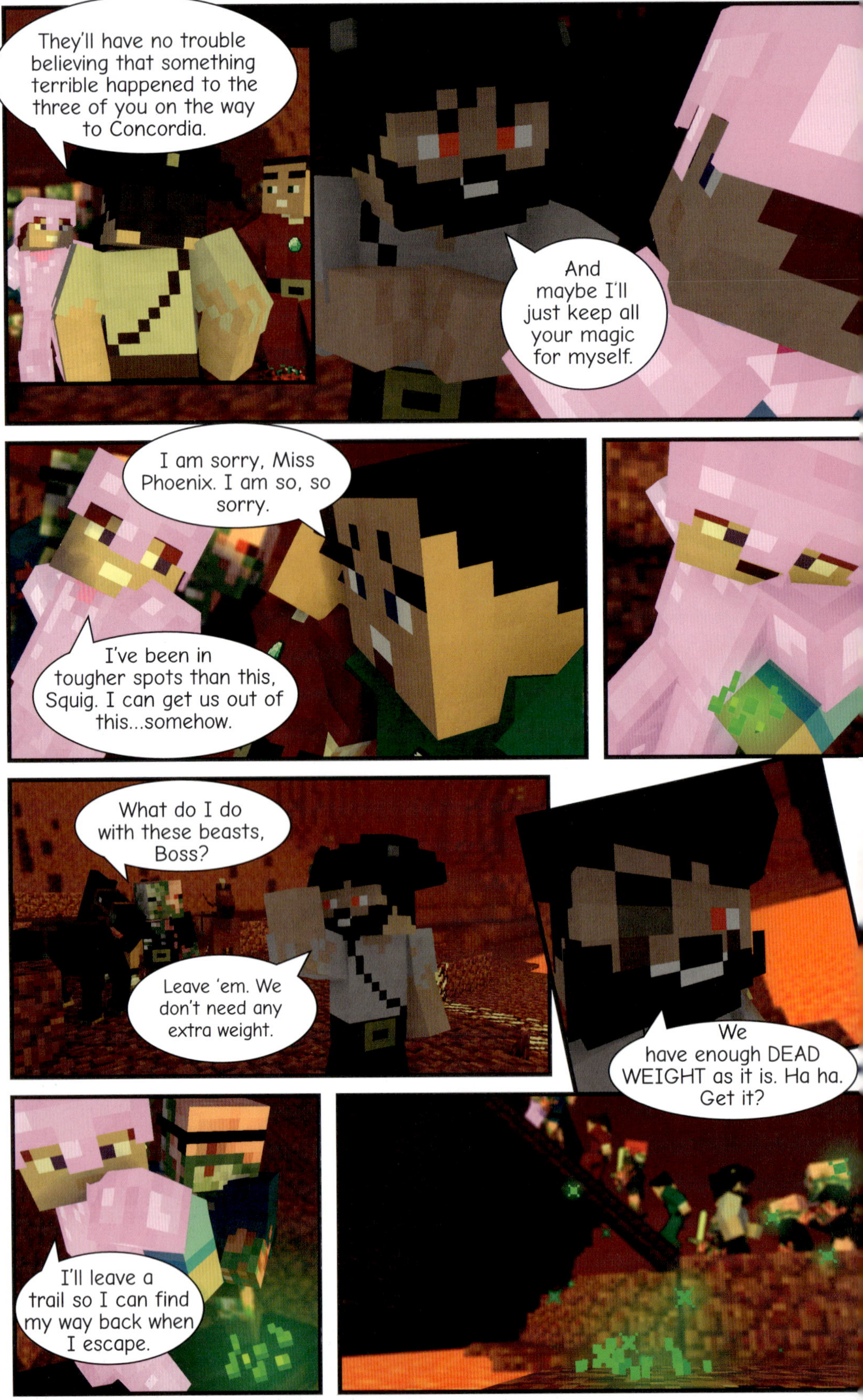
They'll have no trouble believing that something terrible happened to the three of you on the way to Concordia.
And maybe I'll just keep all your magic for myself.
I am sorry, Miss Phoenix. I am so, so sorry.
I've been in tougher spots than this, Squig. I can get us out of this...somehow.
What do I do with these beasts, Boss?
Leave 'em. We don't need any extra weight.
We have enough DEAD WEIGHT as it is. Ha ha. Get it?
I'll leave a trail so I can find my way back when I escape.

CHAPTER 5

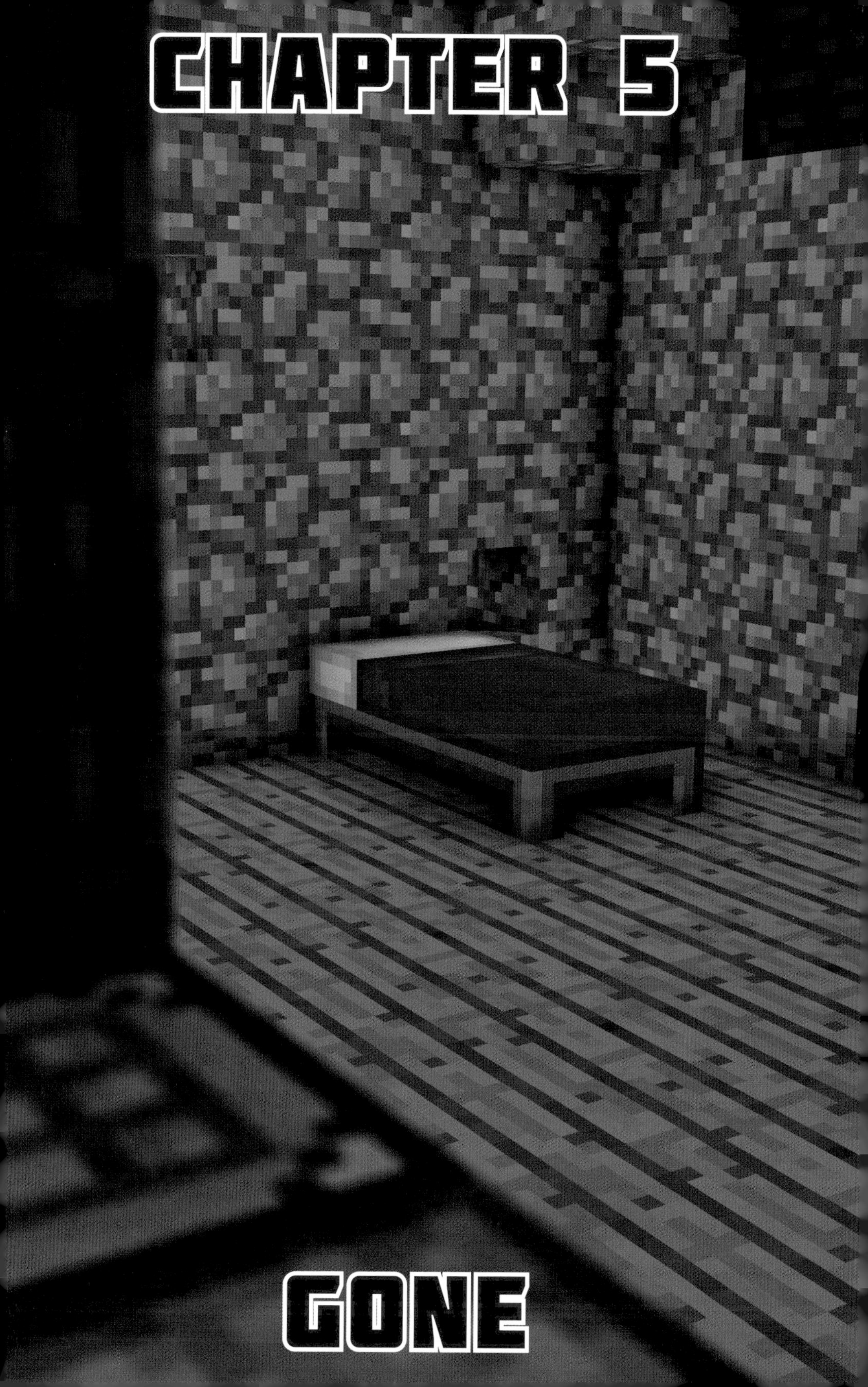

GONE

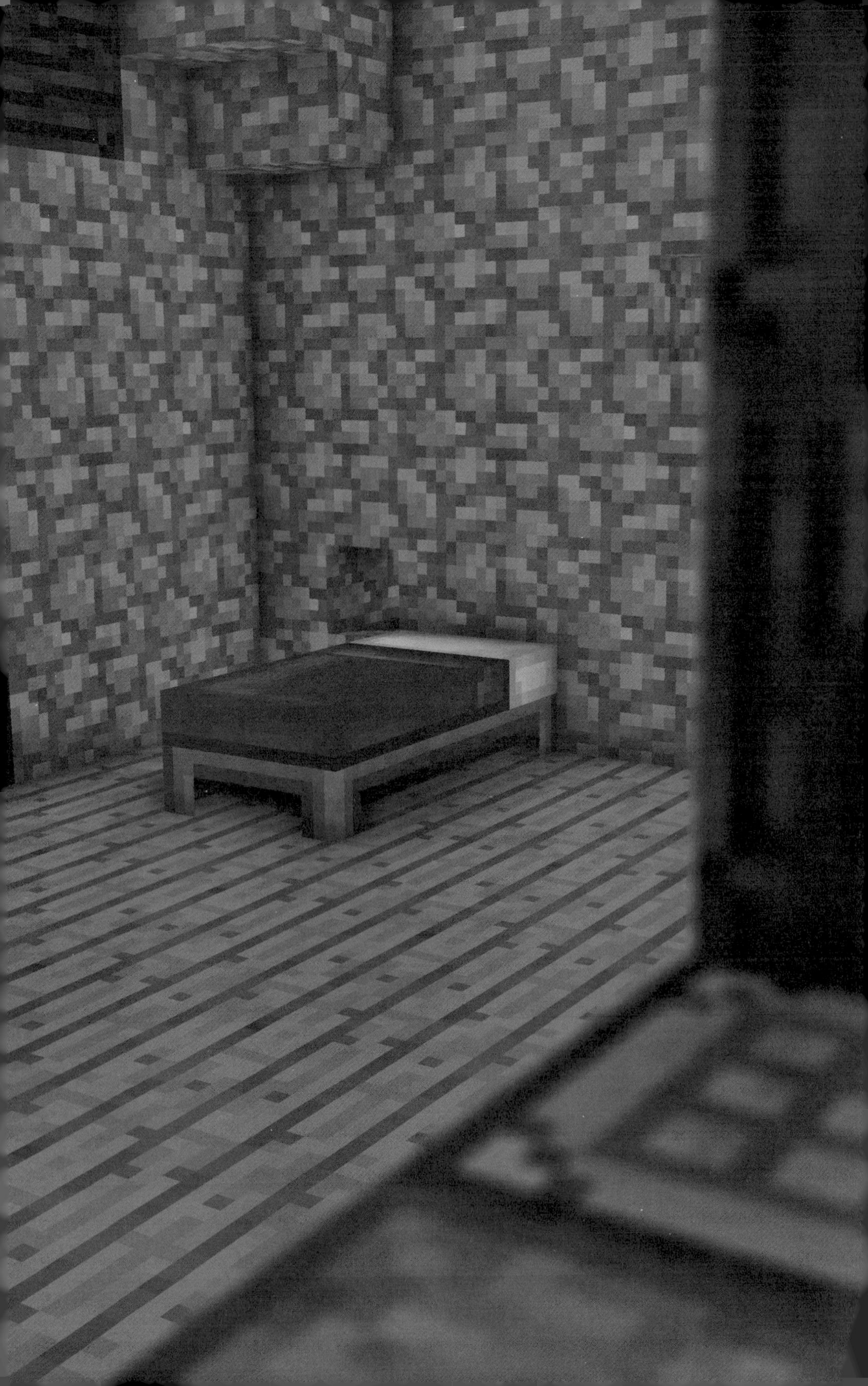

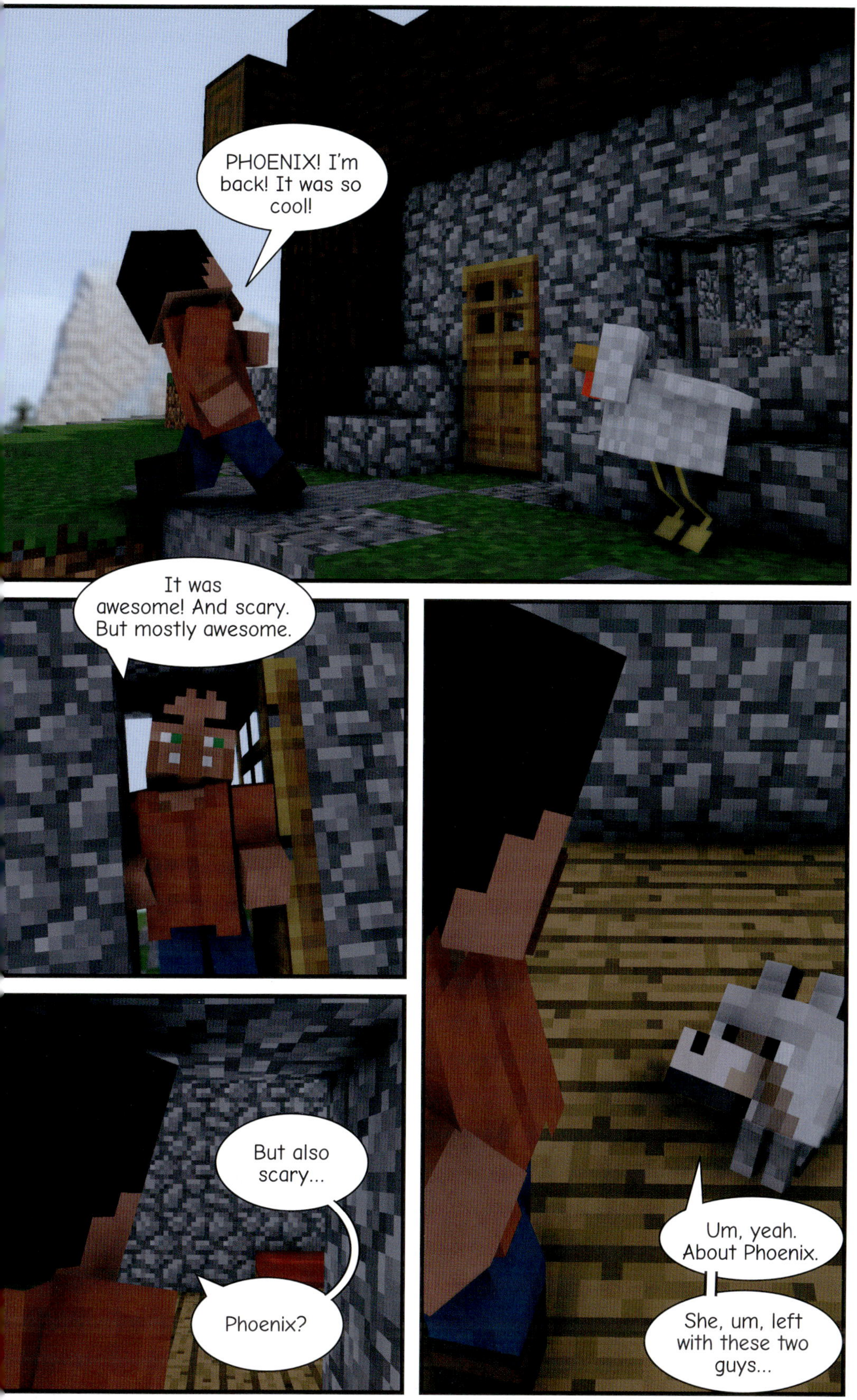
PHOENIX! I'm back! It was so cool!
It was awesome! And scary. But mostly awesome.
But also scary...
Phoenix?
Um, yeah. About Phoenix.
She, um, left with these two guys...

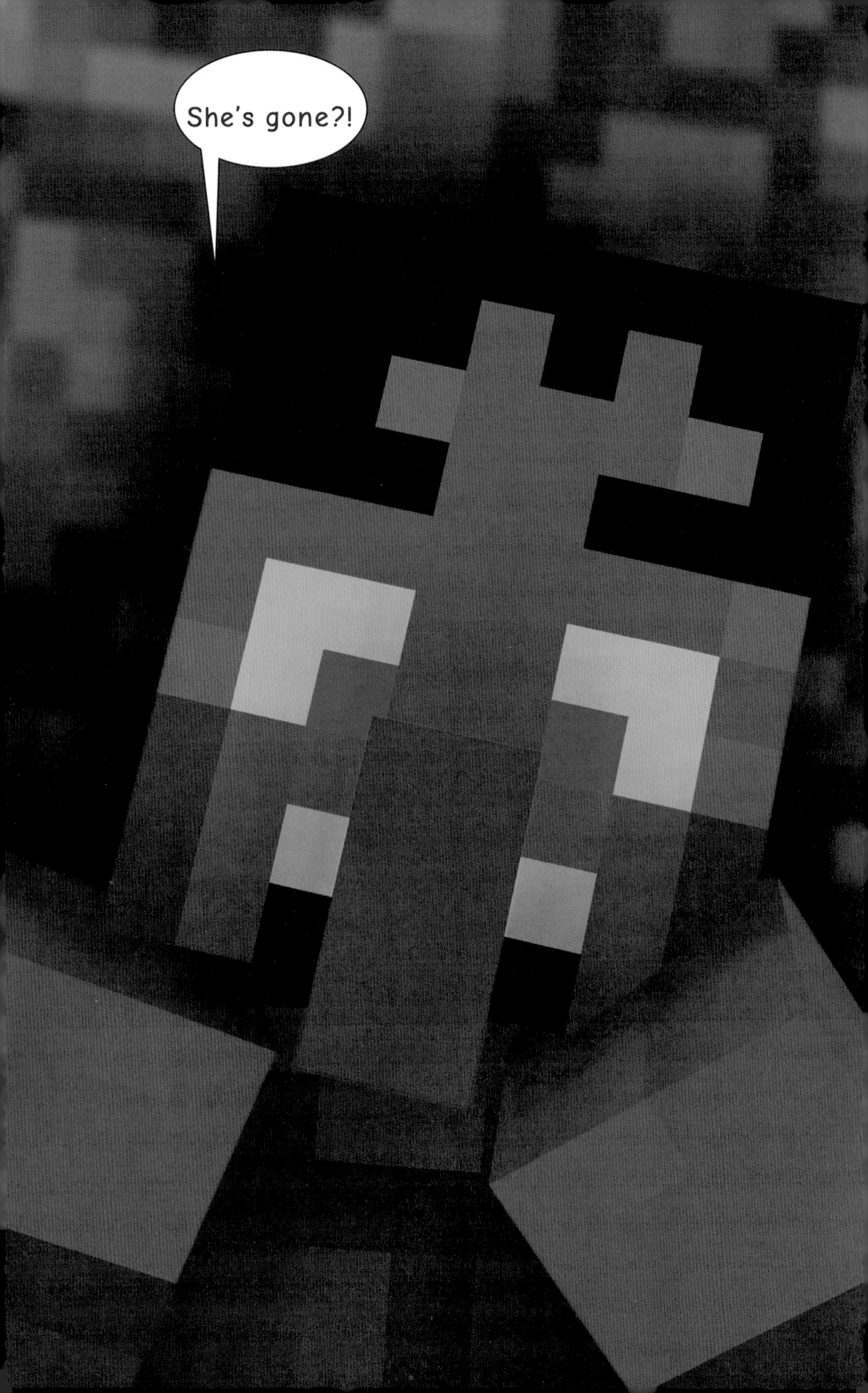
She's gone?!

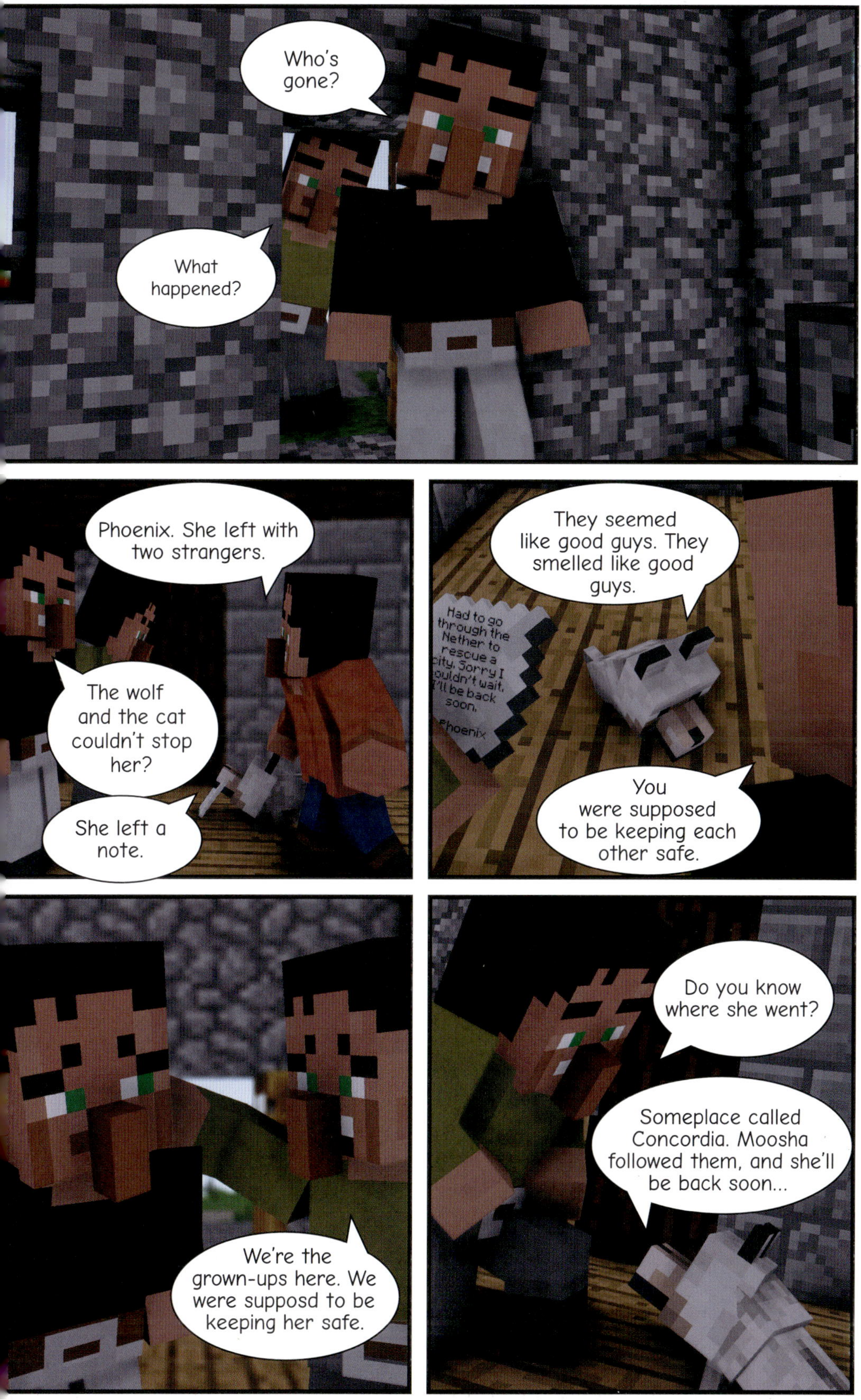
Who's gone?
What happened?
Phoenix. She left with two strangers.
The wolf and the cat couldn't stop her?
She left a note.
They seemed like good guys. They smelled like good guys.
Had to go through the Nether to rescue a ity. Sorry I ouldn't wait. 'll be back soon.
Phoenix
You were supposed to be keeping each other safe.
We're the grown-ups here. We were supposd to be keeping her safe.
Do you know where she went?
Someplace called Concordia. Moosha followed them, and she'll be back soon...

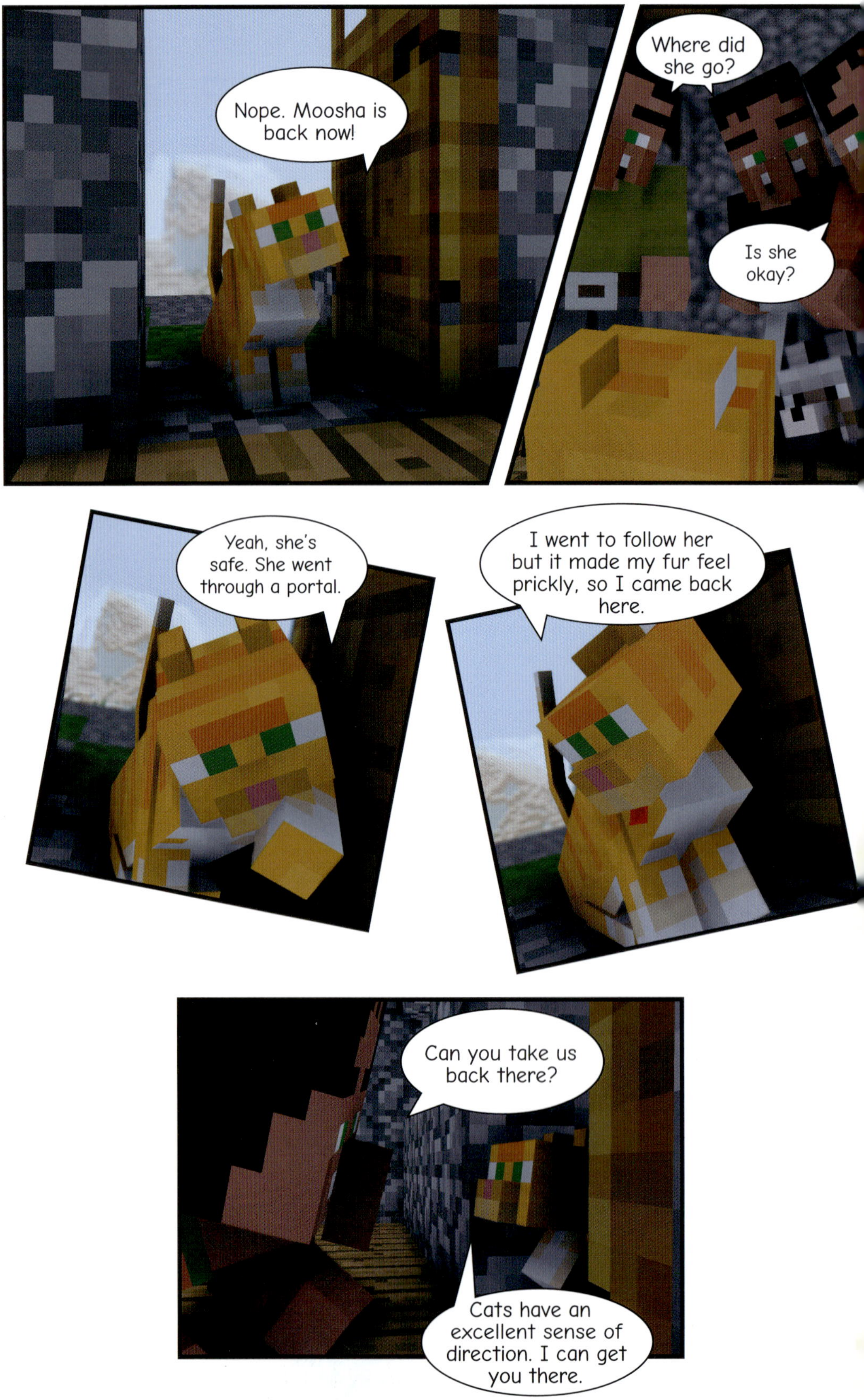
Nope. Moosha is back now!
Where did she go?
Is she okay?
Yeah, she's safe. She went through a portal.
I went to follow her but it made my fur feel prickly, so I came back here.
Can you take us back there?
Cats have an excellent sense of direction. I can get you there.

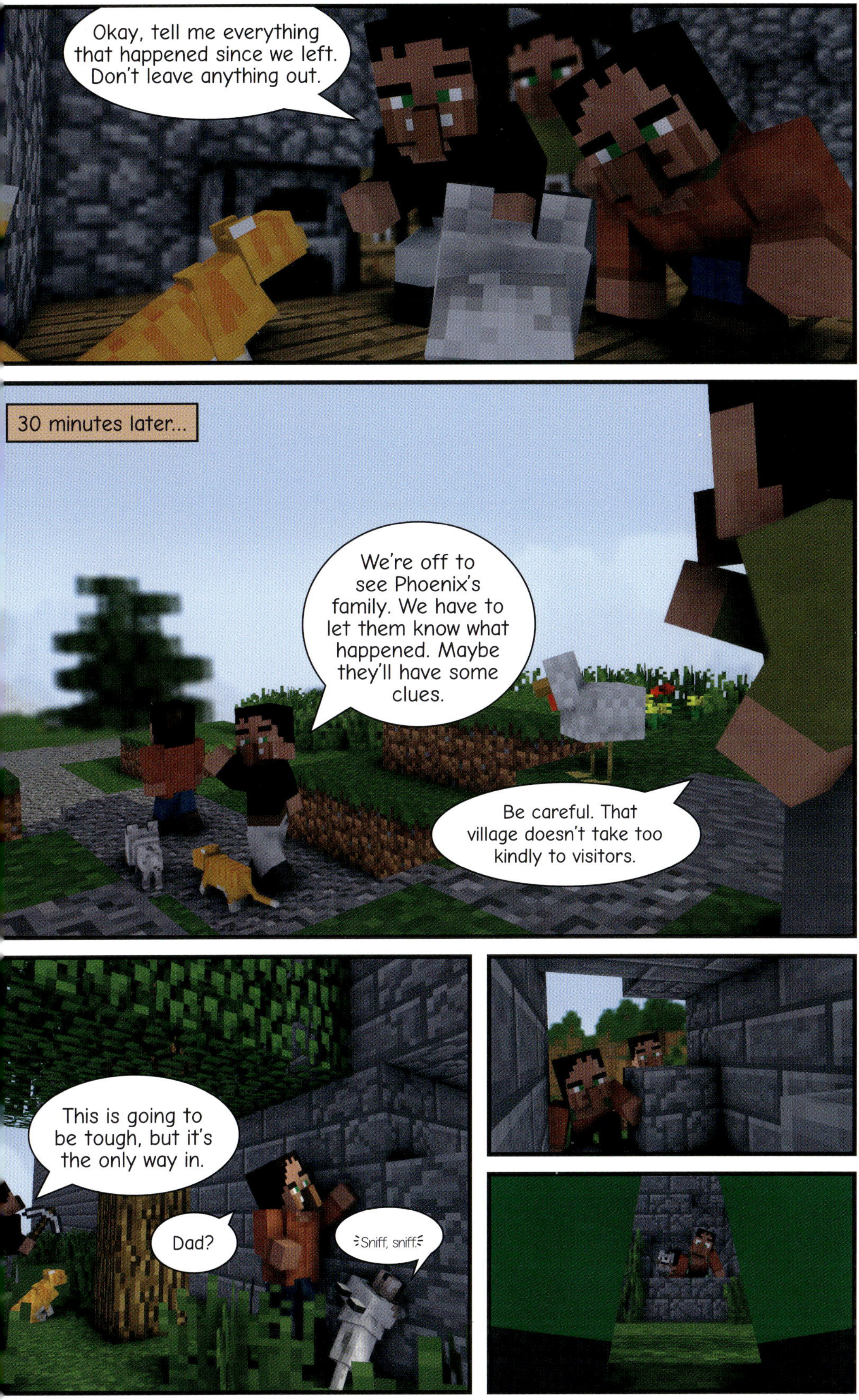
Okay, tell me everything that happened since we left. Don't leave anything out.
30 minutes later...
We're off to see Phoenix's family. We have to let them know what happened. Maybe they'll have some clues.
Be careful. That village doesn't take too kindly to visitors.
This is going to be tough, but it's the only way in.
Dad?
Sniff, sniff.

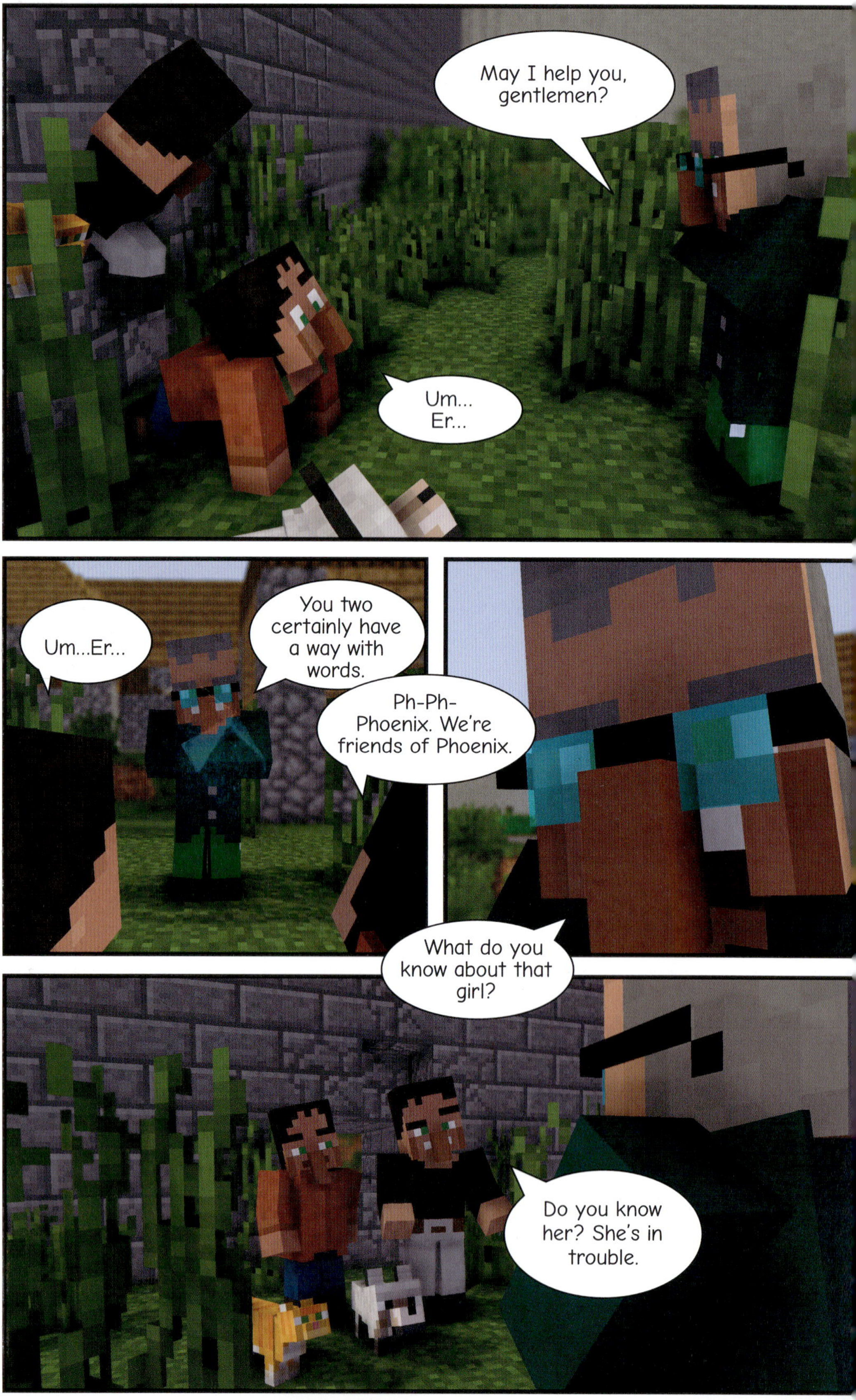
May I help you, gentlemen?
Um... Er...
Um...Er...
You two certainly have a way with words.
Ph-Ph- Phoenix. We're friends of Phoenix.
What do you know about that girl?
Do you know her? She's in trouble.

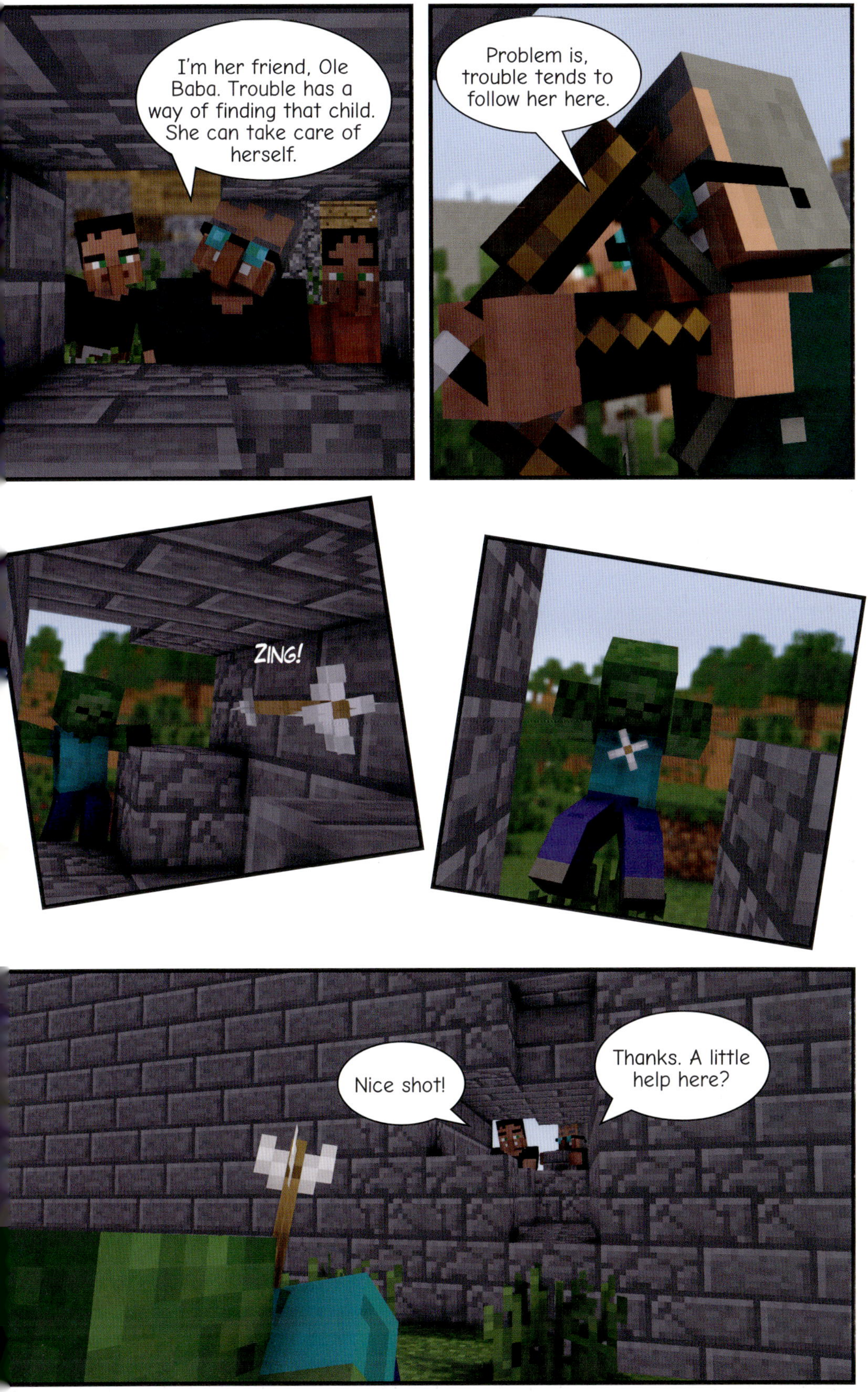
I'm her friend, Ole Baba. Trouble has a way of finding that child. She can take care of herself.
Problem is, trouble tends to follow her here.
ZING!
Nice shot!
Thanks. A little help here?

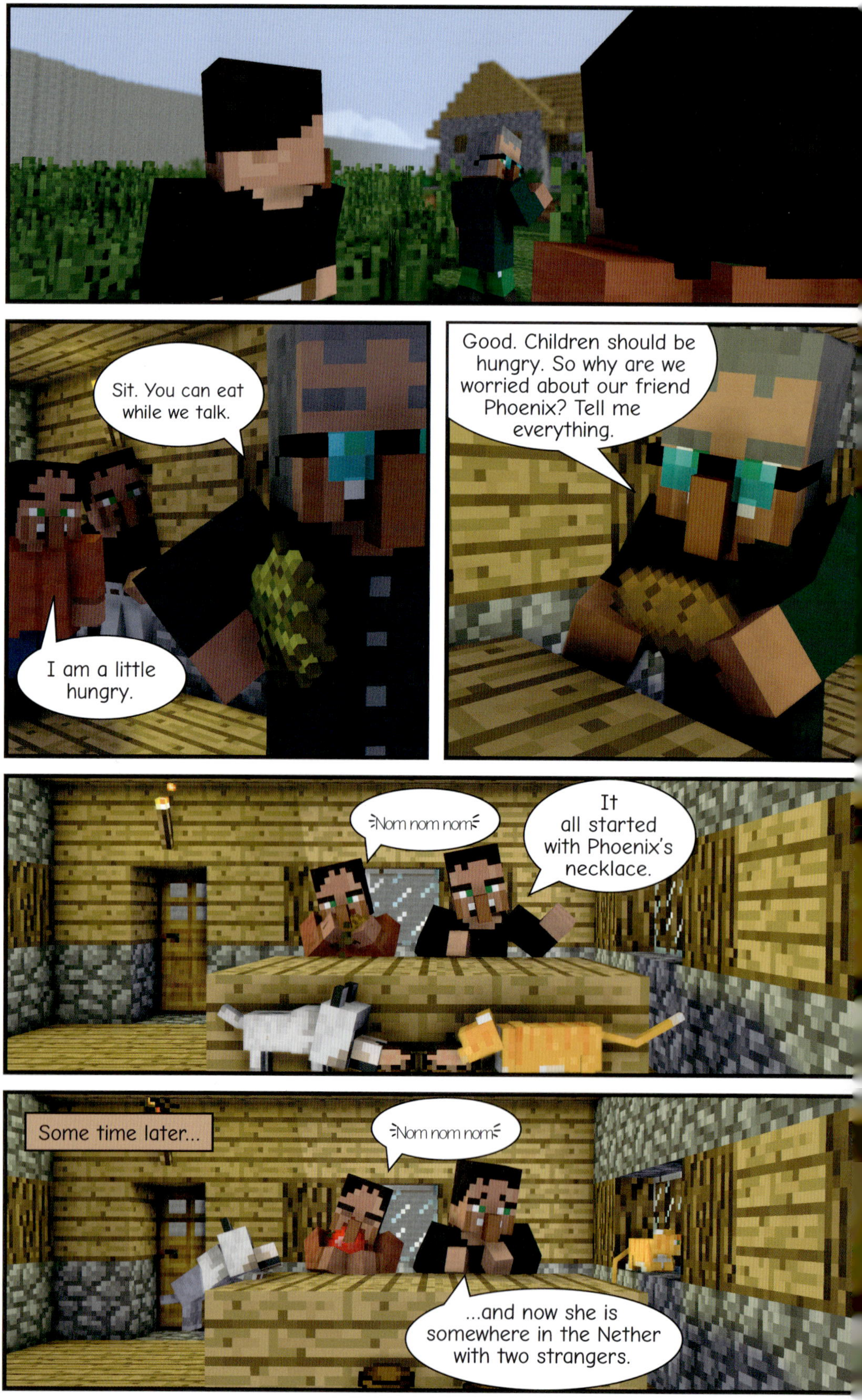
Sit. You can eat while we talk.
I am a little hungry.
Good. Children should be hungry. So why are we worried about our friend Phoenix? Tell me everything.
Nom nom nom
It all started with Phoenix's necklace.
Some time later...
Nom nom nom
...and now she is somewhere in the Nether with two strangers.

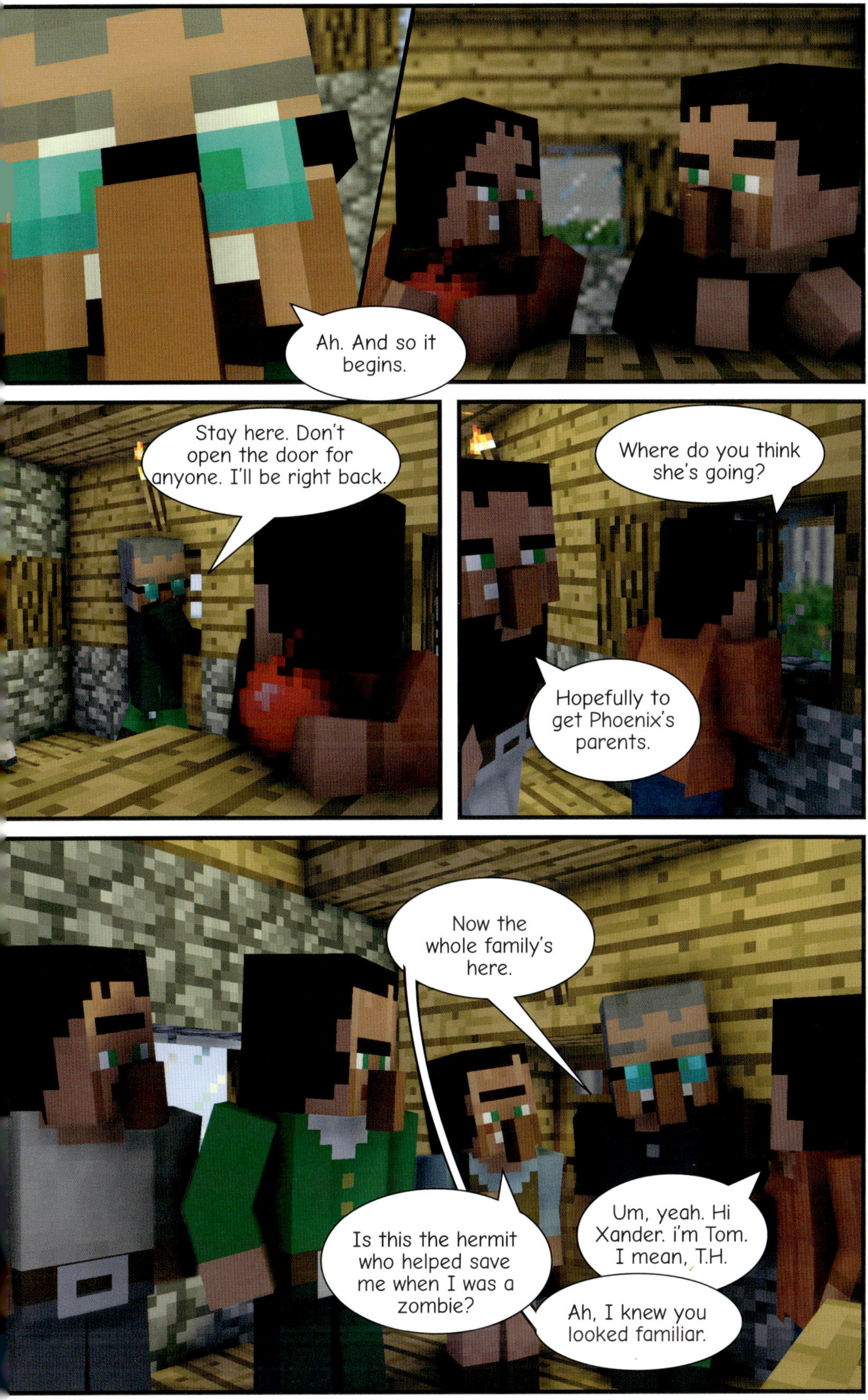
Ah. And so it begins.
Stay here. Don't open the door for anyone. I'll be right back.
Where do you think she's going?
Hopefully to get Phoenix's parents.
Now the whole family's here.
Is this the hermit who helped save me when I was a zombie?
Um, yeah. Hi Xander. i'm Tom. I mean, T.H.
Ah, I knew you looked familiar.

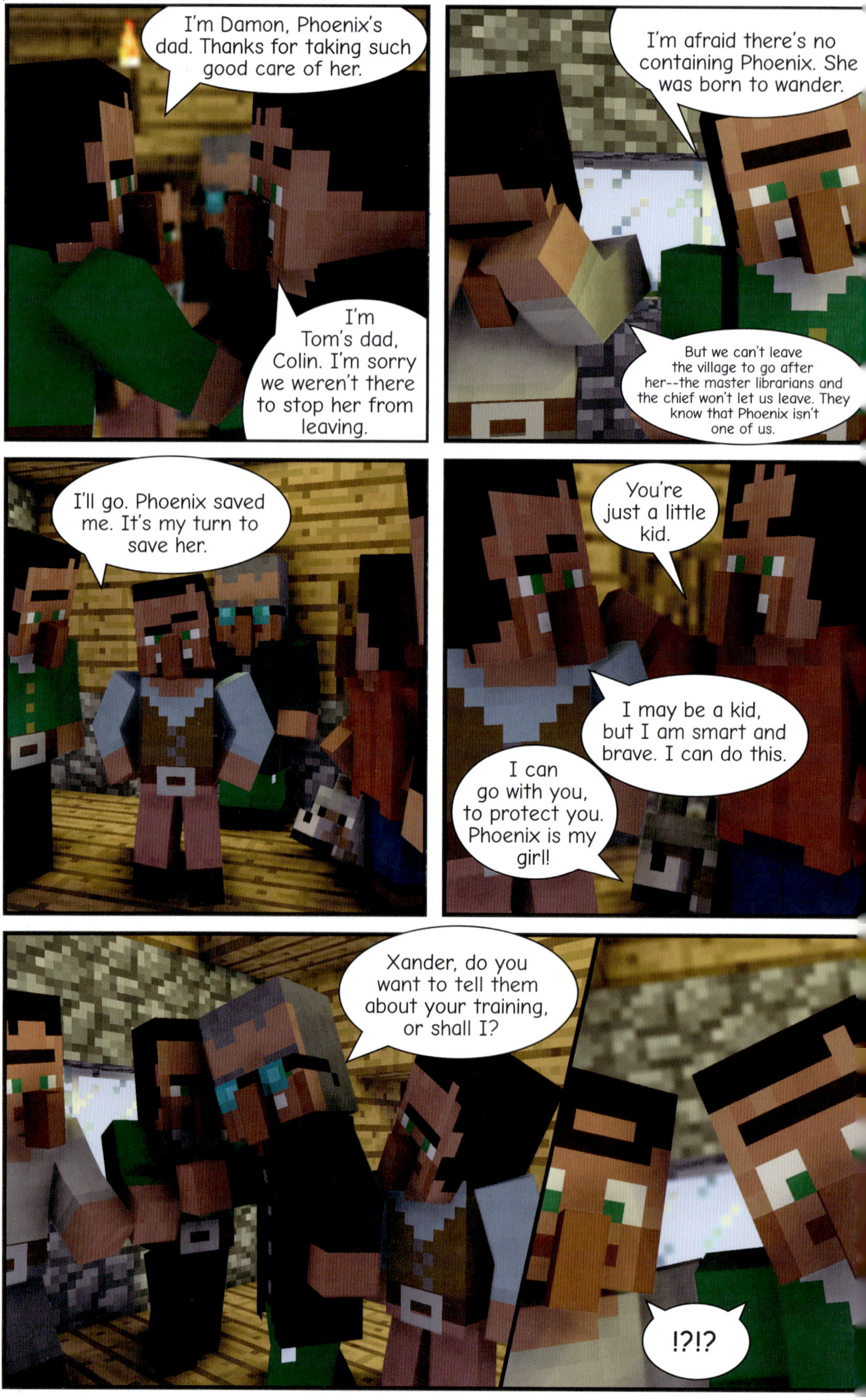
I'm Damon, Phoenix's dad. Thanks for taking such good care of her.
I'm Tom's dad, Colin. I'm sorry we weren't there to stop her from leaving.
I'm afraid there's no containing Phoenix. She was born to wander.
But we can't leave the village to go after her--the master librarians and the chief won't let us leave. They know that Phoenix isn't one of us.
I'll go. Phoenix saved me. It's my turn to save her.
You're just a little kid.
I may be a kid, but I am smart and brave. I can do this.
I can go with you, to protect you. Phoenix is my girl!
Xander, do you want to tell them about your training, or shall I?
!?!?

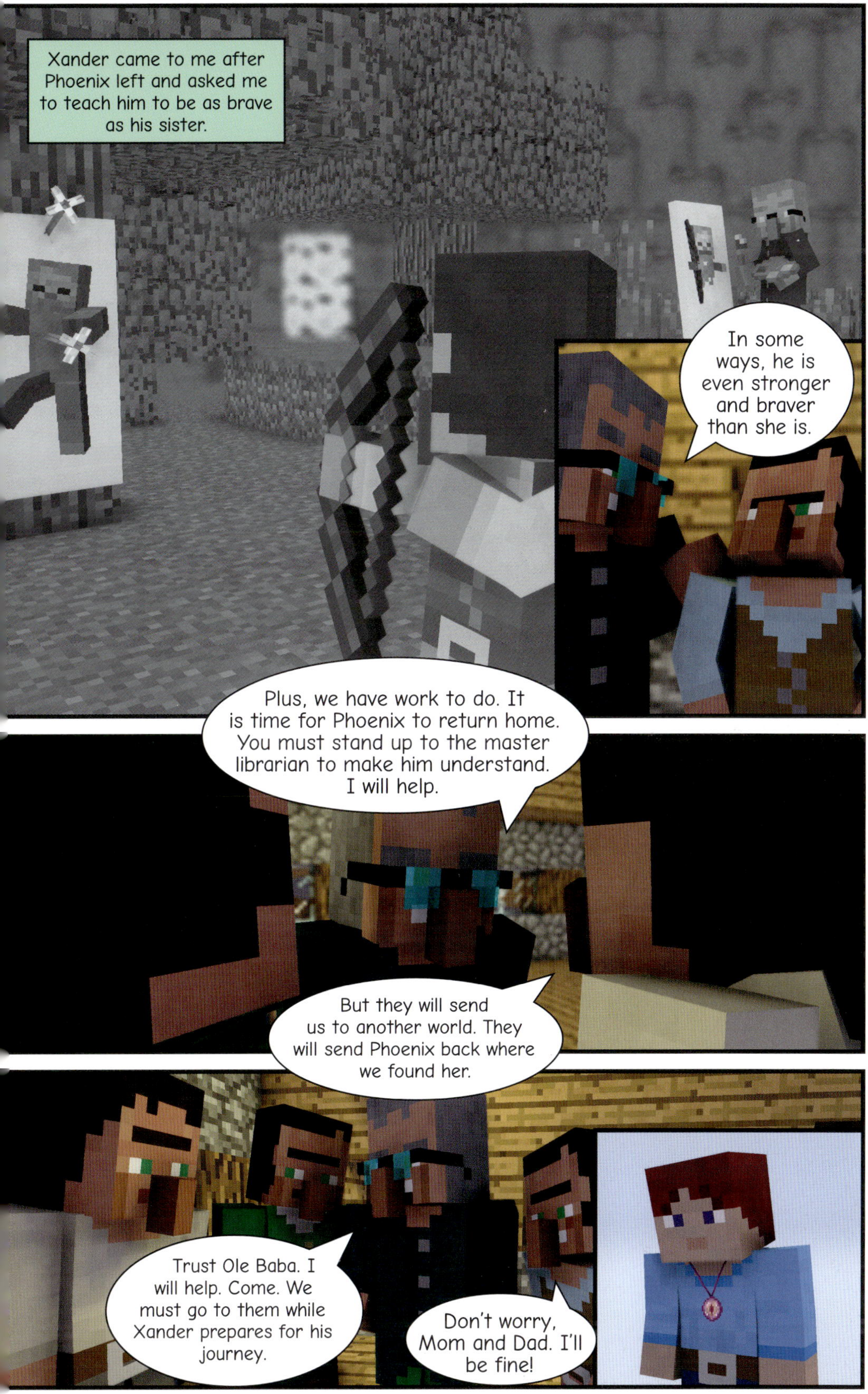
Xander came to me after Phoenix left and asked me to teach him to be as brave as his sister.
In some ways, he is even stronger and braver than she is.
Plus, we have work to do. It is time for Phoenix to return home. You must stand up to the master librarian to make him understand. I will help.
But they will send us to another world. They will send Phoenix back where we found her.
Trust Ole Baba. I will help. Come. We must go to them while Xander prepares for his journey.
Don't worry, Mom and Dad. I'll be fine!

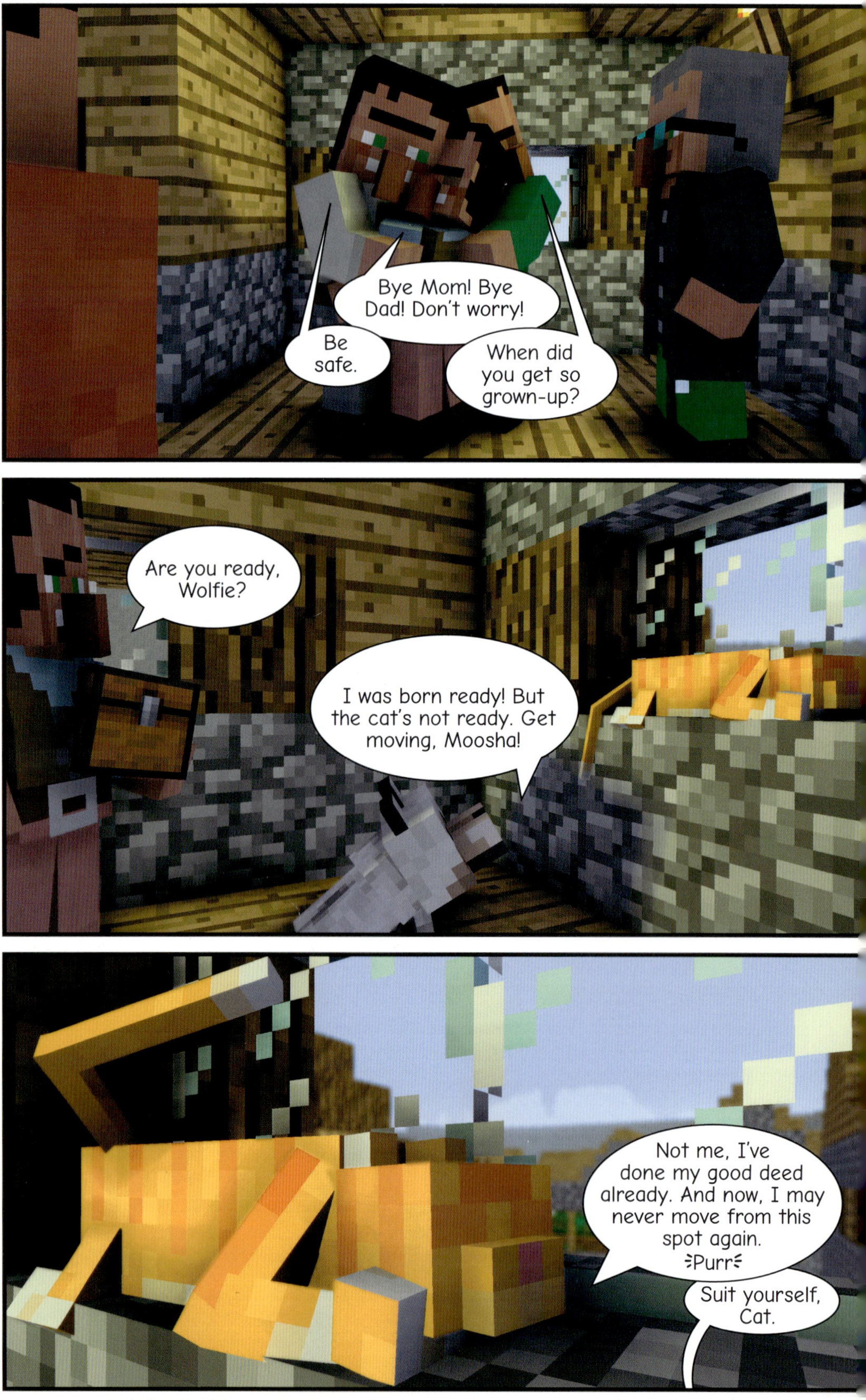
Bye Mom! Bye Dad! Don't worry!
Be safe.
When did you get so grown-up?
Are you ready, Wolfie?
I was born ready! But the cat's not ready. Get moving, Moosha!
Not me, I've done my good deed already. And now, I may never move from this spot again.
Purr
Suit yourself, Cat.

CHAPTER 6

A RIVER OF LAVA

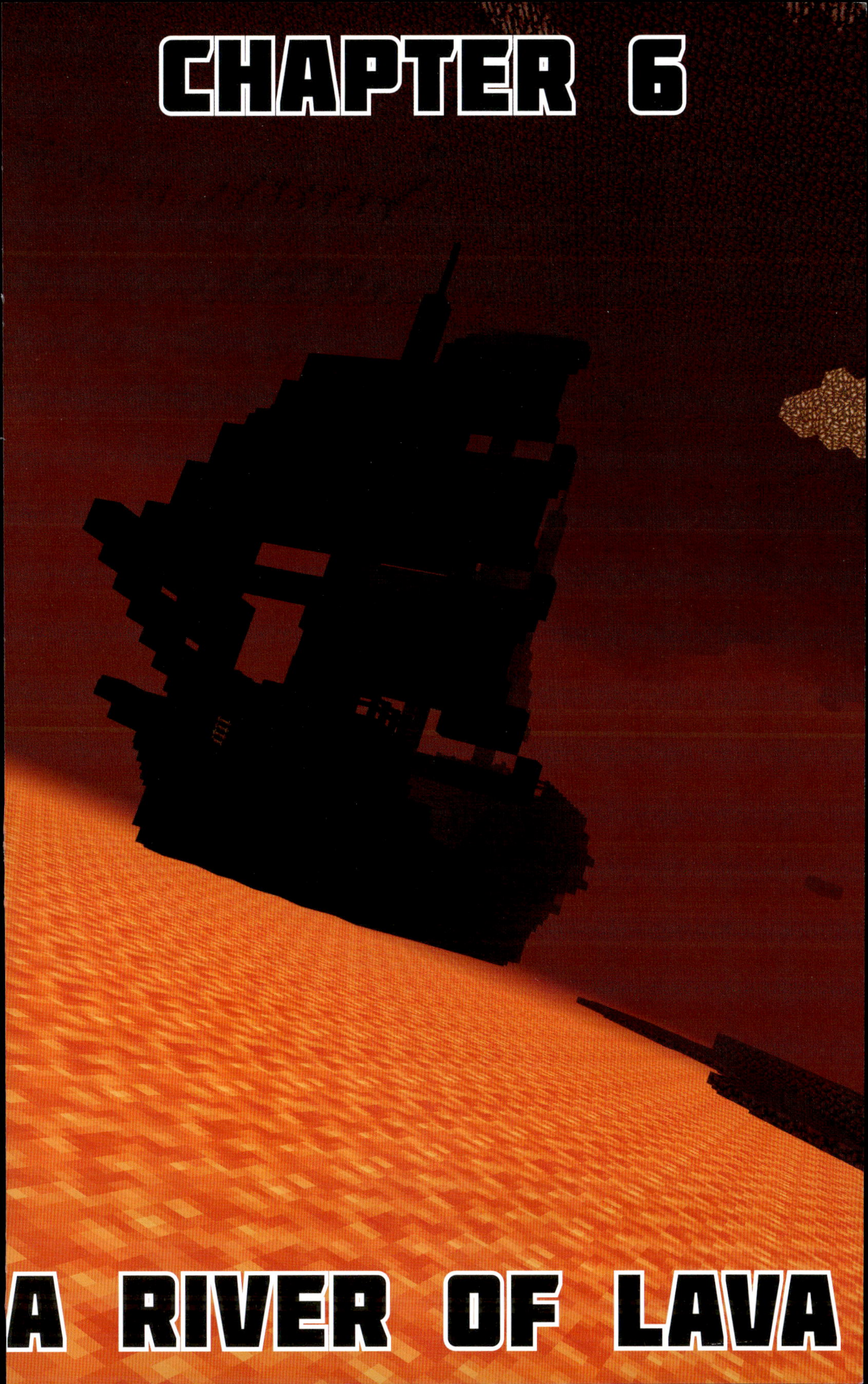

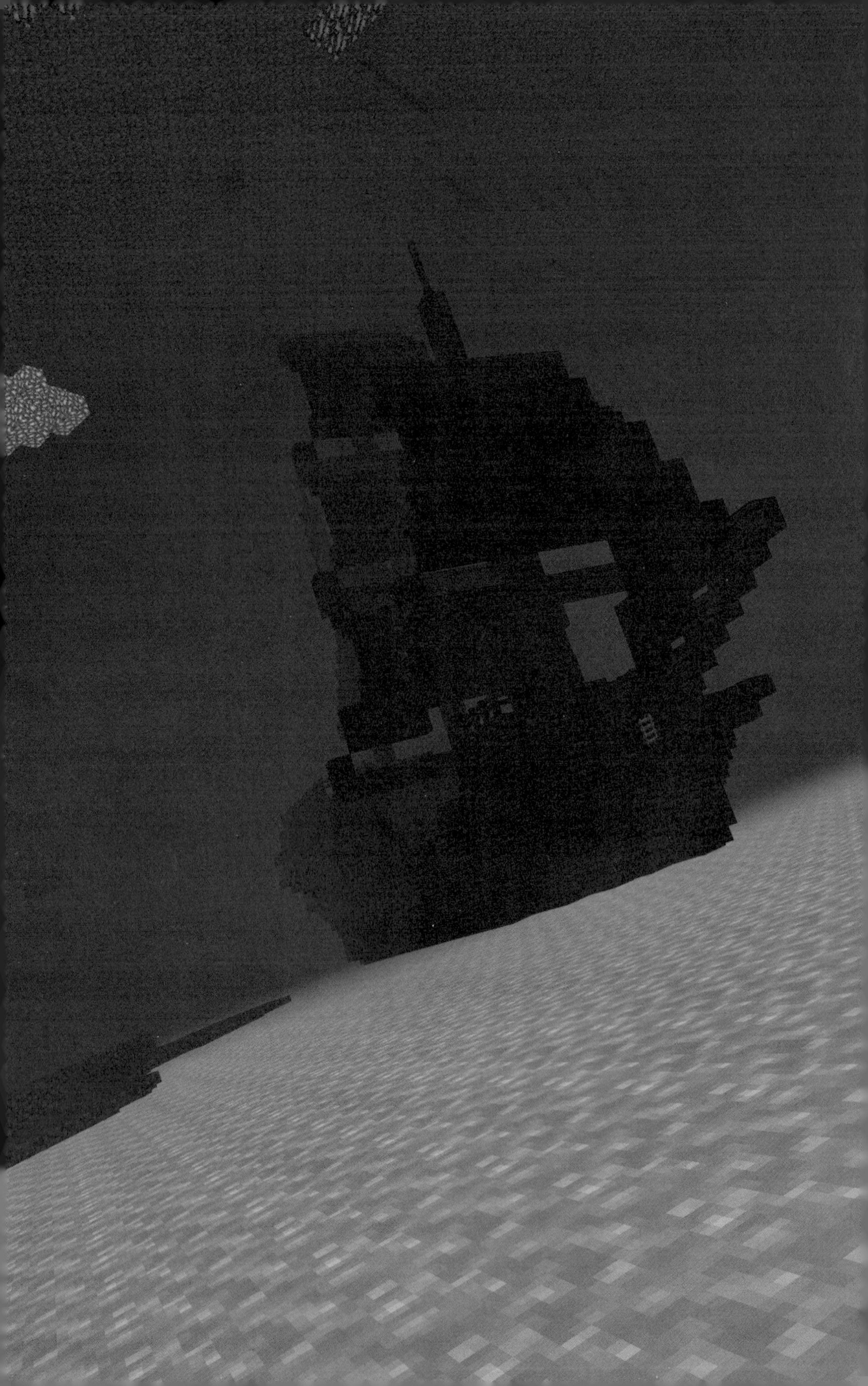

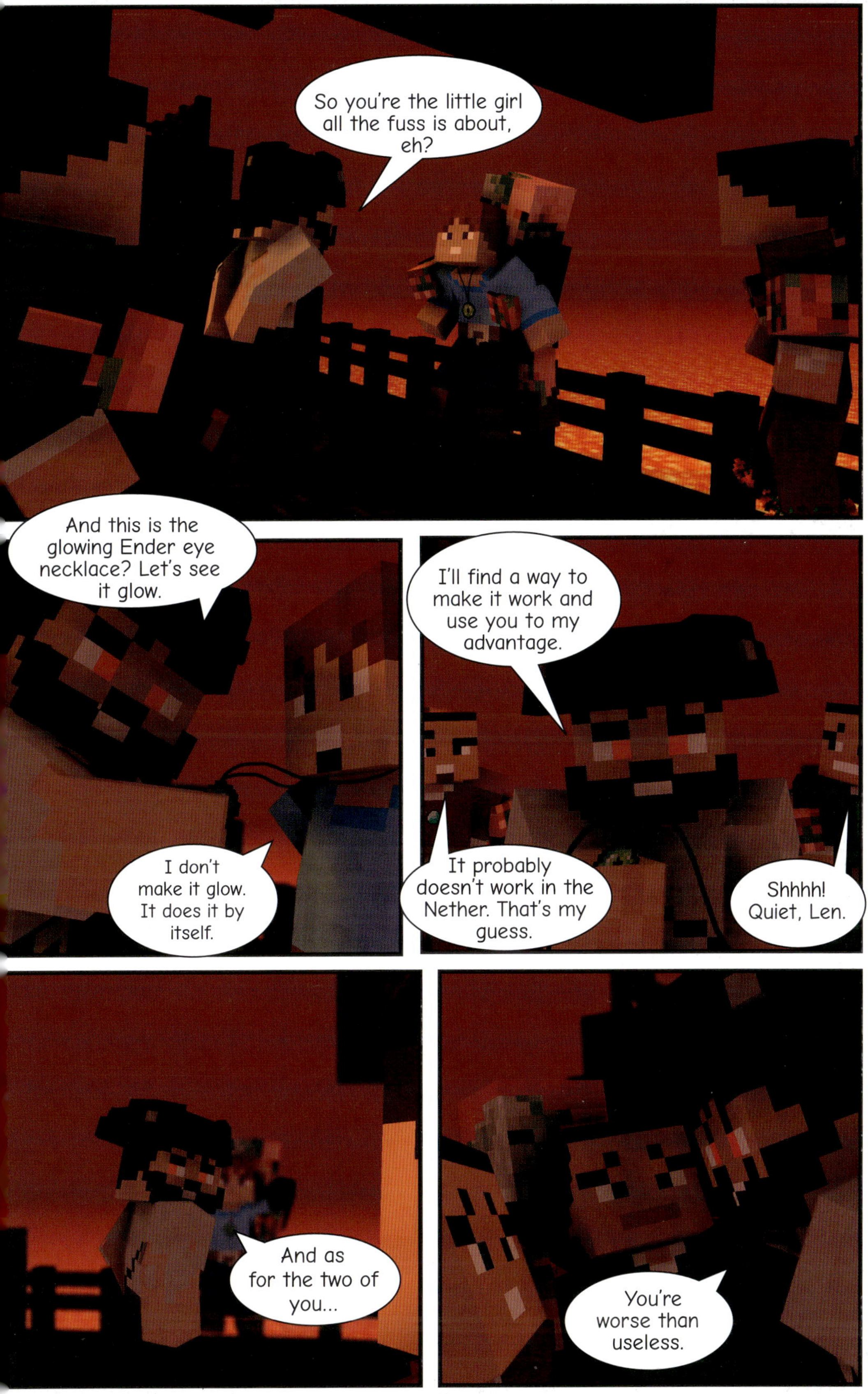
So you're the little girl all the fuss is about, eh?
And this is the glowing Ender eye necklace? Let's see it glow.
I don't make it glow. It does it by itself.
I'll find a way to make it work and use you to my advantage.
It probably doesn't work in the Nether. That's my guess.
Shhhh! Quiet, Len.
And as for the two of you...
You're worse than useless.

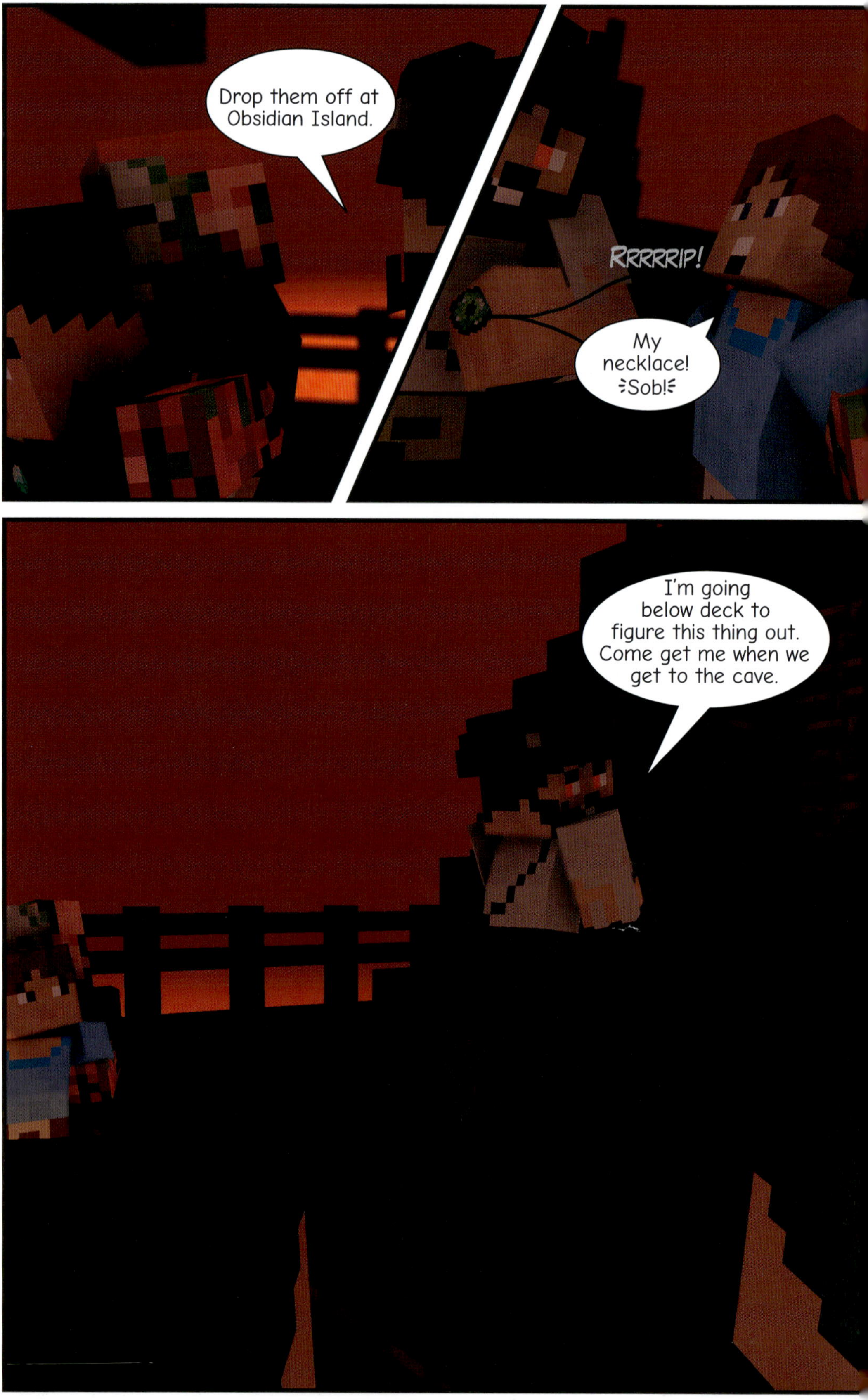
Drop them off at Obsidian Island.
RRRRRIP!
My necklace! Sob!
I'm going below deck to figure this thing out. Come get me when we get to the cave.

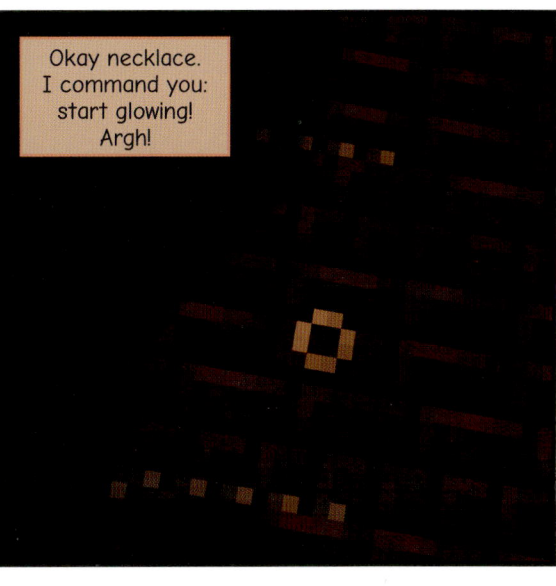

So, do we need to obey now that he's not here?

I think so. Let's head to the island and drop these guys off first.

Ok, D.K., head to Obsisian Island.

Aye, aye, Boss.

Okay necklace. I command you: start glowing! Argh!

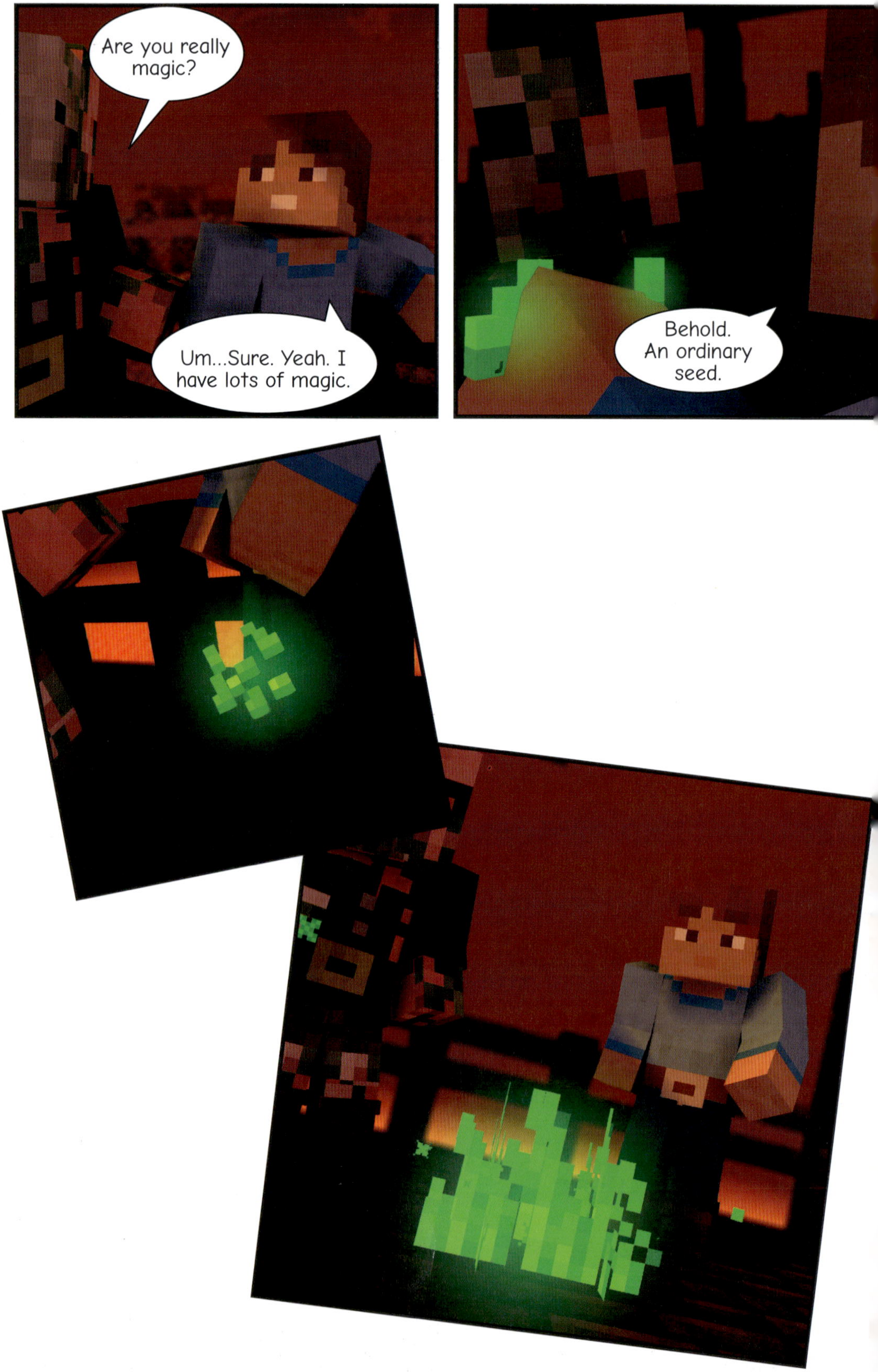
Are you really magic?
Um...Sure. Yeah. I have lots of magic.
Behold. An ordinary seed.

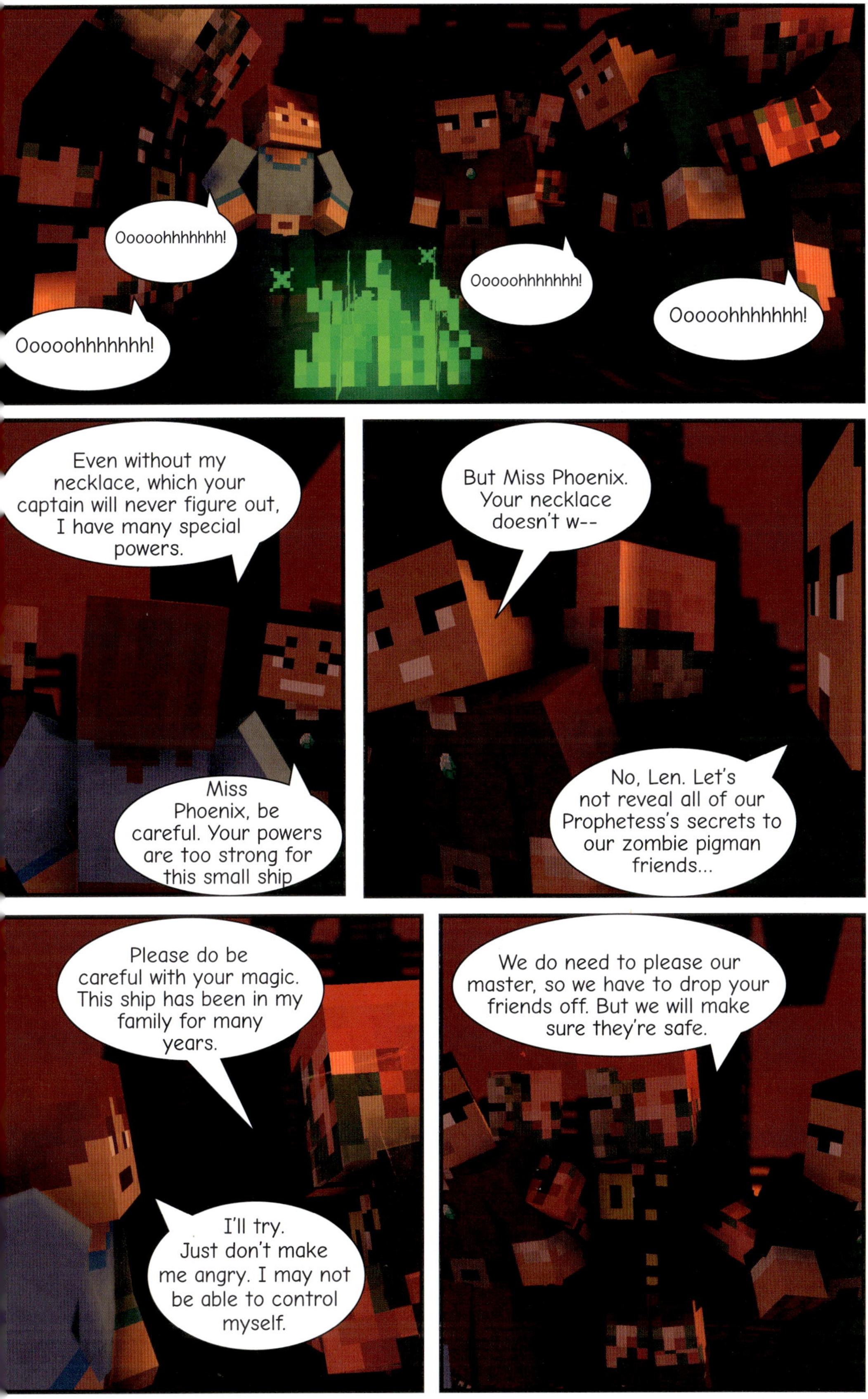
Ooooohhhhhhh!
Ooooohhhhhhh!
Ooooohhhhhhh!
Ooooohhhhhhh!
Even without my necklace, which your captain will never figure out, I have many special powers.
Miss Phoenix, be careful. Your powers are too strong for this small ship
But Miss Phoenix. Your necklace doesn't w--
No, Len. Let's not reveal all of our Prophetess's secrets to our zombie pigman friends...
Please do be careful with your magic. This ship has been in my family for many years.
I'll try. Just don't make me angry. I may not be able to control myself.
We do need to please our master, so we have to drop your friends off. But we will make sure they're safe.

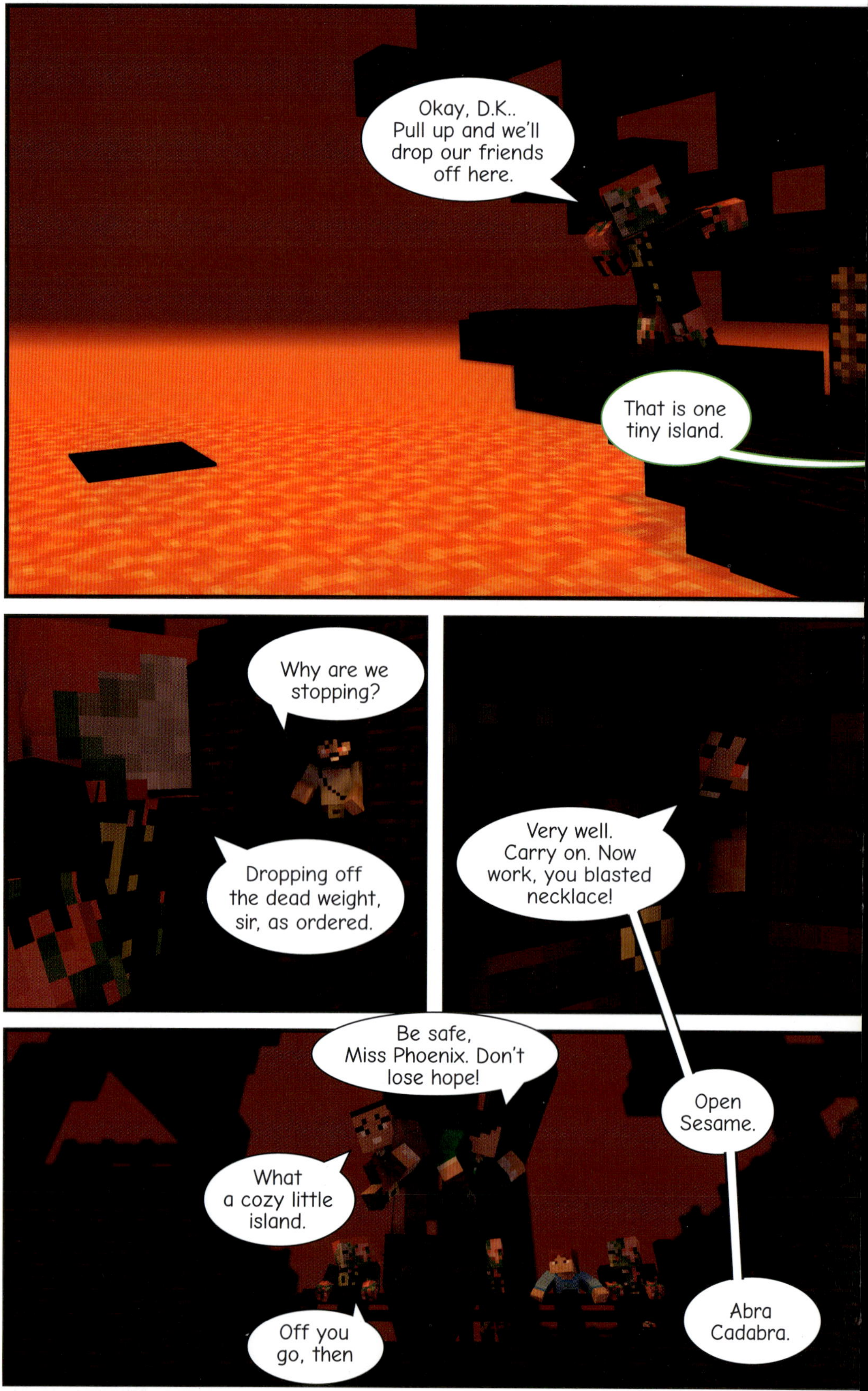
Okay, D.K..
Pull up and we'll drop our friends off here.
That is one tiny island.
Why are we stopping?
Dropping off the dead weight, sir, as ordered.
Very well. Carry on. Now work, you blasted necklace!
Open Sesame.
Abra Cadabra.
Be safe, Miss Phoenix. Don't lose hope!
What a cozy little island.
Off you go, then

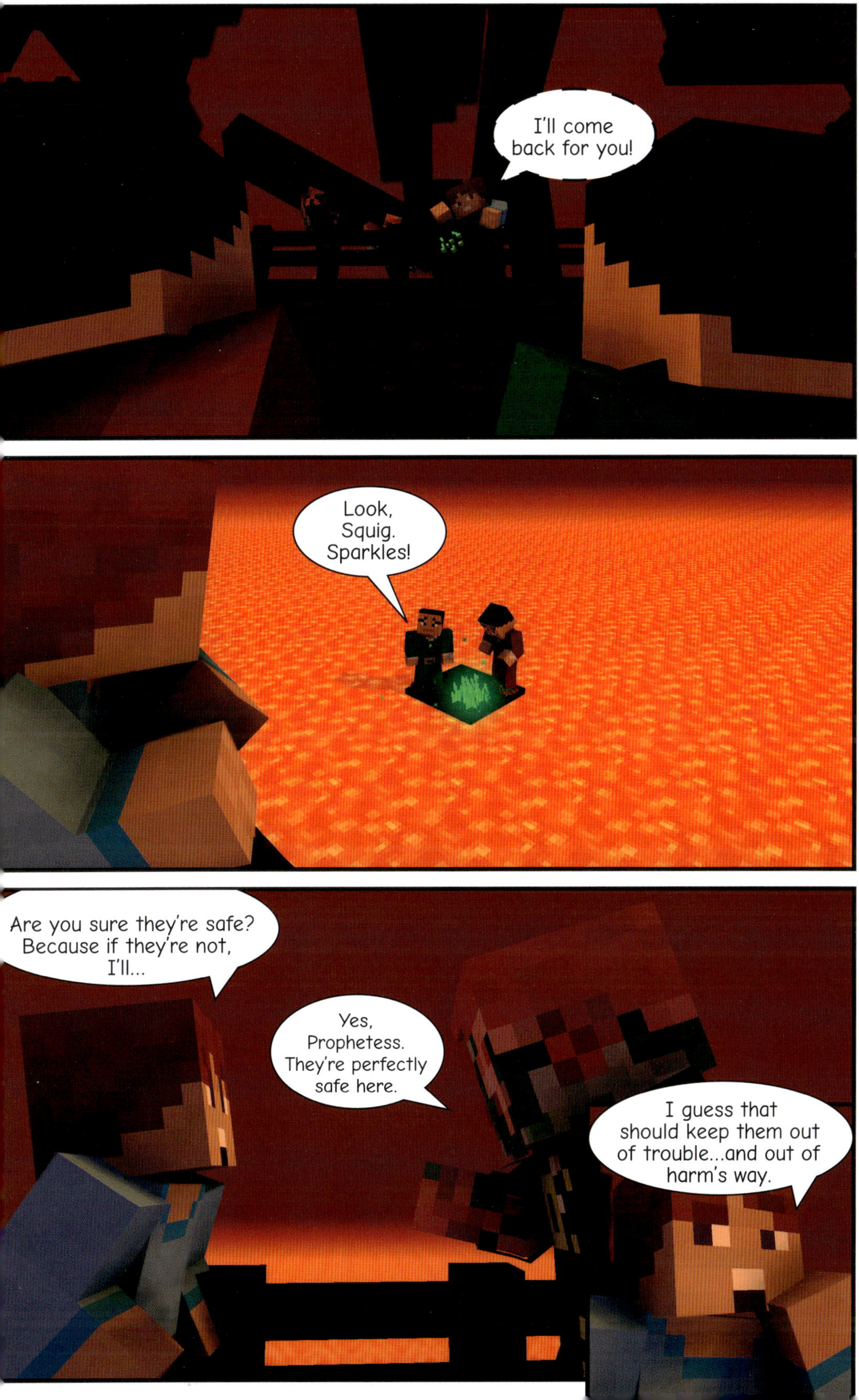
I'll come back for you!
Look, Squig. Sparkles!
Are you sure they're safe? Because if they're not, I'll...
Yes, Prophetess. They're perfectly safe here.
I guess that should keep them out of trouble...and out of harm's way.

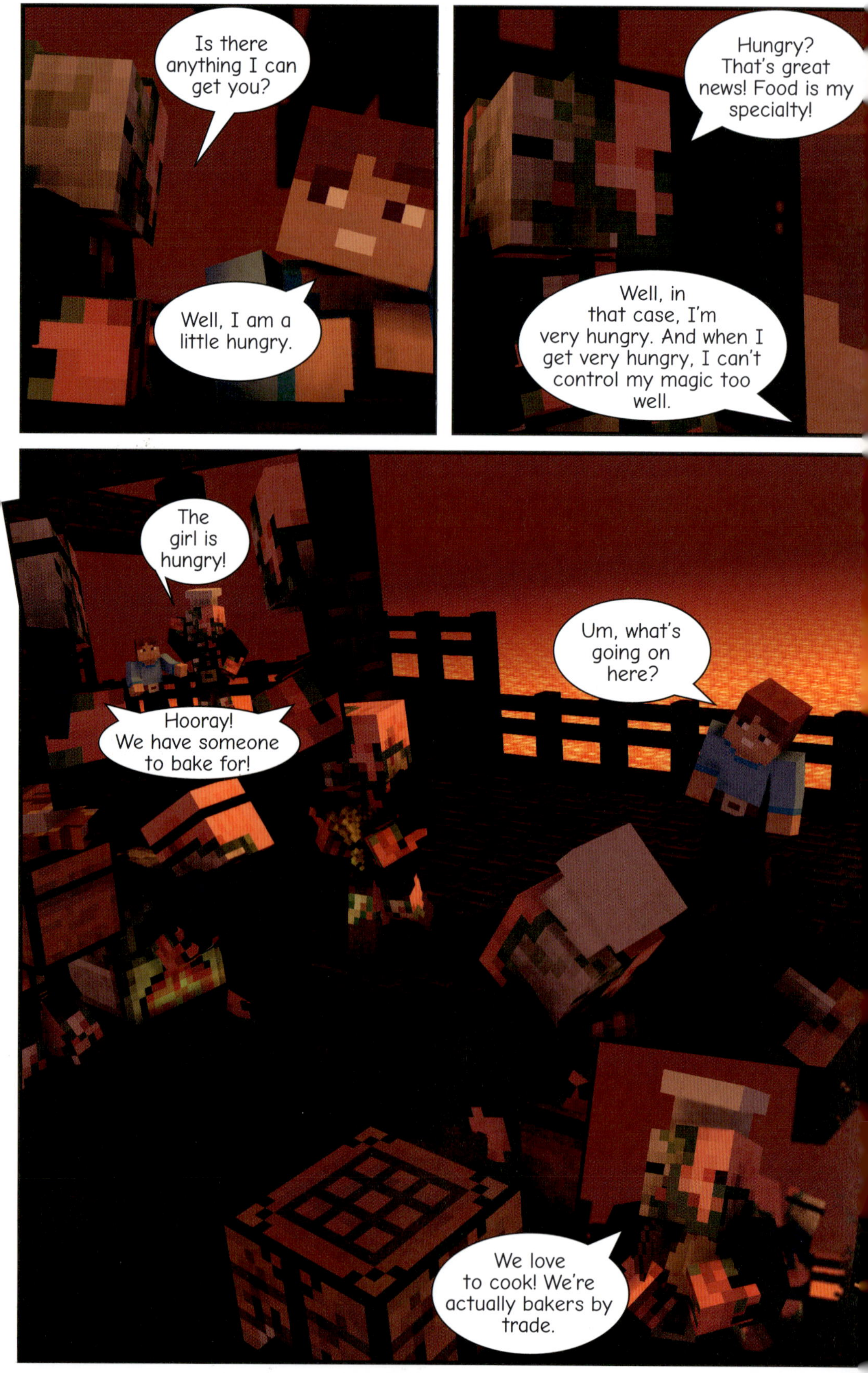
Is there anything I can get you?
Well, I am a little hungry.
Hungry? That's great news! Food is my specialty!
Well, in that case, I'm very hungry. And when I get very hungry, I can't control my magic too well.
The girl is hungry!
Um, what's going on here?
Hooray! We have someone to bake for!
We love to cook! We're actually bakers by trade.

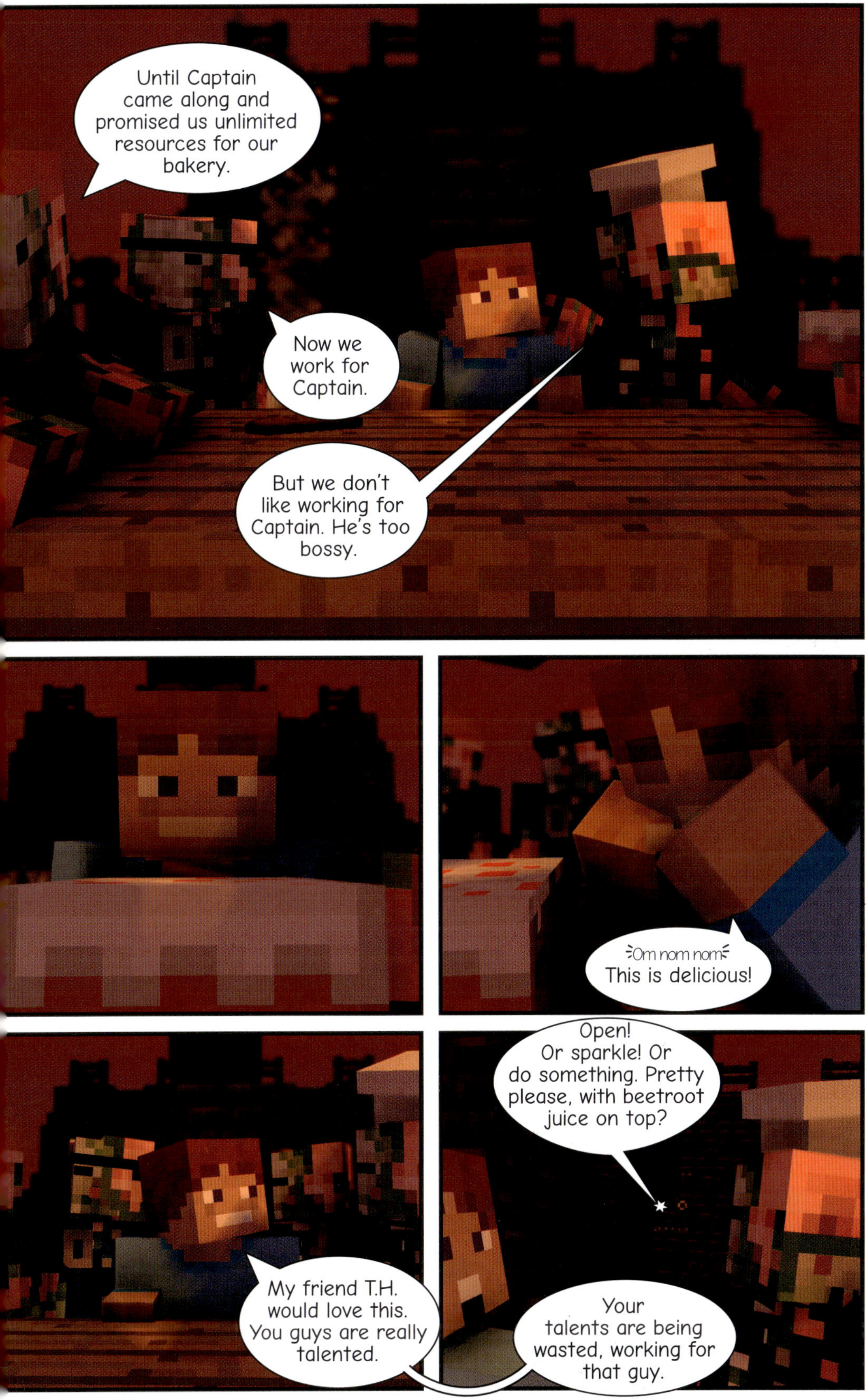
Until Captain came along and promised us unlimited resources for our bakery.
Now we work for Captain.
But we don't like working for Captain. He's too bossy.
Om nom nom
This is delicious!
My friend T.H. would love this. You guys are really talented.
Your talents are being wasted, working for that guy.
Open! Or sparkle! Or do something. Pretty please, with beetroot juice on top?

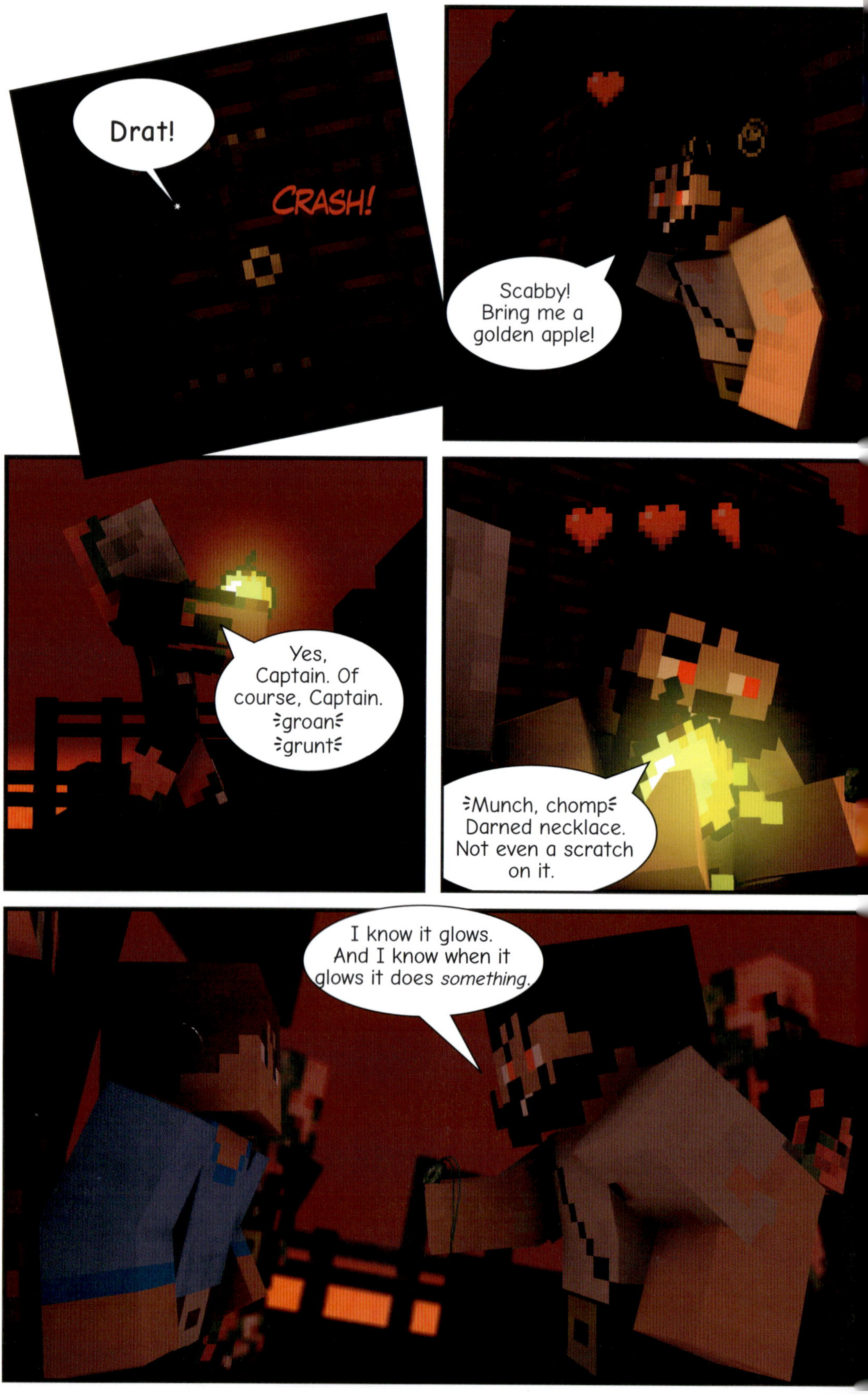
Drat!
CRASH!
Scabby! Bring me a golden apple!
Yes, Captain. Of course, Captain. ⁼groan⁼ ⁼grunt⁼
⁼Munch, chomp⁼ Darned necklace. Not even a scratch on it.
I know it glows. And I know when it glows it does *something*.

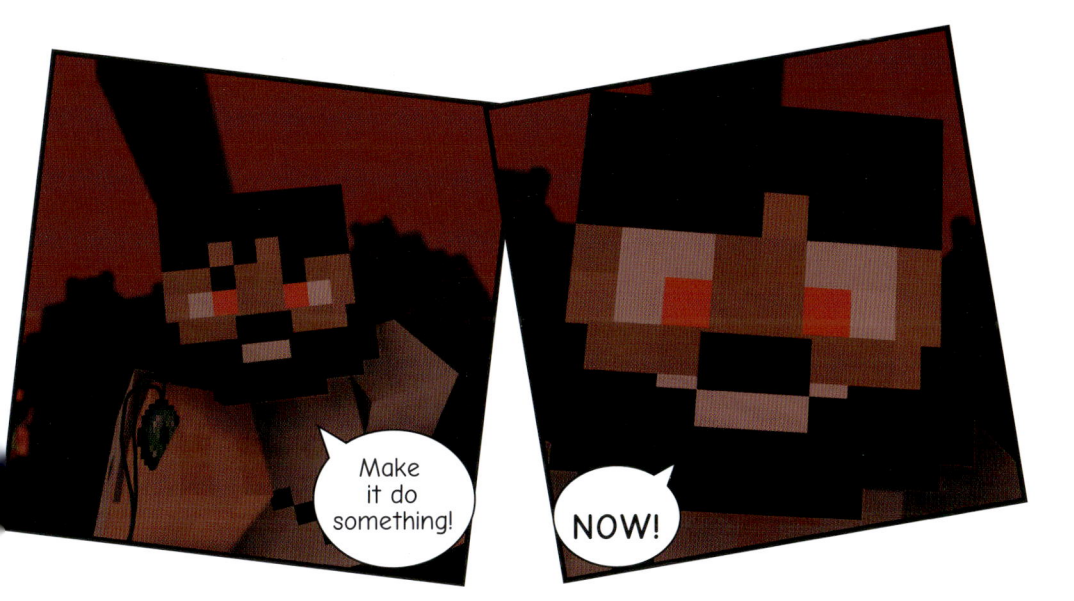

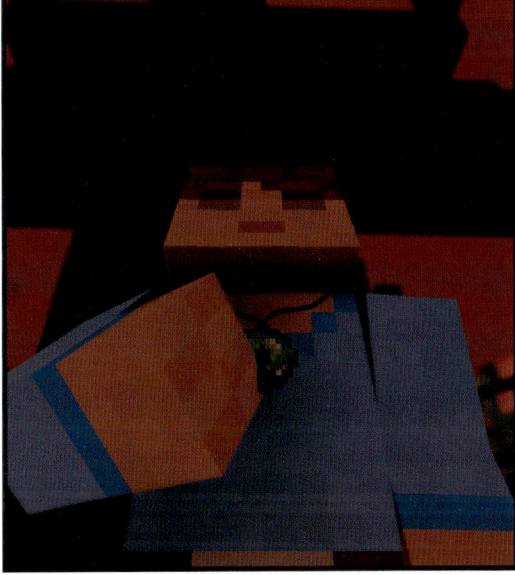

Make it do something!

NOW!

I'll need the necklace back if it's going to do my bidding.

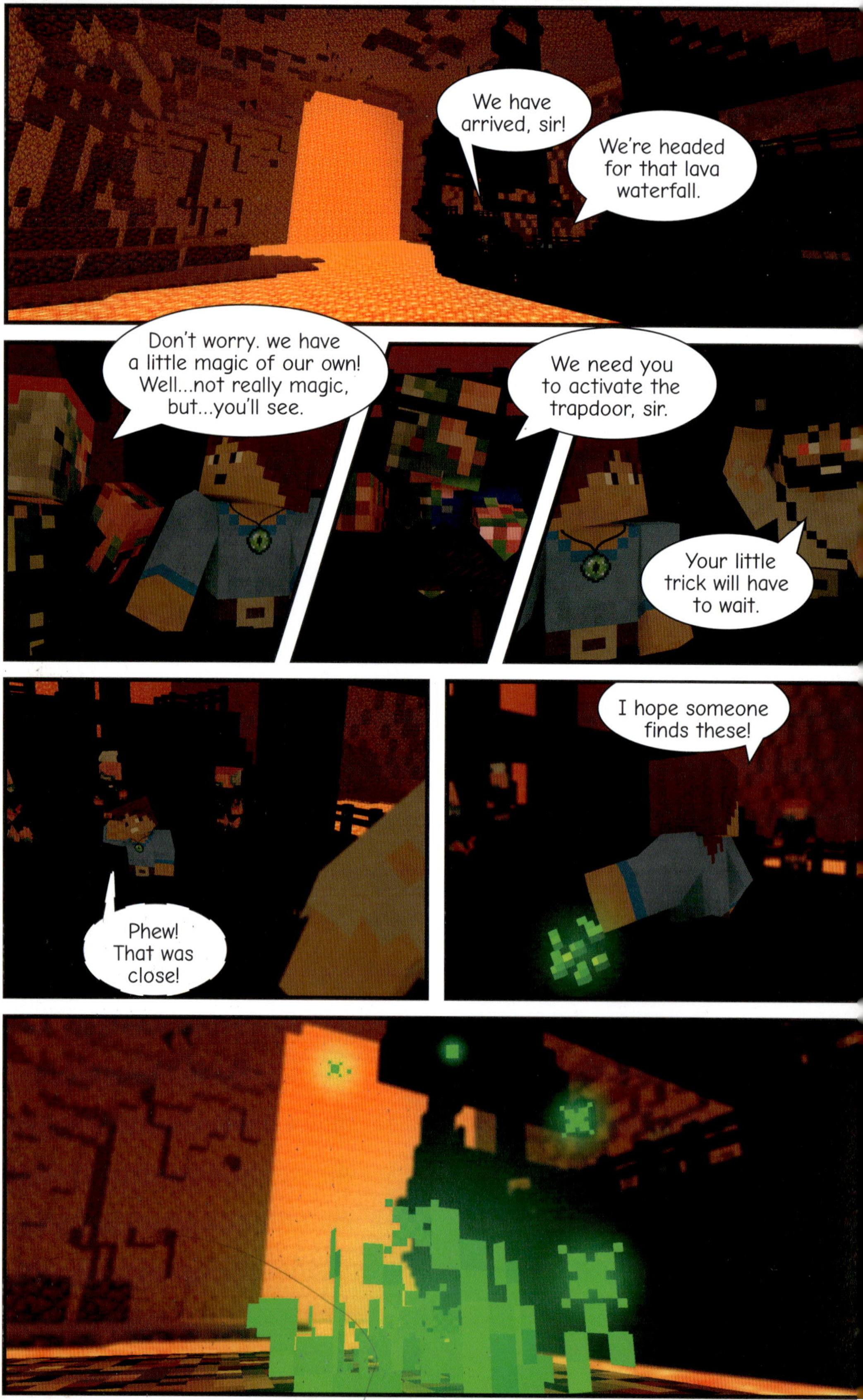

We have arrived, sir!
We're headed for that lava waterfall.
Don't worry. we have a little magic of our own! Well...not really magic, but...you'll see.
We need you to activate the trapdoor, sir.
Your little trick will have to wait.
Phew! That was close!
I hope someone finds these!

CHAPTER 7

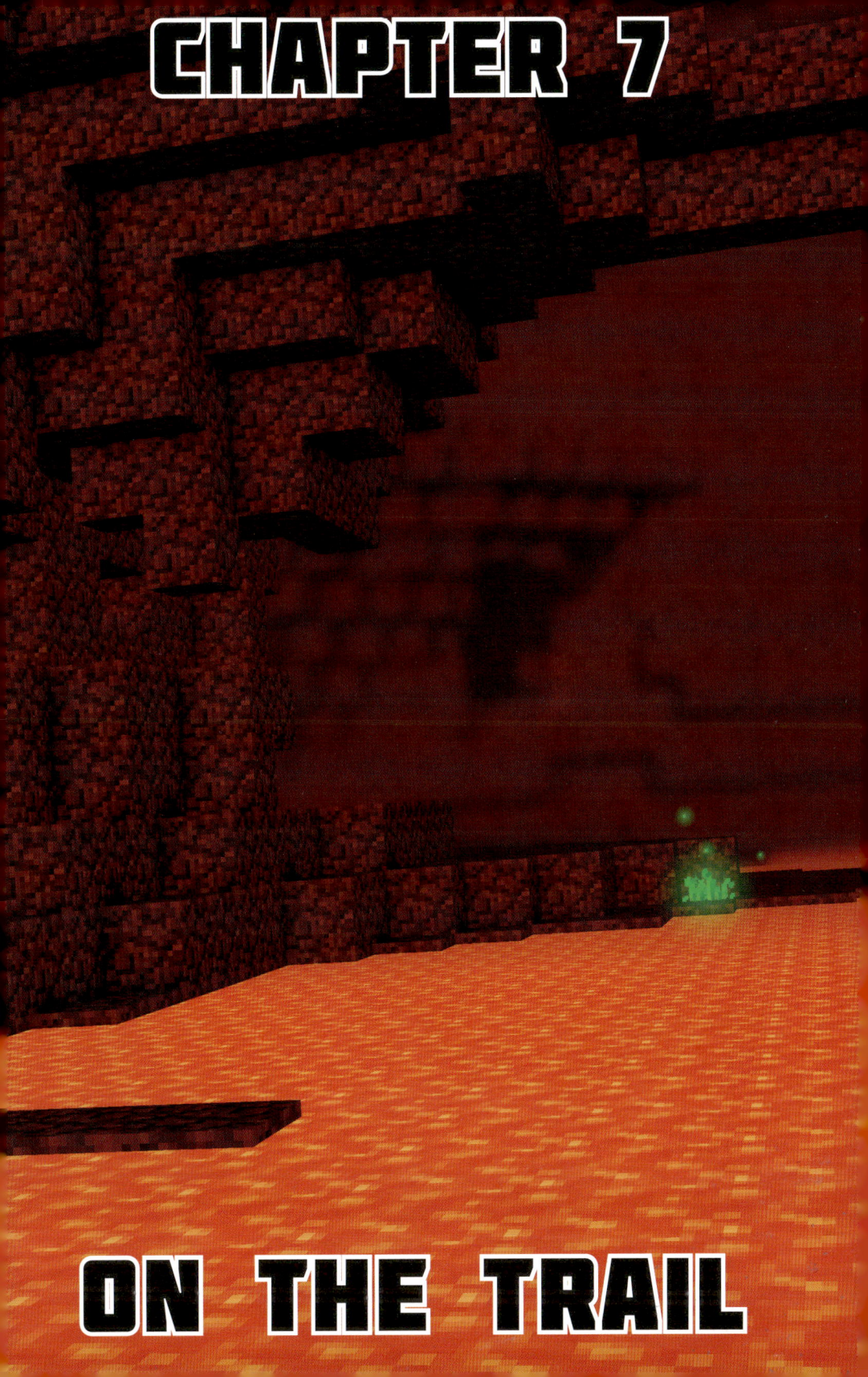

ON THE TRAIL

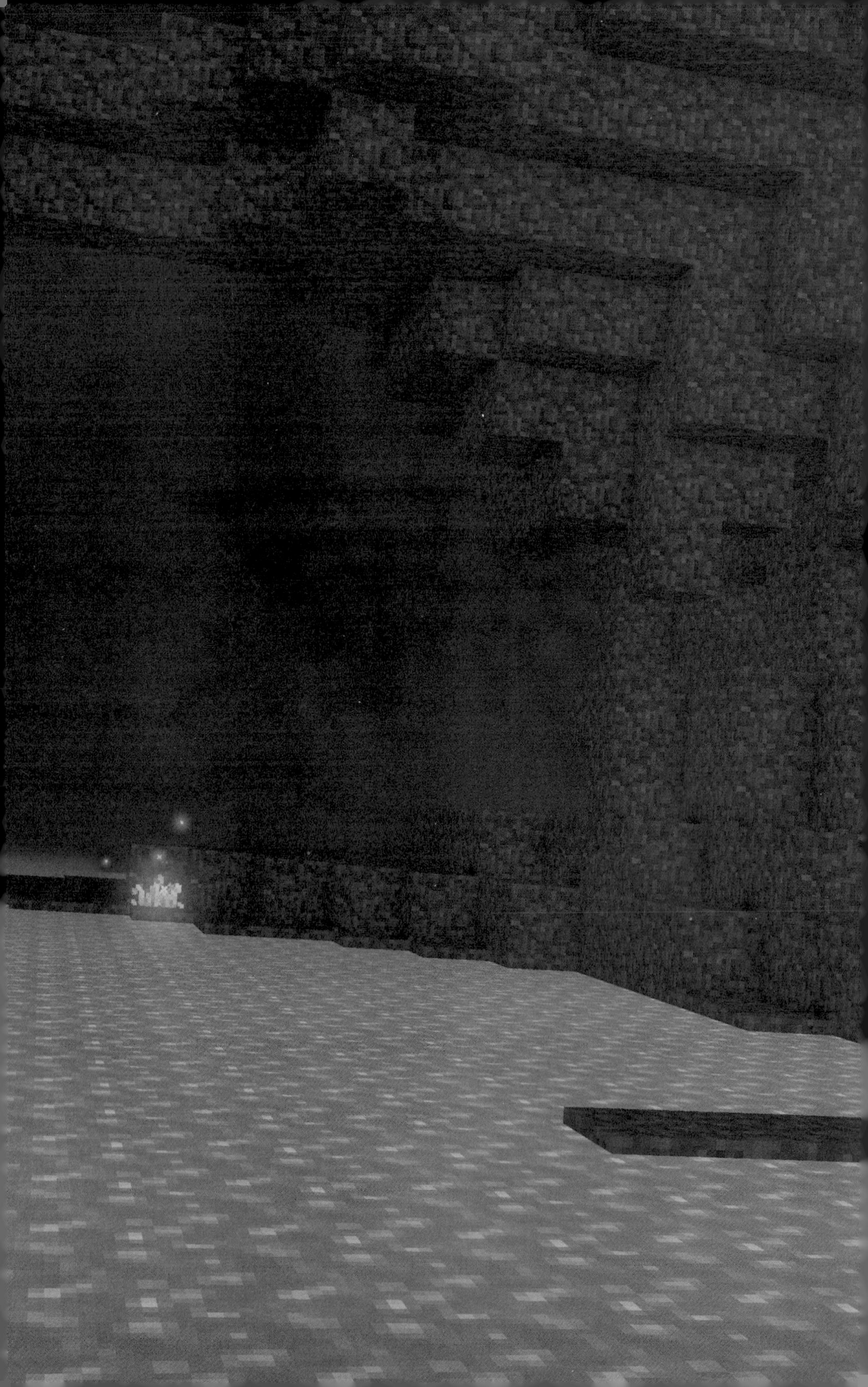

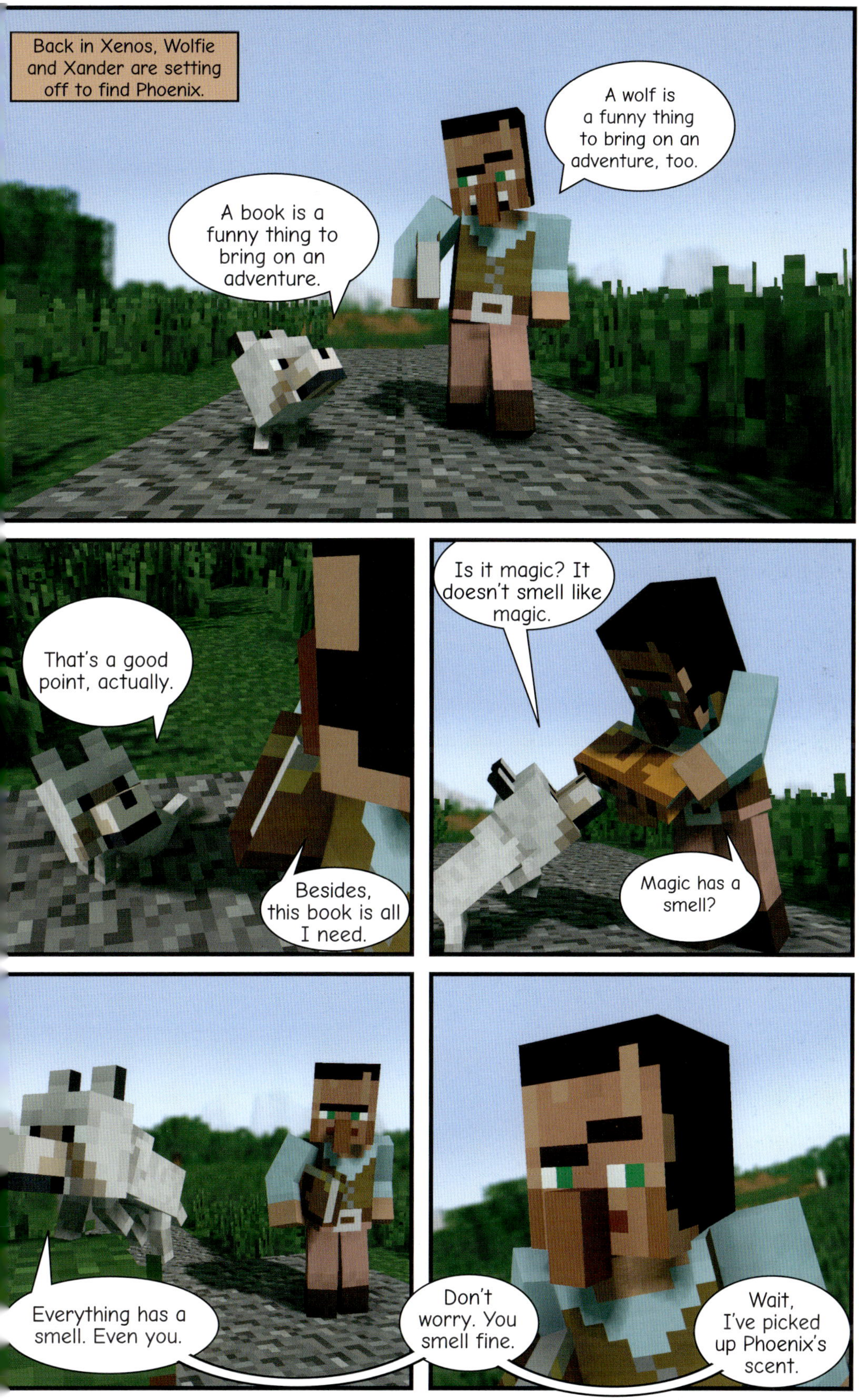
Back in Xenos, Wolfie and Xander are setting off to find Phoenix.
A book is a funny thing to bring on an adventure.
A wolf is a funny thing to bring on an adventure, too.
That's a good point, actually.
Besides, this book is all I need.
Is it magic? It doesn't smell like magic.
Magic has a smell?
Everything has a smell. Even you.
Don't worry. You smell fine.
Wait, I've picked up Phoenix's scent.

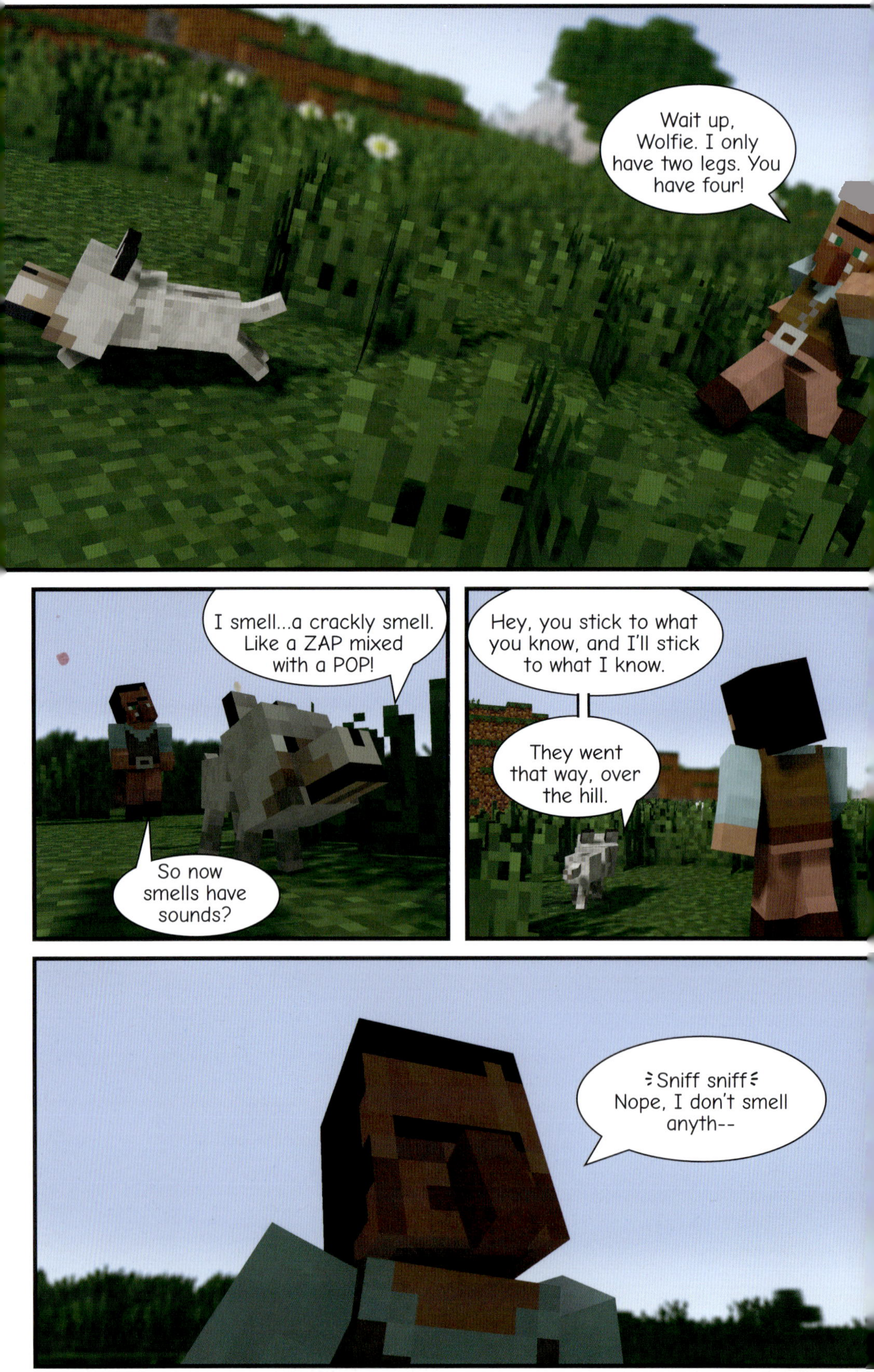

Wait up, Wolfie. I only have two legs. You have four!
I smell...a crackly smell. Like a ZAP mixed with a POP!
So now smells have sounds?
Hey, you stick to what you know, and I'll stick to what I know.
They went that way, over the hill.
Sniff sniff
Nope, I don't smell anyth--

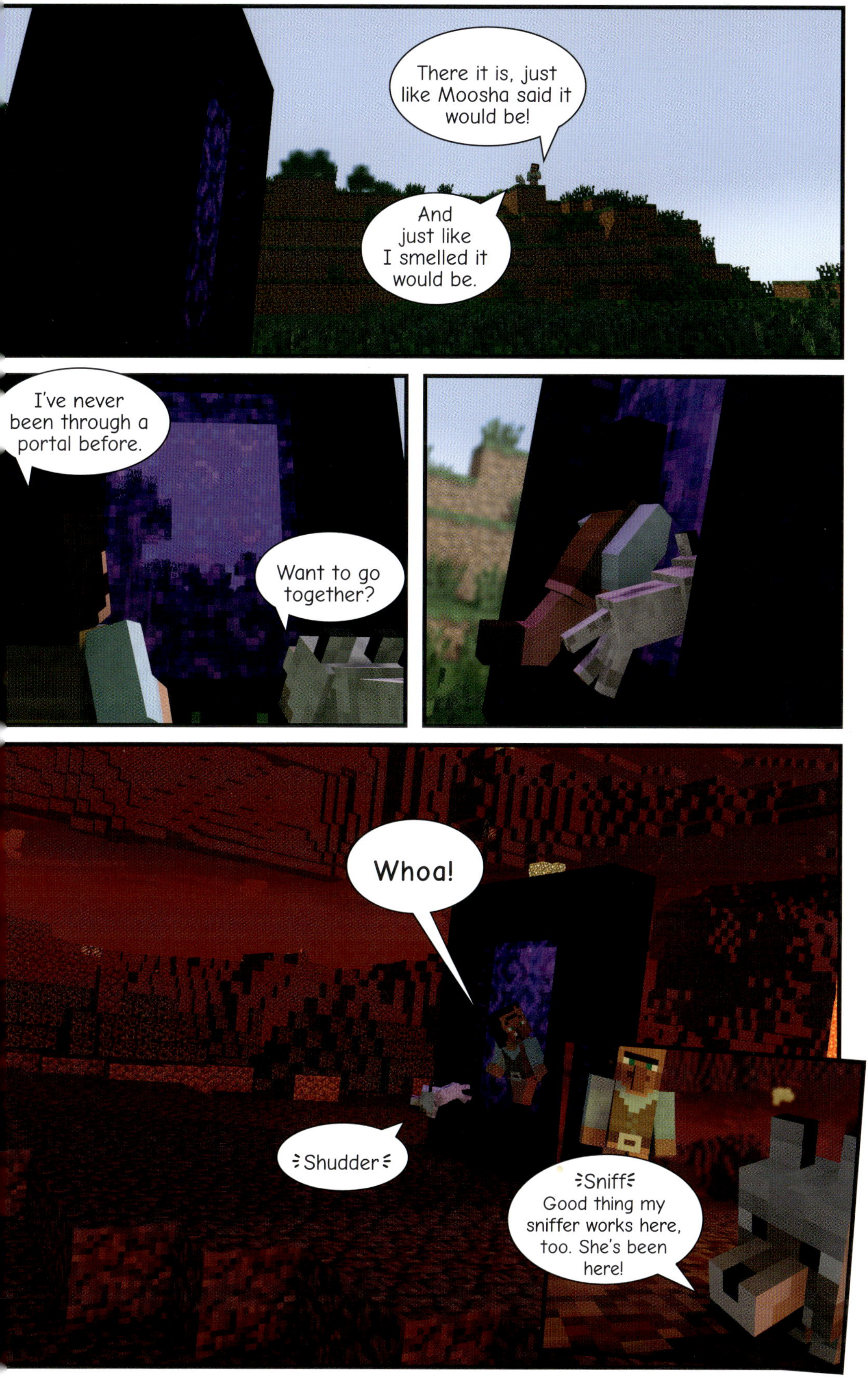
There it is, just like Moosha said it would be!
And just like I smelled it would be.
I've never been through a portal before.
Want to go together?
Whoa!
⁼Shudder⁼
⁼Sniff⁼ Good thing my sniffer works here, too. She's been here!

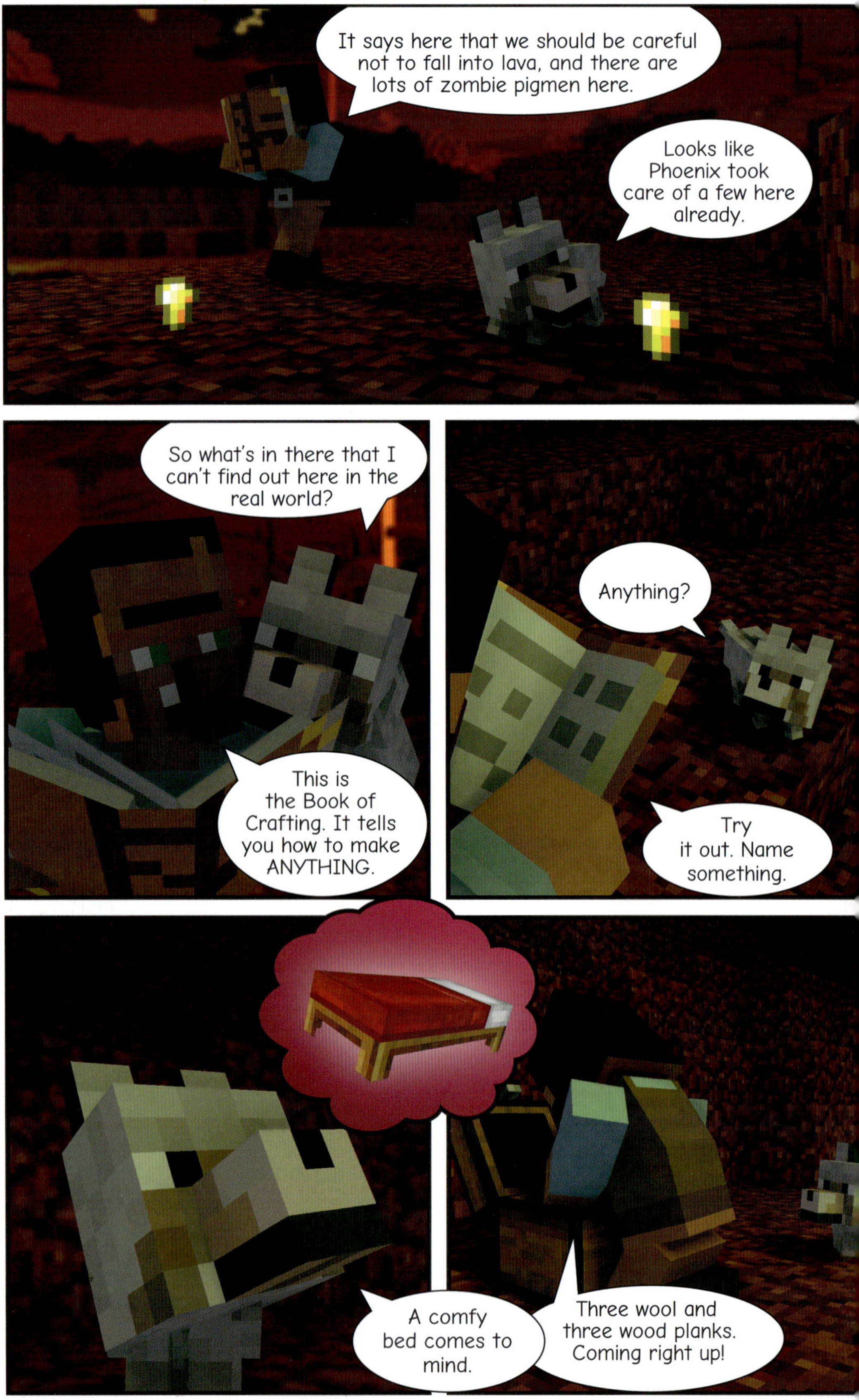
It says here that we should be careful not to fall into lava, and there are lots of zombie pigmen here.
Looks like Phoenix took care of a few here already.
So what's in there that I can't find out here in the real world?
This is the Book of Crafting. It tells you how to make ANYTHING.
Anything?
Try it out. Name something.
A comfy bed comes to mind.
Three wool and three wood planks. Coming right up!

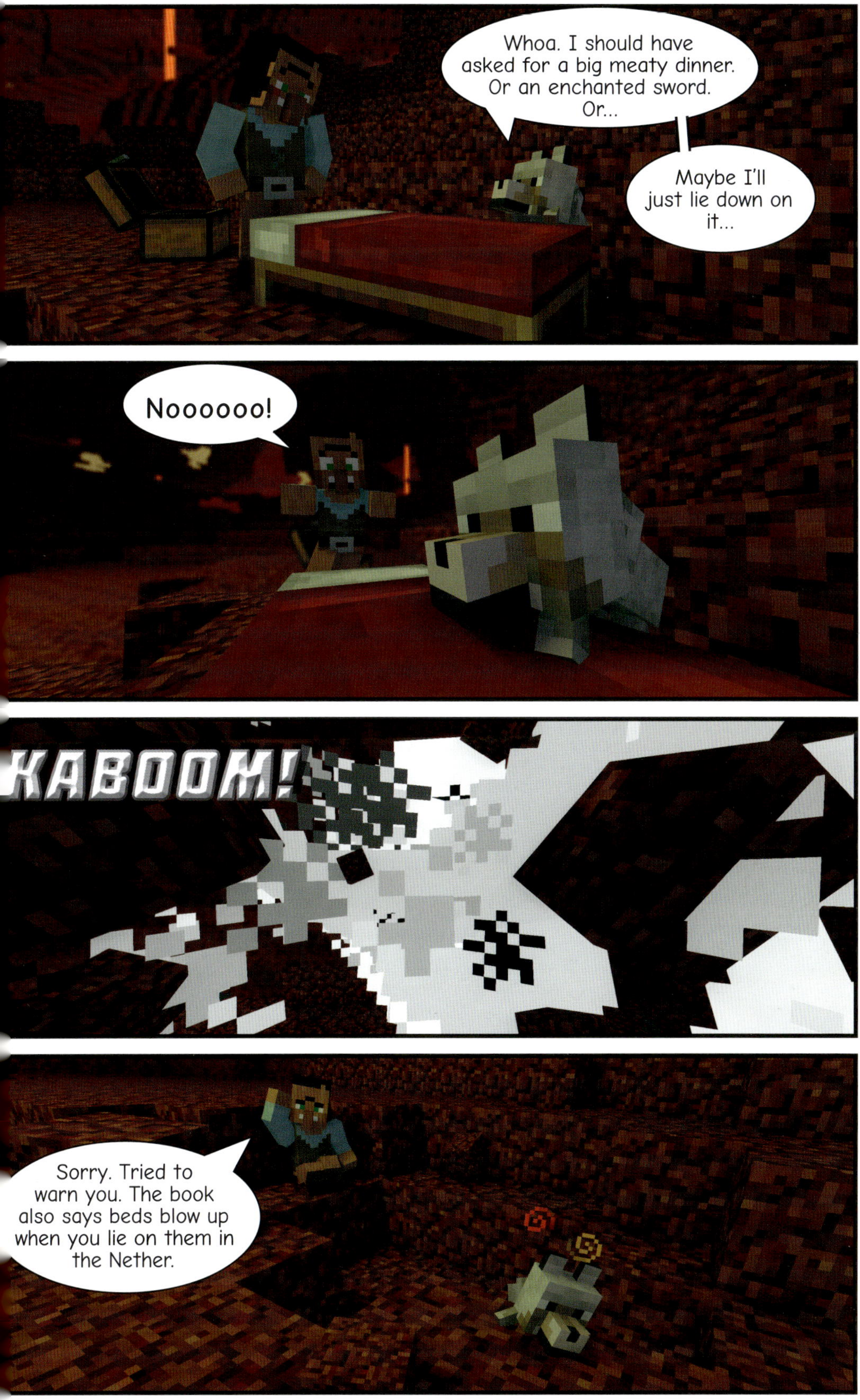
Whoa. I should have asked for a big meaty dinner. Or an enchanted sword. Or...
Maybe I'll just lie down on it...
Noooooo!
KABOOM!
Sorry. Tried to warn you. The book also says beds blow up when you lie on them in the Nether.

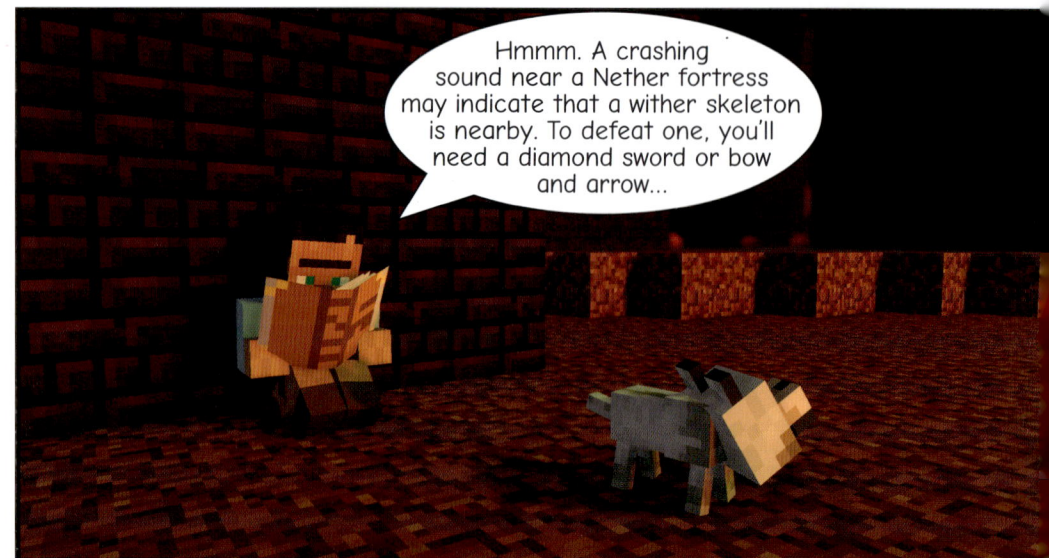

Hey, what's that cool thing?

Whatever it is, it's in the opposite direction of where Phoenix went.

Come on.

Maybe we can climb to the top to get a better view. We could find Phoenix.

It says here that this is a Nether fortress.

CRASH

ROAR

What's that sound?

Hmmm. A crashing sound near a Nether fortress may indicate that a wither skeleton is nearby. To defeat one, you'll need a diamond sword or bow and arrow...

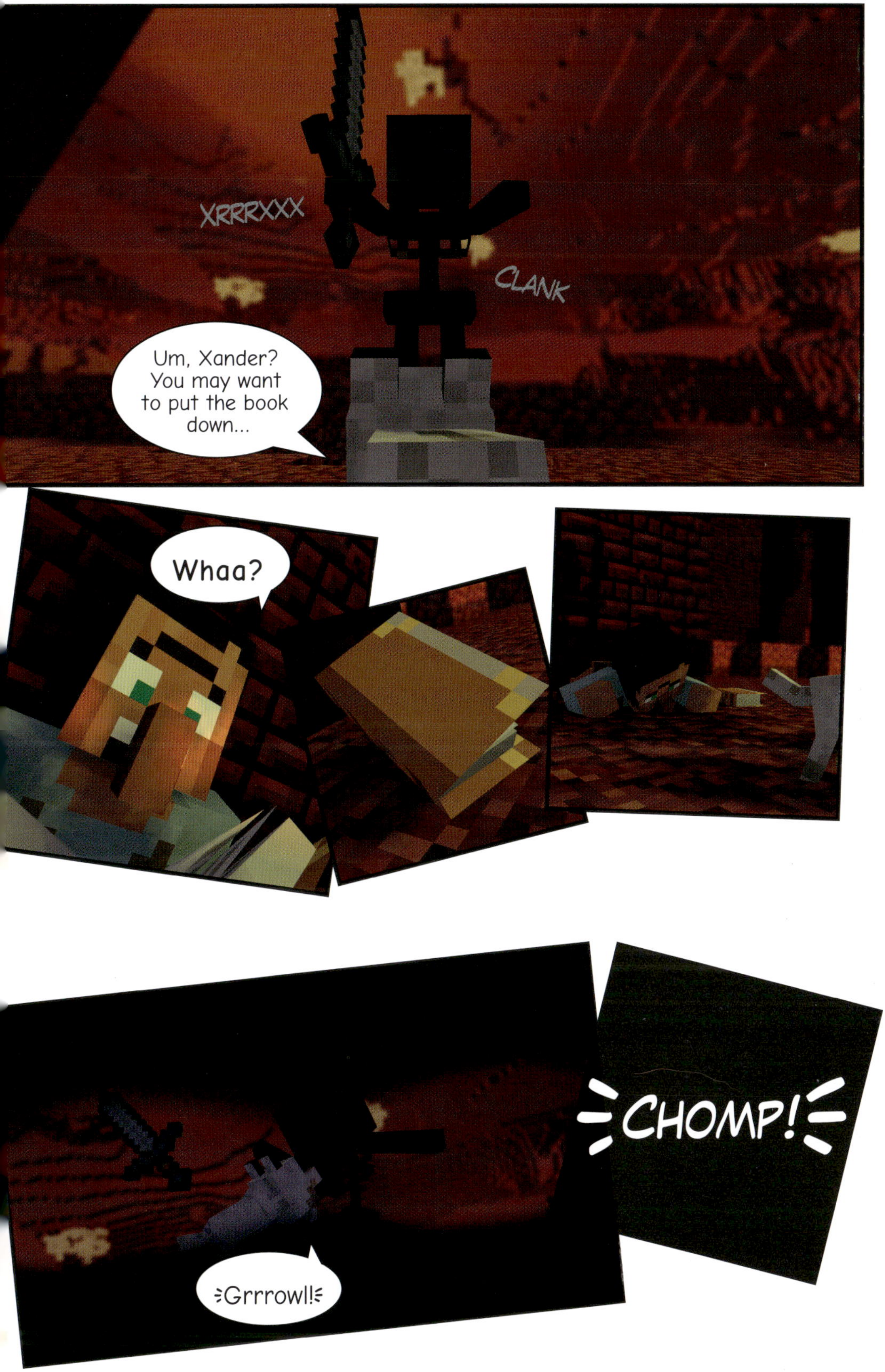
XRRRXXX
CLANK
Um, Xander? You may want to put the book down...
Whaa?
CHOMP!
Grrrowl!

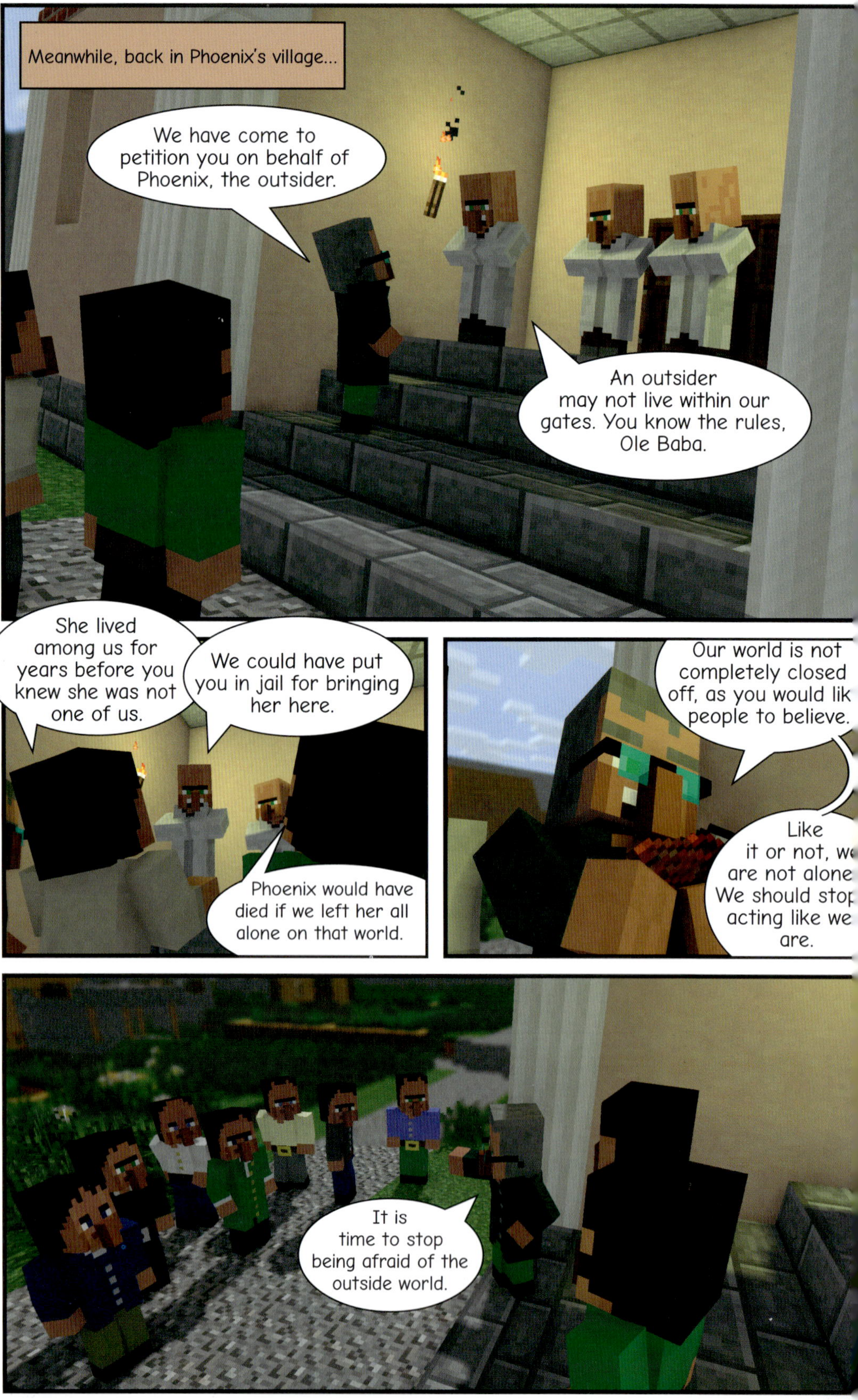
Meanwhile, back in Phoenix's village...
We have come to petition you on behalf of Phoenix, the outsider.
An outsider may not live within our gates. You know the rules, Ole Baba.
She lived among us for years before you knew she was not one of us.
We could have put you in jail for bringing her here.
Phoenix would have died if we left her all alone on that world.
Our world is not completely closed off, as you would lik people to believe.
Like it or not, w are not alone We should sto acting like we are.
It is time to stop being afraid of the outside world.

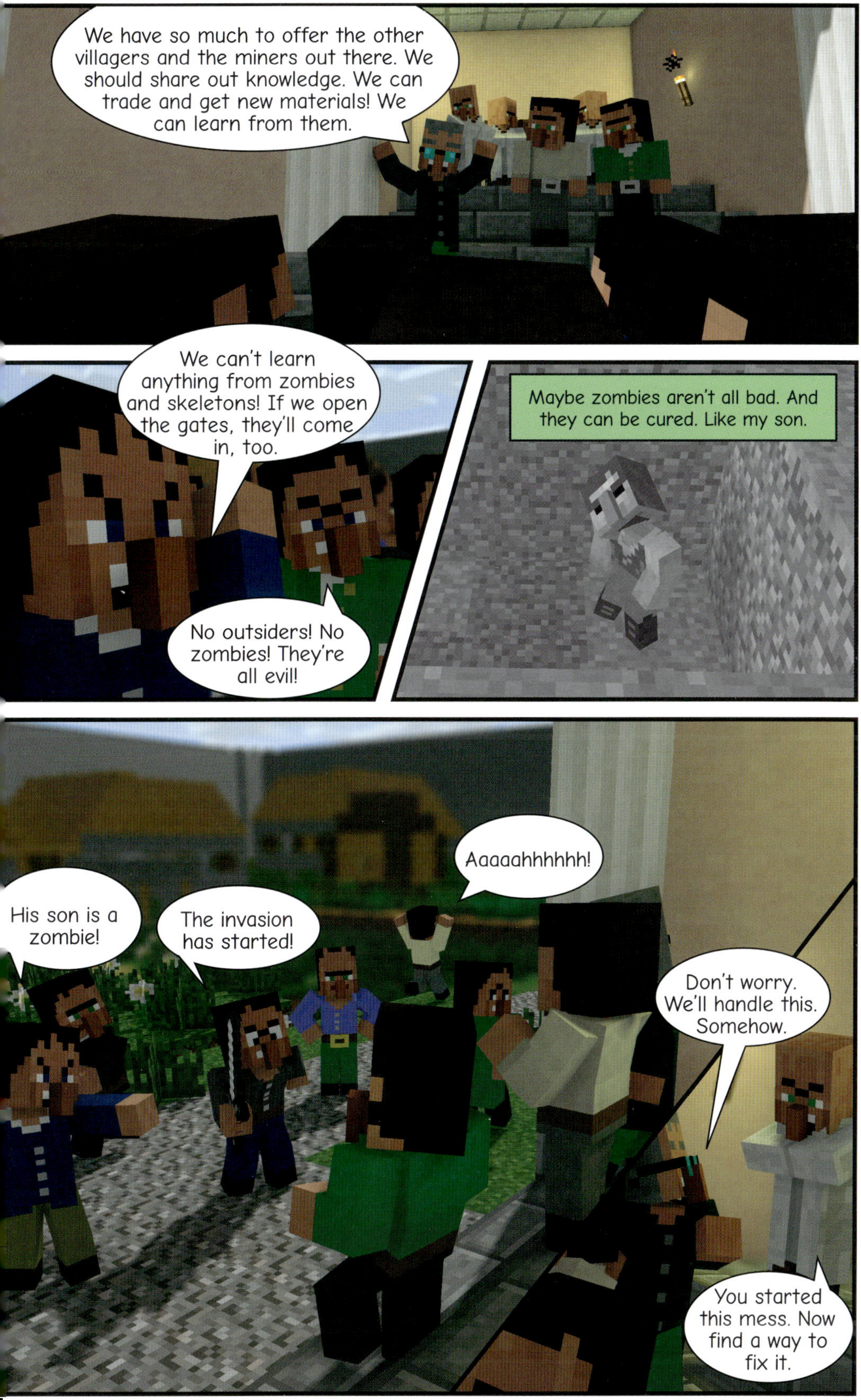
We have so much to offer the other villagers and the miners out there. We should share out knowledge. We can trade and get new materials! We can learn from them.
We can't learn anything from zombies and skeletons! If we open the gates, they'll come in, too.
No outsiders! No zombies! They're all evil!
Maybe zombies aren't all bad. And they can be cured. Like my son.
His son is a zombie!
The invasion has started!
Aaaaahhhhh!
Don't worry. We'll handle this. Somehow.
You started this mess. Now find a way to fix it.

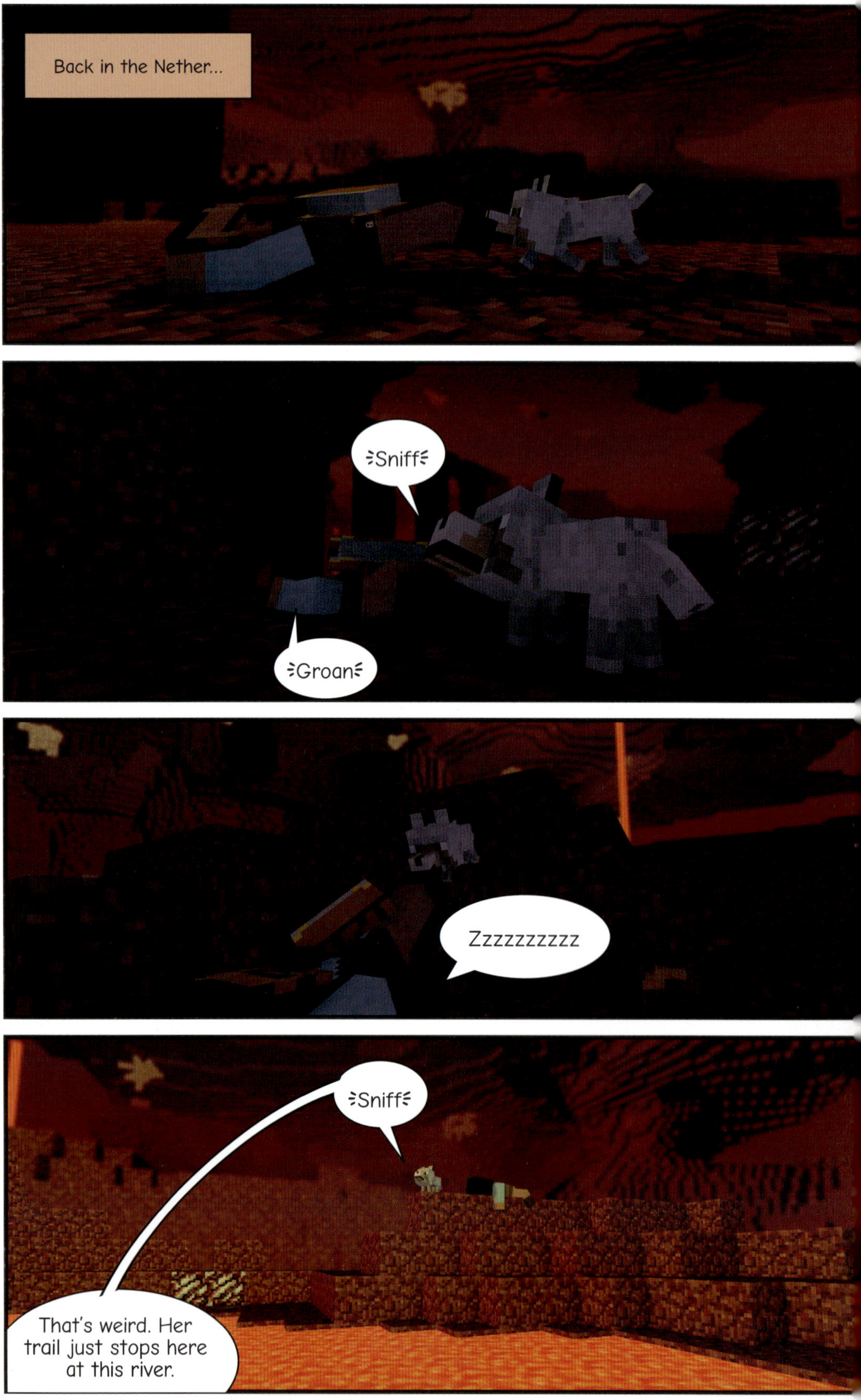
Back in the Nether...
Sniff
Groan
Zzzzzzzzzz
Sniff
That's weird. Her trail just stops here at this river.

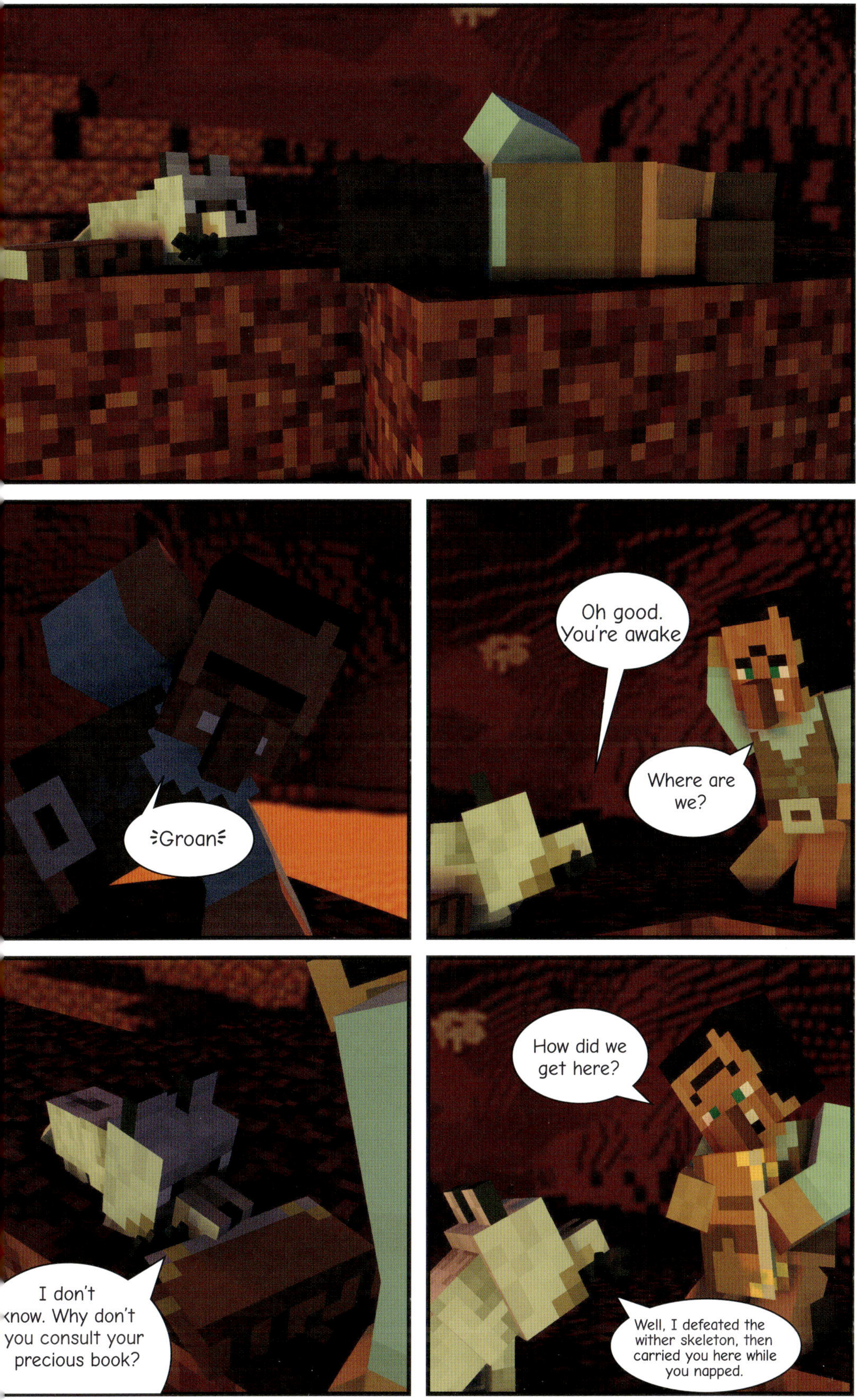

Groan
Oh good. You're awake
Where are we?
I don't know. Why don't you consult your precious book?
How did we get here?
Well, I defeated the wither skeleton, then carried you here while you napped.

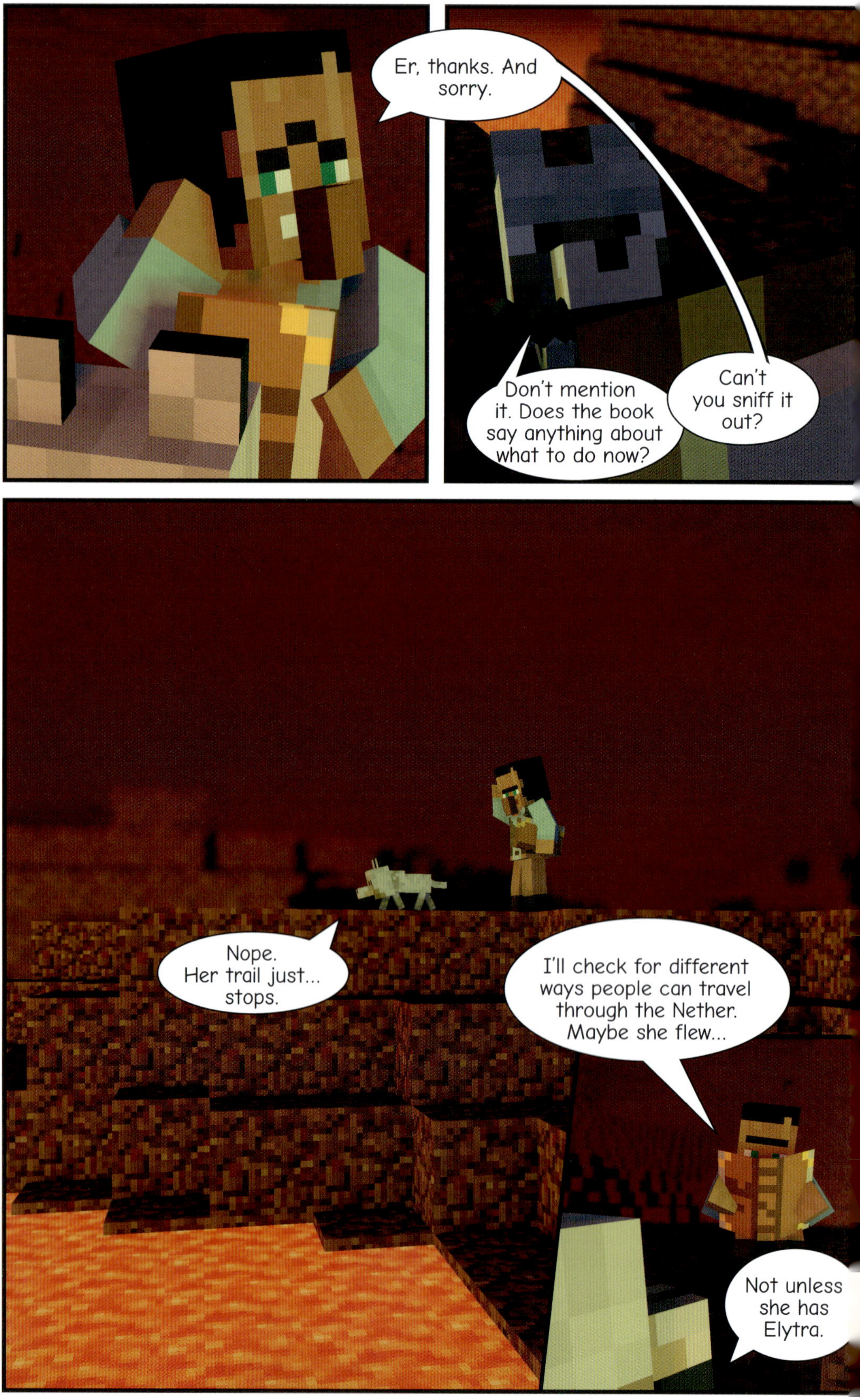
Er, thanks. And sorry.
Don't mention it. Does the book say anything about what to do now?
Can't you sniff it out?
Nope. Her trail just... stops.
I'll check for different ways people can travel through the Nether. Maybe she flew...
Not unless she has Elytra.

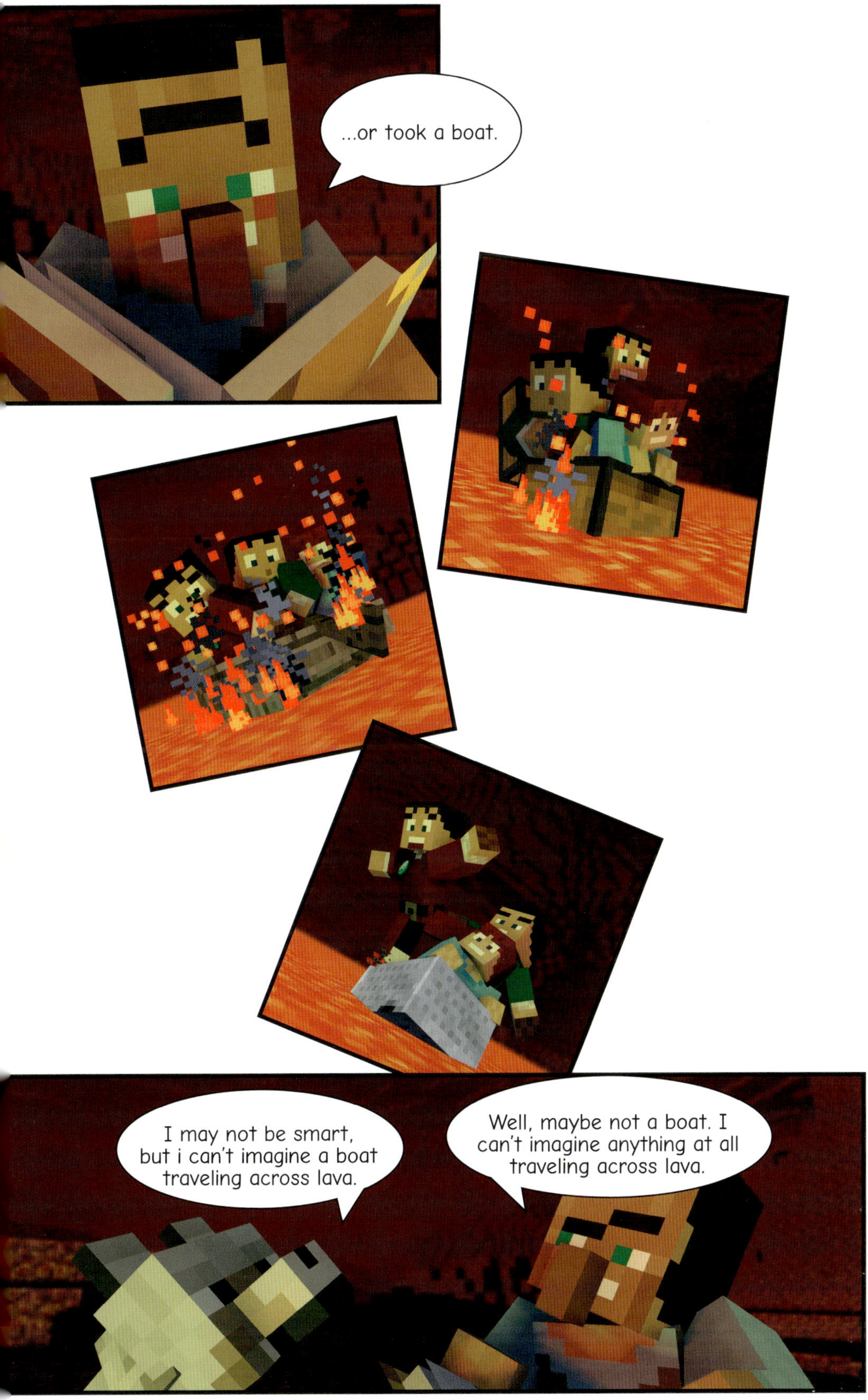
...or took a boat.
I may not be smart, but i can't imagine a boat traveling across lava.
Well, maybe not a boat. I can't imagine anything at all traveling across lava.

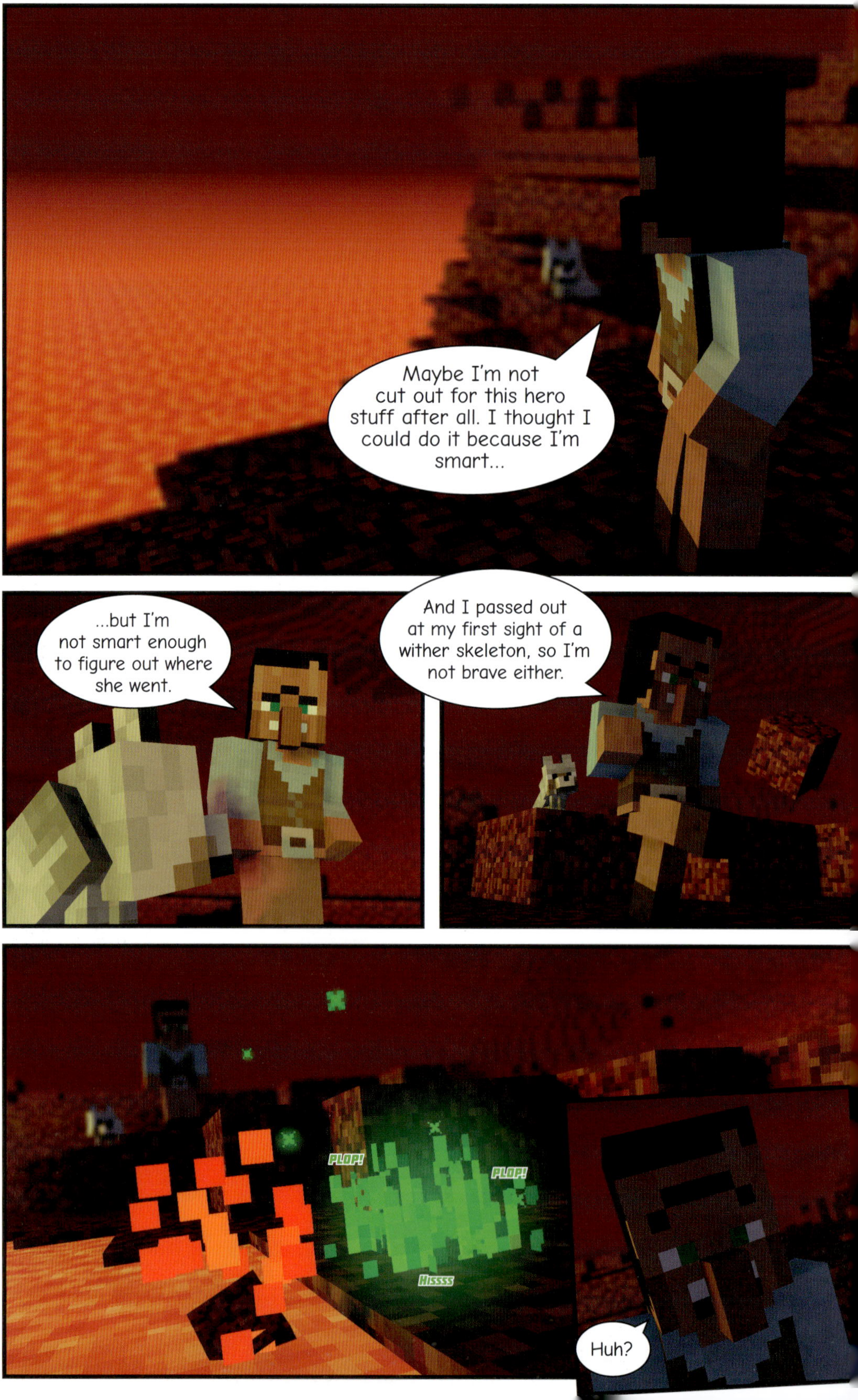
Maybe I'm not cut out for this hero stuff after all. I thought I could do it because I'm smart...
...but I'm not smart enough to figure out where she went.
And I passed out at my first sight of a wither skeleton, so I'm not brave either.
PLOP!
PLOP!
HISSSS
Huh?

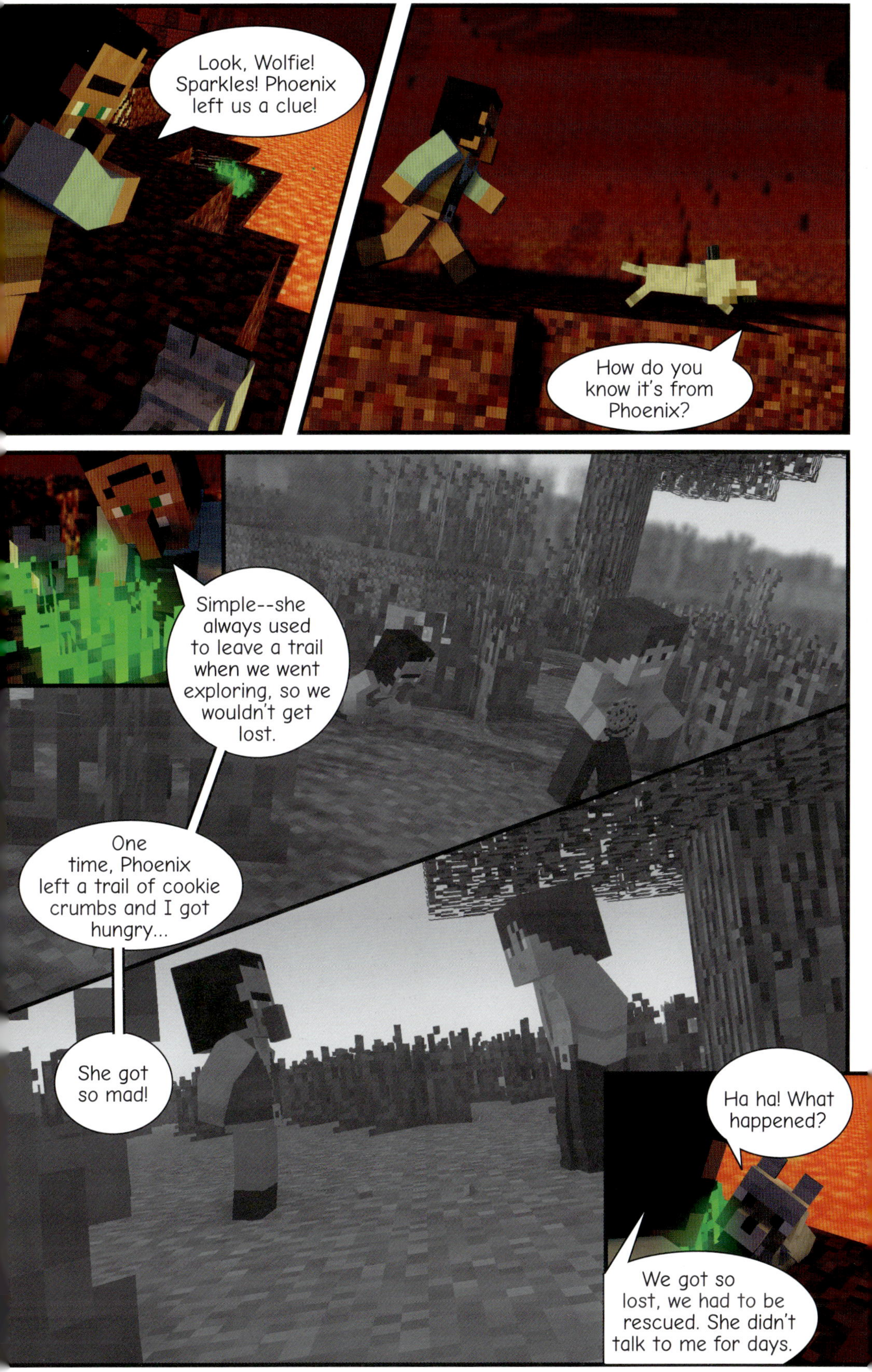
Look, Wolfie! Sparkles! Phoenix left us a clue!
How do you know it's from Phoenix?
Simple--she always used to leave a trail when we went exploring, so we wouldn't get lost.
One time, Phoenix left a trail of cookie crumbs and I got hungry...
She got so mad!
Ha ha! What happened?
We got so lost, we had to be rescued. She didn't talk to me for days.

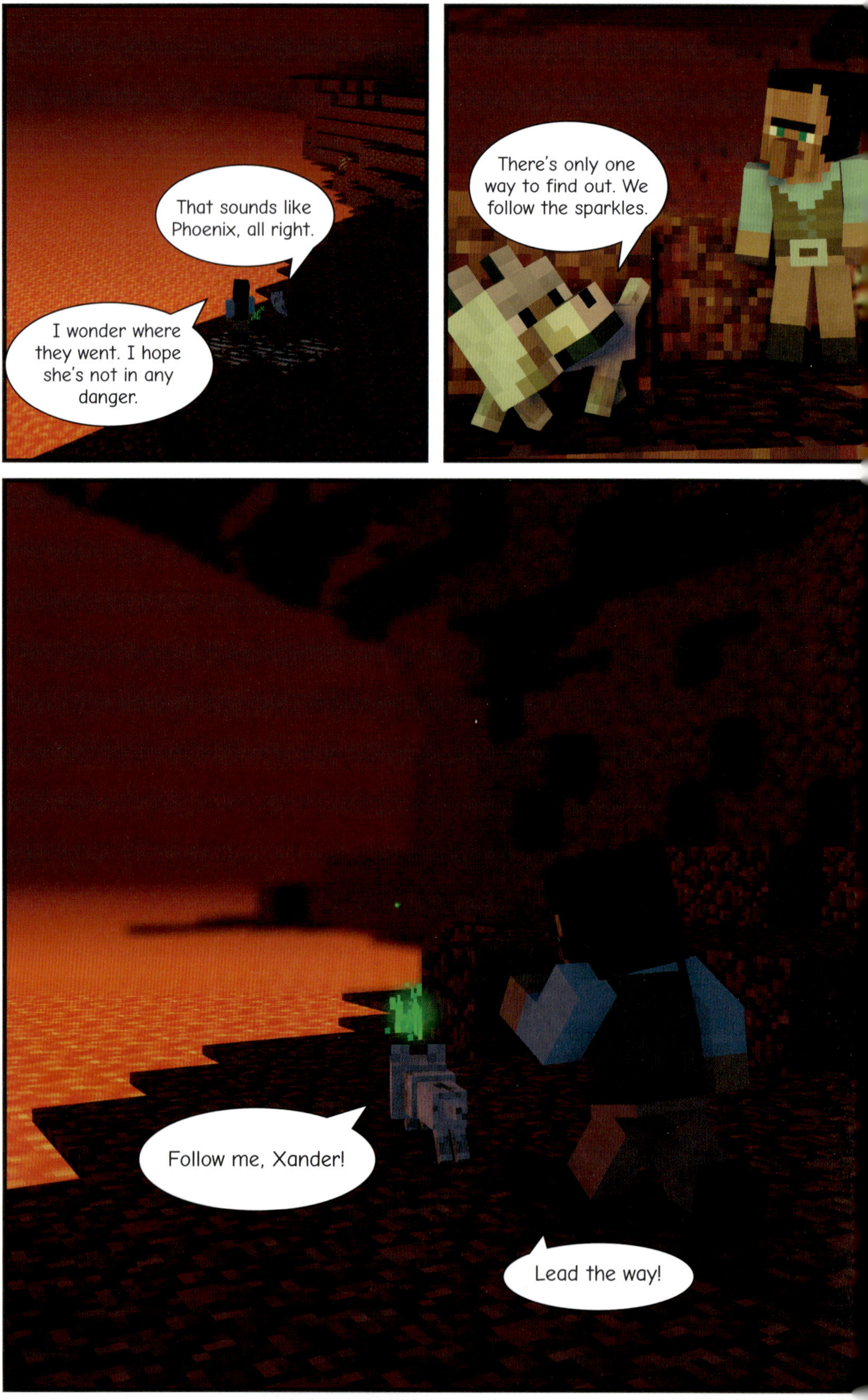
I wonder where they went. I hope she's not in any danger.
That sounds like Phoenix, all right.
There's only one way to find out. We follow the sparkles.
Follow me, Xander!
Lead the way!

CHAPTER 8

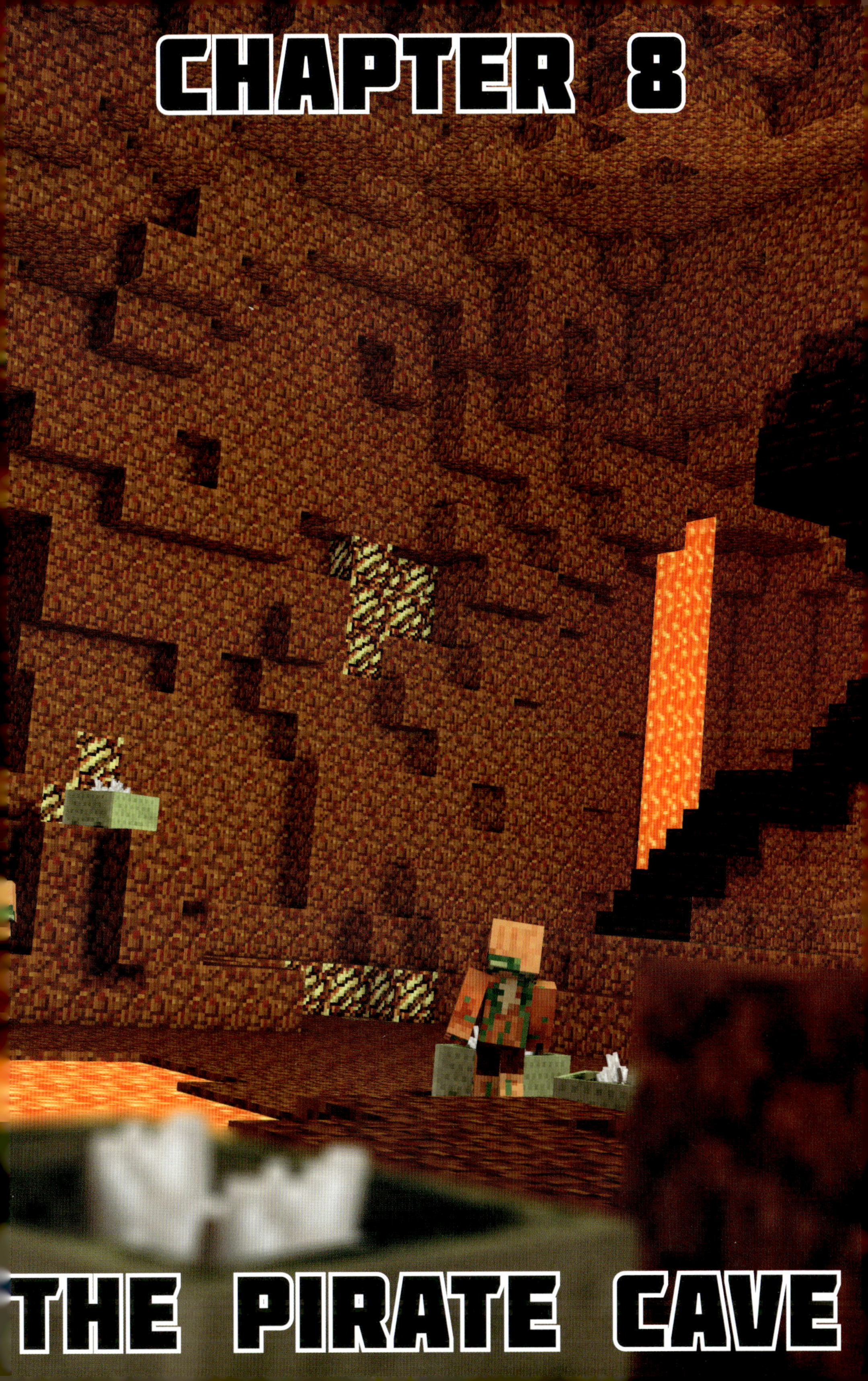

THE PIRATE CAVE

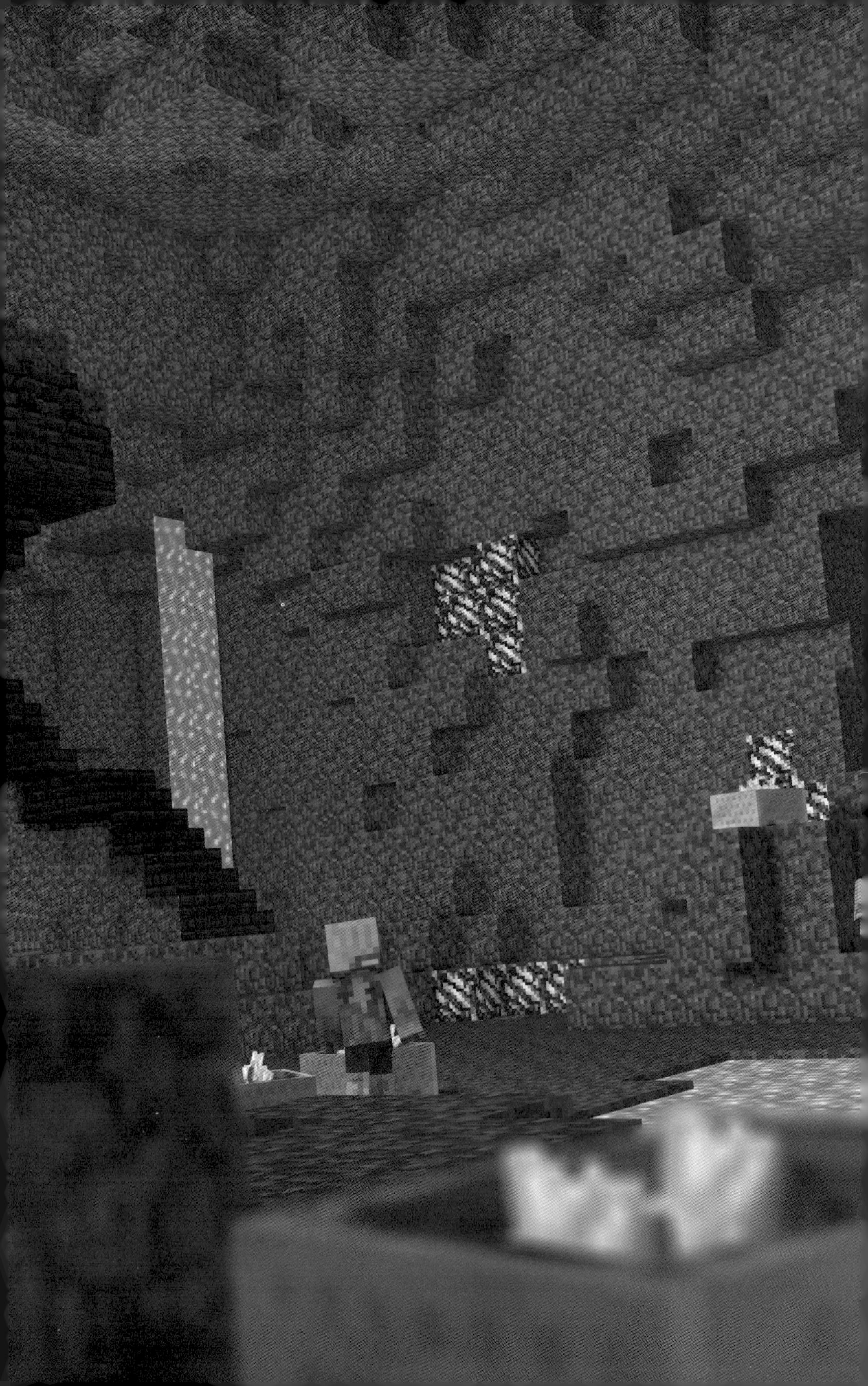

Back at Captain Killigrew's Secret Lair...

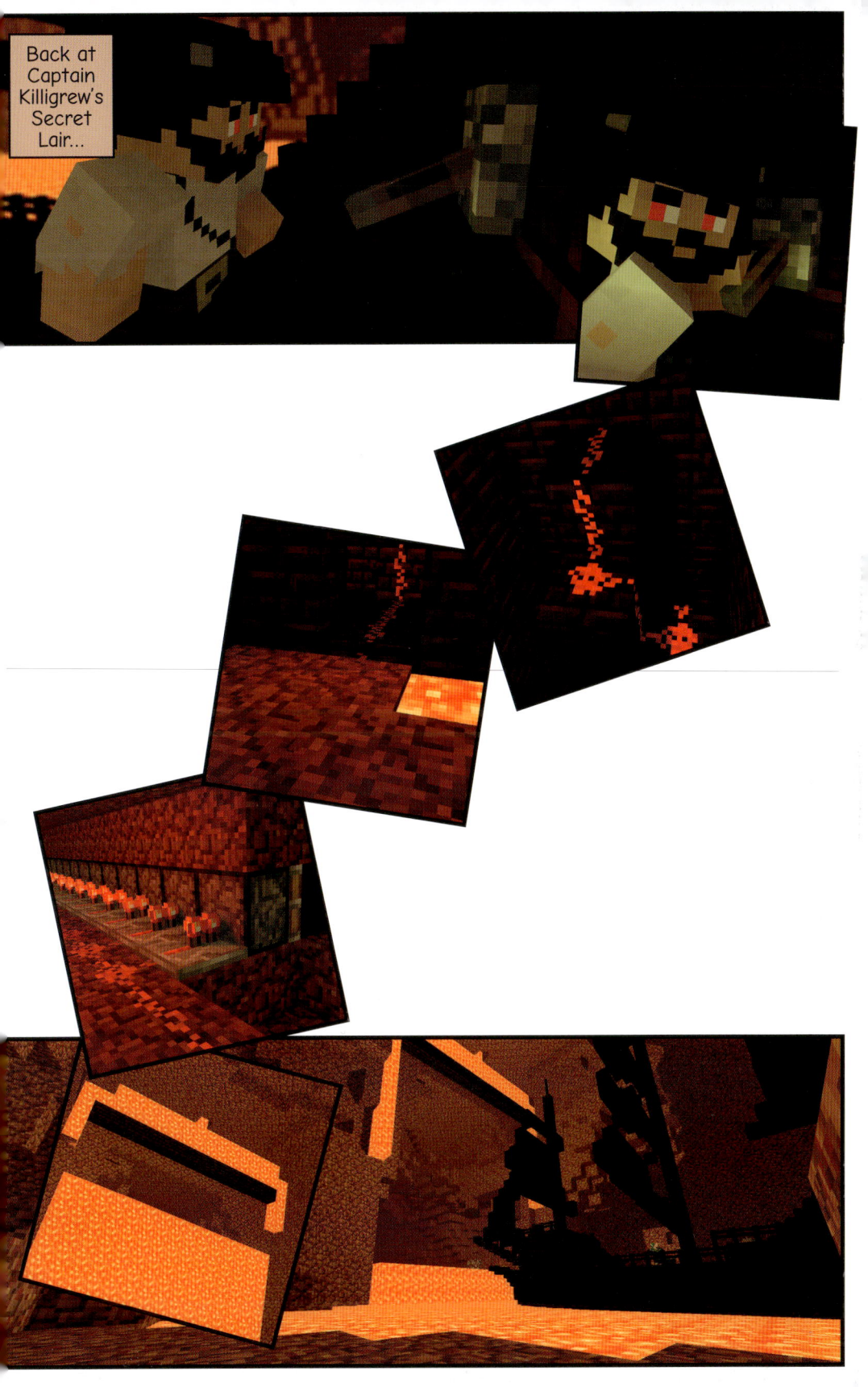

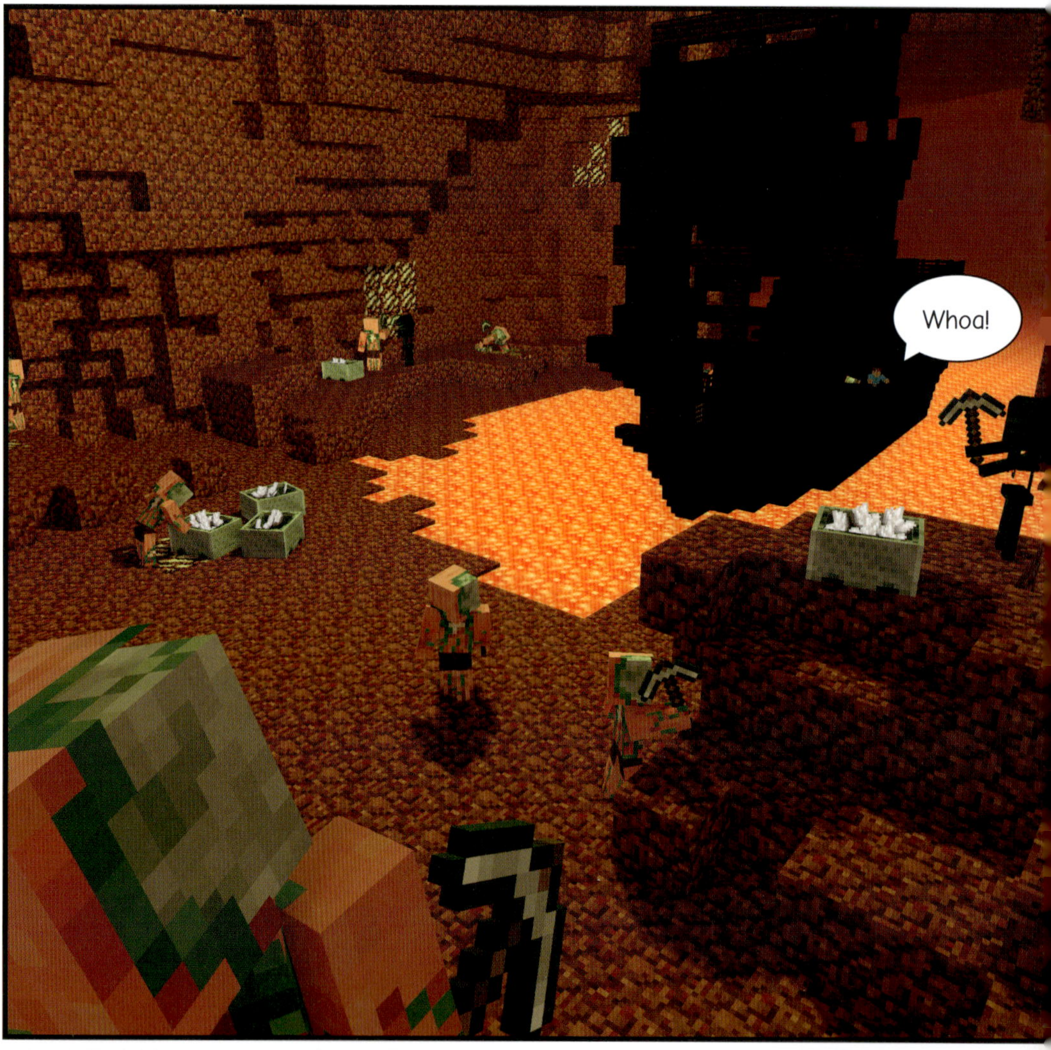
Whoa!

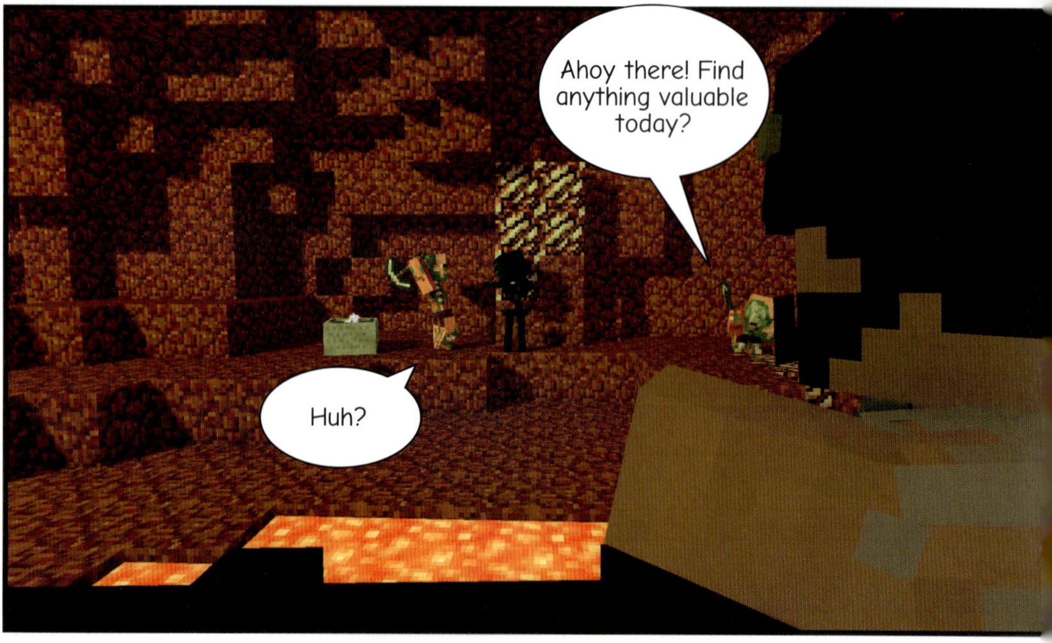
Ahoy there! Find anything valuable today?
Huh?

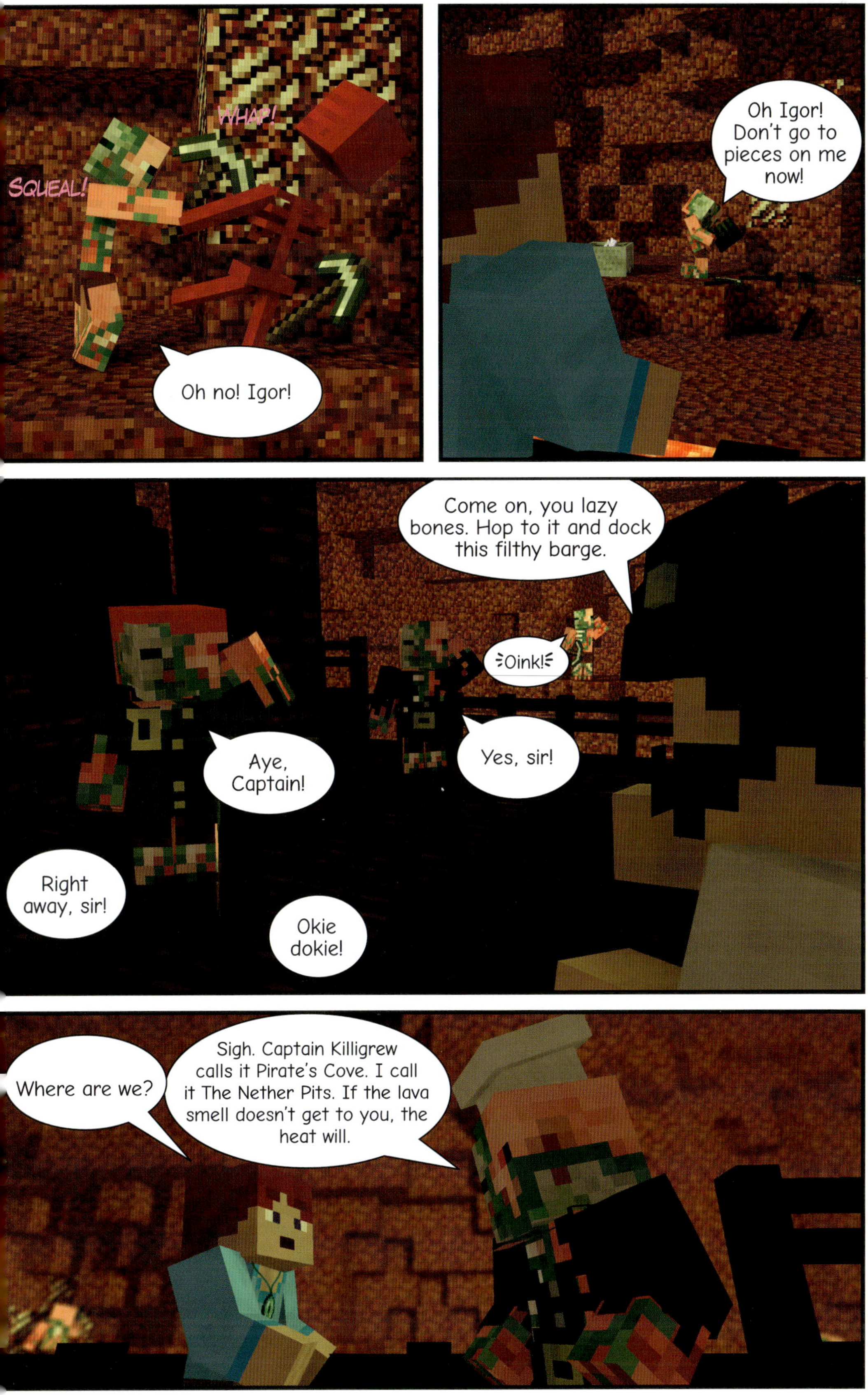
WHAP!
SQUEAL!
Oh no! Igor!
Oh Igor! Don't go to pieces on me now!
Come on, you lazy bones. Hop to it and dock this filthy barge.
Oink!
Aye, Captain!
Yes, sir!
Right away, sir!
Okie dokie!
Where are we?
Sigh. Captain Killigrew calls it Pirate's Cove. I call it The Nether Pits. If the lava smell doesn't get to you, the heat will.

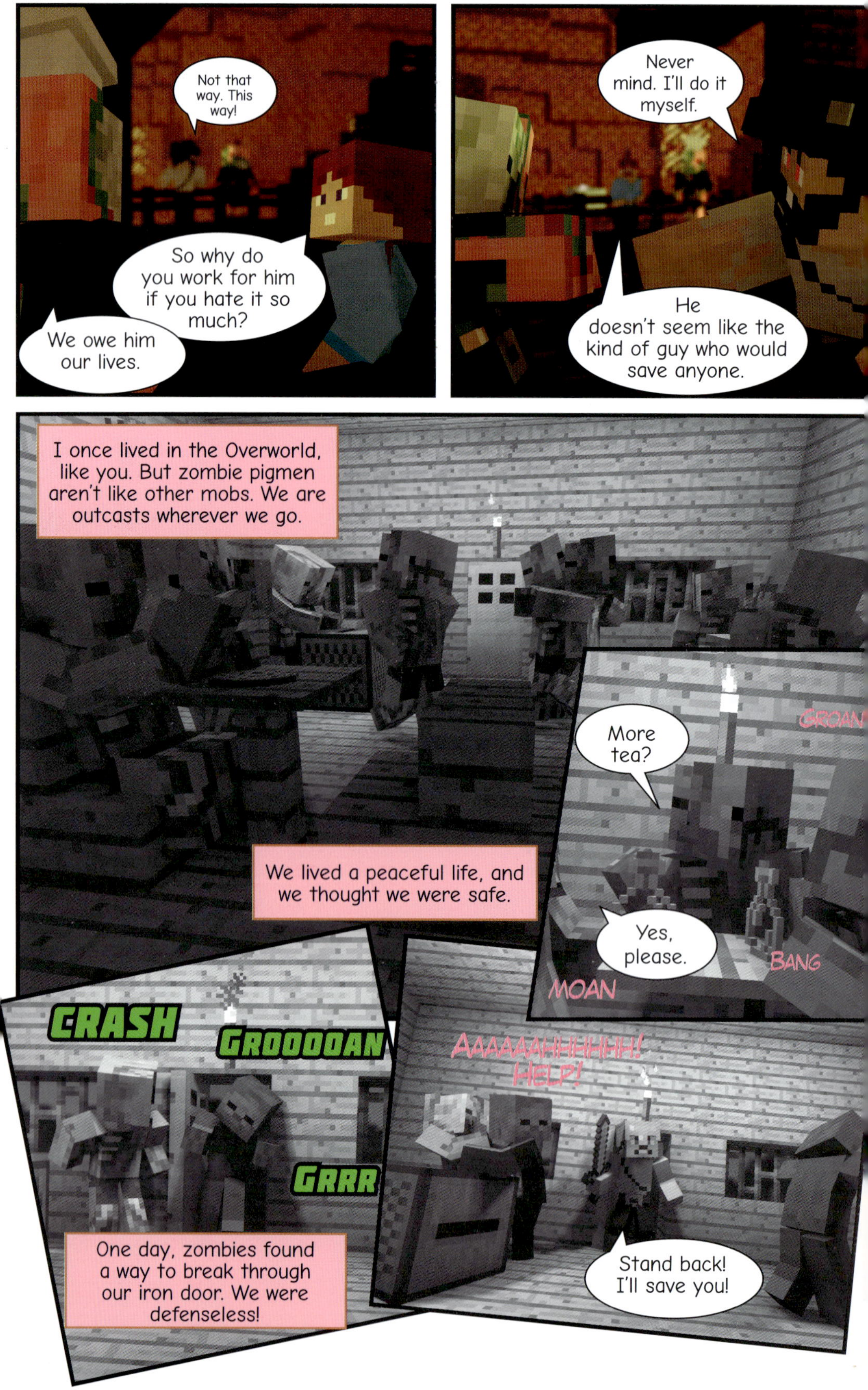

Not that way. This way!
So why do you work for him if you hate it so much?
We owe him our lives.
Never mind. I'll do it myself.
He doesn't seem like the kind of guy who would save anyone.
I once lived in the Overworld, like you. But zombie pigmen aren't like other mobs. We are outcasts wherever we go.
We lived a peaceful life, and we thought we were safe.
GROAN
More tea?
Yes, please.
BANG
MOAN
CRASH
GROOOOAN
GRRR
One day, zombies found a way to break through our iron door. We were defenseless!
AAAAAAHHHHHH! HELP!
Stand back! I'll save you!

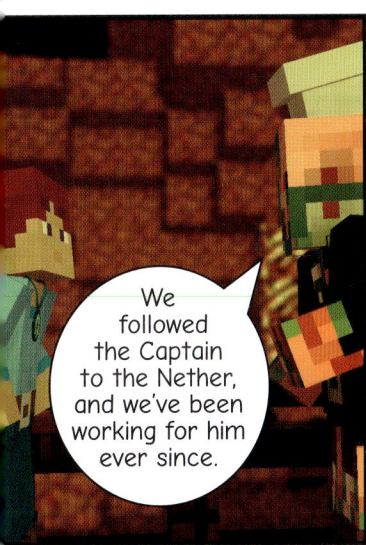

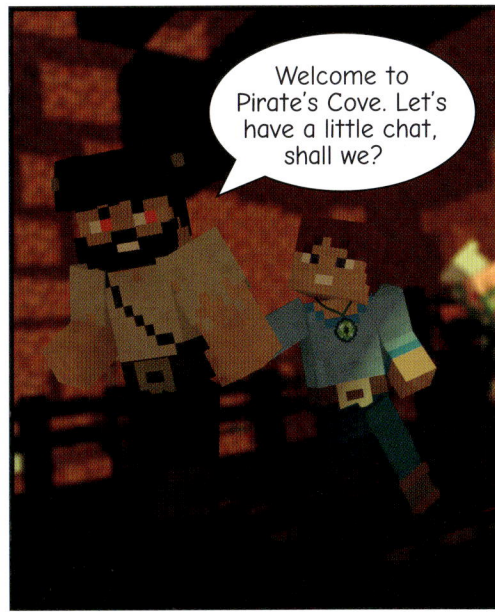

Good thing I was here to protect you.

You saved our lives!

How can we ever repay you?

We followed the Captain to the Nether, and we've been working for him ever since.

Zombies can't go through an iron door on their own, you know.

Is it possible the Captain let them in?

Welcome to Pirate's Cove. Let's have a little chat, shall we?

!!!

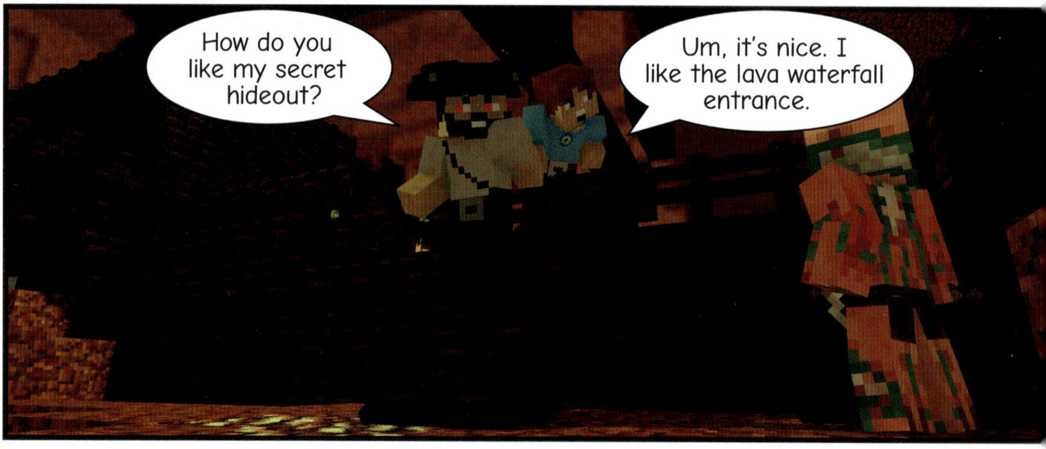
How do you like my secret hideout?
Um, it's nice. I like the lava waterfall entrance.

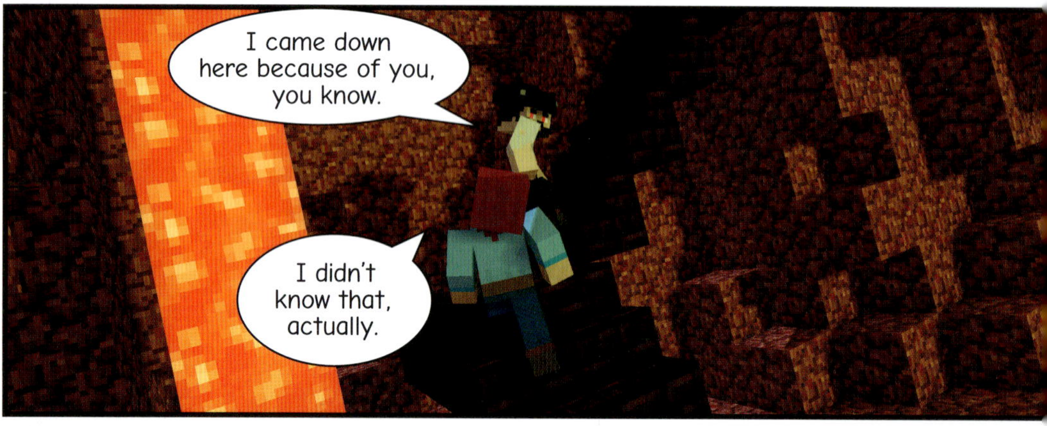
I came down here because of you, you know.
I didn't know that, actually.

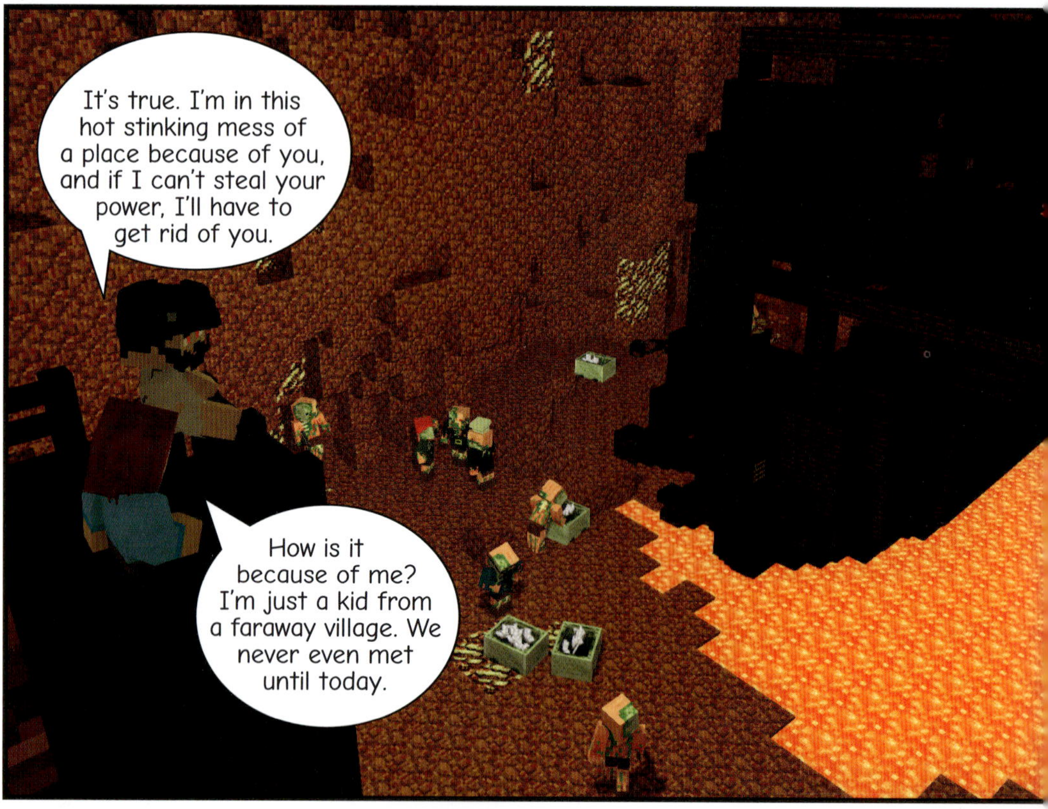
It's true. I'm in this hot stinking mess of a place because of you, and if I can't steal your power, I'll have to get rid of you.
How is it because of me? I'm just a kid from a faraway village. We never even met until today.

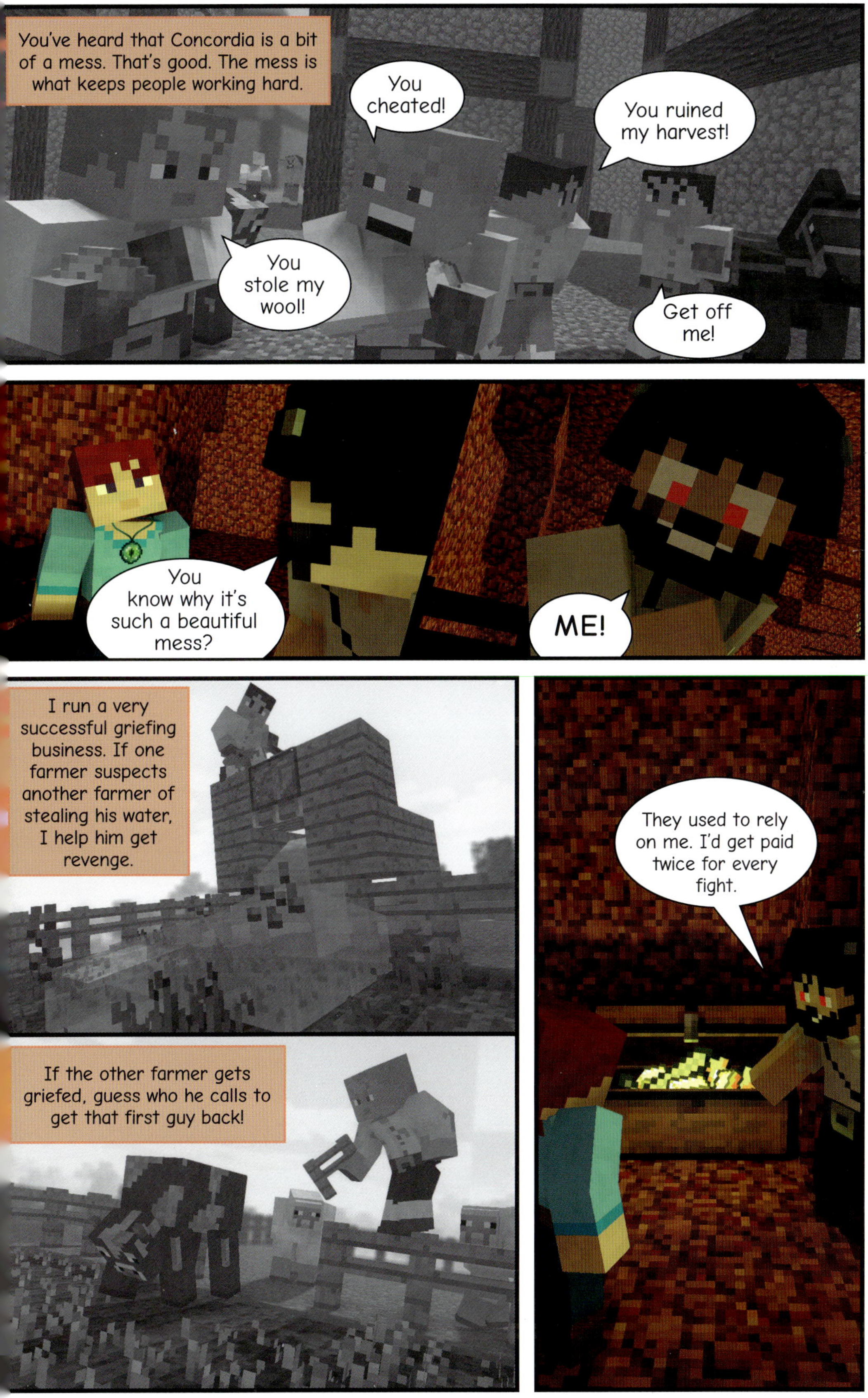
You've heard that Concordia is a bit of a mess. That's good. The mess is what keeps people working hard.
You cheated!
You ruined my harvest!
You stole my wool!
Get off me!
You know why it's such a beautiful mess?
ME!
I run a very successful griefing business. If one farmer suspects another farmer of stealing his water, I help him get revenge.
If the other farmer gets griefed, guess who he calls to get that first guy back!
They used to rely on me. I'd get paid twice for every fight.

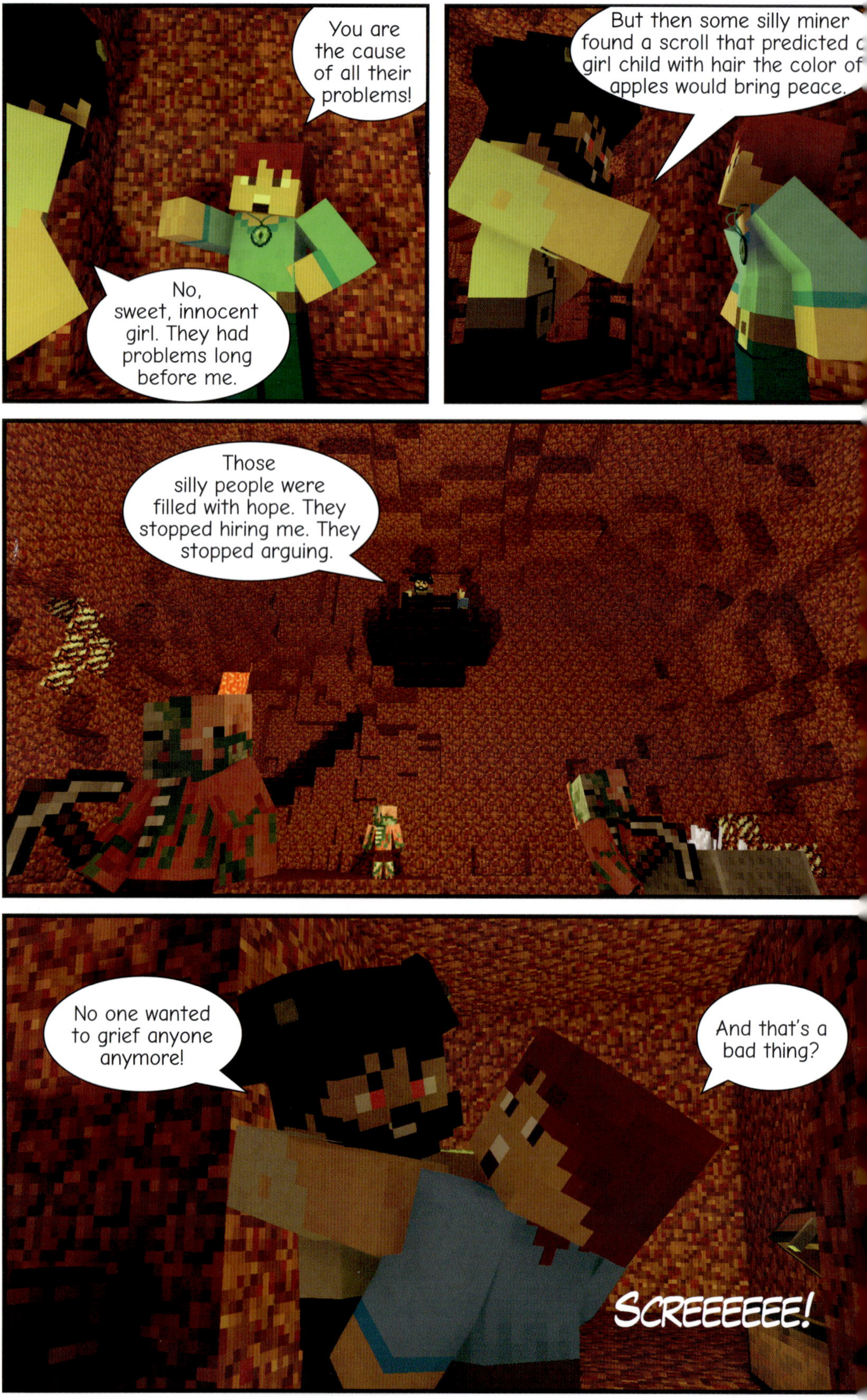
You are the cause of all their problems!
No, sweet, innocent girl. They had problems long before me.
But then some silly miner found a scroll that predicted a girl child with hair the color of apples would bring peace.
Those silly people were filled with hope. They stopped hiring me. They stopped arguing.
No one wanted to grief anyone anymore!
And that's a bad thing?
SCREEEEEEE!

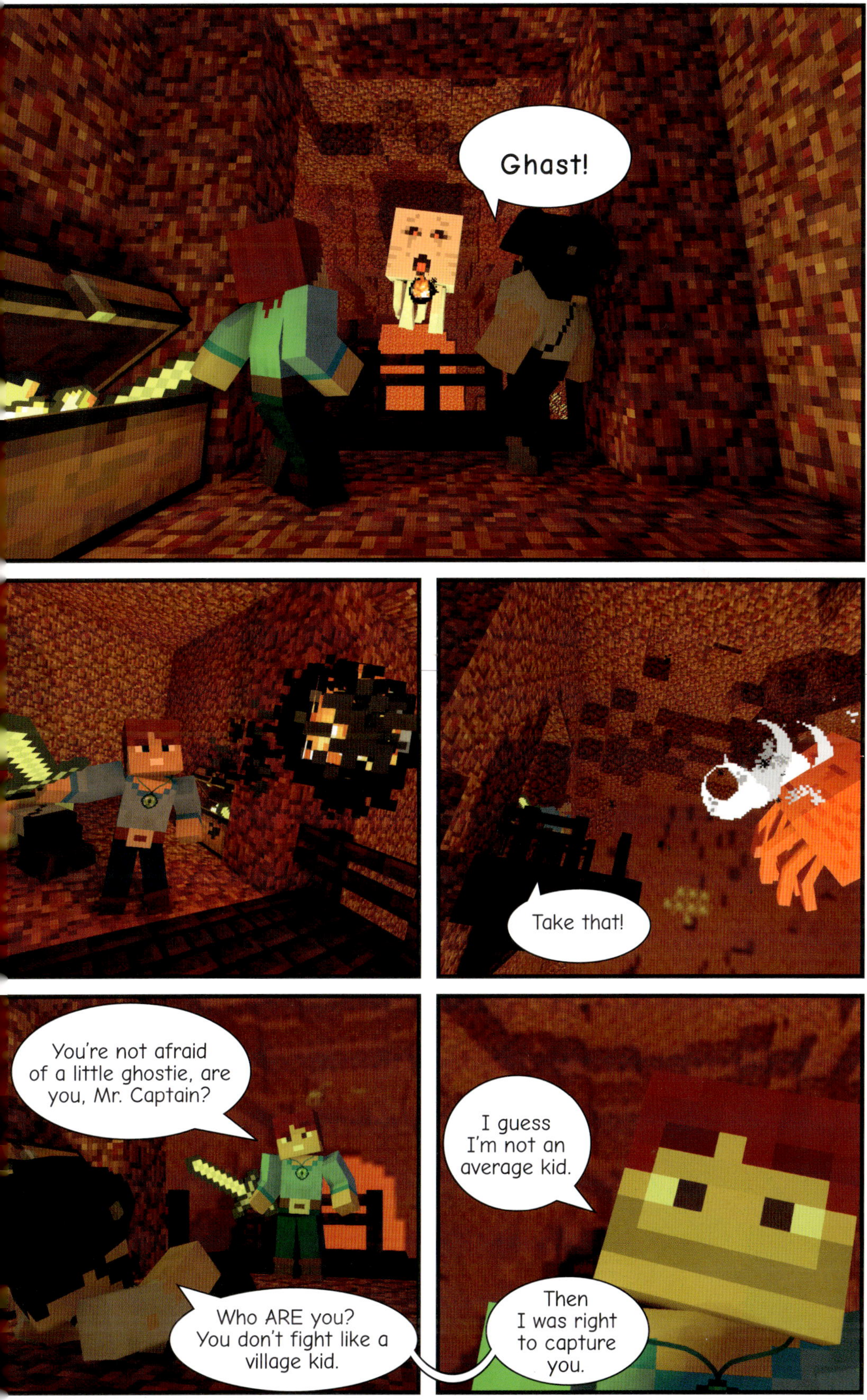
Ghast!
Take that!
You're not afraid of a little ghostie, are you, Mr. Captain?
Who ARE you? You don't fight like a village kid.
I guess I'm not an average kid.
Then I was right to capture you.

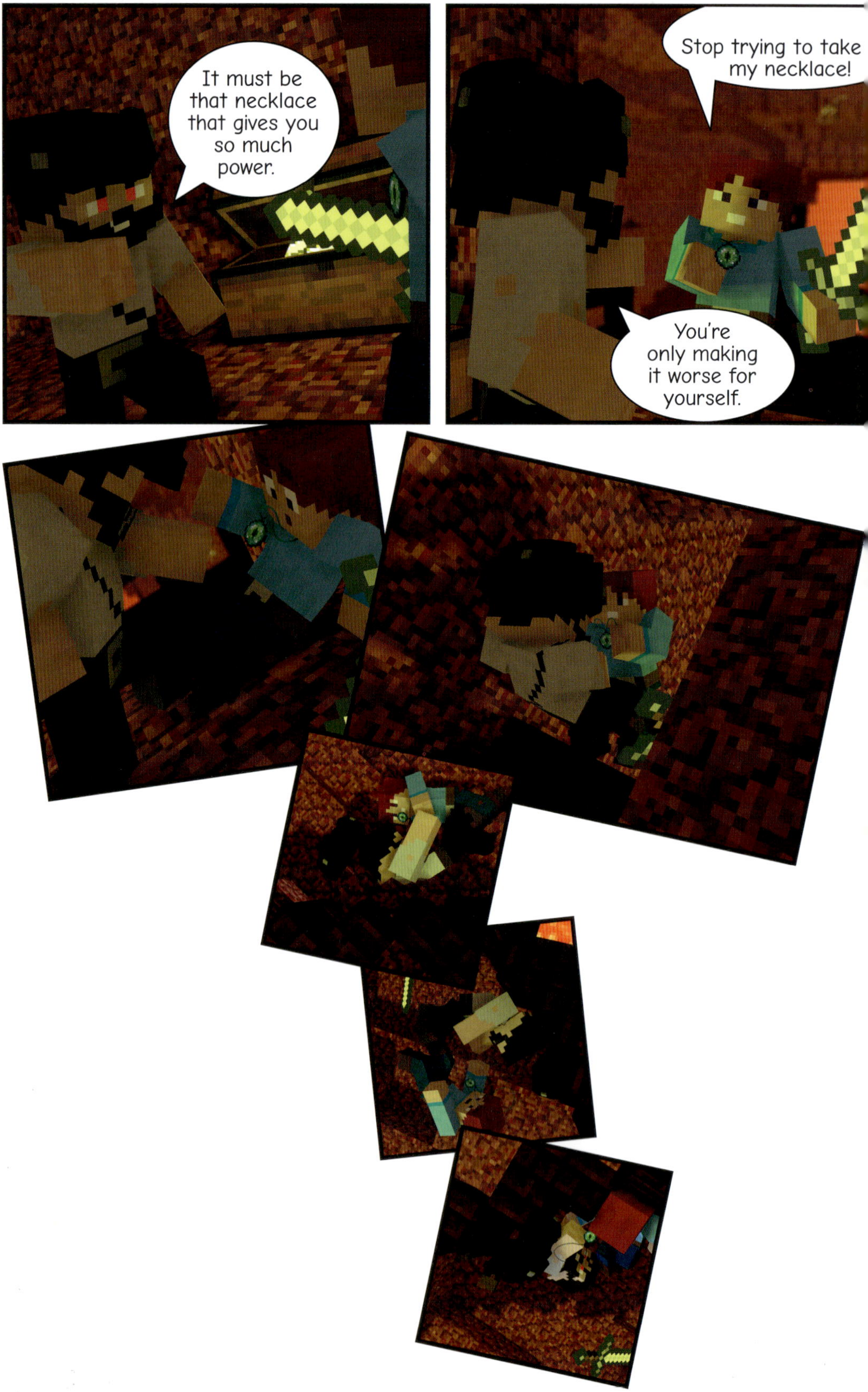
It must be that necklace that gives you so much power.
Stop trying to take my necklace!
You're only making it worse for yourself.

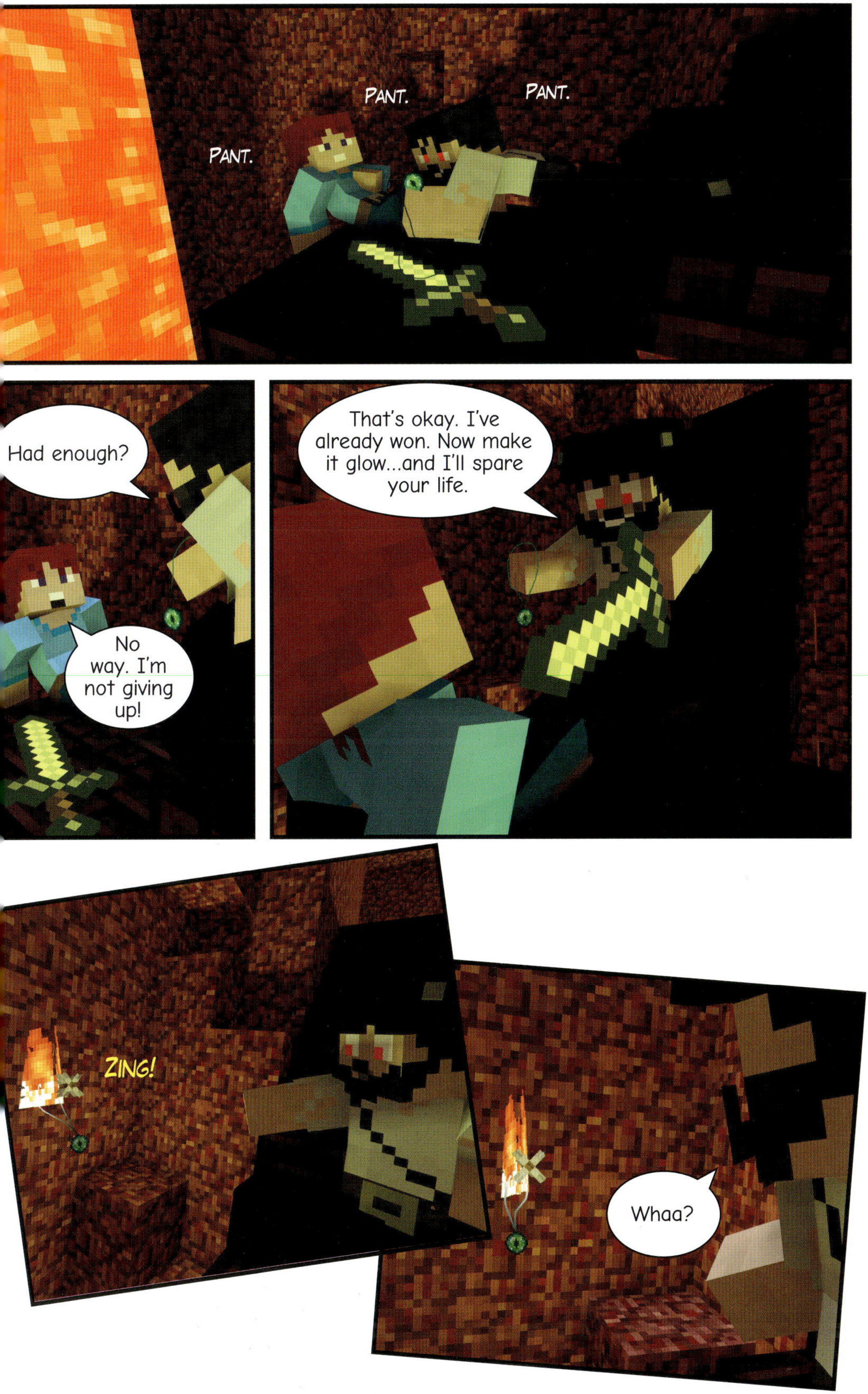
PANT.
PANT.
PANT.
Had enough?
No way. I'm not giving up!
That's okay. I've already won. Now make it glow...and I'll spare your life.
ZING!
Whaa?

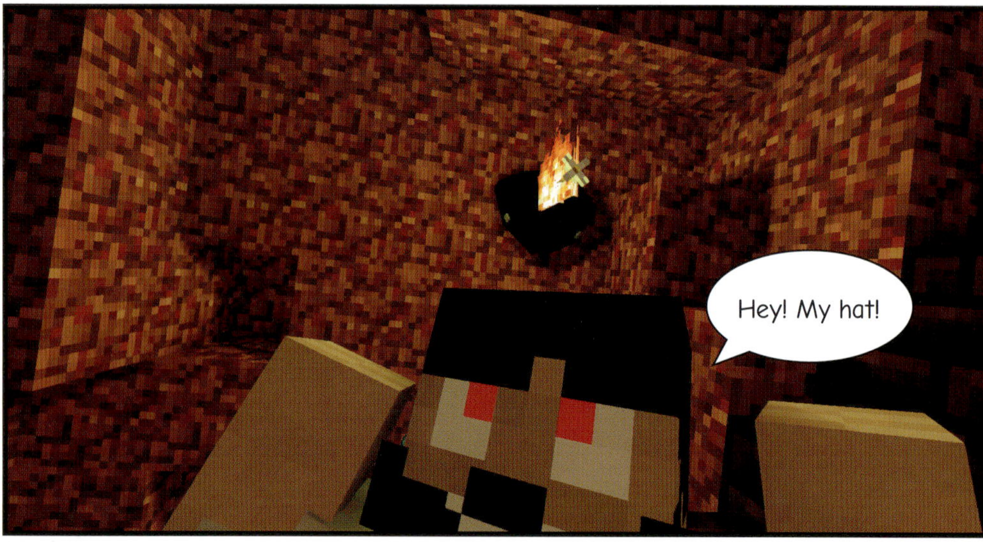
Hey! My hat!

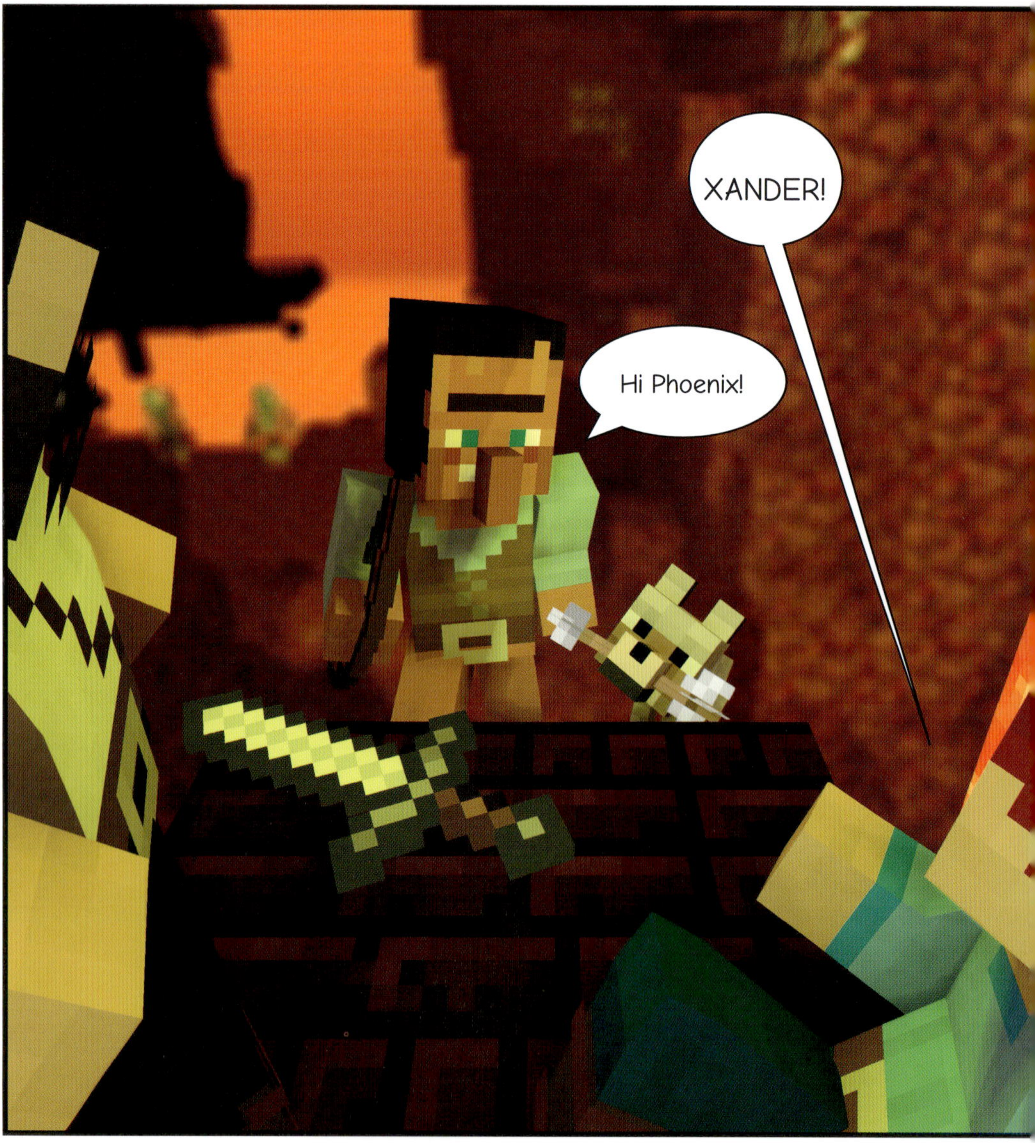
XANDER!
Hi Phoenix!

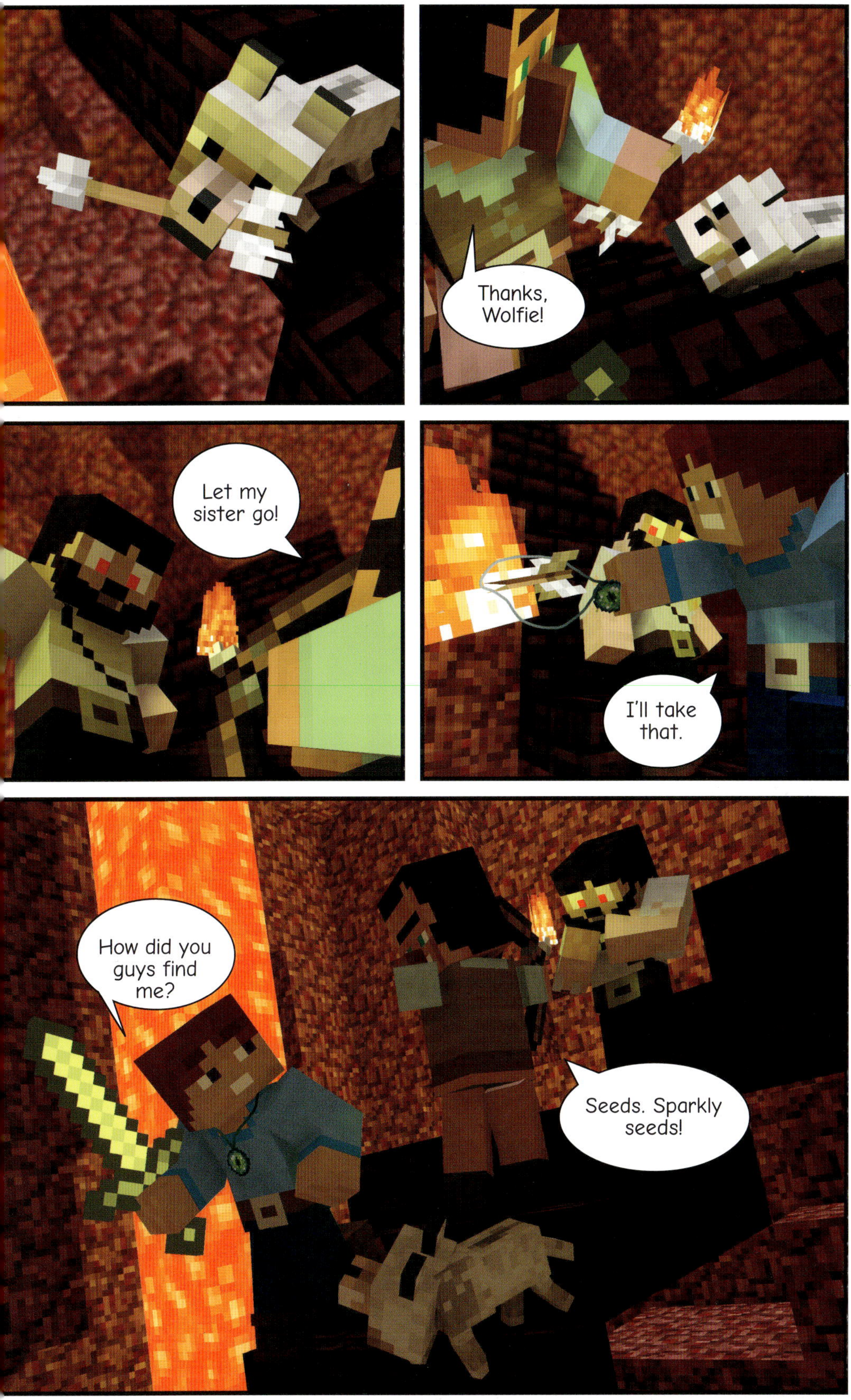
Thanks, Wolfie!
Let my sister go!
I'll take that.
How did you guys find me?
Seeds. Sparkly seeds!

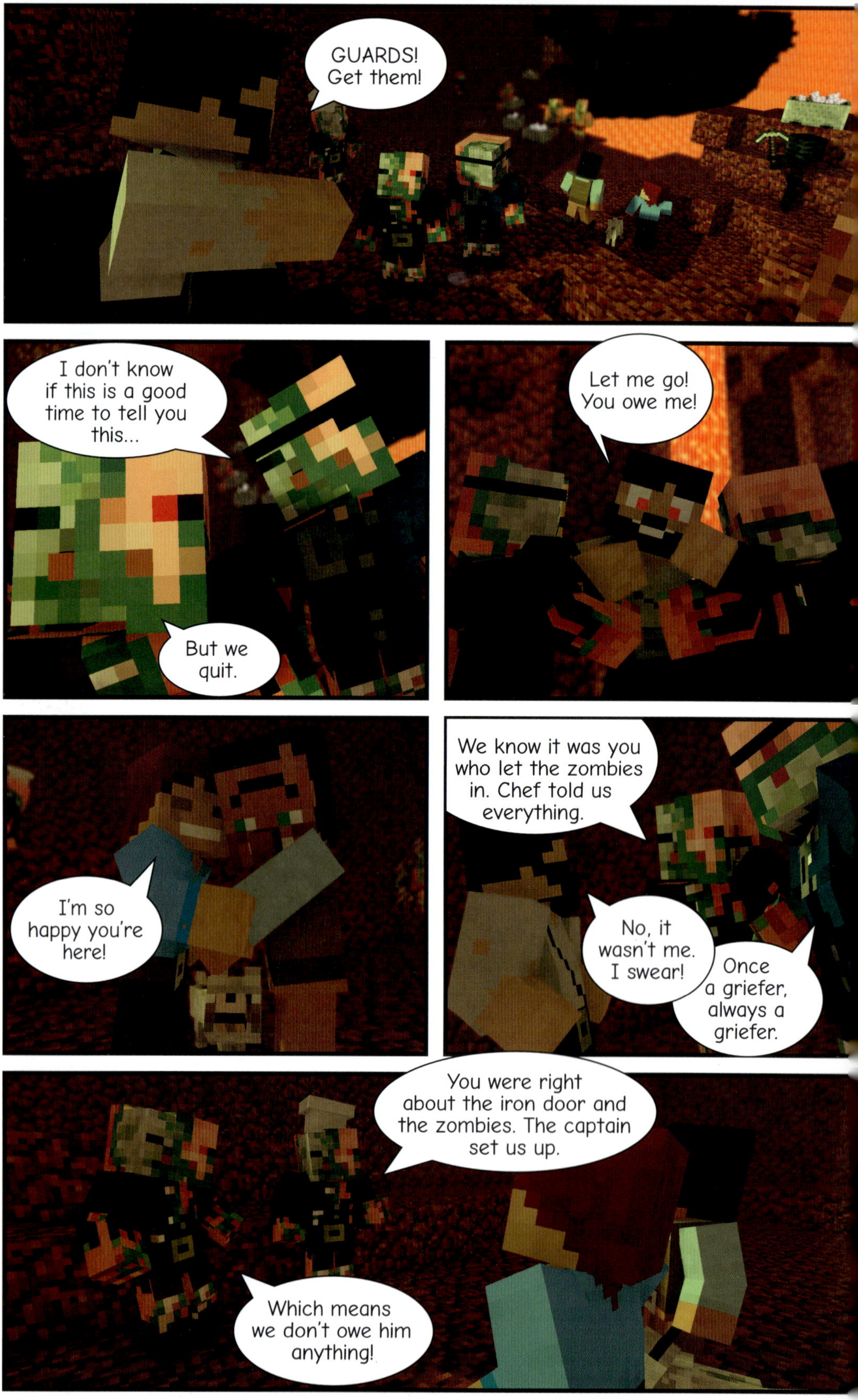
GUARDS! Get them!
I don't know if this is a good time to tell you this...
But we quit.
Let me go! You owe me!
I'm so happy you're here!
We know it was you who let the zombies in. Chef told us everything.
No, it wasn't me. I swear!
Once a griefer, always a griefer.
You were right about the iron door and the zombies. The captain set us up.
Which means we don't owe him anything!

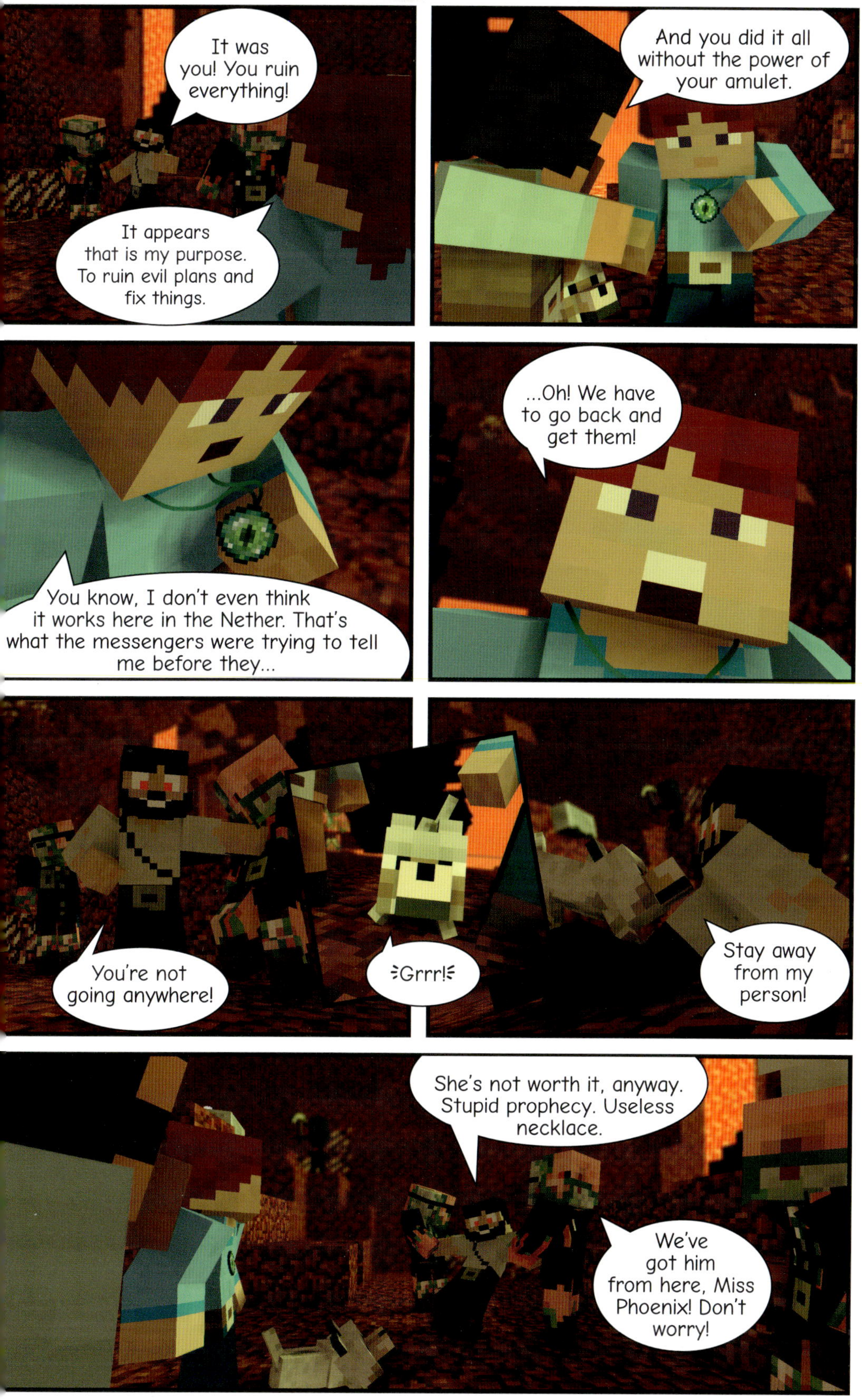

It was you! You ruin everything!
It appears that is my purpose. To ruin evil plans and fix things.
And you did it all without the power of your amulet.
You know, I don't even think it works here in the Nether. That's what the messengers were trying to tell me before they...
...Oh! We have to go back and get them!
You're not going anywhere!
Grrr!
Stay away from my person!
She's not worth it, anyway. Stupid prophecy. Useless necklace.
We've got him from here, Miss Phoenix! Don't worry!

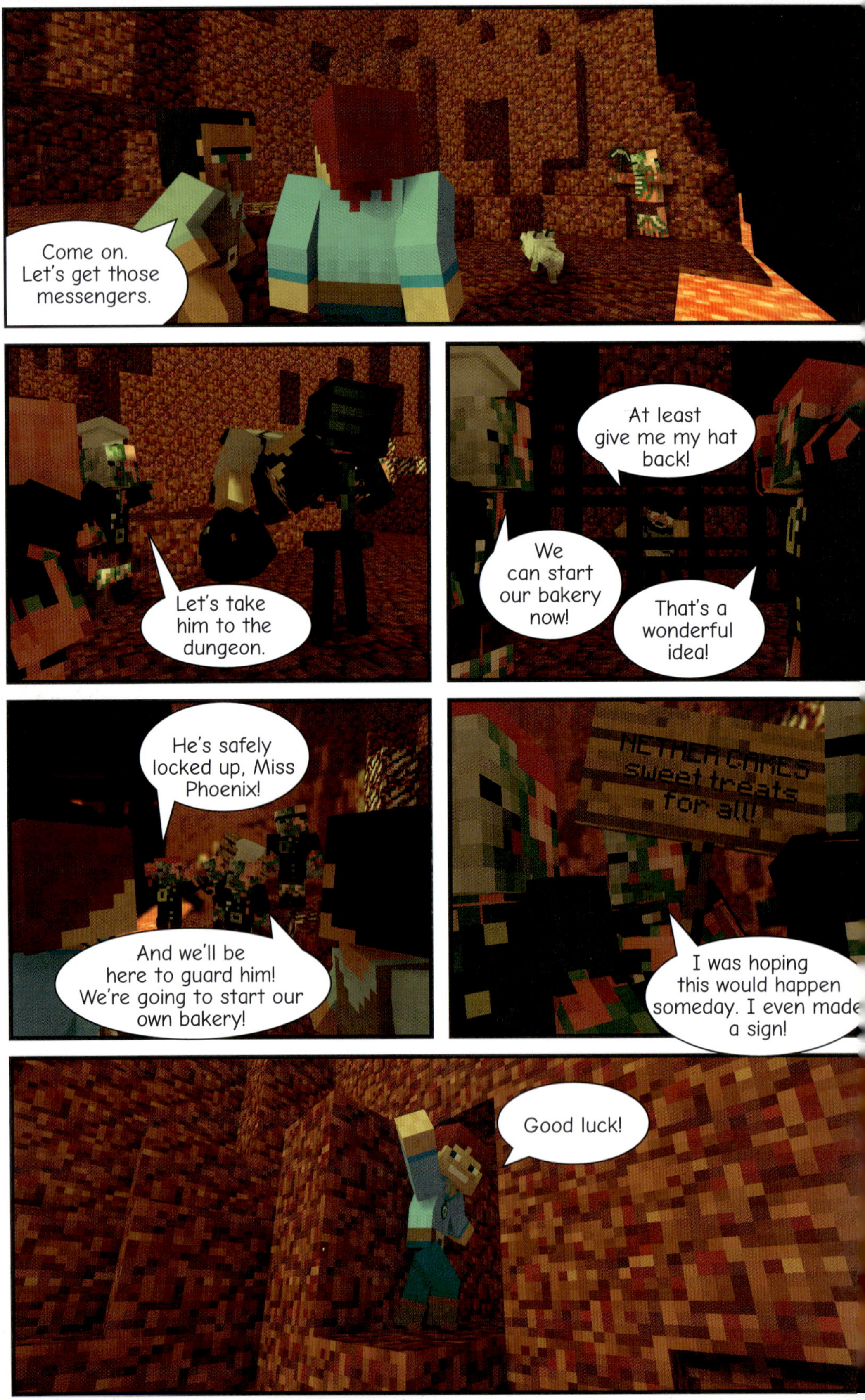
Come on. Let's get those messengers.
Let's take him to the dungeon.
At least give me my hat back!
We can start our bakery now!
That's a wonderful idea!
He's safely locked up, Miss Phoenix!
And we'll be here to guard him! We're going to start our own bakery!
NETHER CAKES sweet treats for all!
I was hoping this would happen someday. I even made a sign!
Good luck!

CHAPTER 9
REUNITED

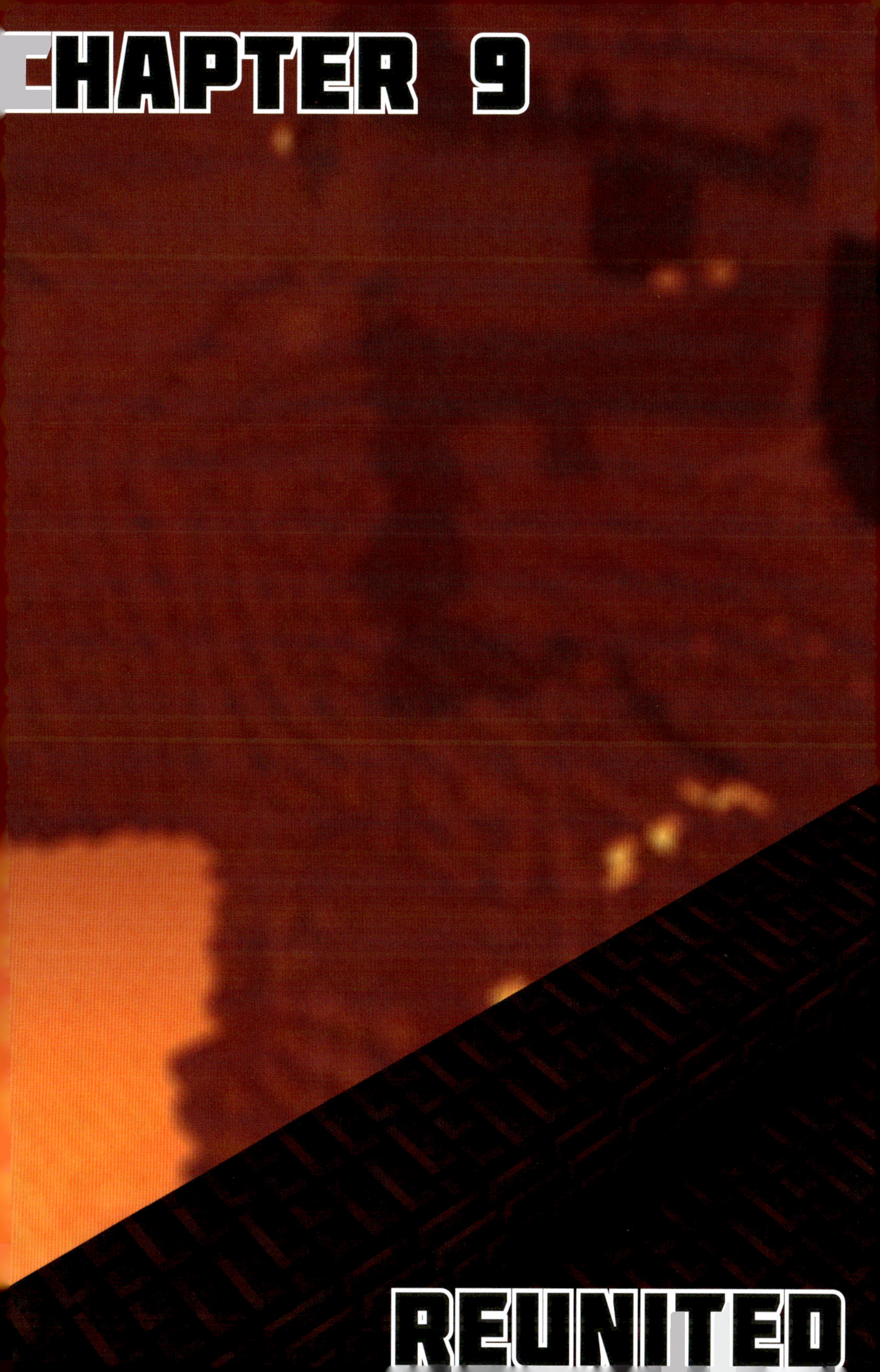

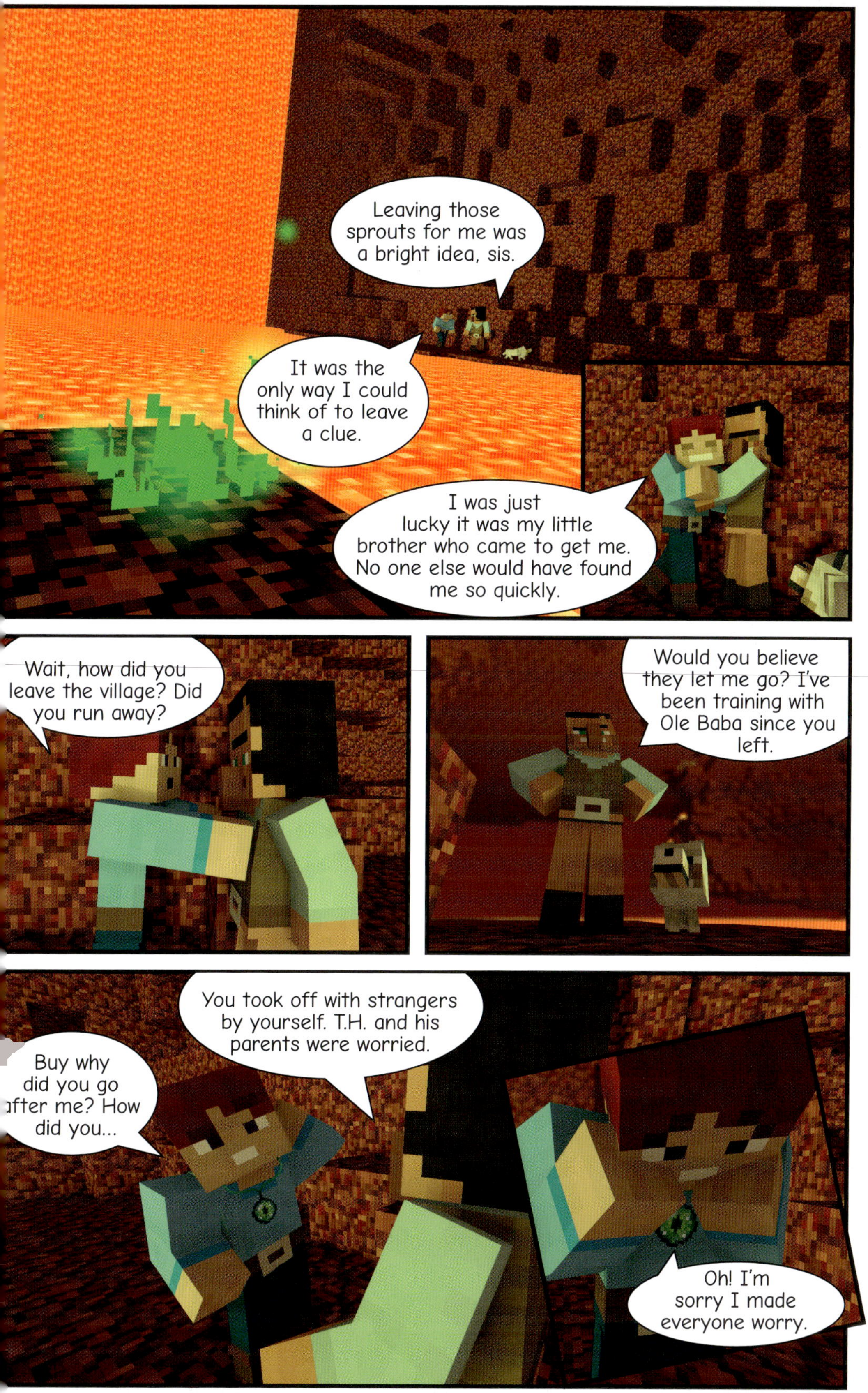
Leaving those sprouts for me was a bright idea, sis.
It was the only way I could think of to leave a clue.
I was just lucky it was my little brother who came to get me. No one else would have found me so quickly.
Wait, how did you leave the village? Did you run away?
Would you believe they let me go? I've been training with Ole Baba since you left.
Buy why did you go after me? How did you...
You took off with strangers by yourself. T.H. and his parents were worried.
Oh! I'm sorry I made everyone worry.

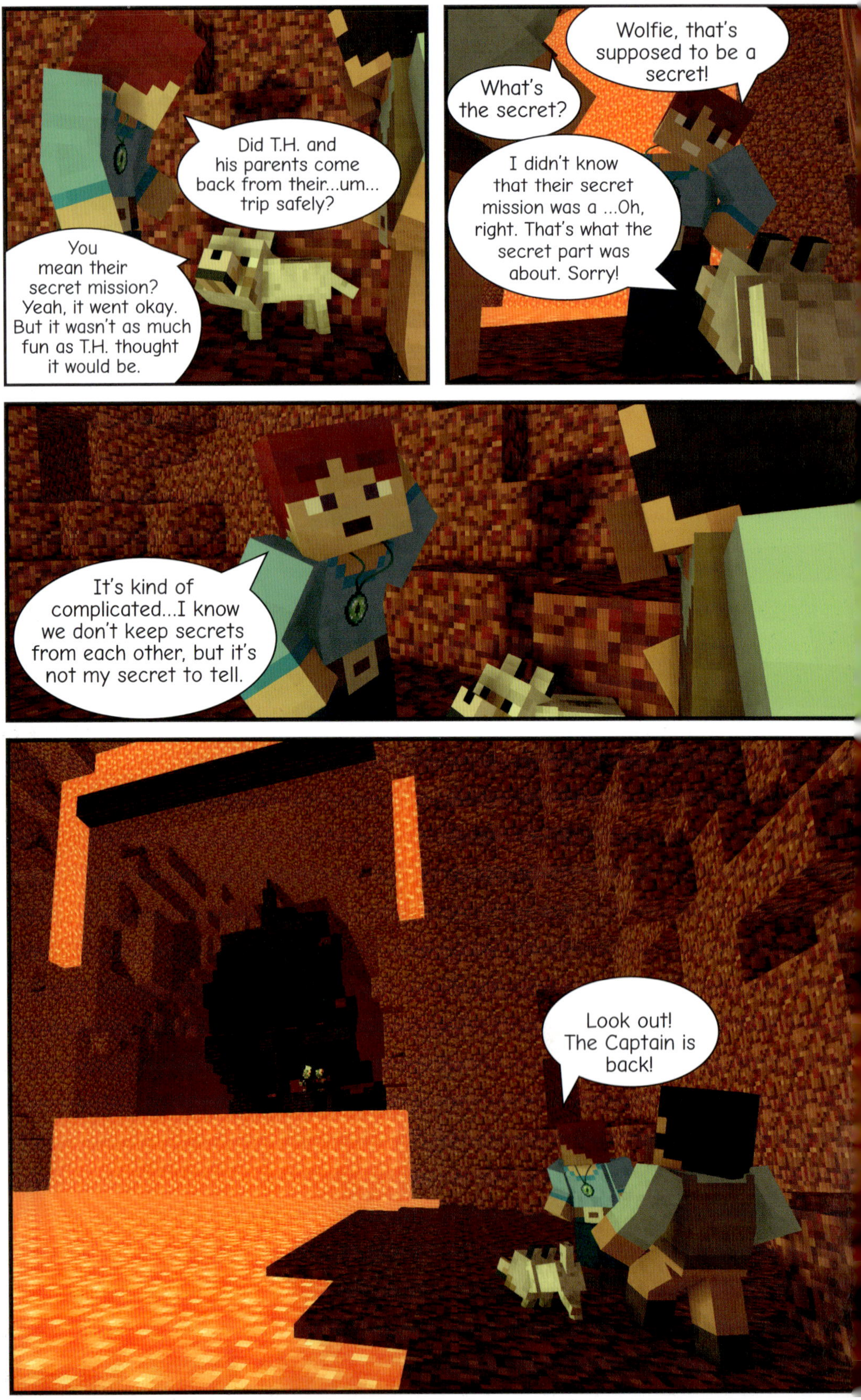
Did T.H. and his parents come back from their...um... trip safely?
You mean their secret mission? Yeah, it went okay. But it wasn't as much fun as T.H. thought it would be.
Wolfie, that's supposed to be a secret!
What's the secret?
I didn't know that their secret mission was a ...Oh, right. That's what the secret part was about. Sorry!
It's kind of complicated...I know we don't keep secrets from each other, but it's not my secret to tell.
Look out! The Captain is back!

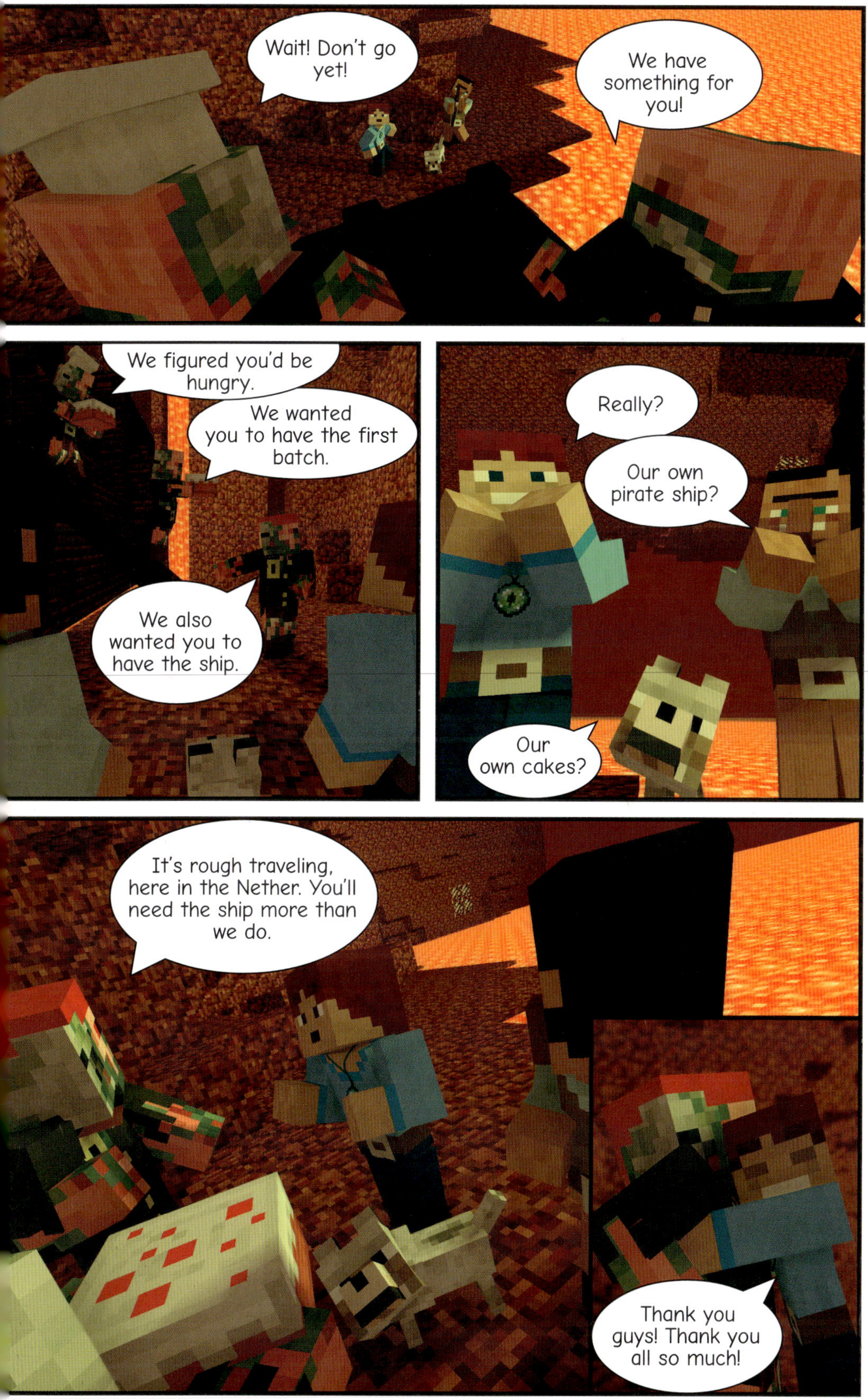
Wait! Don't go yet!
We have something for you!
We figured you'd be hungry.
We wanted you to have the first batch.
We also wanted you to have the ship.
Really?
Our own pirate ship?
Our own cakes?
It's rough traveling, here in the Nether. You'll need the ship more than we do.
Thank you guys! Thank you all so much!

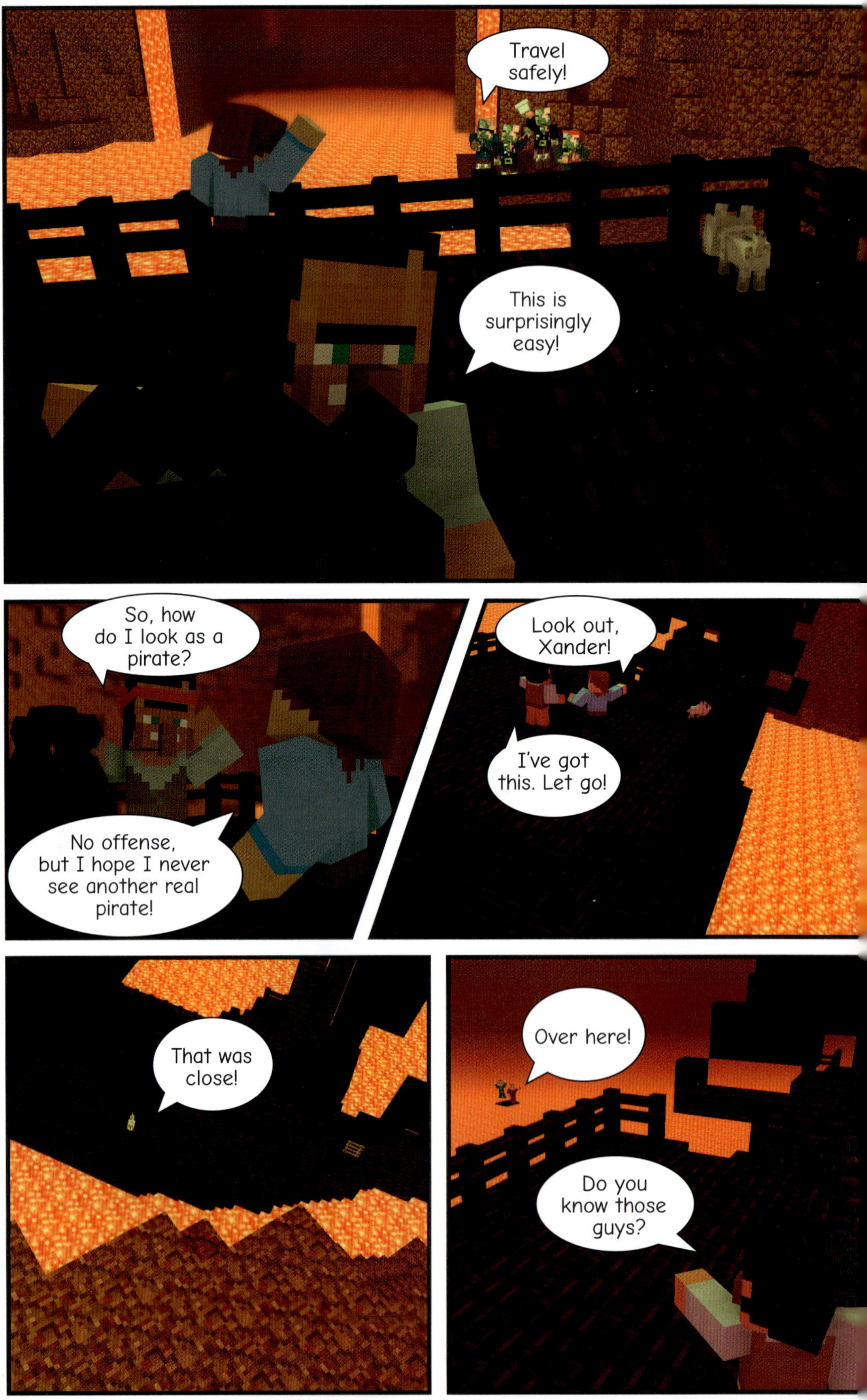
Travel safely!
This is surprisingly easy!
So, how do I look as a pirate?
No offense, but I hope I never see another real pirate!
Look out, Xander!
I've got this. Let go!
That was close!
Over here!
Do you know those guys?

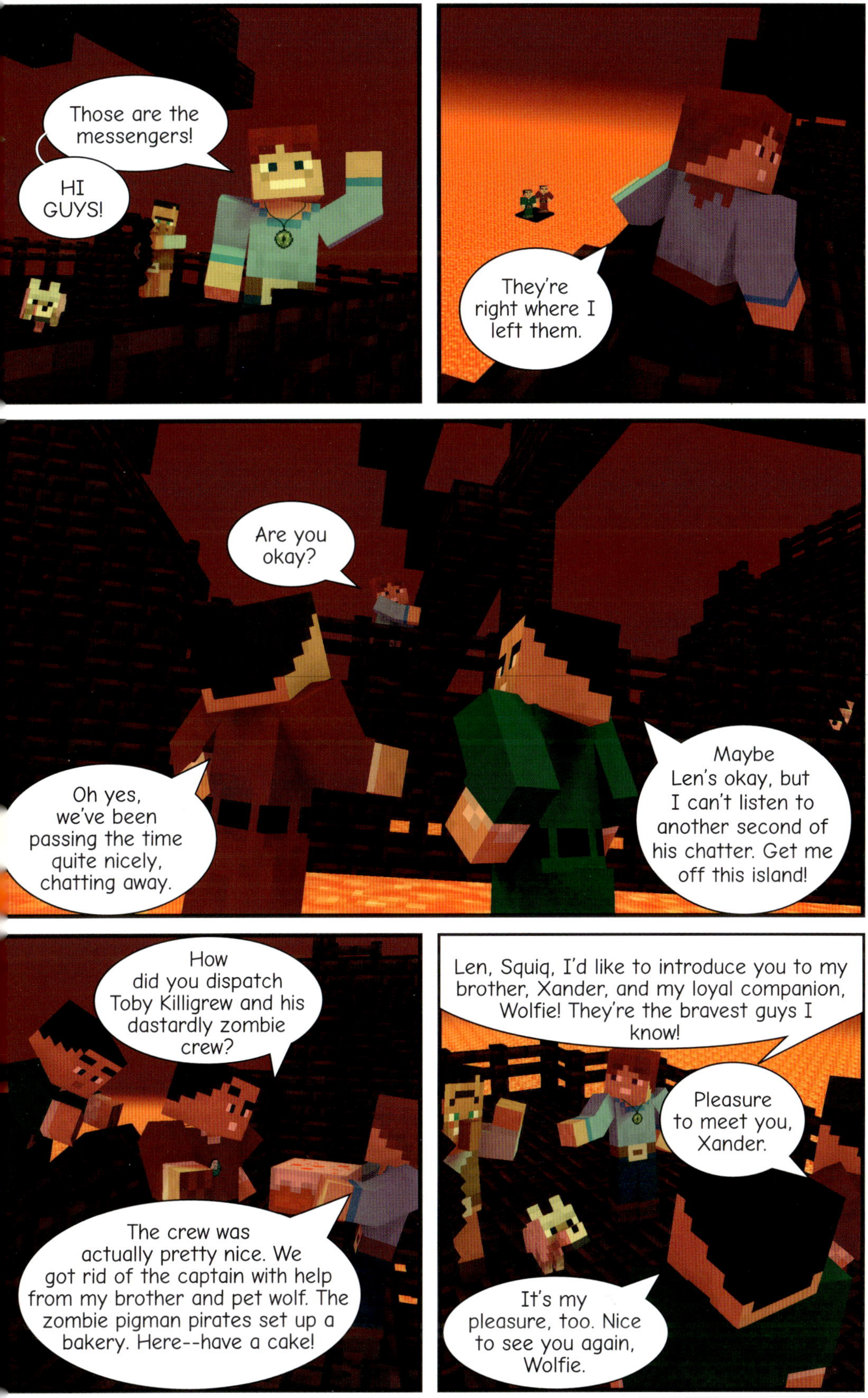
Those are the messengers!
HI GUYS!
They're right where I left them.
Are you okay?
Oh yes, we've been passing the time quite nicely, chatting away.
Maybe Len's okay, but I can't listen to another second of his chatter. Get me off this island!
How did you dispatch Toby Killigrew and his dastardly zombie crew?
The crew was actually pretty nice. We got rid of the captain with help from my brother and pet wolf. The zombie pigman pirates set up a bakery. Here--have a cake!
Len, Squiq, I'd like to introduce you to my brother, Xander, and my loyal companion, Wolfie! They're the bravest guys I know!
Pleasure to meet you, Xander.
It's my pleasure, too. Nice to see you again, Wolfie.

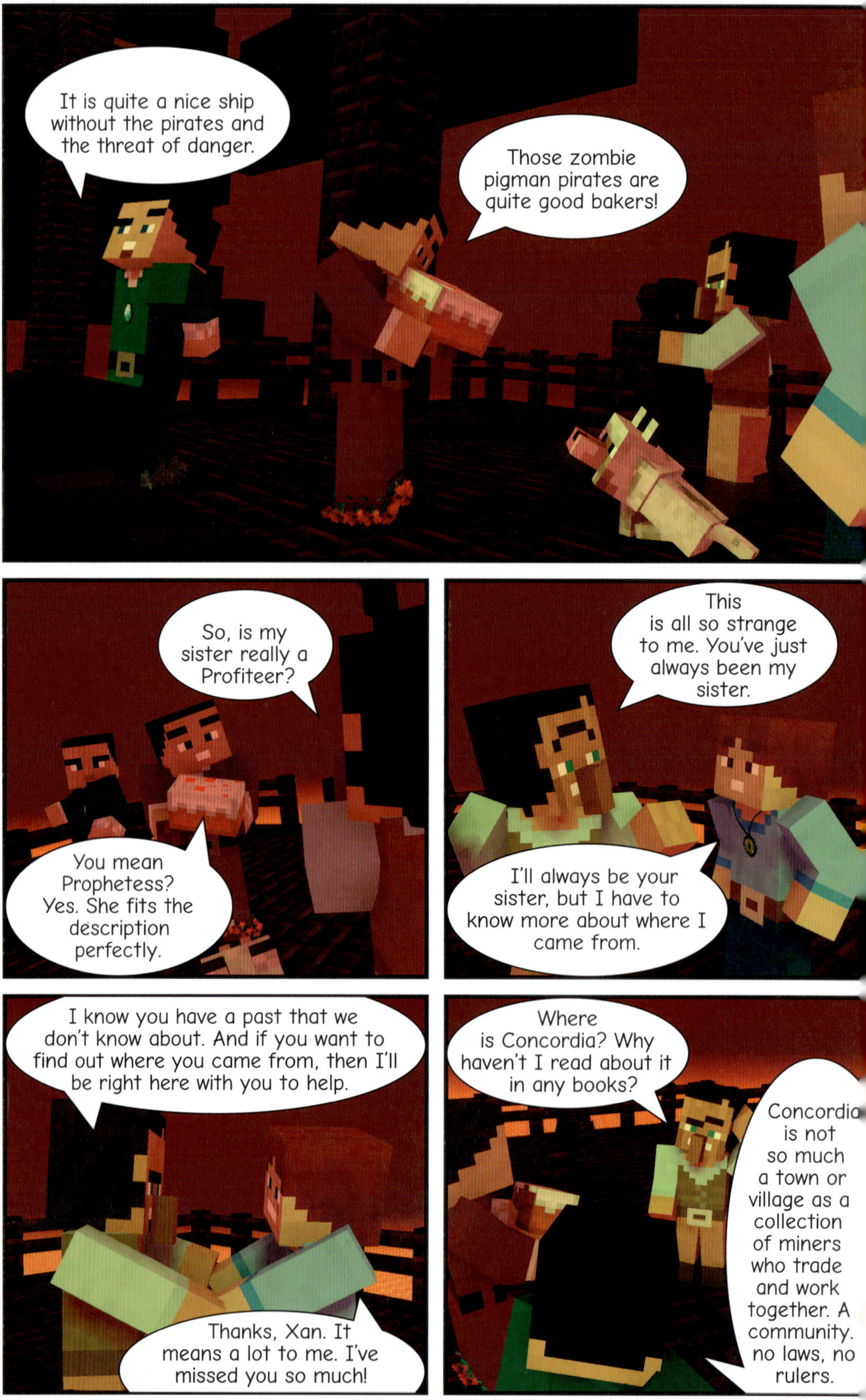

It is quite a nice ship without the pirates and the threat of danger.
Those zombie pigman pirates are quite good bakers!
So, is my sister really a Profiteer?
You mean Prophetess? Yes. She fits the description perfectly.
This is all so strange to me. You've just always been my sister.
I'll always be your sister, but I have to know more about where I came from.
I know you have a past that we don't know about. And if you want to find out where you came from, then I'll be right here with you to help.
Thanks, Xan. It means a lot to me. I've missed you so much!
Where is Concordia? Why haven't I read about it in any books?
Concordia is not so much a town or village as a collection of miners who trade and work together. A community. no laws, no rulers.

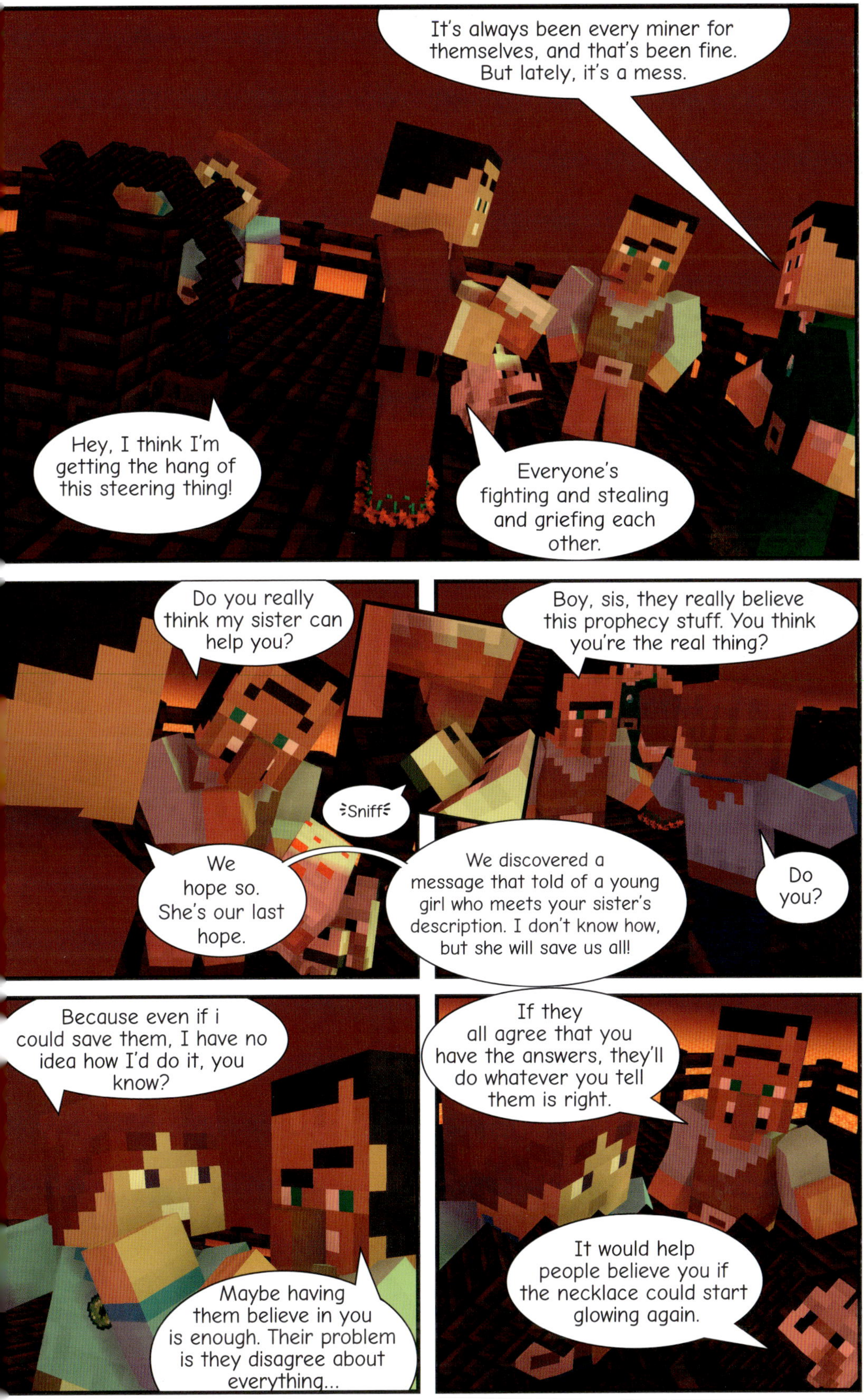
It's always been every miner for themselves, and that's been fine. But lately, it's a mess.
Hey, I think I'm getting the hang of this steering thing!
Everyone's fighting and stealing and griefing each other.
Do you really think my sister can help you?
Sniff
We hope so. She's our last hope.
We discovered a message that told of a young girl who meets your sister's description. I don't know how, but she will save us all!
Boy, sis, they really believe this prophecy stuff. You think you're the real thing?
Do you?
Because even if i could save them, I have no idea how I'd do it, you know?
Maybe having them believe in you is enough. Their problem is they disagree about everything...
If they all agree that you have the answers, they'll do whatever you tell them is right.
It would help people believe you if the necklace could start glowing again.

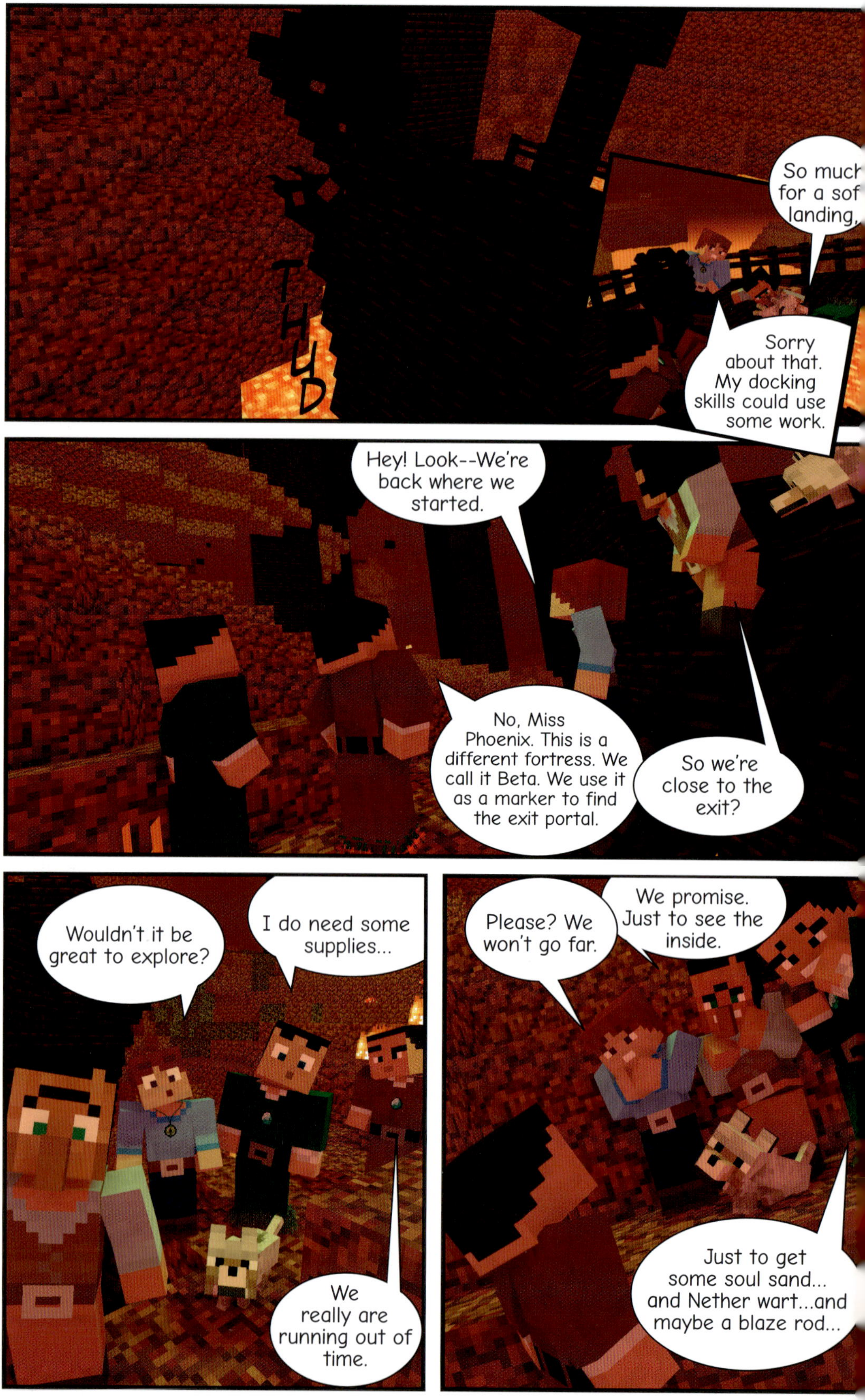
THUD
So much for a sof landing,
Sorry about that. My docking skills could use some work.
Hey! Look--We're back where we started.
No, Miss Phoenix. This is a different fortress. We call it Beta. We use it as a marker to find the exit portal.
So we're close to the exit?
Wouldn't it be great to explore?
I do need some supplies...
We really are running out of time.
Please? We won't go far.
We promise. Just to see the inside.
Just to get some soul sand... and Nether wart...and maybe a blaze rod...

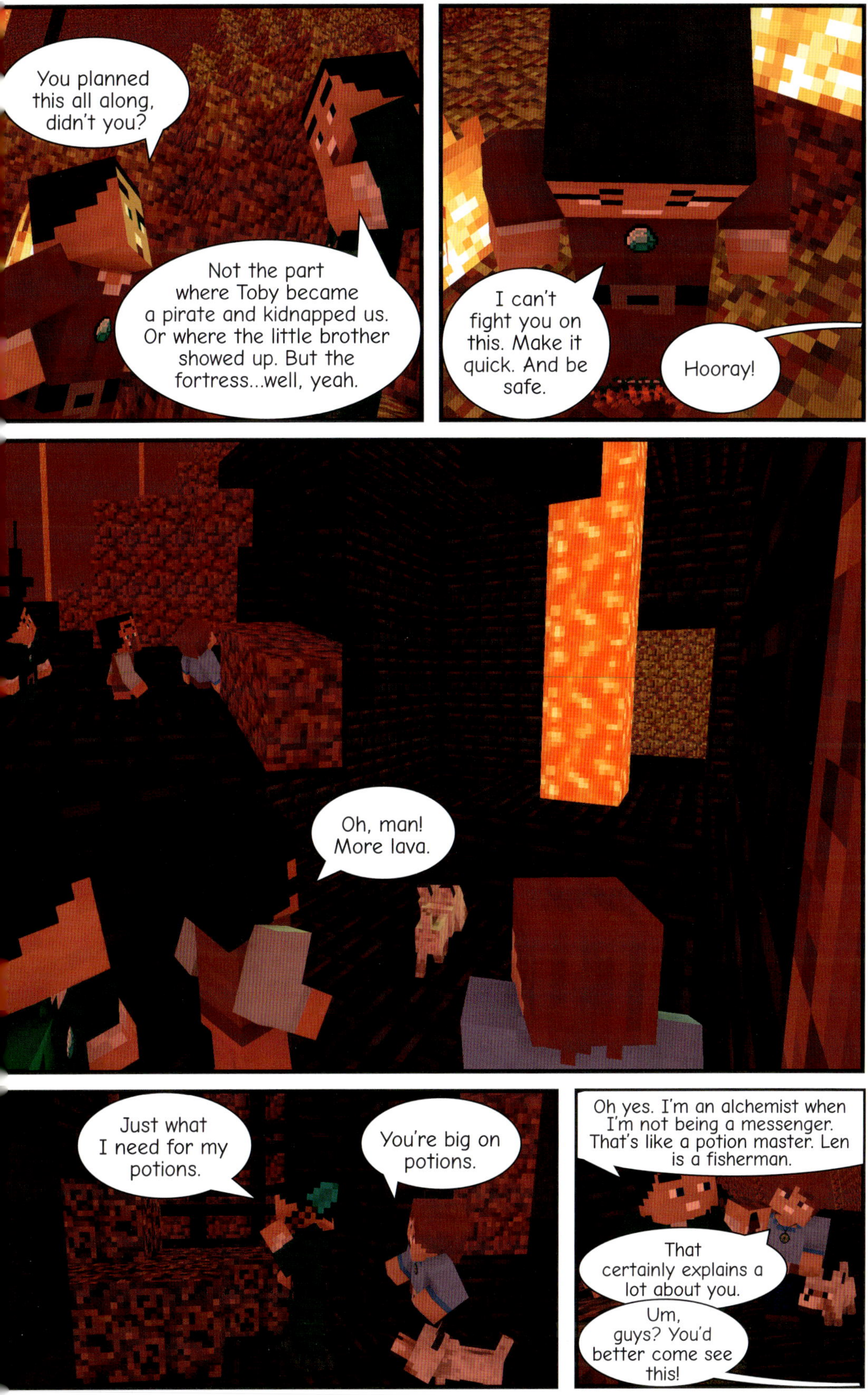
You planned this all along, didn't you?
Not the part where Toby became a pirate and kidnapped us. Or where the little brother showed up. But the fortress...well, yeah.
I can't fight you on this. Make it quick. And be safe.
Hooray!
Oh, man! More lava.
Just what I need for my potions.
You're big on potions.
Oh yes. I'm an alchemist when I'm not being a messenger. That's like a potion master. Len is a fisherman.
That certainly explains a lot about you.
Um, guys? You'd better come see this!

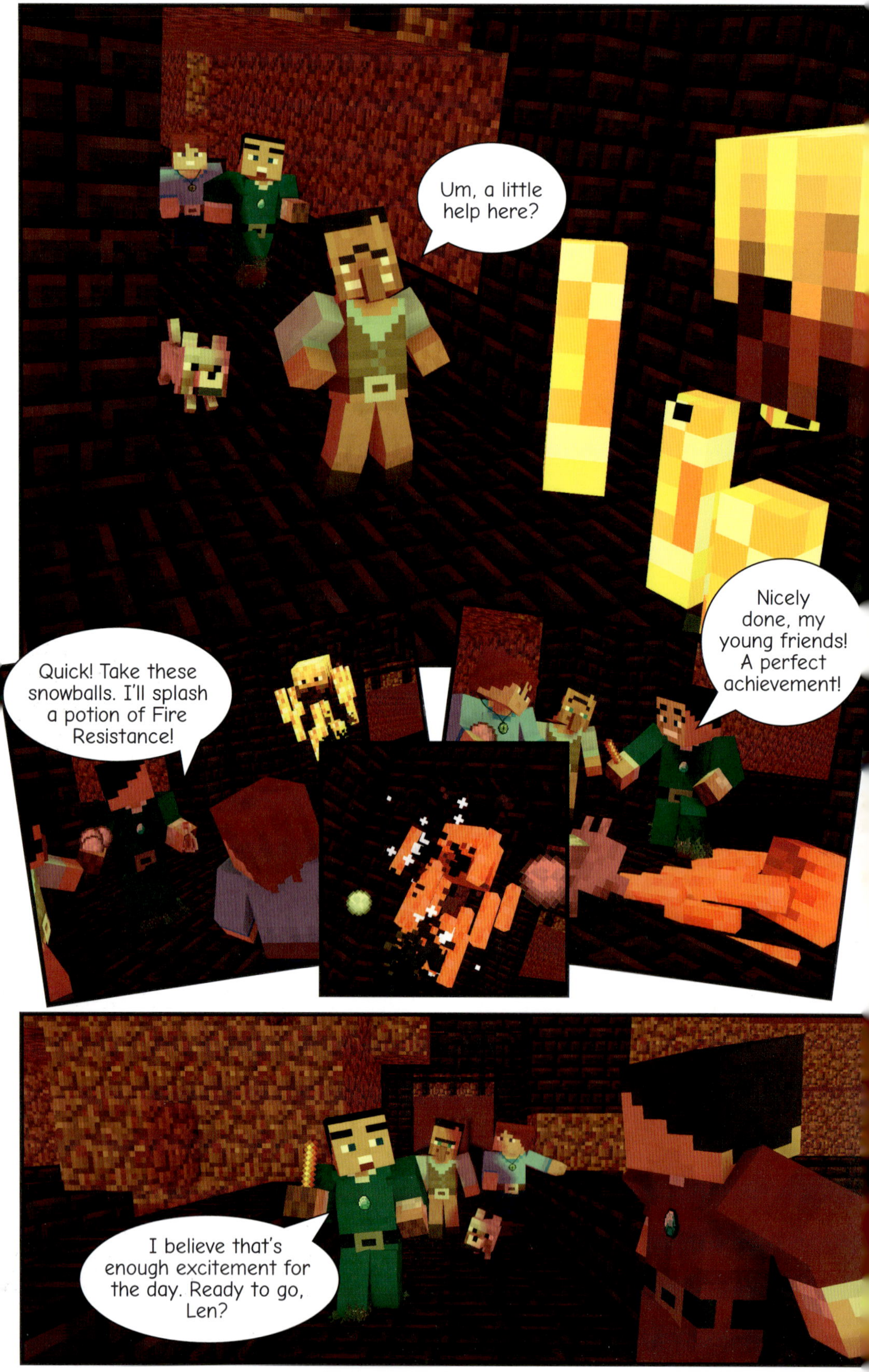
Um, a little help here?
Quick! Take these snowballs. I'll splash a potion of Fire Resistance!
Nicely done, my young friends! A perfect achievement!
I believe that's enough excitement for the day. Ready to go, Len?

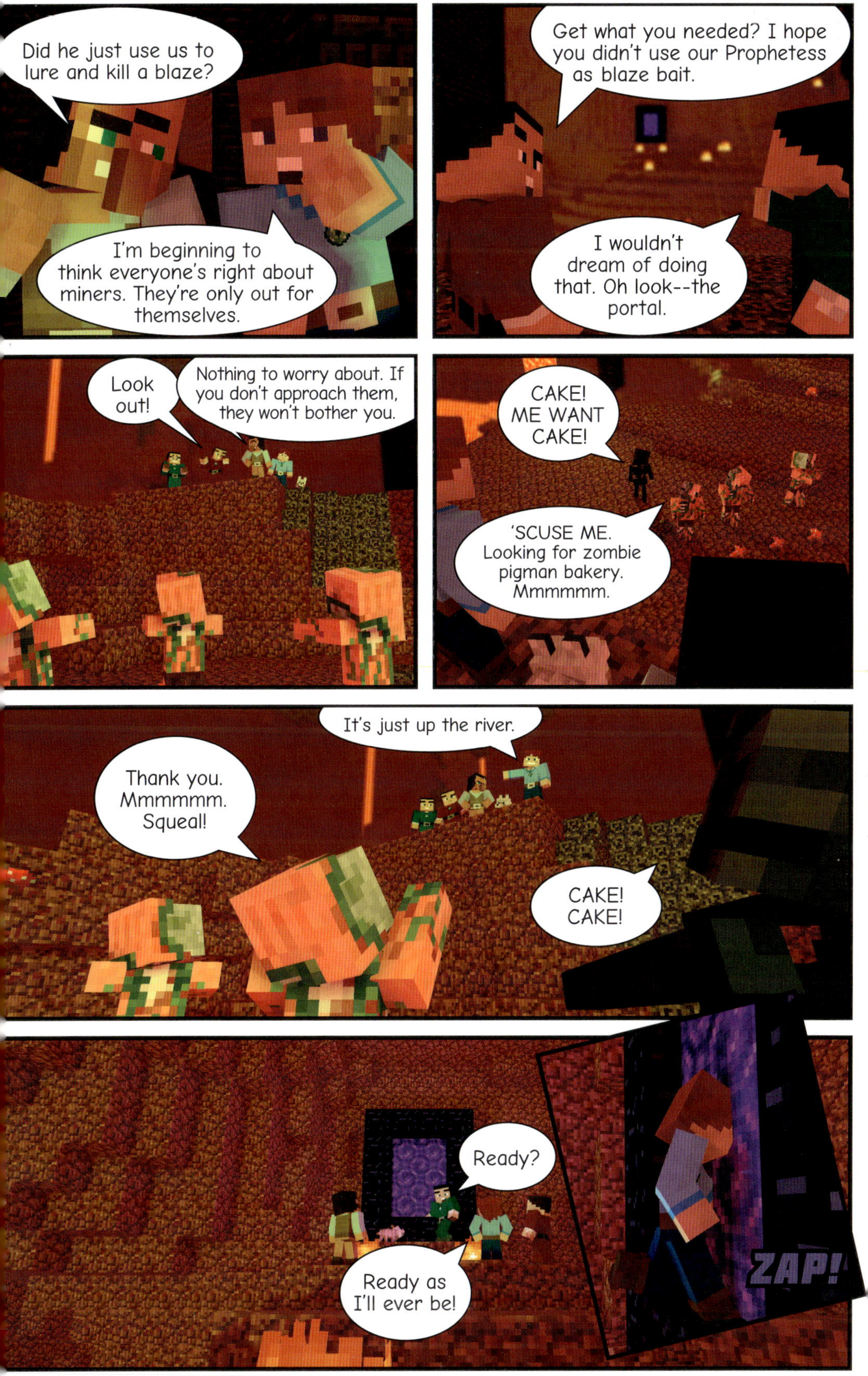
Did he just use us to lure and kill a blaze?
I'm beginning to think everyone's right about miners. They're only out for themselves.
Get what you needed? I hope you didn't use our Prophetess as blaze bait.
I wouldn't dream of doing that. Oh look--the portal.
Look out!
Nothing to worry about. If you don't approach them, they won't bother you.
CAKE! ME WANT CAKE!
'SCUSE ME. Looking for zombie pigman bakery. Mmmmmm.
It's just up the river.
Thank you. Mmmmmm. Squeal!
CAKE! CAKE!
Ready?
Ready as I'll ever be!
ZAP!

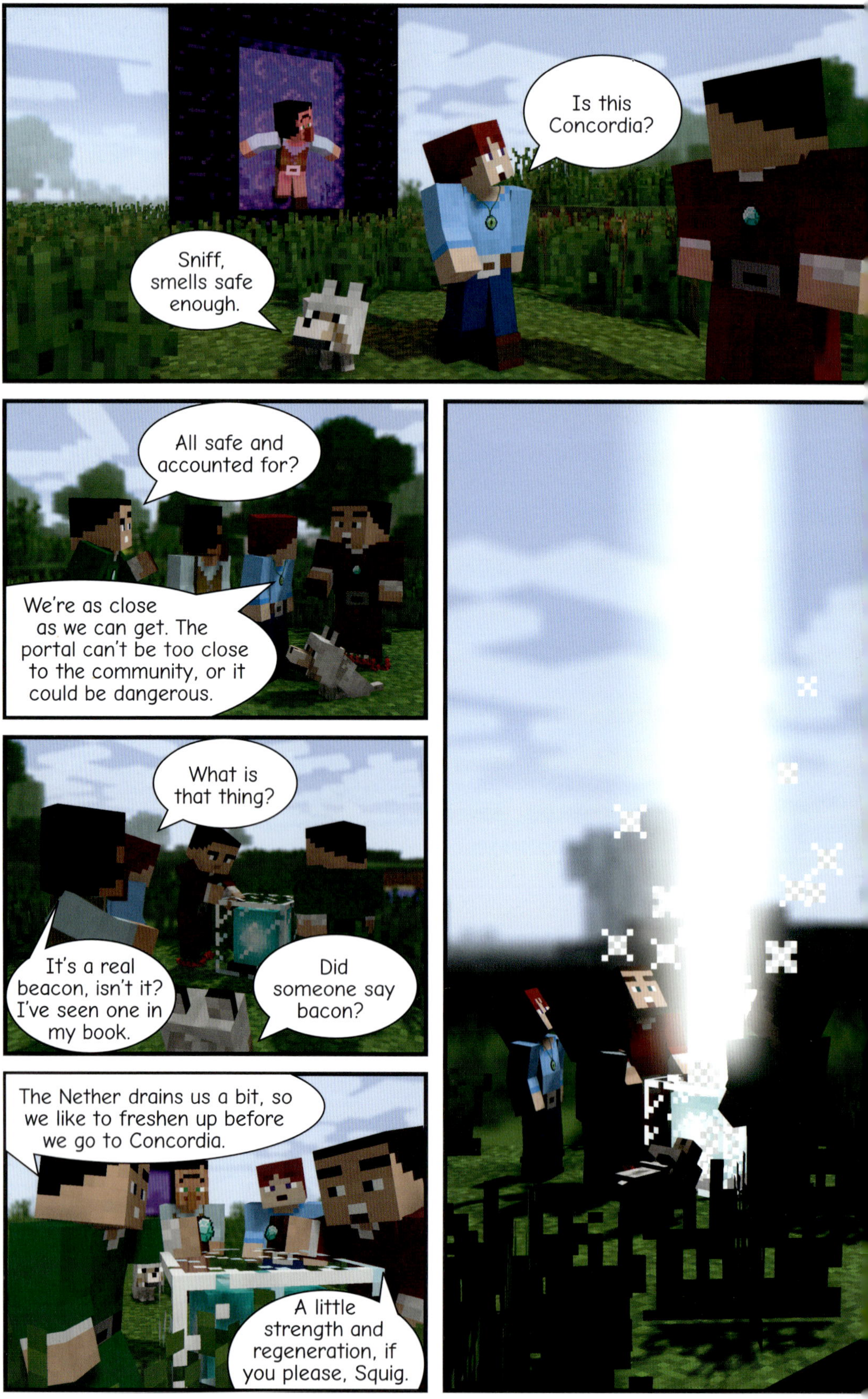
Is this Concordia?
Sniff, smells safe enough.
All safe and accounted for?
We're as close as we can get. The portal can't be too close to the community, or it could be dangerous.
What is that thing?
It's a real beacon, isn't it? I've seen one in my book.
Did someone say bacon?
The Nether drains us a bit, so we like to freshen up before we go to Concordia.
A little strength and regeneration, if you please, Squig.

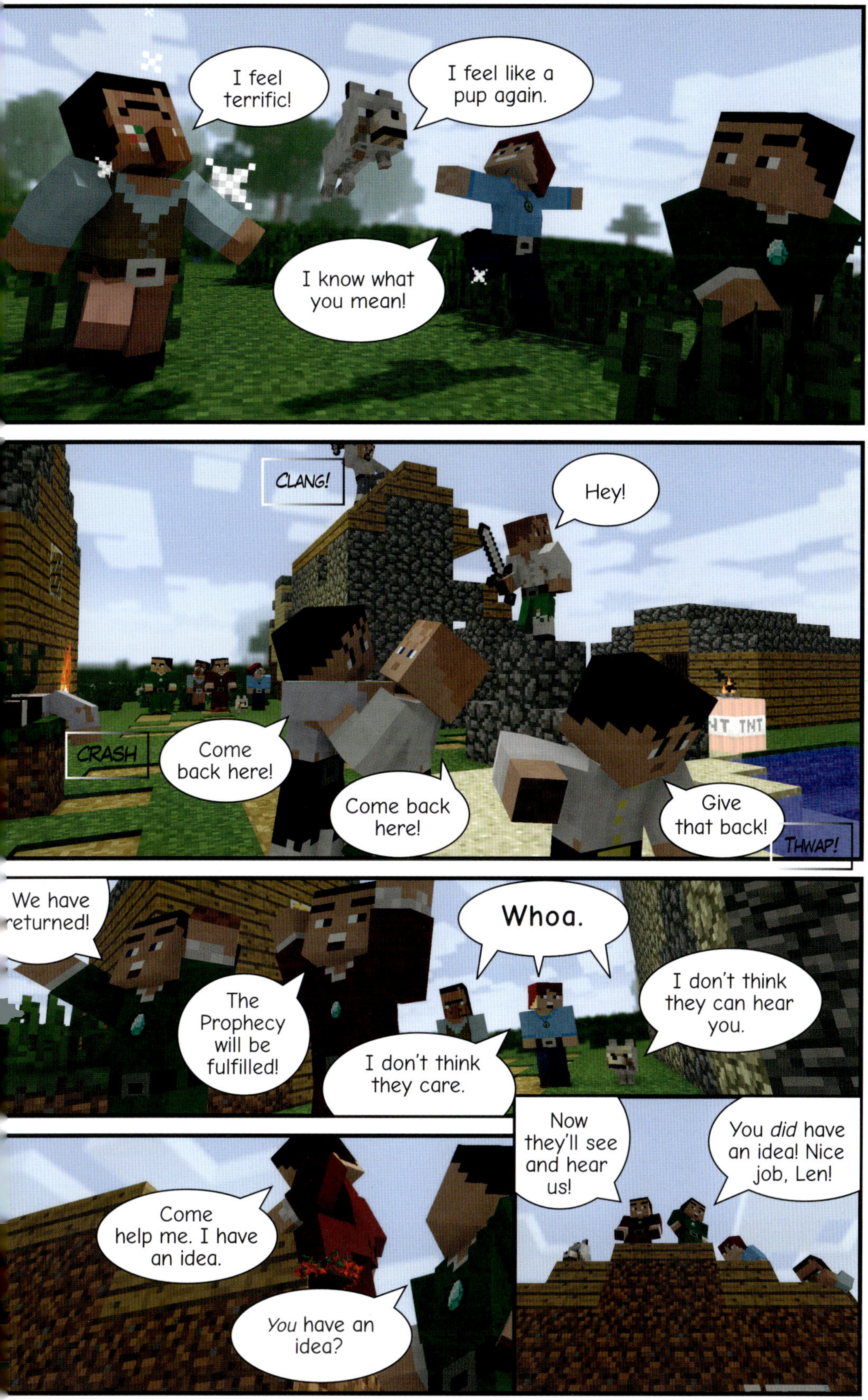
I feel terrific!
I feel like a pup again.
I know what you mean!
CLANG!
Hey!
CRASH
Come back here!
Come back here!
Give that back!
THWAP!
We have returned!
The Prophecy will be fulfilled!
Whoa.
I don't think they care.
I don't think they can hear you.
Come help me. I have an idea.
You have an idea?
Now they'll see and hear us!
You *did* have an idea! Nice job, Len!

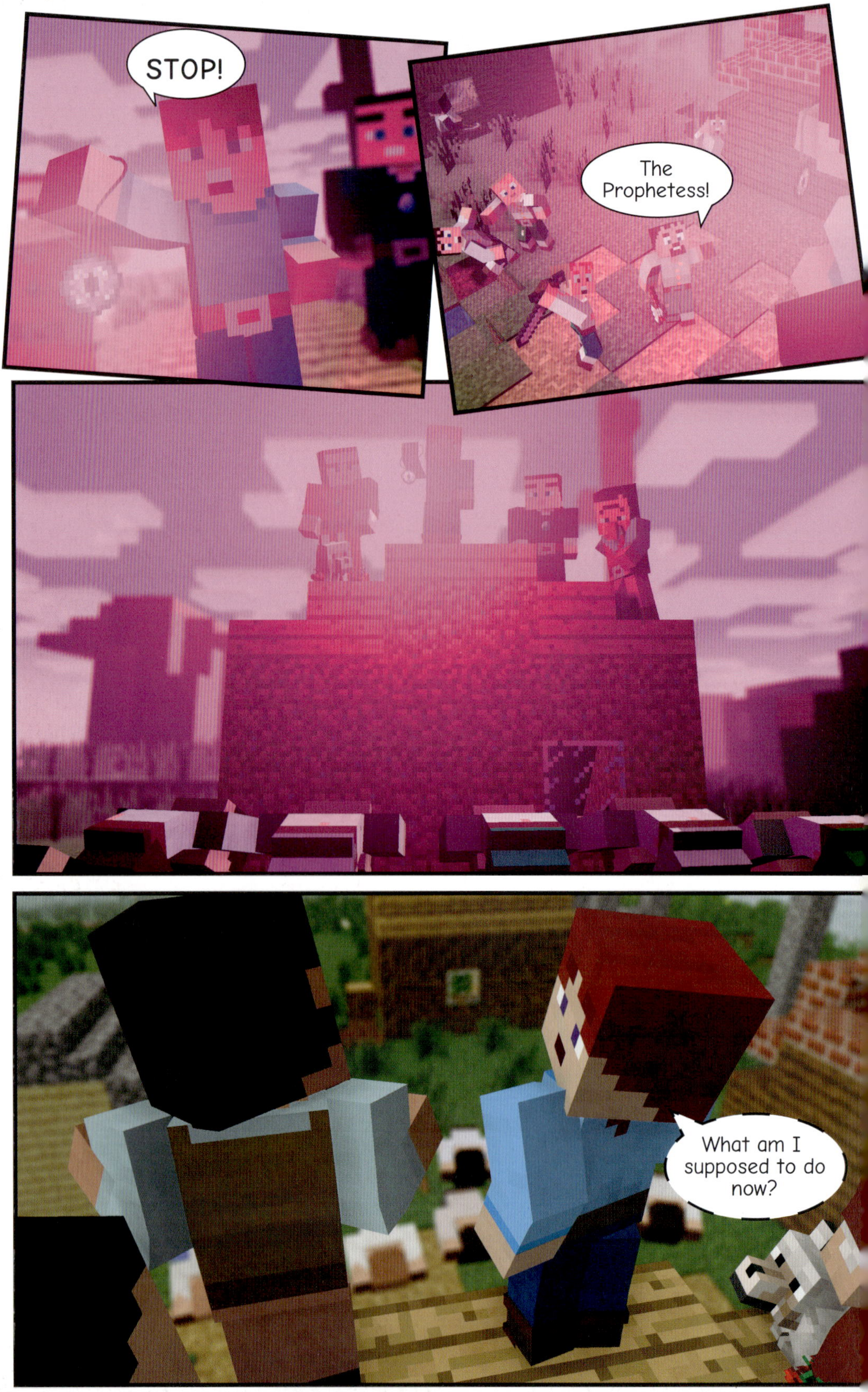
STOP!
The Prophetess!
What am I supposed to do now?

CHAPTER 10

THE PROPHETESS

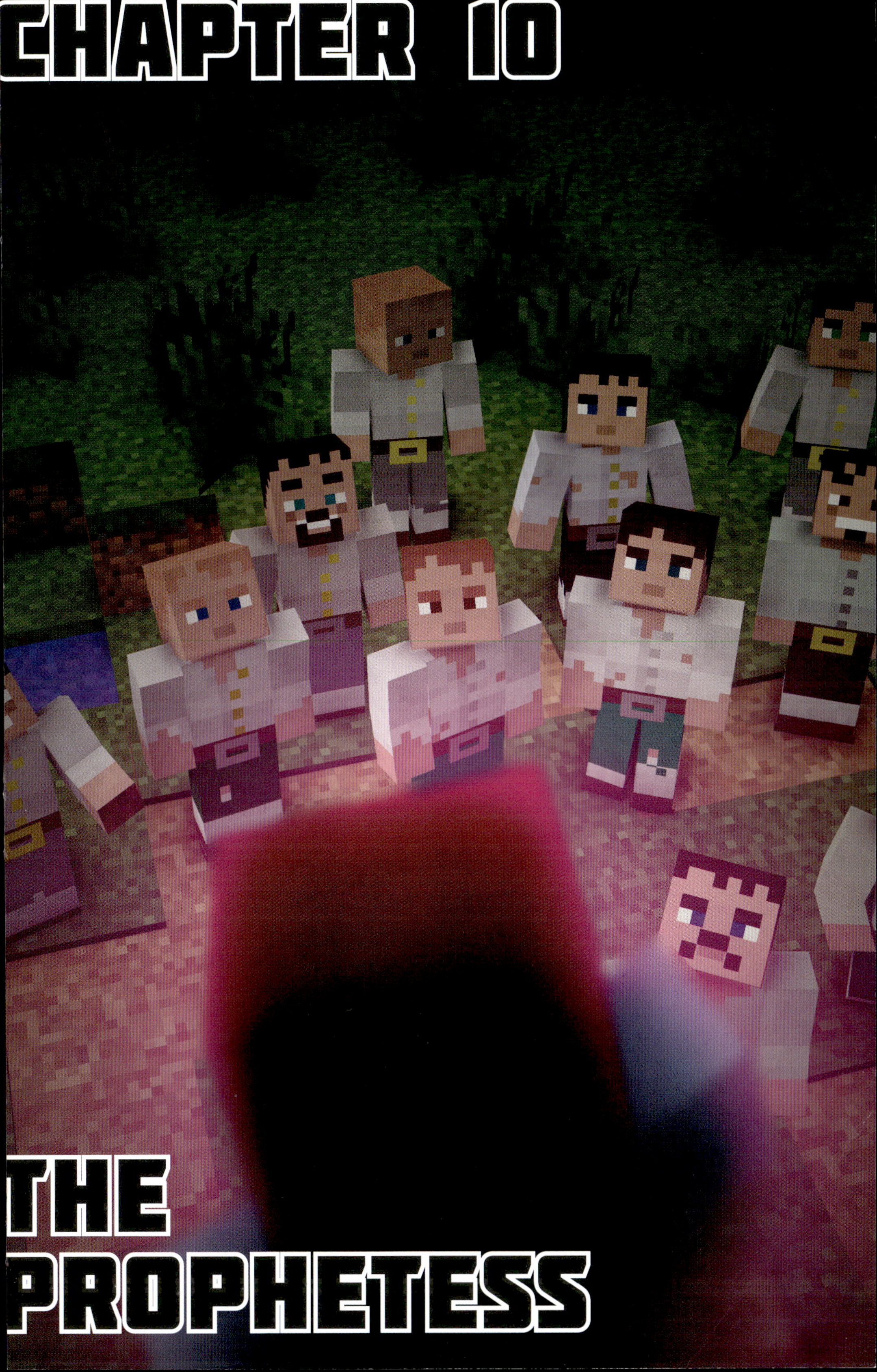

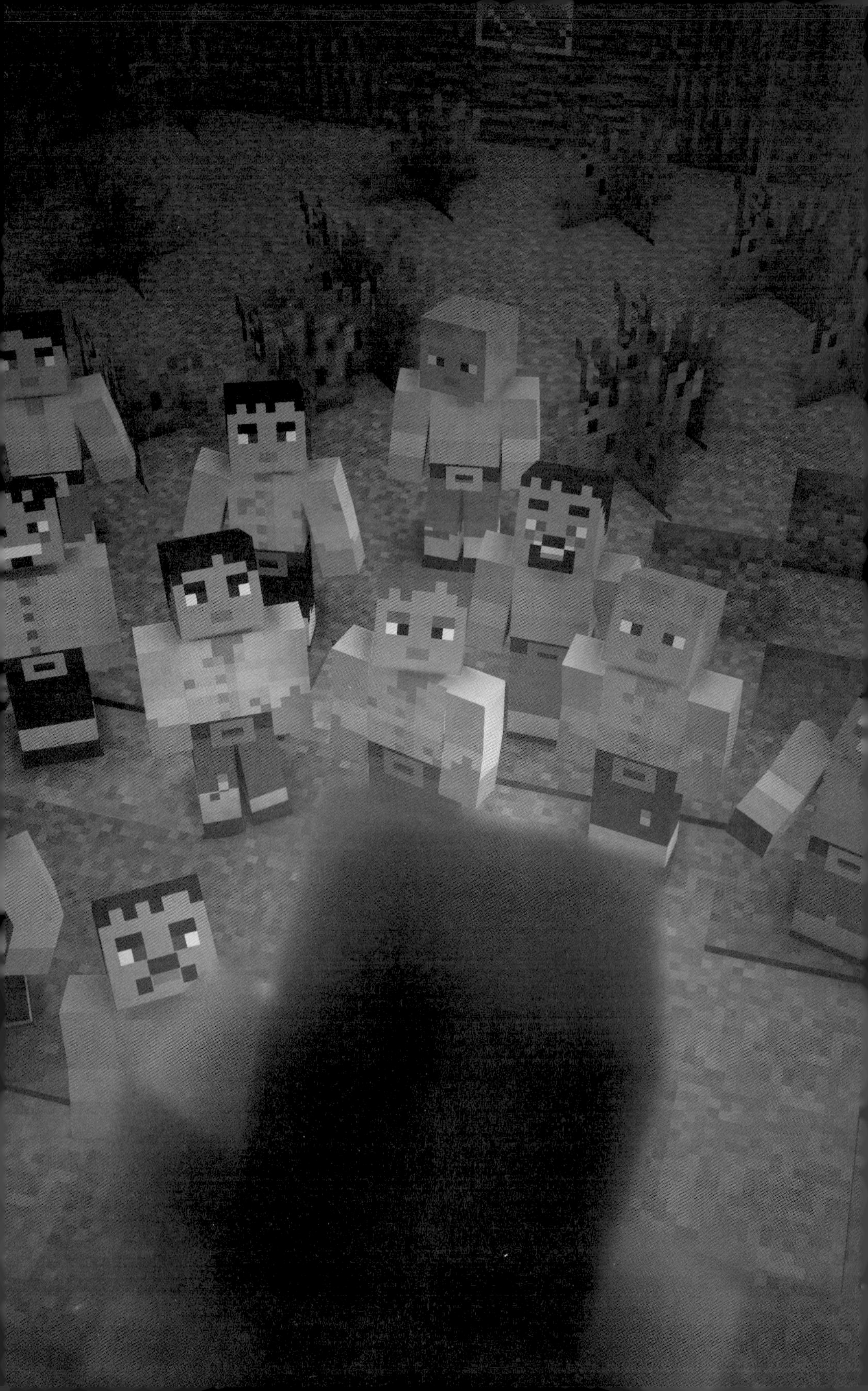

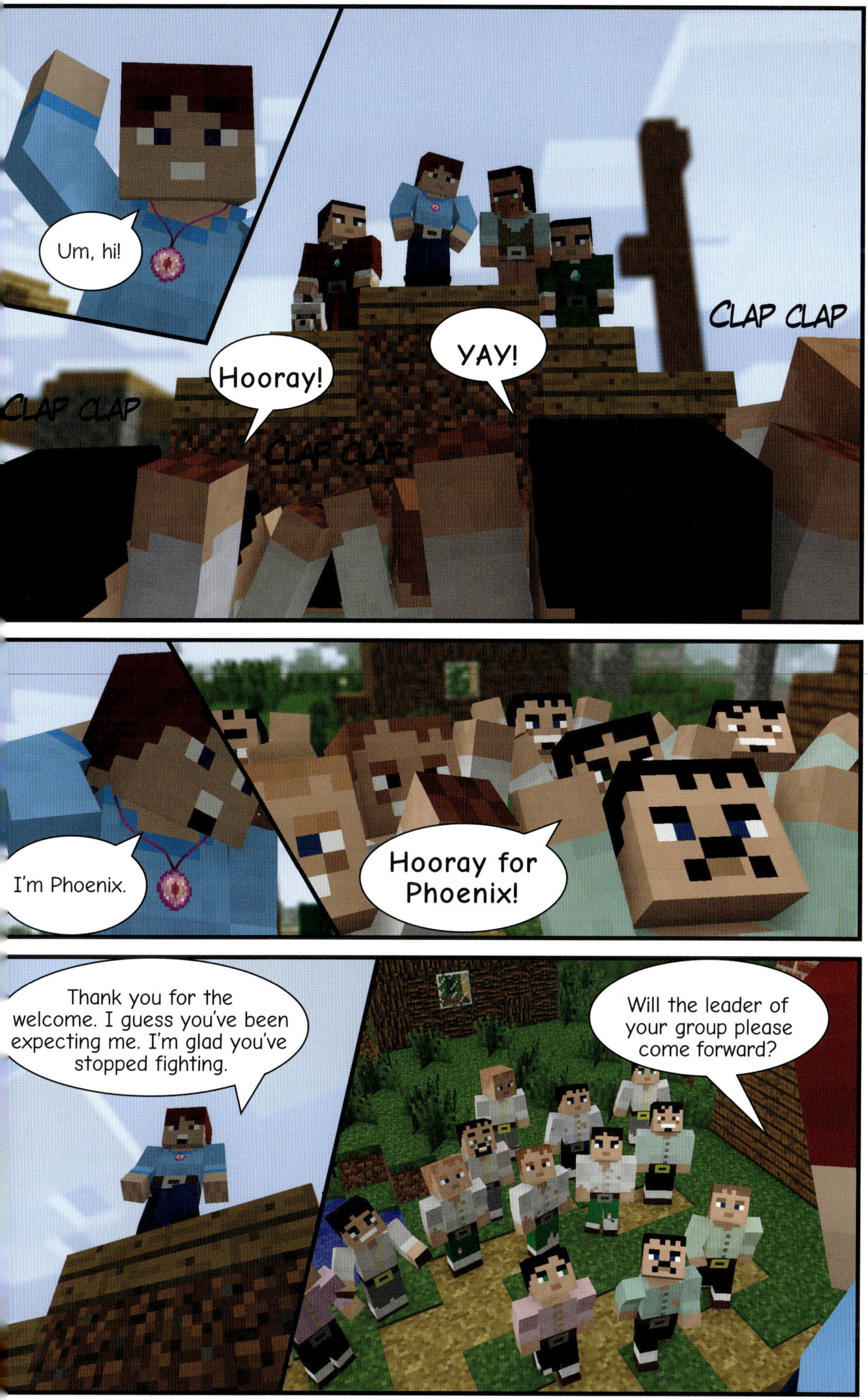
Um, hi!
CLAP CLAP
Hooray!
YAY!
CLAP CLAP
CLAP CLAP
I'm Phoenix.
Hooray for Phoenix!
Thank you for the welcome. I guess you've been expecting me. I'm glad you've stopped fighting.
Will the leader of your group please come forward?

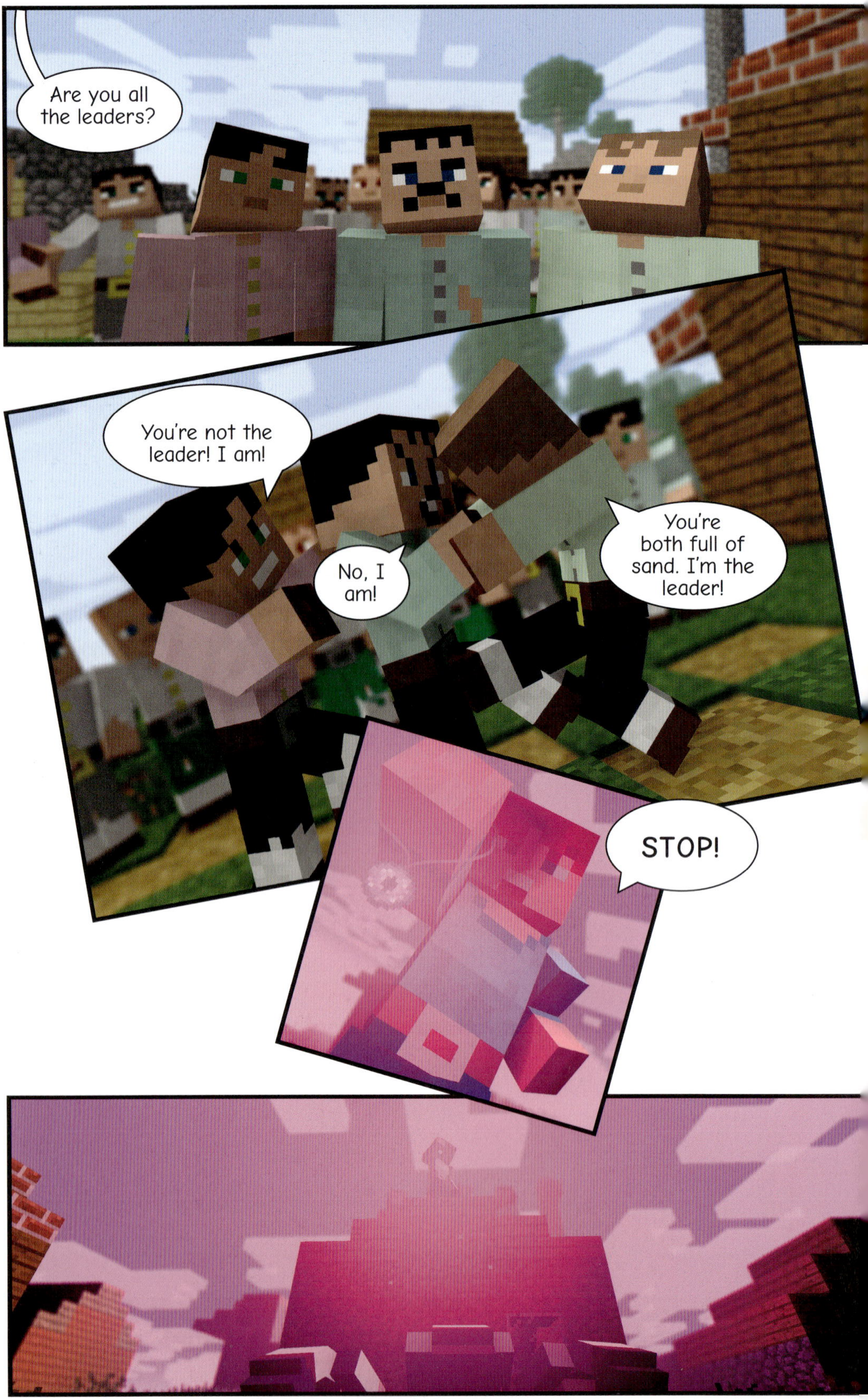
Are you all the leaders?
You're not the leader! I am!
No, I am!
You're both full of sand. I'm the leader!
STOP!

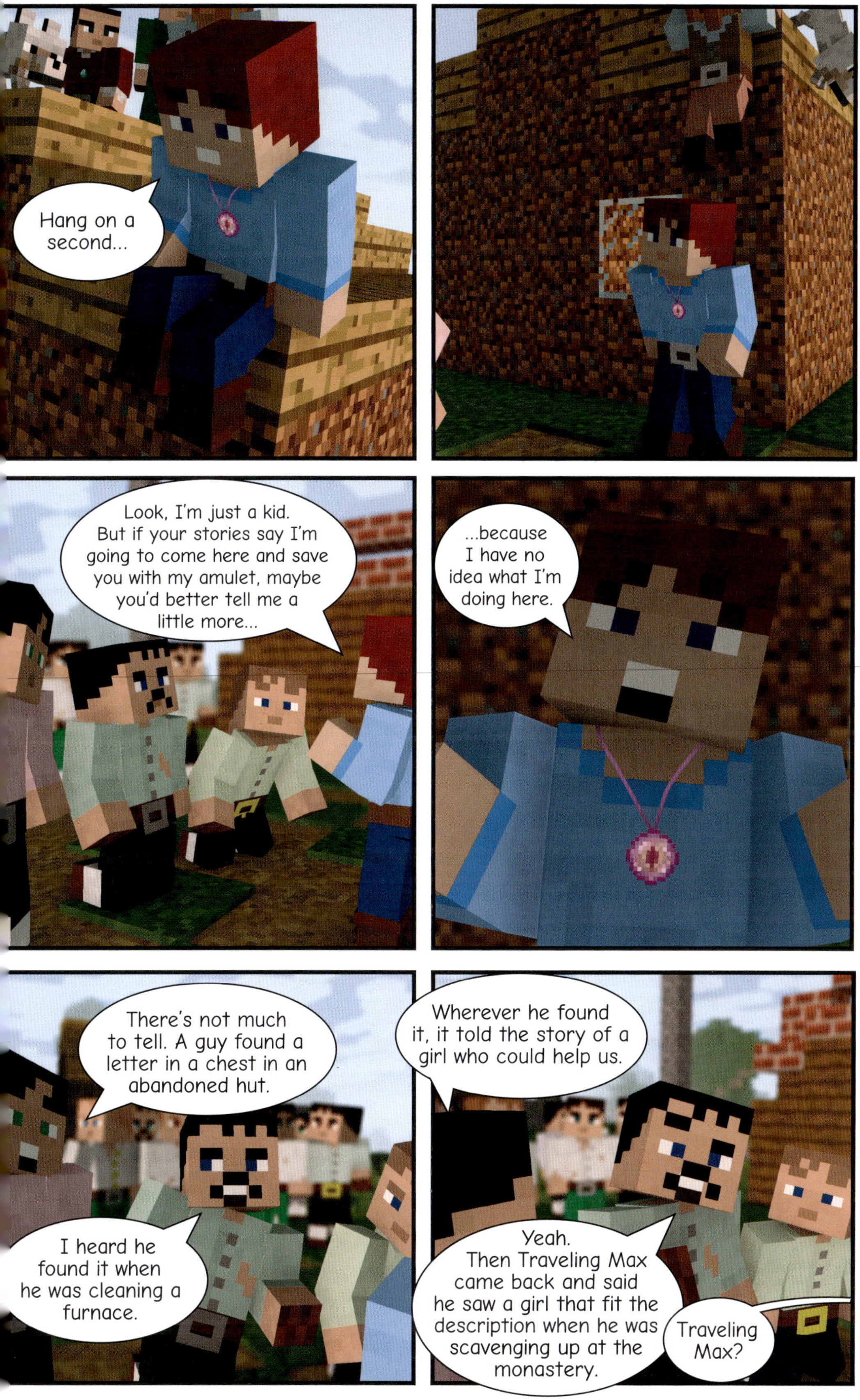
Hang on a second...
Look, I'm just a kid. But if your stories say I'm going to come here and save you with my amulet, maybe you'd better tell me a little more...
...because I have no idea what I'm doing here.
There's not much to tell. A guy found a letter in a chest in an abandoned hut.
I heard he found it when he was cleaning a furnace.
Wherever he found it, it told the story of a girl who could help us.
Yeah. Then Traveling Max came back and said he saw a girl that fit the description when he was scavenging up at the monastery.
Traveling Max?

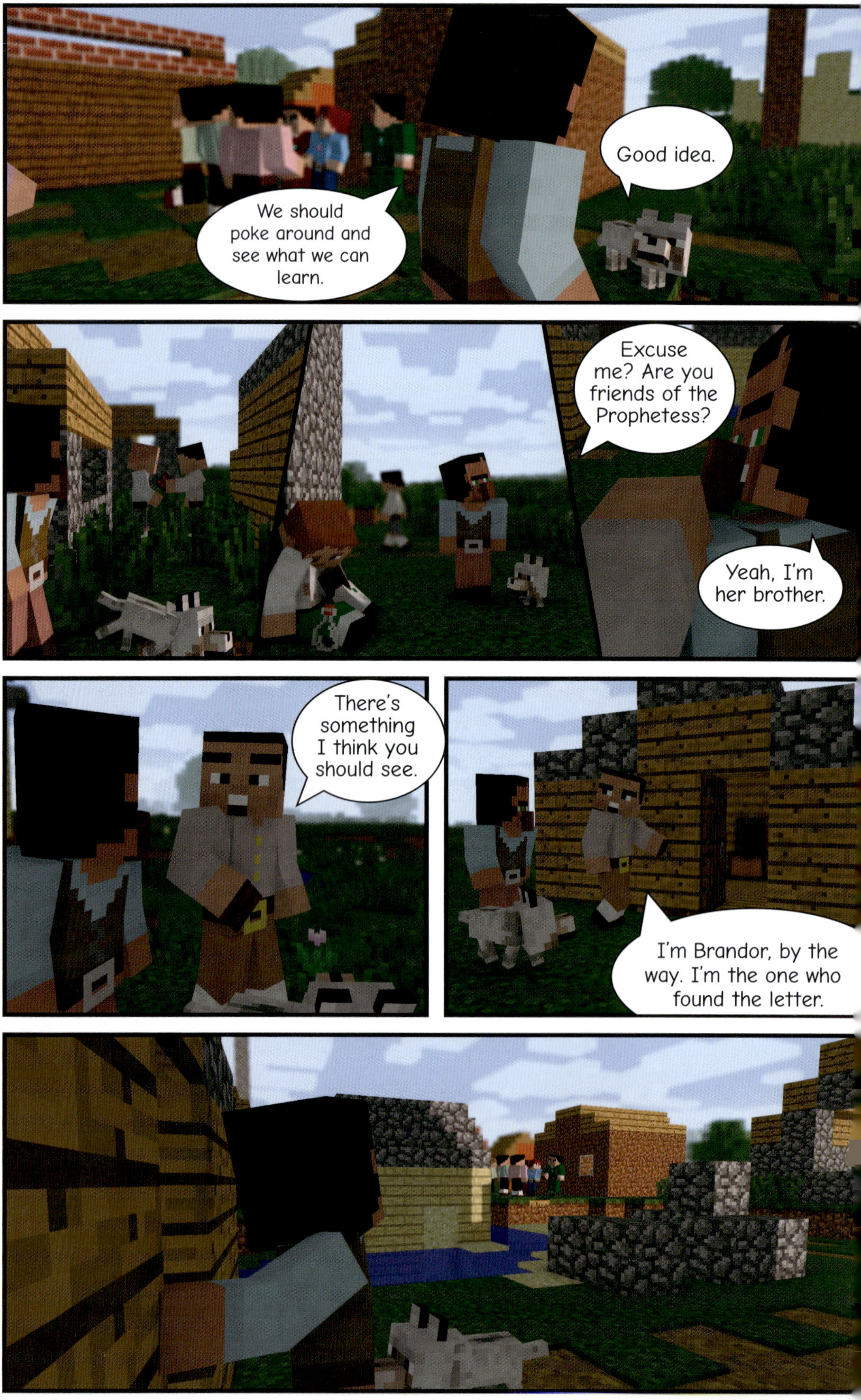
We should poke around and see what we can learn.
Good idea.
Excuse me? Are you friends of the Prophetess?
Yeah, I'm her brother.
There's something I think you should see.
I'm Brandor, by the way. I'm the one who found the letter.

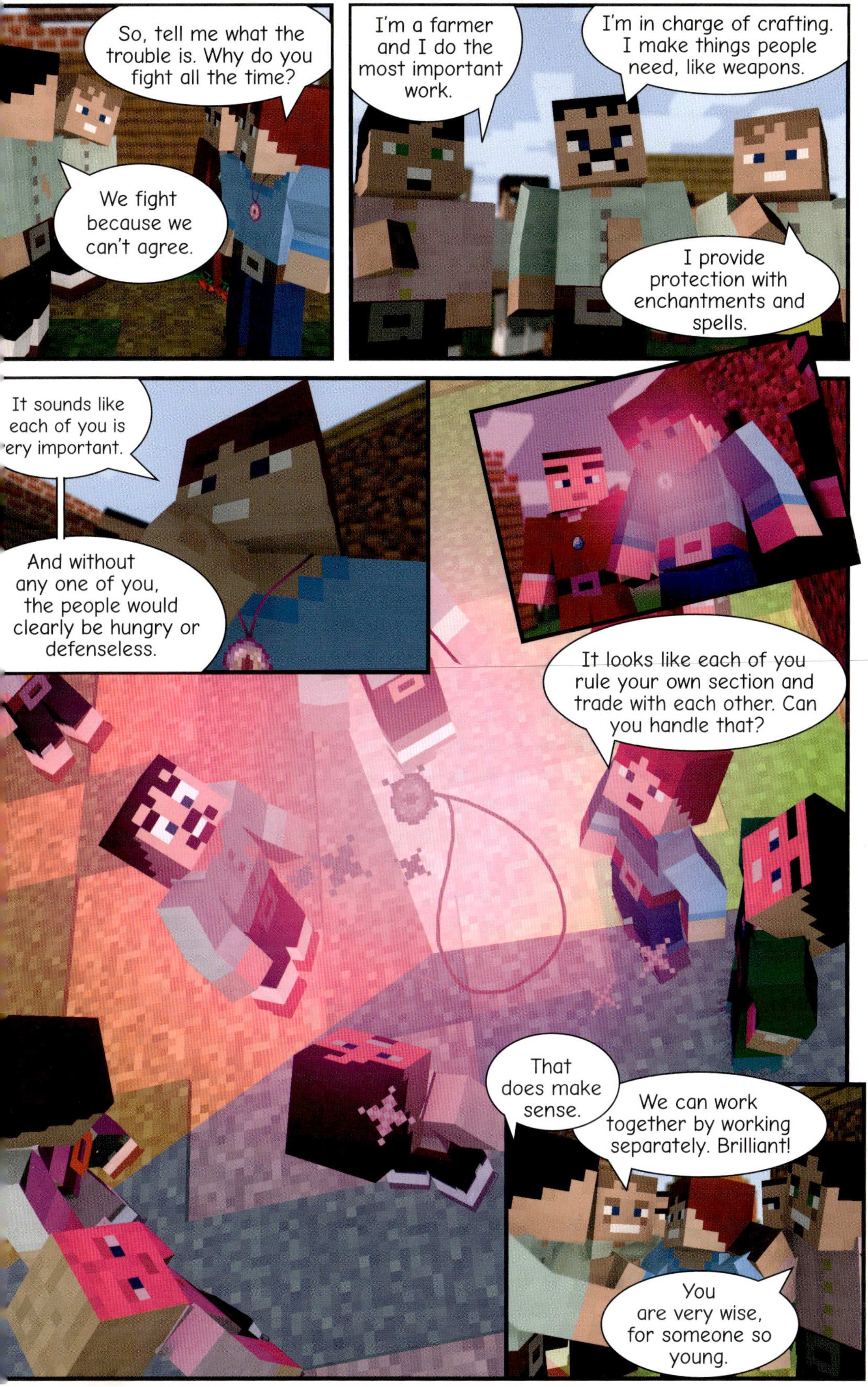
So, tell me what the trouble is. Why do you fight all the time?
We fight because we can't agree.
I'm a farmer and I do the most important work.
I'm in charge of crafting. I make things people need, like weapons.
I provide protection with enchantments and spells.
It sounds like each of you is ery important.
And without any one of you, the people would clearly be hungry or defenseless.
It looks like each of you rule your own section and trade with each other. Can you handle that?
That does make sense.
We can work together by working separately. Brilliant!
You are very wise, for someone so young.

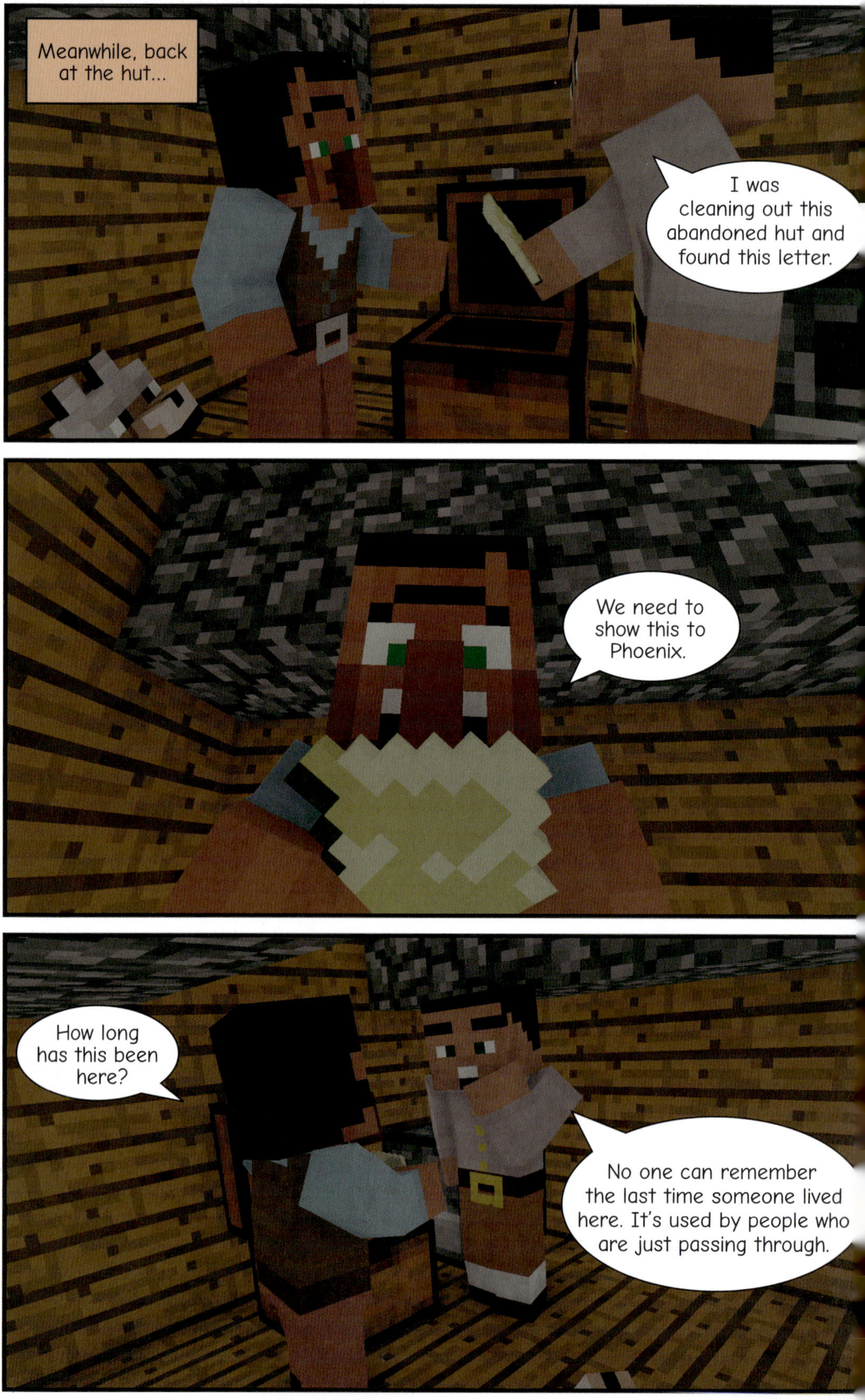
Meanwhile, back at the hut...
I was cleaning out this abandoned hut and found this letter.
We need to show this to Phoenix.
How long has this been here?
No one can remember the last time someone lived here. It's used by people who are just passing through.

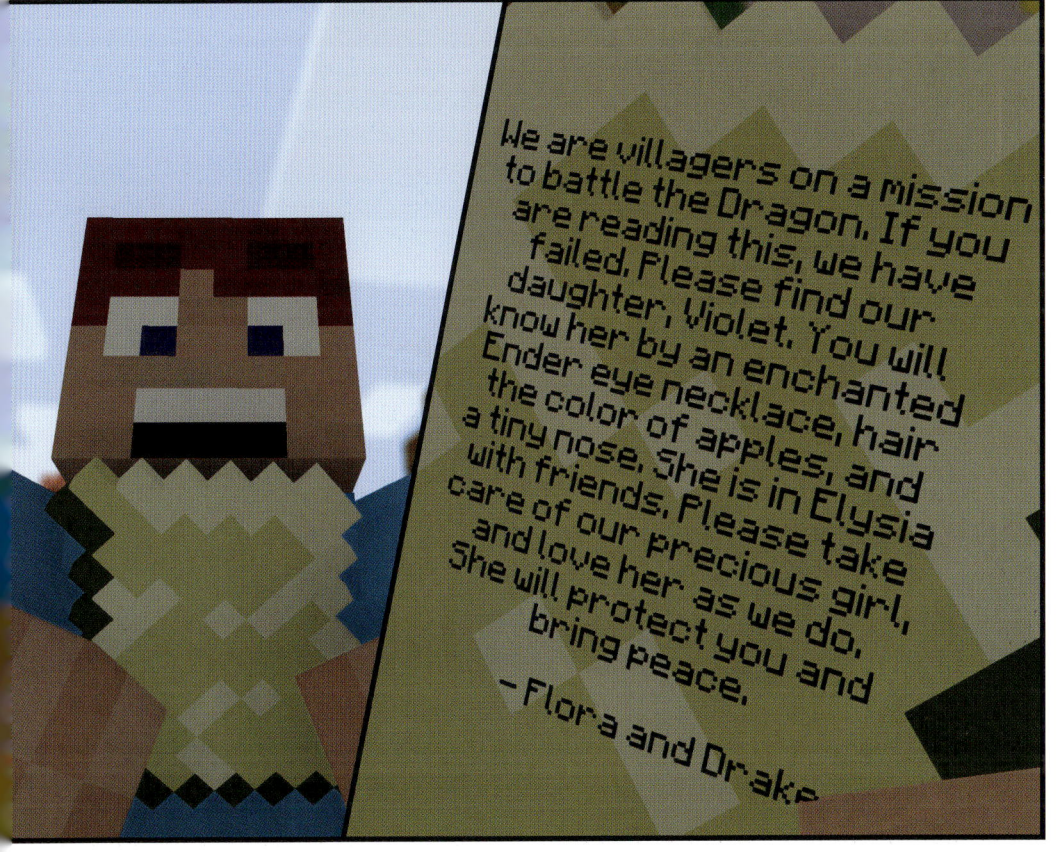

Panel 1: "Thank you, everyone. But really, I can't accept these gifts. I have nowhere to put them, and no way to get them home."

Panel 2: "Pssst! Phoenix, over here!"

Panel 3: "Excuse me everyone."

Panel 4: "Phoenix, this is Brandor. He's the one who found the prophecy."

"This is the letter I found. It was in an abandoned hut."

Panel 5:

We are villagers on a mission to battle the Dragon. If you are reading this, we have failed. Please find our daughter, Violet. You will know her by an enchanted Ender eye necklace, hair the color of apples, and a tiny nose. She is in Elysia with friends. Please take care of our precious girl, and love her as we do. She will protect you and bring peace.

— Flora and Drake

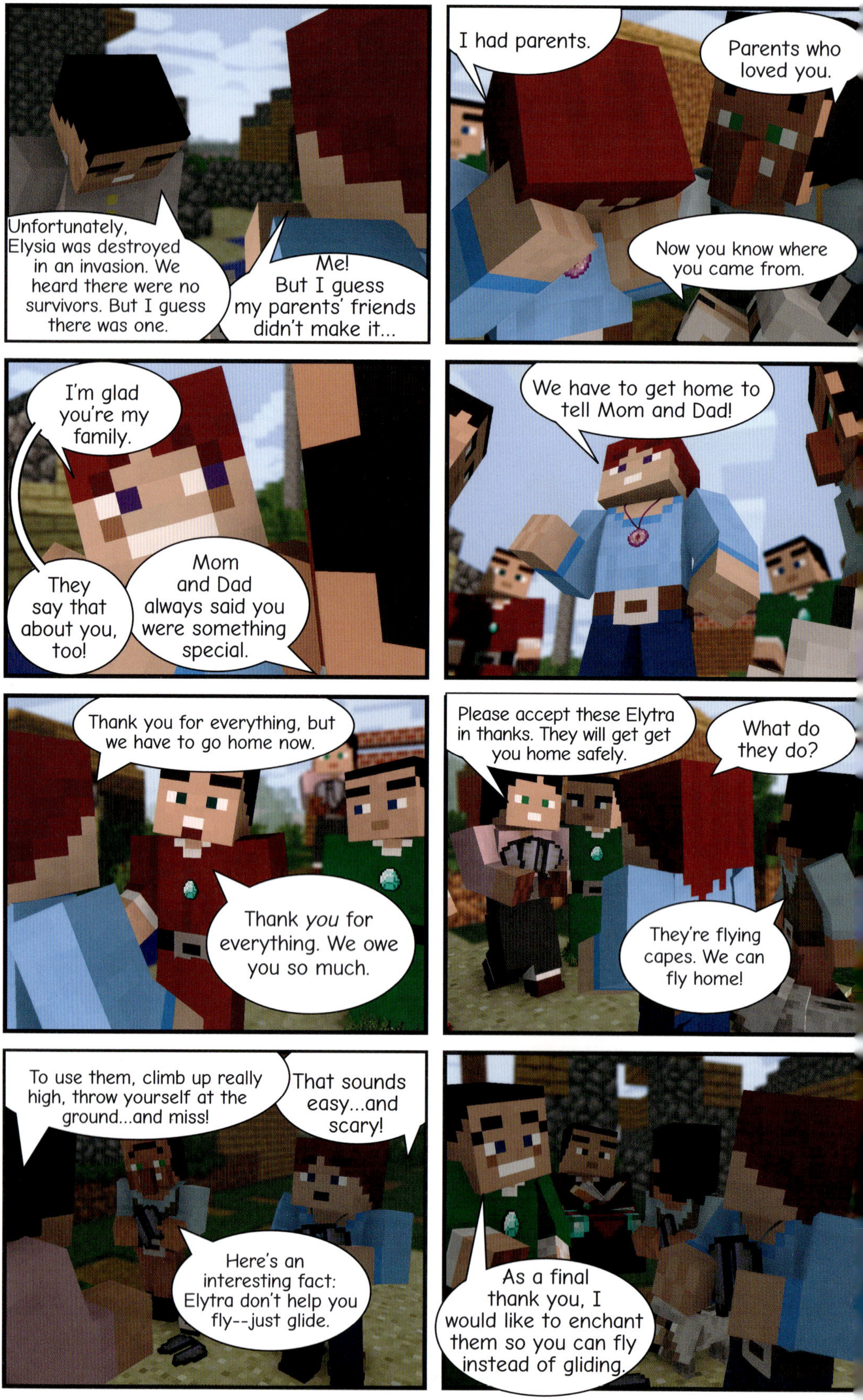
Unfortunately, Elysia was destroyed in an invasion. We heard there were no survivors. But I guess there was one.
Me! But I guess my parents' friends didn't make it...
I had parents.
Parents who loved you.
Now you know where you came from.
I'm glad you're my family.
Mom and Dad always said you were something special.
They say that about you, too!
We have to get home to tell Mom and Dad!
Thank you for everything, but we have to go home now.
Thank *you* for everything. We owe you so much.
Please accept these Elytra in thanks. They will get get you home safely.
What do they do?
They're flying capes. We can fly home!
To use them, climb up really high, throw yourself at the ground...and miss!
That sounds easy...and scary!
Here's an interesting fact: Elytra don't help you fly--just glide.
As a final thank you, I would like to enchant them so you can fly instead of gliding.

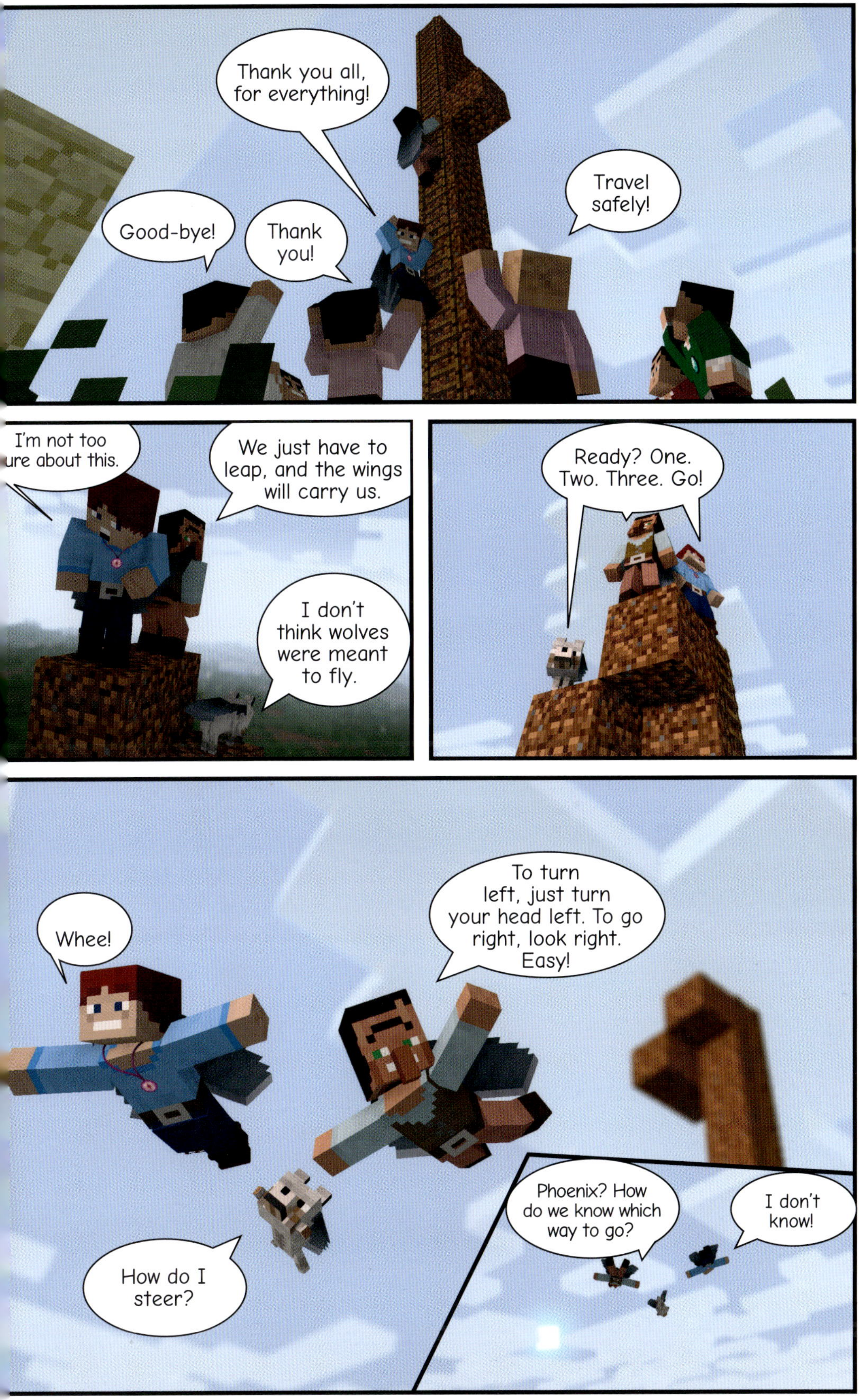
Thank you all, for everything!
Good-bye!
Thank you!
Travel safely!
I'm not too ure about this.
We just have to leap, and the wings will carry us.
I don't think wolves were meant to fly.
Ready? One. Two. Three. Go!
Whee!
To turn left, just turn your head left. To go right, look right. Easy!
How do I steer?
Phoenix? How do we know which way to go?
I don't know!

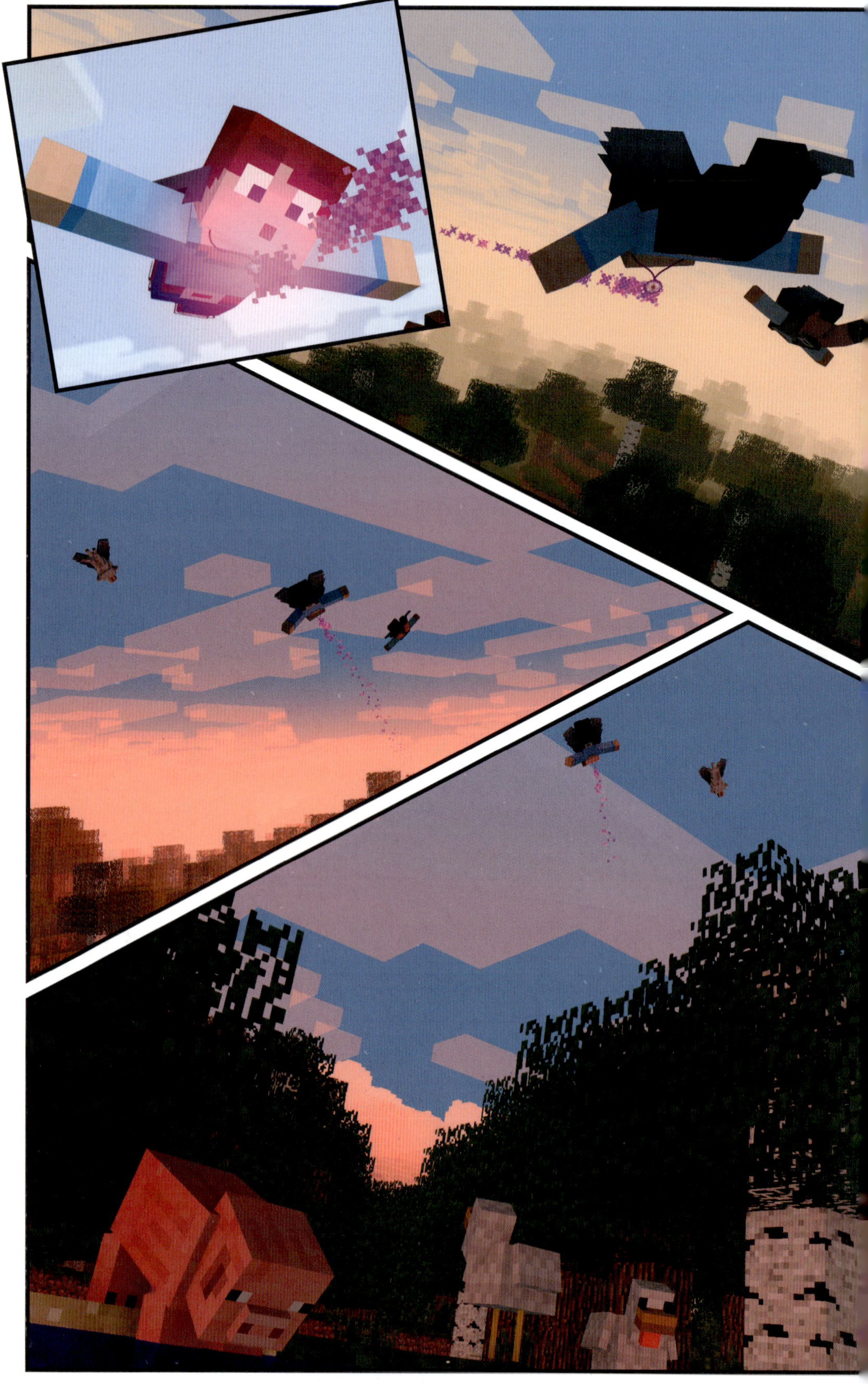

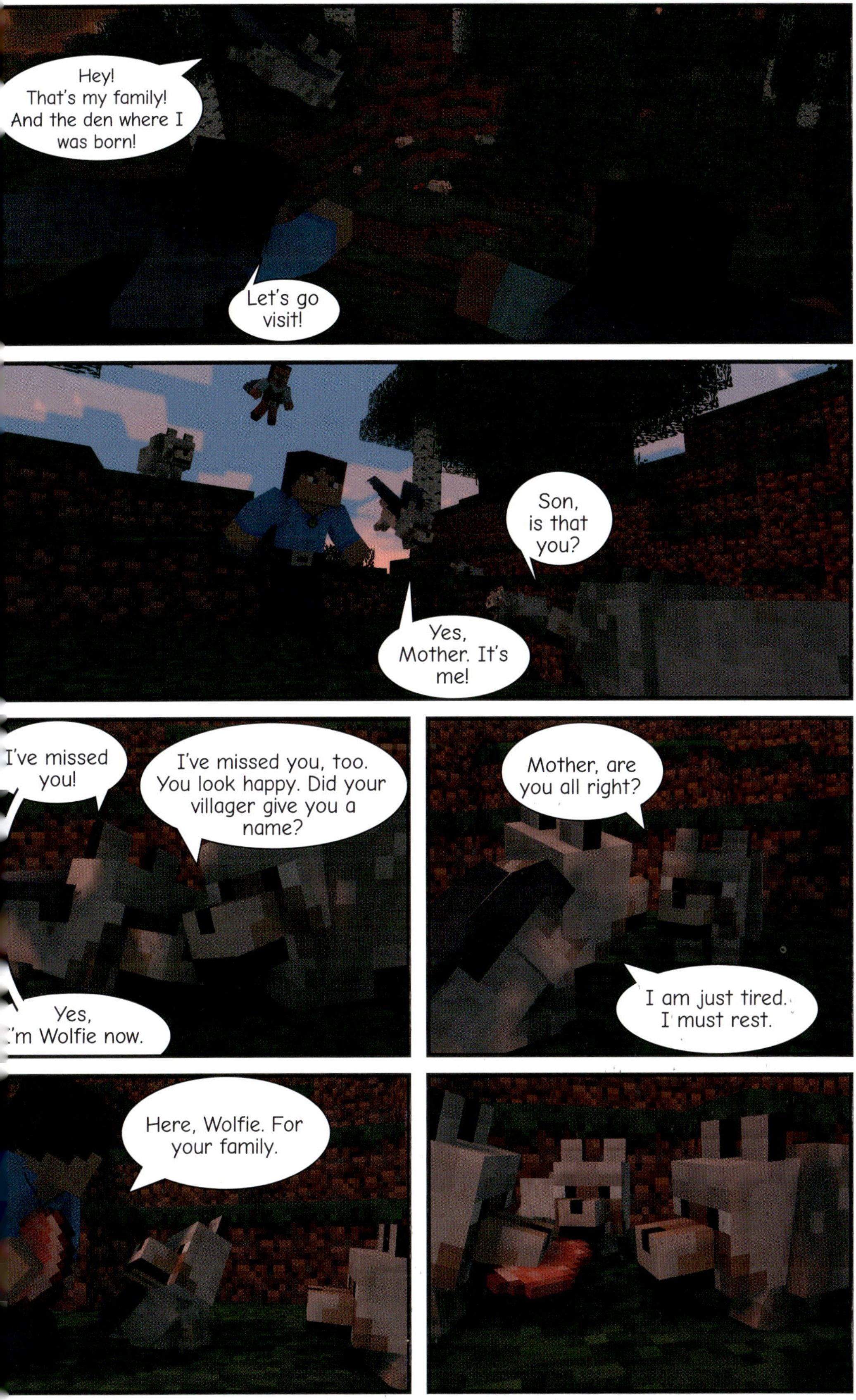
Hey! That's my family! And the den where I was born!
Let's go visit!
Son, is that you?
Yes, Mother. It's me!
I've missed you!
I've missed you, too. You look happy. Did your villager give you a name?
Yes, I'm Wolfie now.
Mother, are you all right?
I am just tired. I must rest.
Here, Wolfie. For your family.

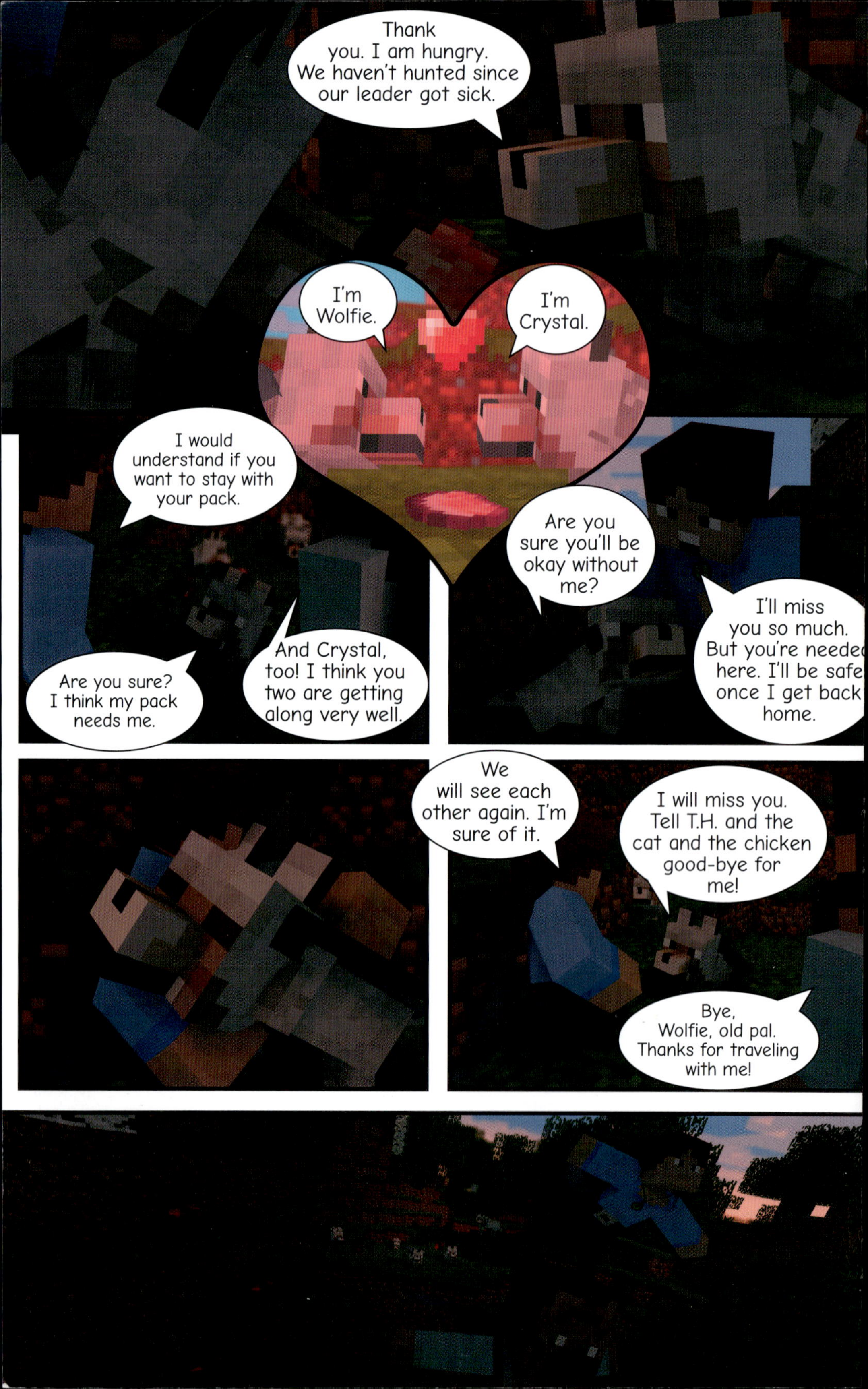
Thank you. I am hungry. We haven't hunted since our leader got sick.
I'm Wolfie.
I'm Crystal.
I would understand if you want to stay with your pack.
Are you sure? I think my pack needs me.
And Crystal, too! I think you two are getting along very well.
Are you sure you'll be okay without me?
I'll miss you so much. But you're needed here. I'll be safe once I get back home.
We will see each other again. I'm sure of it.
I will miss you. Tell T.H. and the cat and the chicken good-bye for me!
Bye, Wolfie, old pal. Thanks for traveling with me!

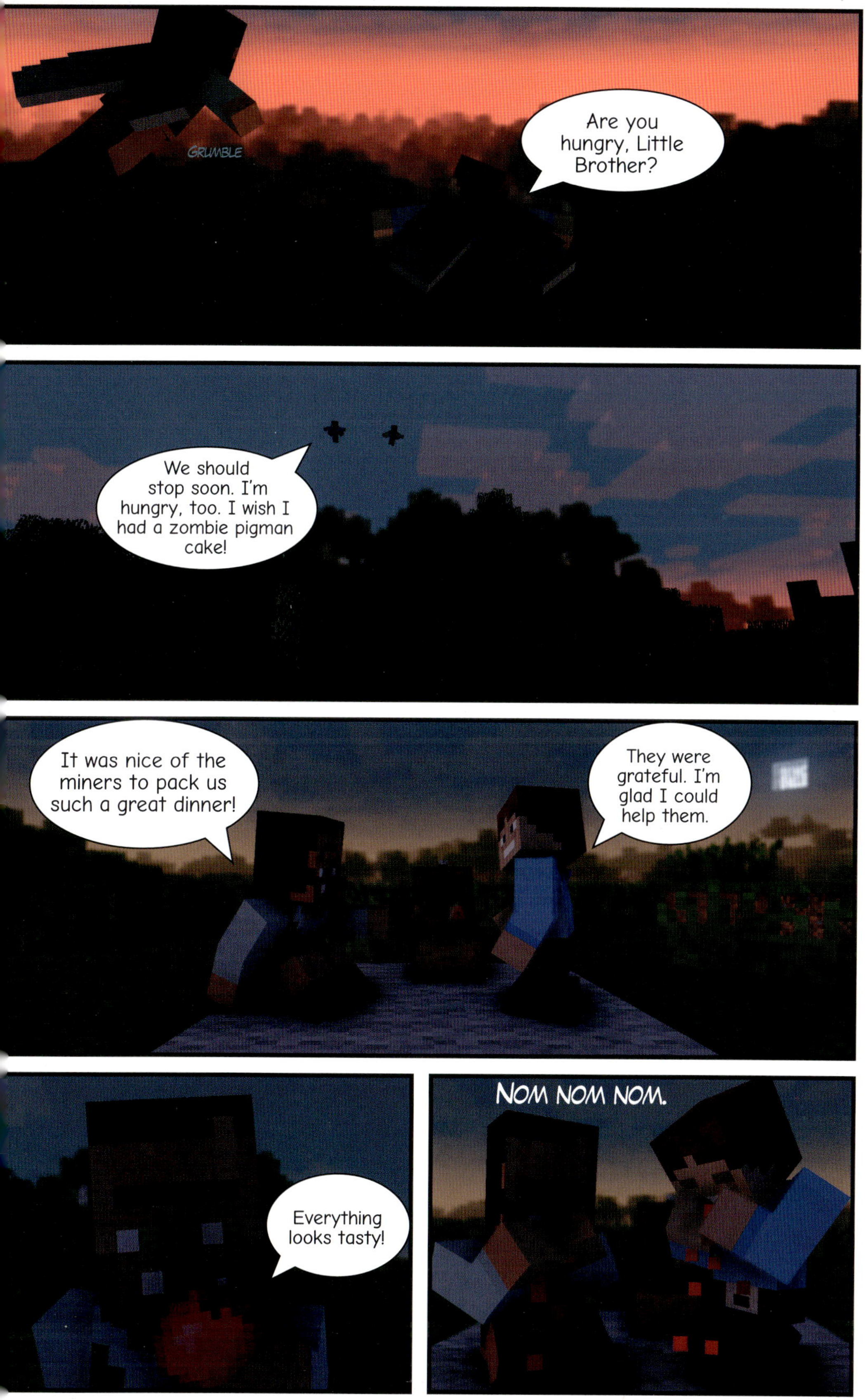
GRUMBLE
Are you hungry, Little Brother?
We should stop soon. I'm hungry, too. I wish I had a zombie pigman cake!
It was nice of the miners to pack us such a great dinner!
They were grateful. I'm glad I could help them.
Everything looks tasty!
NOM NOM NOM.

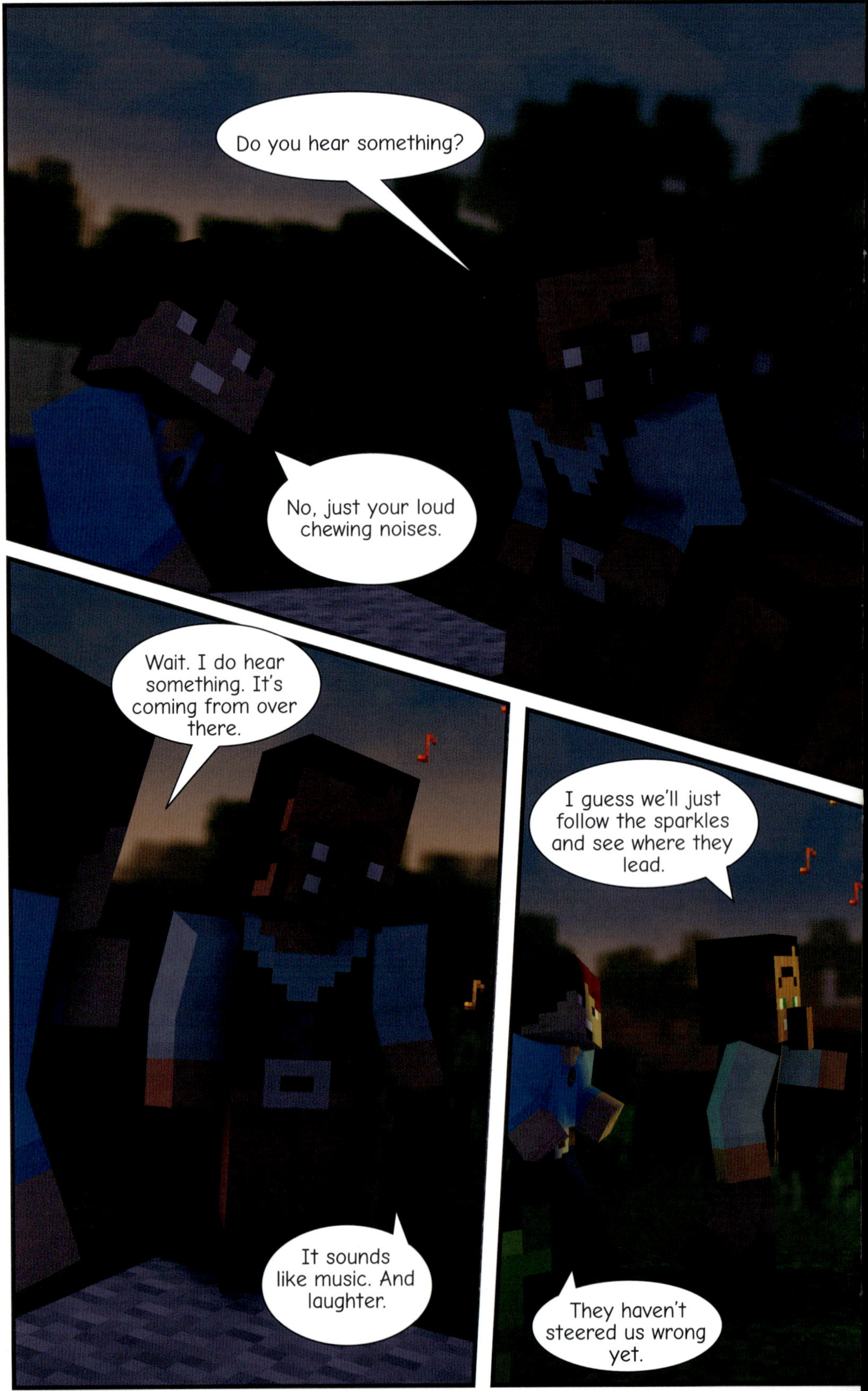
Do you hear something?
No, just your loud chewing noises.
Wait. I do hear something. It's coming from over there.
It sounds like music. And laughter.
I guess we'll just follow the sparkles and see where they lead.
They haven't steered us wrong yet.

CHAPTER 11

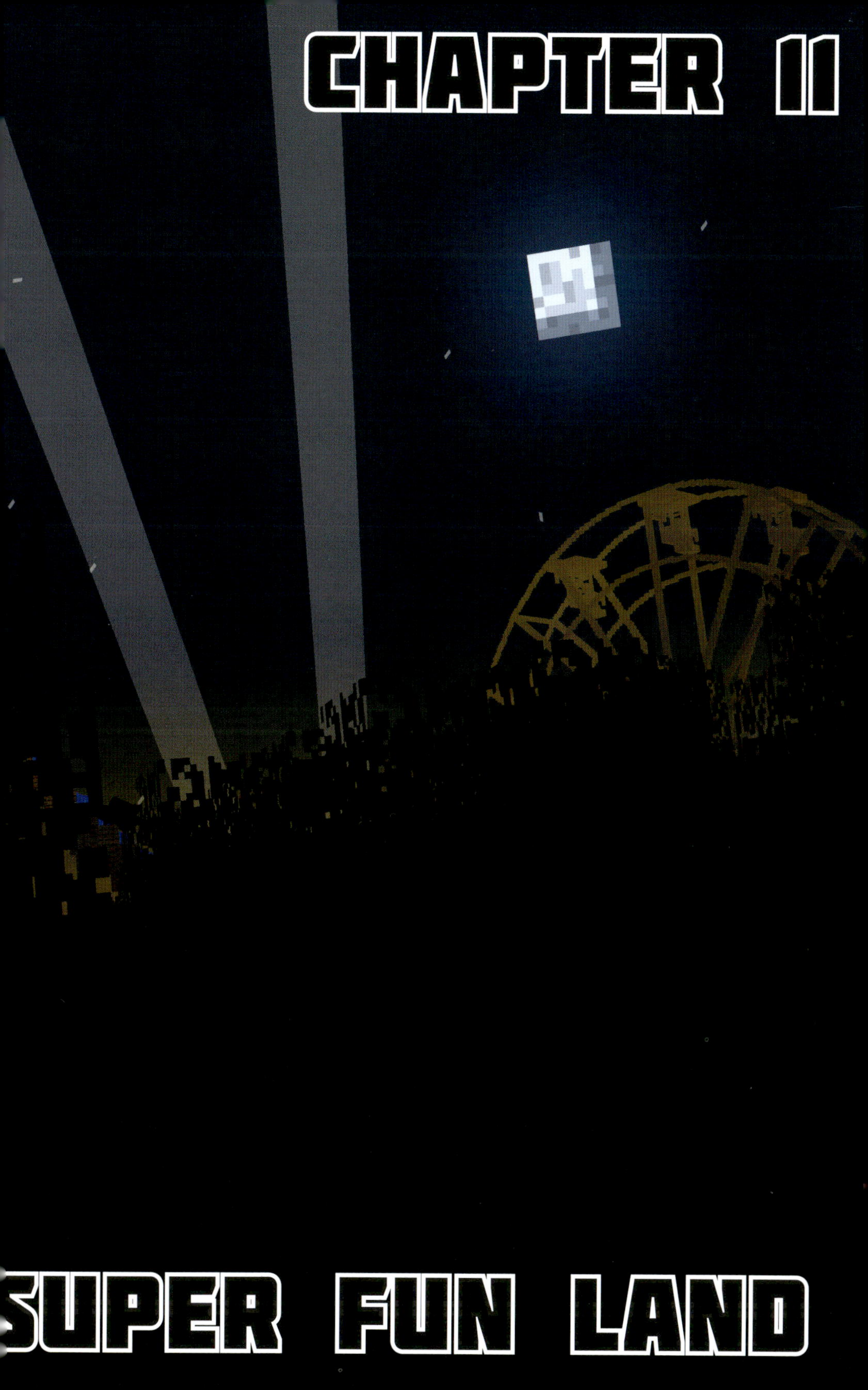

SUPER FUN LAND

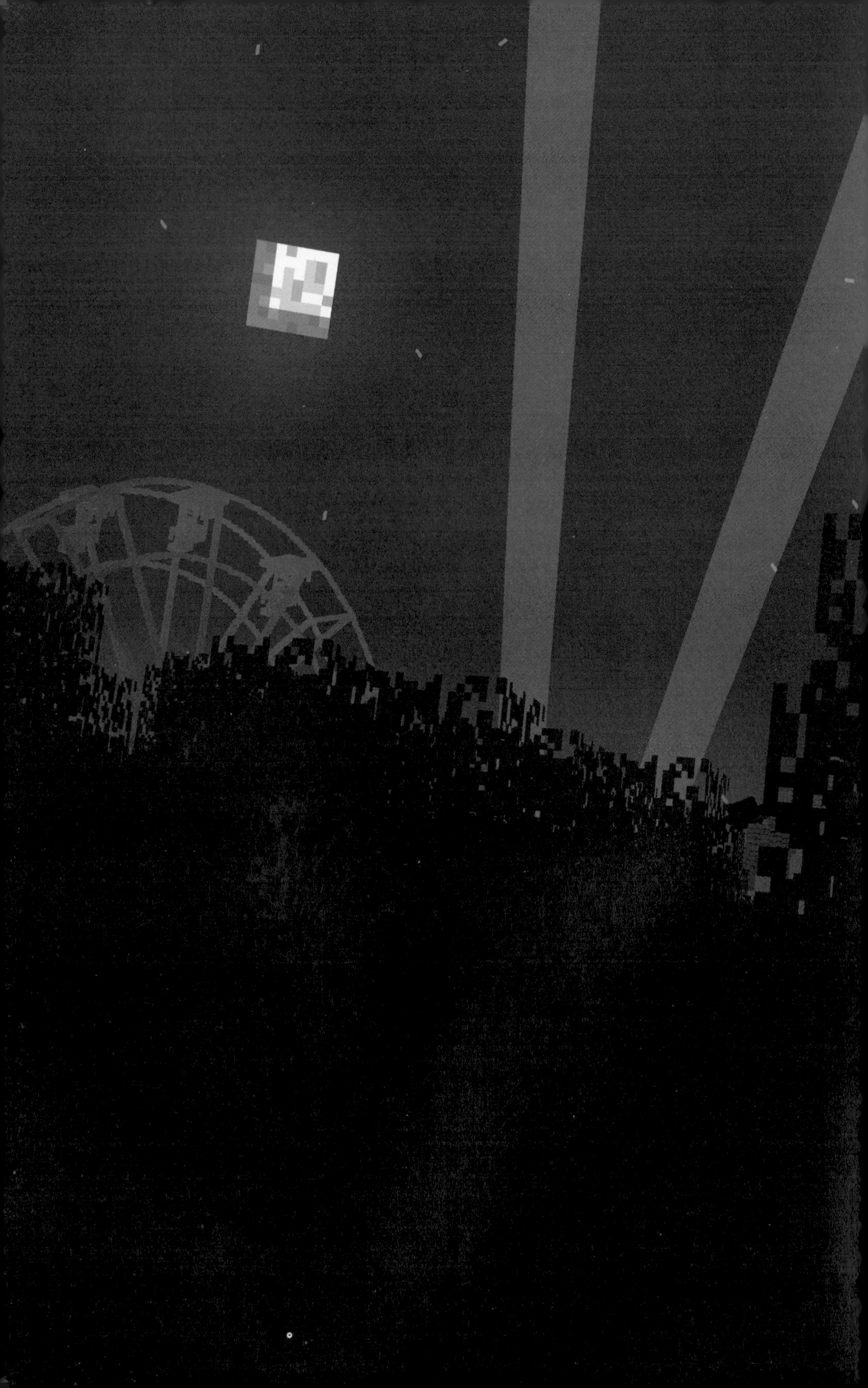

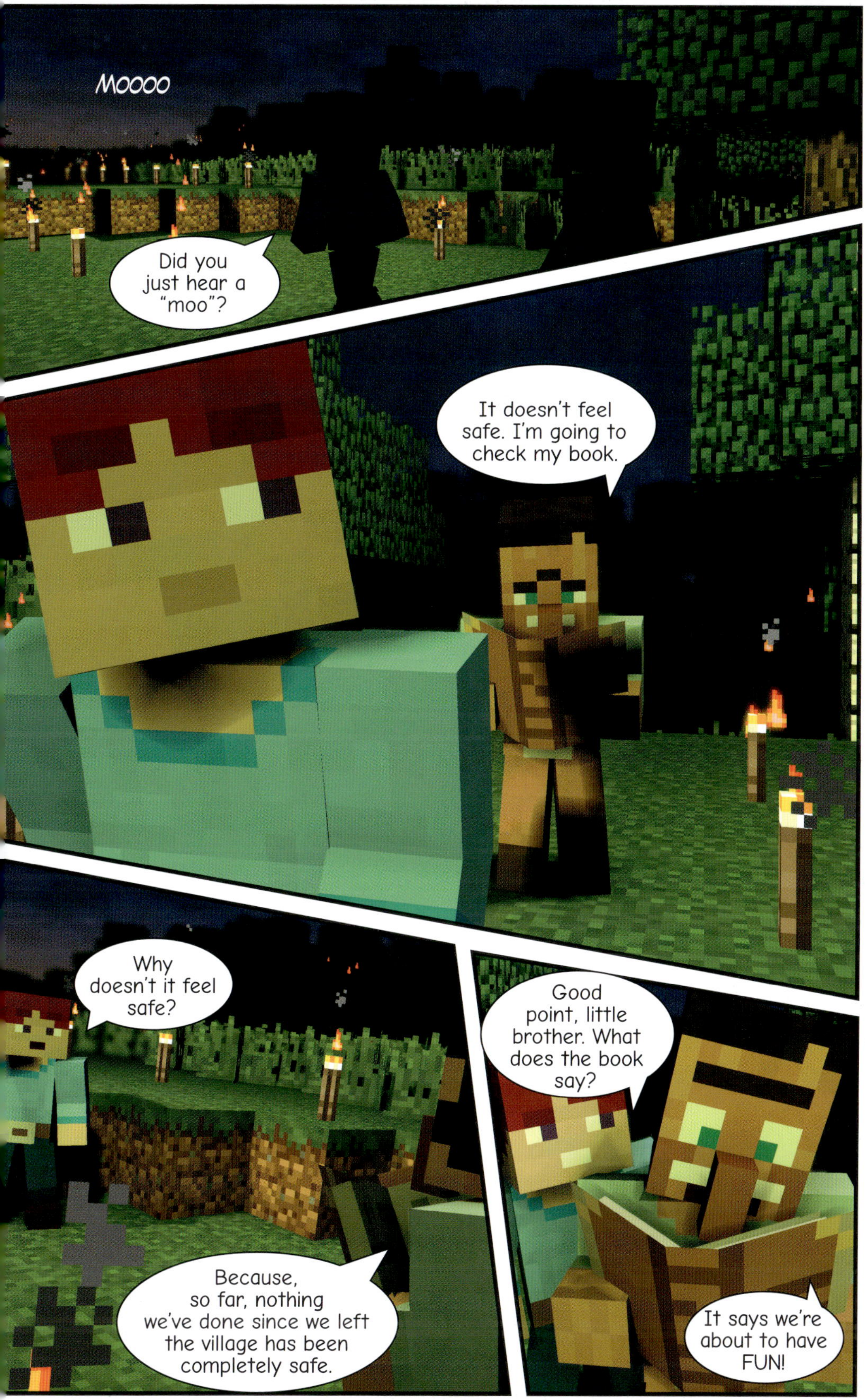
MOOOO
Did you just hear a "moo"?
It doesn't feel safe. I'm going to check my book.
Why doesn't it feel safe?
Because, so far, nothing we've done since we left the village has been completely safe.
Good point, little brother. What does the book say?
It says we're about to have FUN!

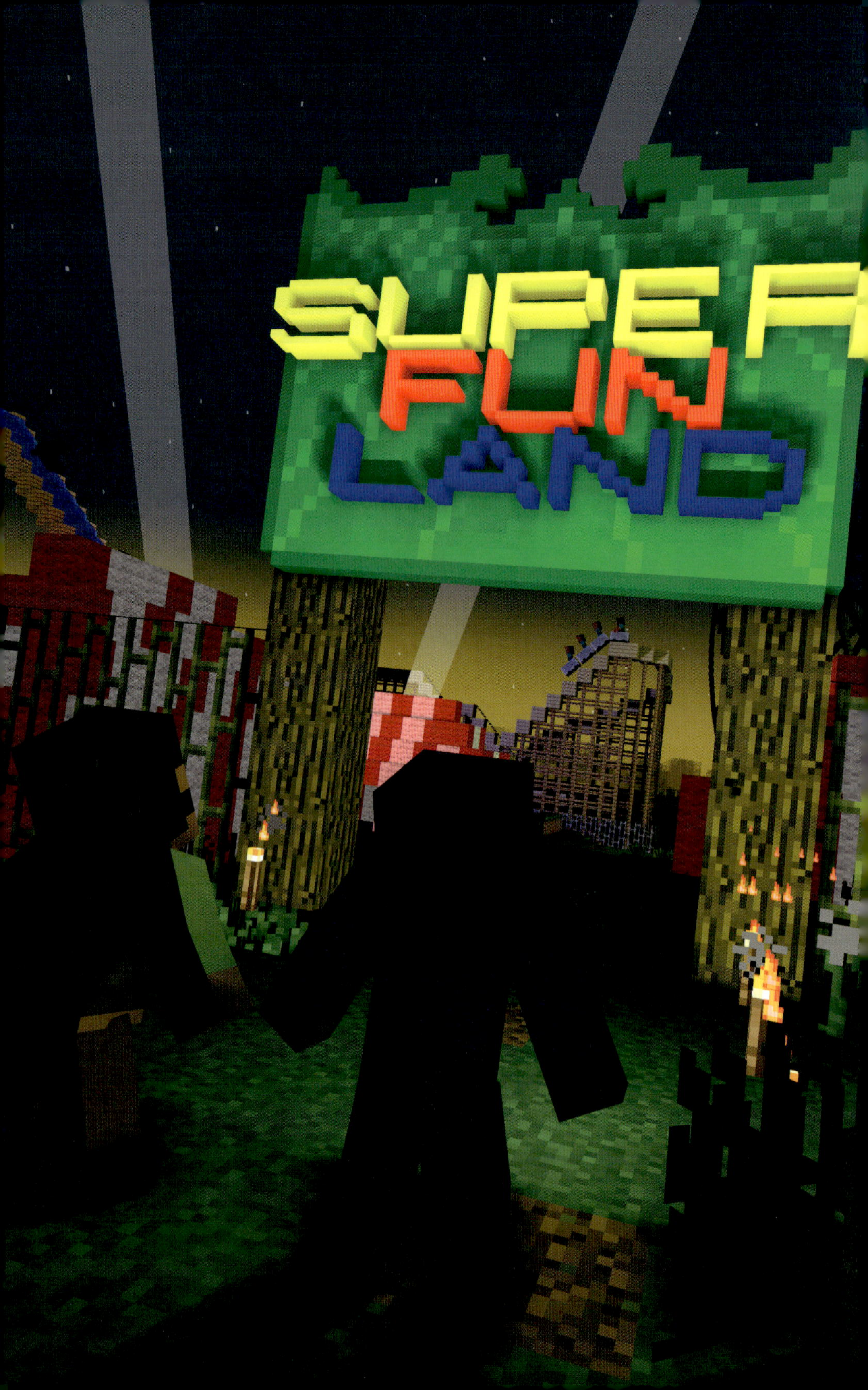
SUPER
FUN
LAND

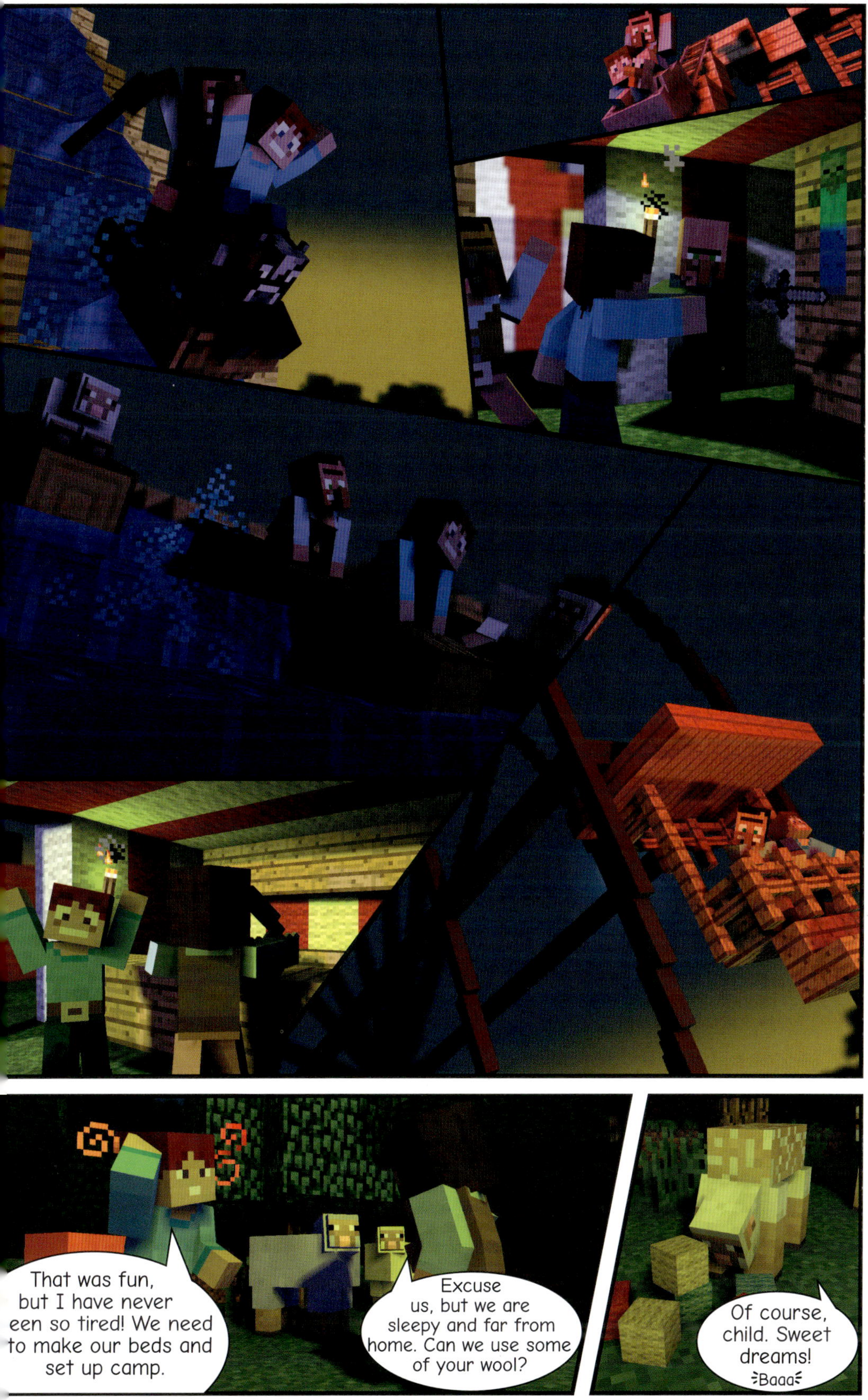

That was fun, but I have never een so tired! We need to make our beds and set up camp.
Excuse us, but we are sleepy and far from home. Can we use some of your wool?
Of course, child. Sweet dreams!
Baaa

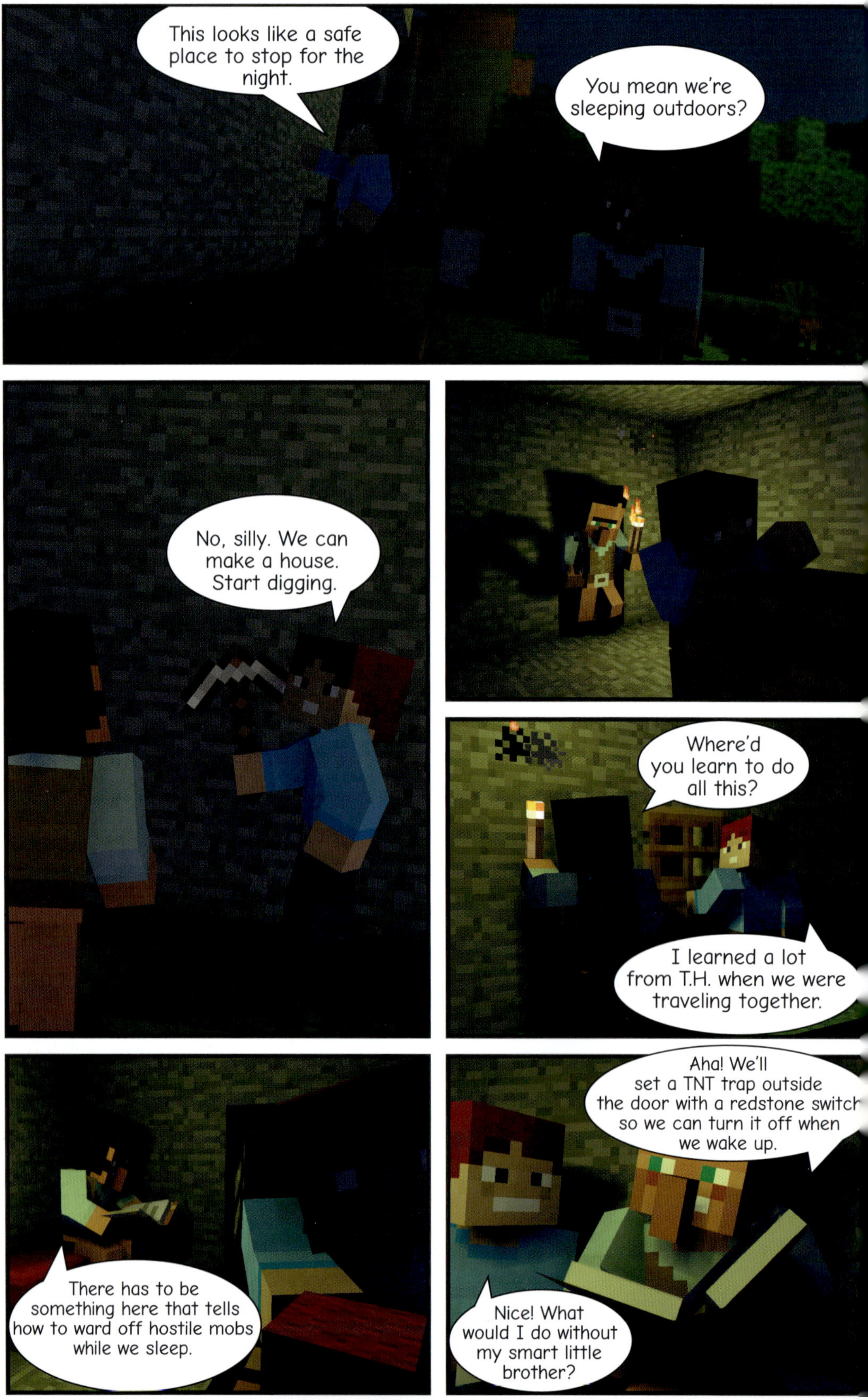
This looks like a safe place to stop for the night.
You mean we're sleeping outdoors?
No, silly. We can make a house. Start digging.
Where'd you learn to do all this?
I learned a lot from T.H. when we were traveling together.
There has to be something here that tells how to ward off hostile mobs while we sleep.
Aha! We'll set a TNT trap outside the door with a redstone switch so we can turn it off when we wake up.
Nice! What would I do without my smart little brother?

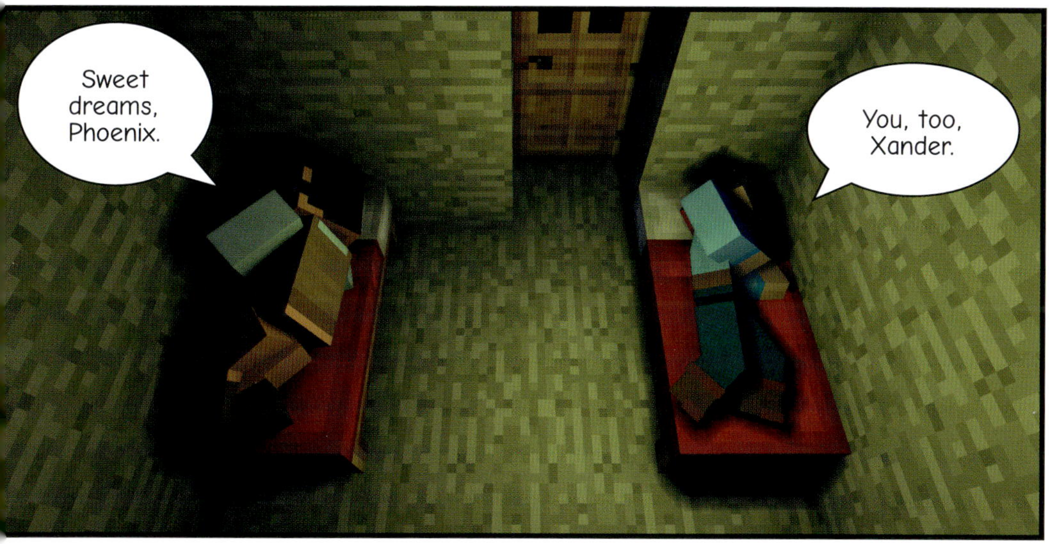
Sweet dreams, Phoenix.
You, too, Xander.

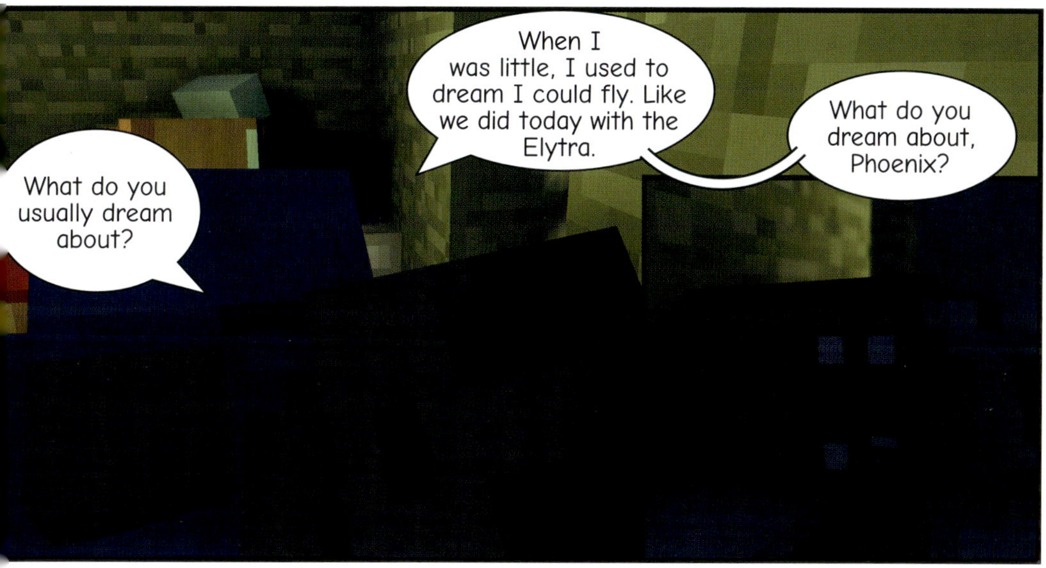
What do you usually dream about?
When I was little, I used to dream I could fly. Like we did today with the Elytra.
What do you dream about, Phoenix?

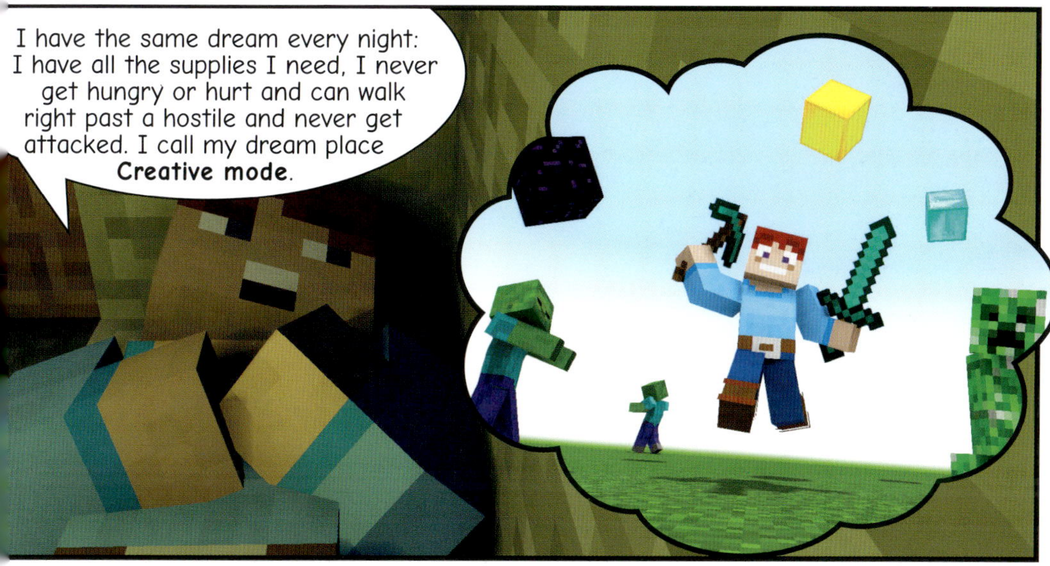
I have the same dream every night: I have all the supplies I need, I never get hungry or hurt and can walk right past a hostile and never get attacked. I call my dream place **Creative mode**.

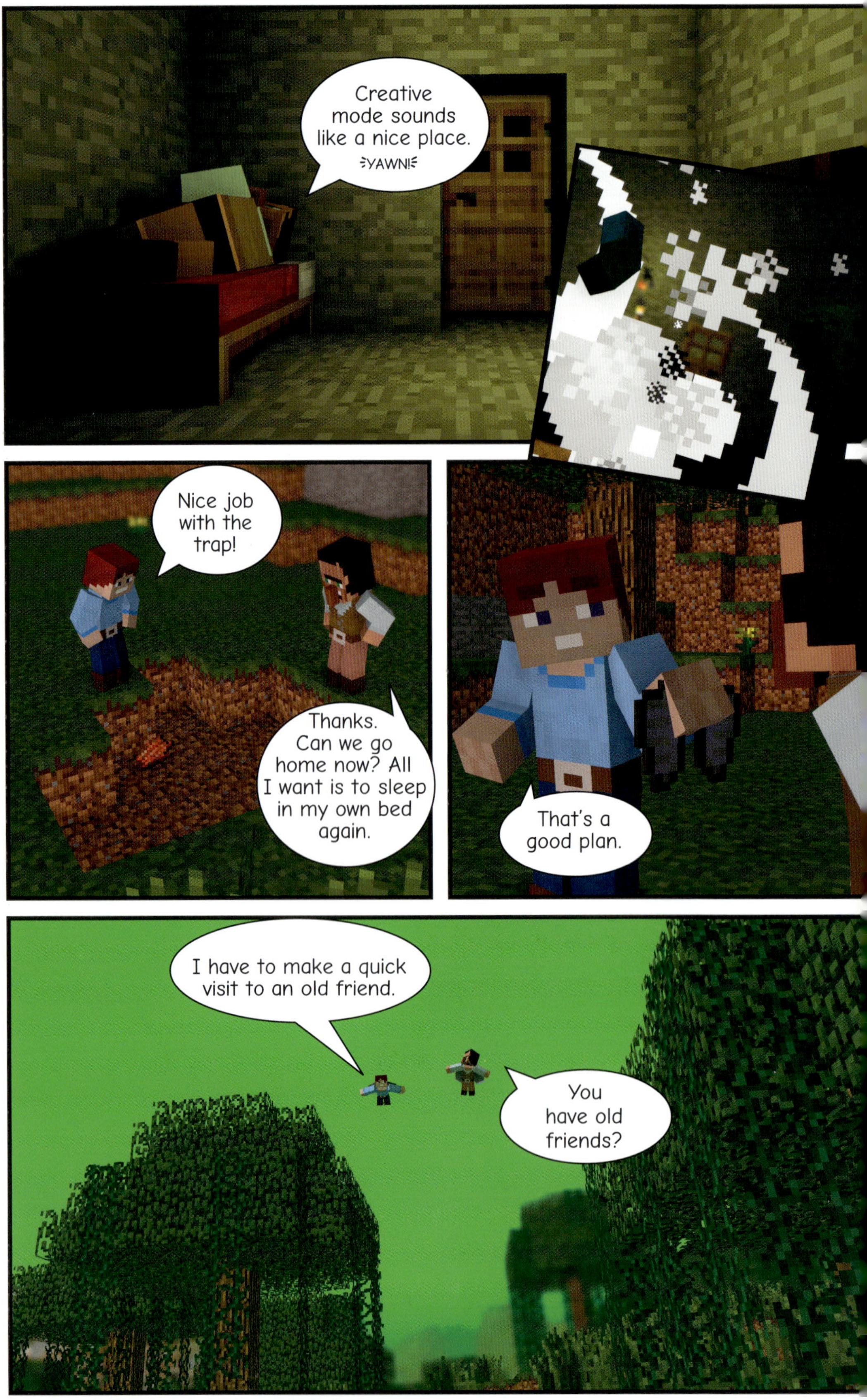
Creative mode sounds like a nice place.
YAWN!
Nice job with the trap!
Thanks. Can we go home now? All I want is to sleep in my own bed again.
That's a good plan.
I have to make a quick visit to an old friend.
You have old friends?

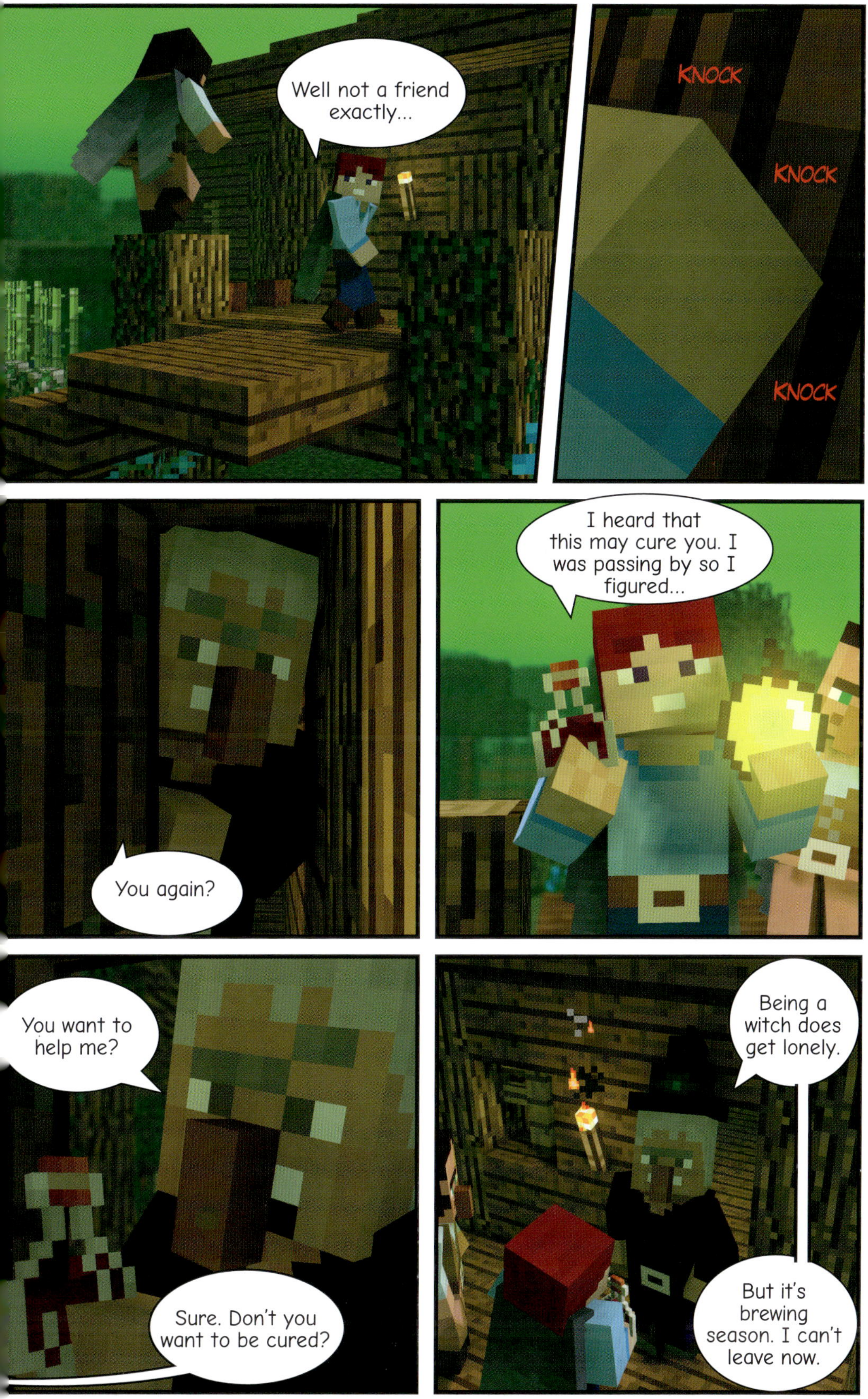
Well not a friend exactly...
KNOCK
KNOCK
KNOCK
You again?
I heard that this may cure you. I was passing by so I figured...
You want to help me?
Sure. Don't you want to be cured?
Being a witch does get lonely.
But it's brewing season. I can't leave now.

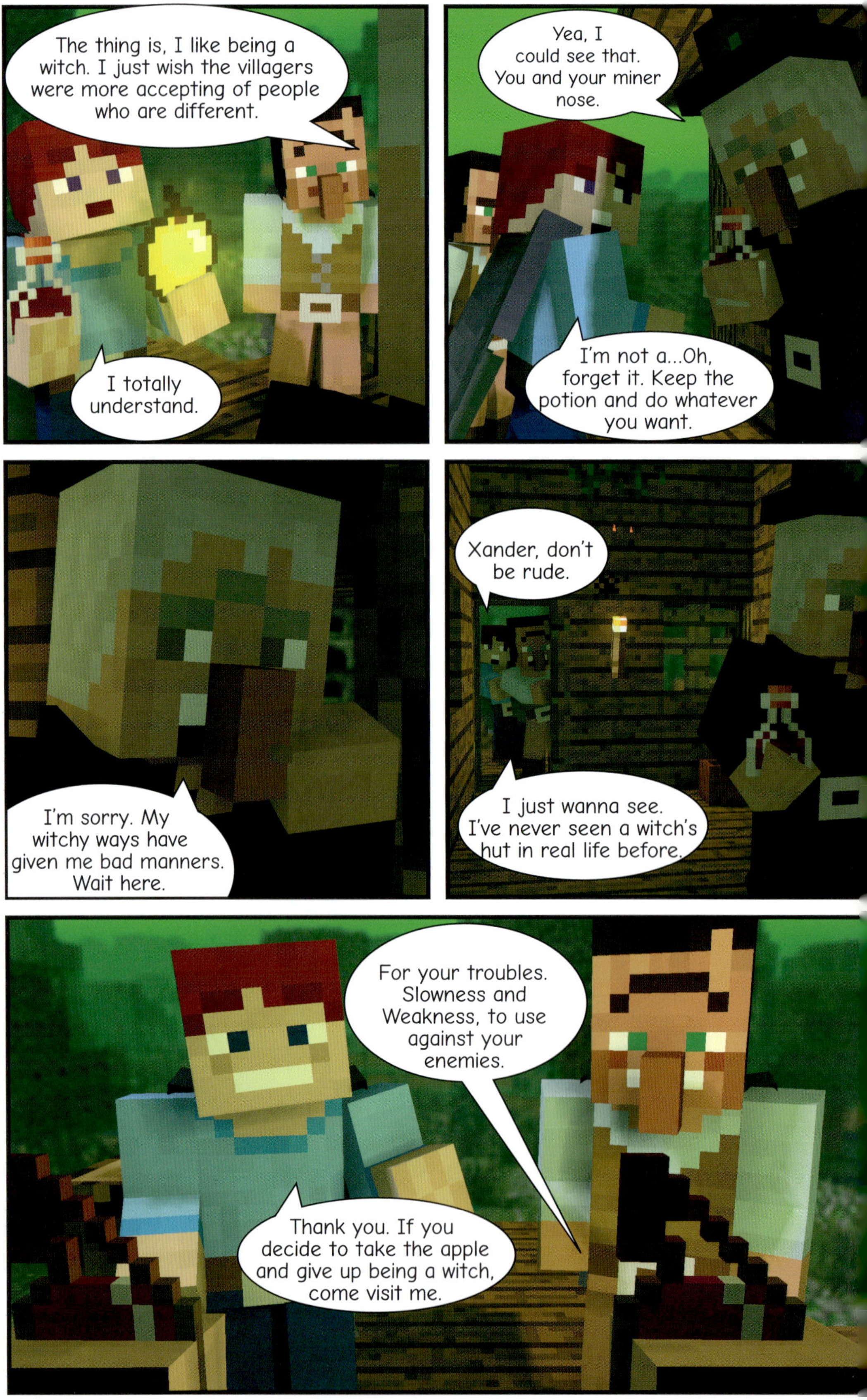
The thing is, I like being a witch. I just wish the villagers were more accepting of people who are different.
I totally understand.
Yea, I could see that. You and your miner nose.
I'm not a...Oh, forget it. Keep the potion and do whatever you want.
I'm sorry. My witchy ways have given me bad manners. Wait here.
Xander, don't be rude.
I just wanna see. I've never seen a witch's hut in real life before.
For your troubles. Slowness and Weakness, to use against your enemies.
Thank you. If you decide to take the apple and give up being a witch, come visit me.

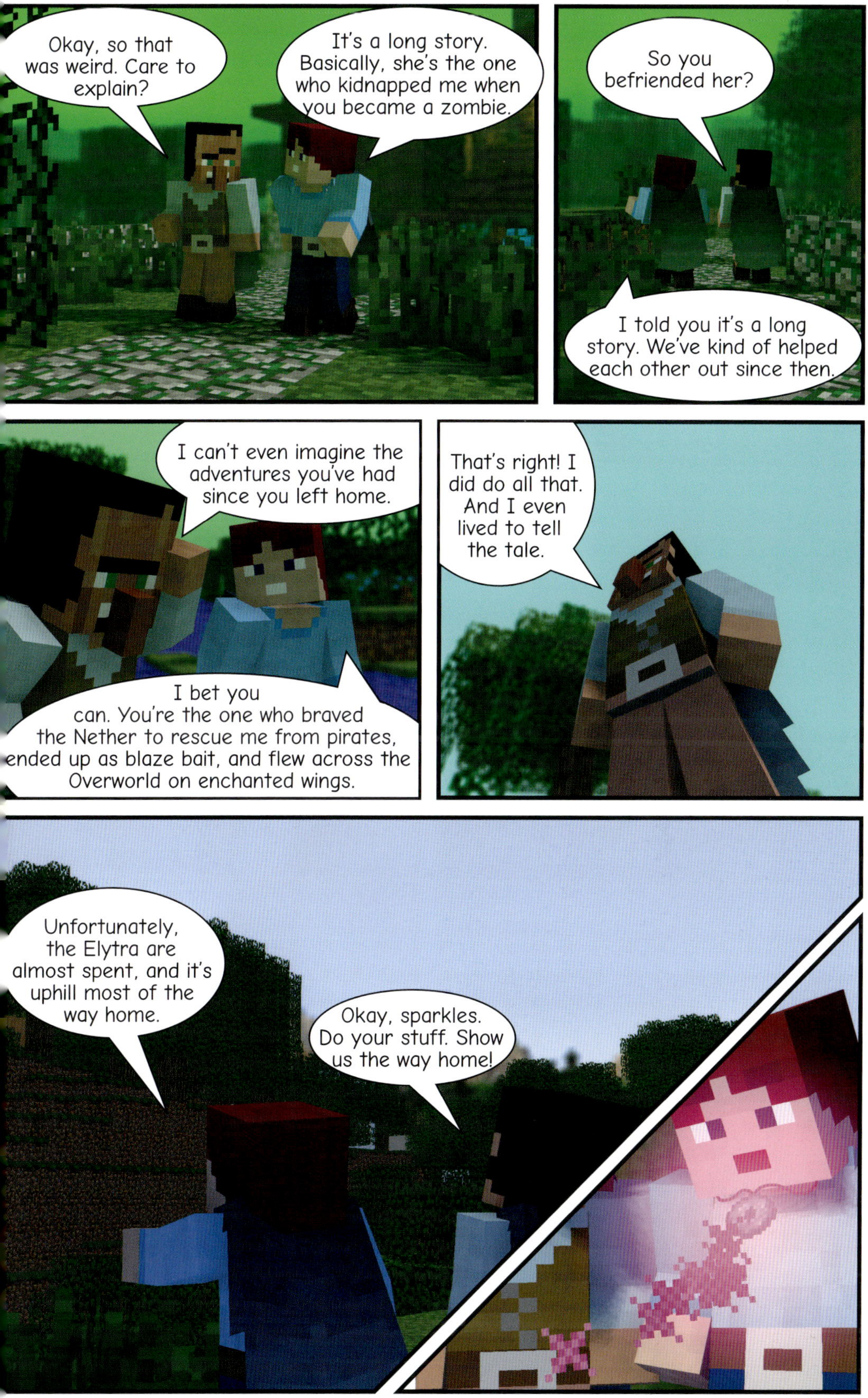
Okay, so that was weird. Care to explain?
It's a long story. Basically, she's the one who kidnapped me when you became a zombie.
So you befriended her?
I told you it's a long story. We've kind of helped each other out since then.
I can't even imagine the adventures you've had since you left home.
I bet you can. You're the one who braved the Nether to rescue me from pirates, ended up as blaze bait, and flew across the Overworld on enchanted wings.
That's right! I did do all that. And I even lived to tell the tale.
Unfortunately, the Elytra are almost spent, and it's uphill most of the way home.
Okay, sparkles. Do your stuff. Show us the way home!

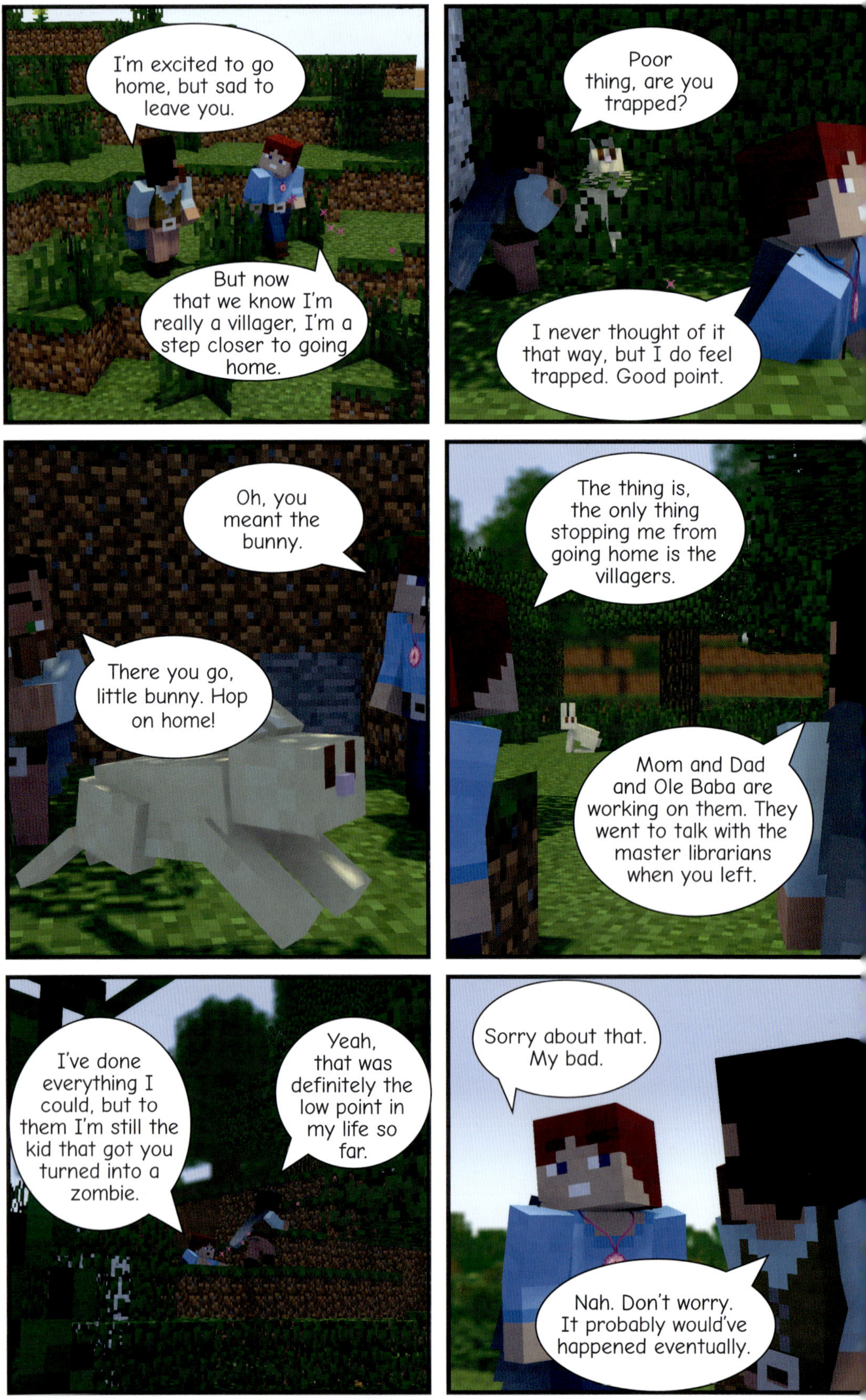
I'm excited to go home, but sad to leave you.
But now that we know I'm really a villager, I'm a step closer to going home.
Poor thing, are you trapped?
I never thought of it that way, but I do feel trapped. Good point.
Oh, you meant the bunny.
There you go, little bunny. Hop on home!
The thing is, the only thing stopping me from going home is the villagers.
Mom and Dad and Ole Baba are working on them. They went to talk with the master librarians when you left.
I've done everything I could, but to them I'm still the kid that got you turned into a zombie.
Yeah, that was definitely the low point in my life so far.
Sorry about that. My bad.
Nah. Don't worry. It probably would've happened eventually.

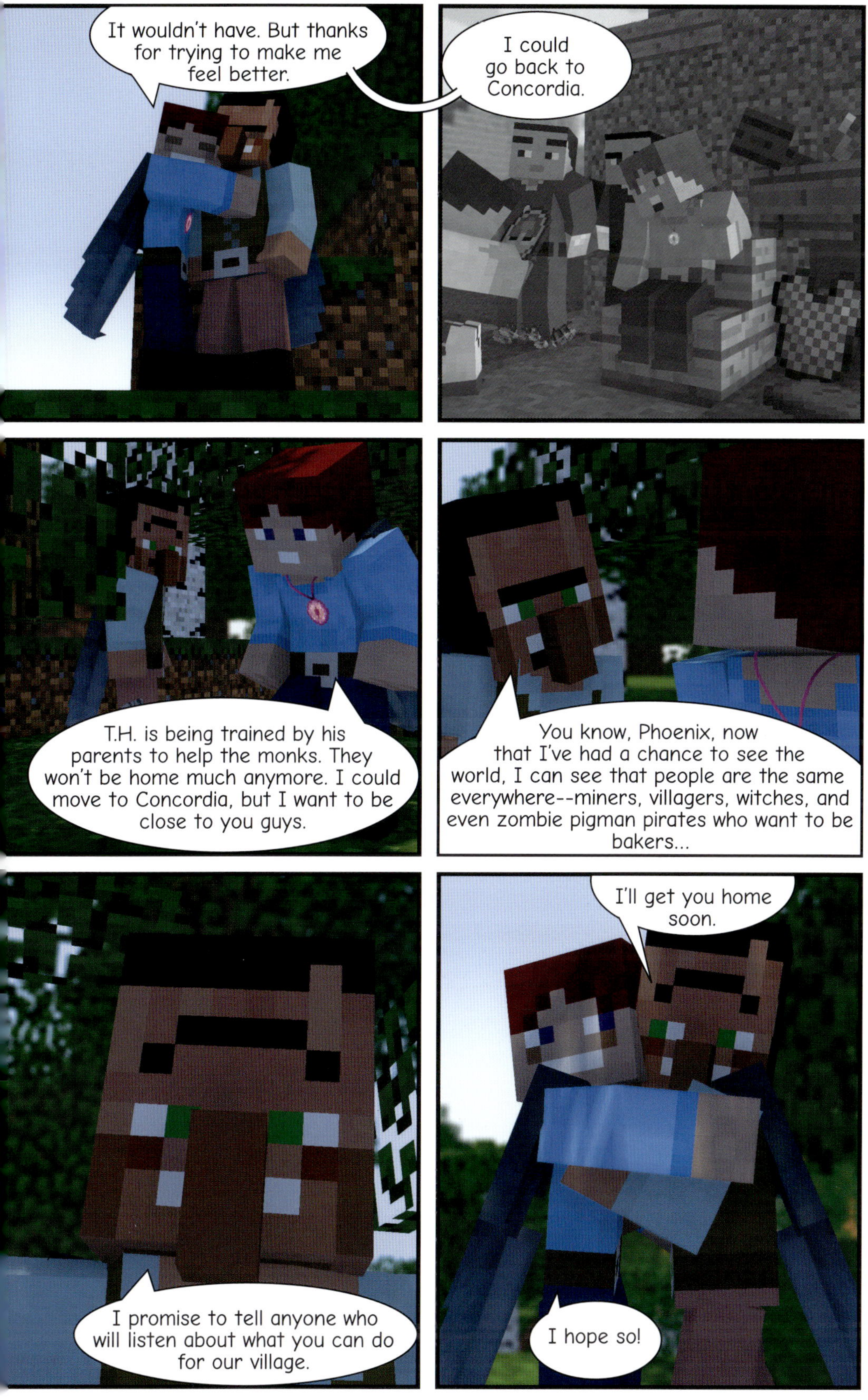
It wouldn't have. But thanks for trying to make me feel better.
I could go back to Concordia.
T.H. is being trained by his parents to help the monks. They won't be home much anymore. I could move to Concordia, but I want to be close to you guys.
You know, Phoenix, now that I've had a chance to see the world, I can see that people are the same everywhere--miners, villagers, witches, and even zombie pigman pirates who want to be bakers...
I promise to tell anyone who will listen about what you can do for our village.
I'll get you home soon.
I hope so!

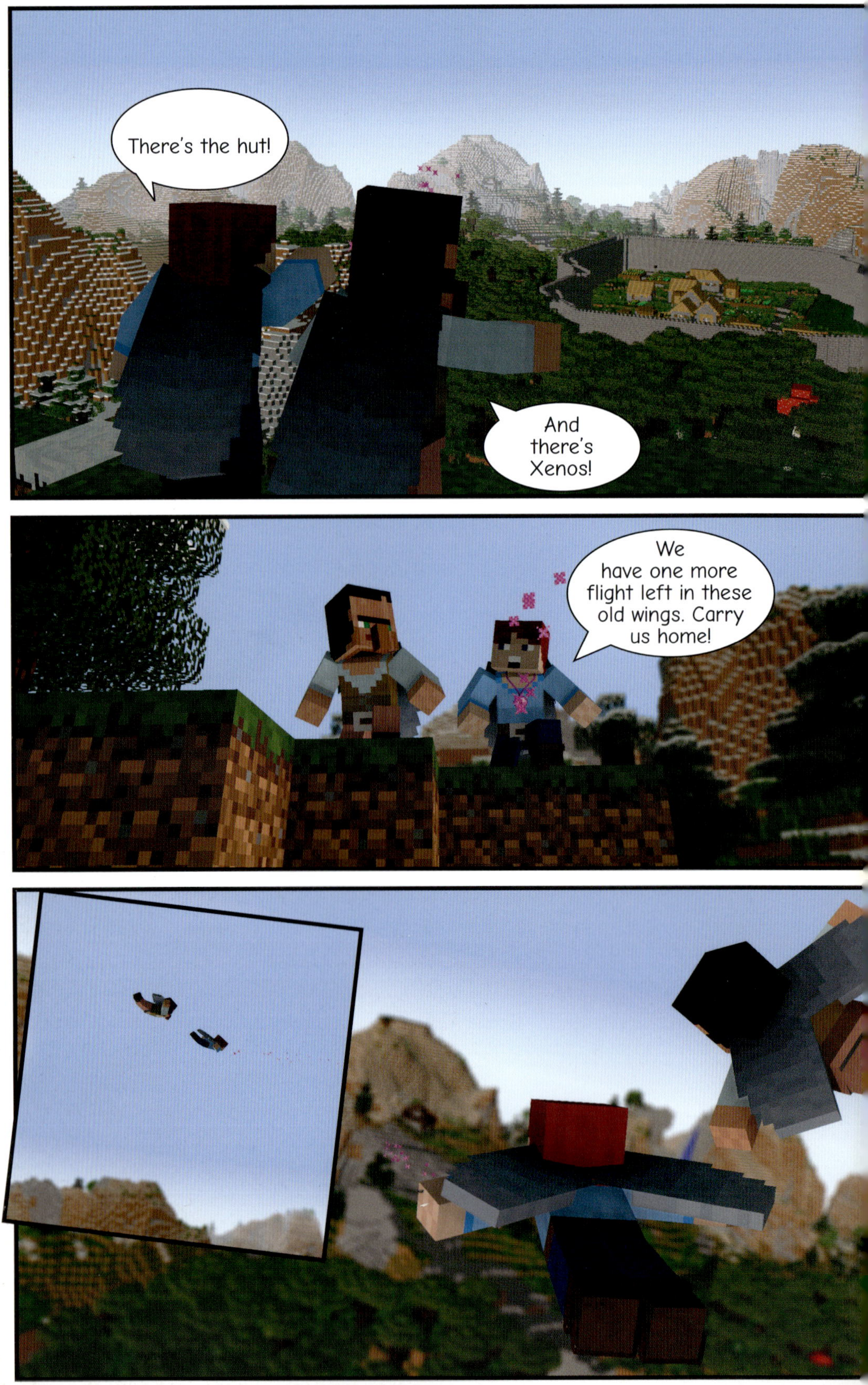
There's the hut!
And there's Xenos!
We have one more flight left in these old wings. Carry us home!

CHAPTER 12

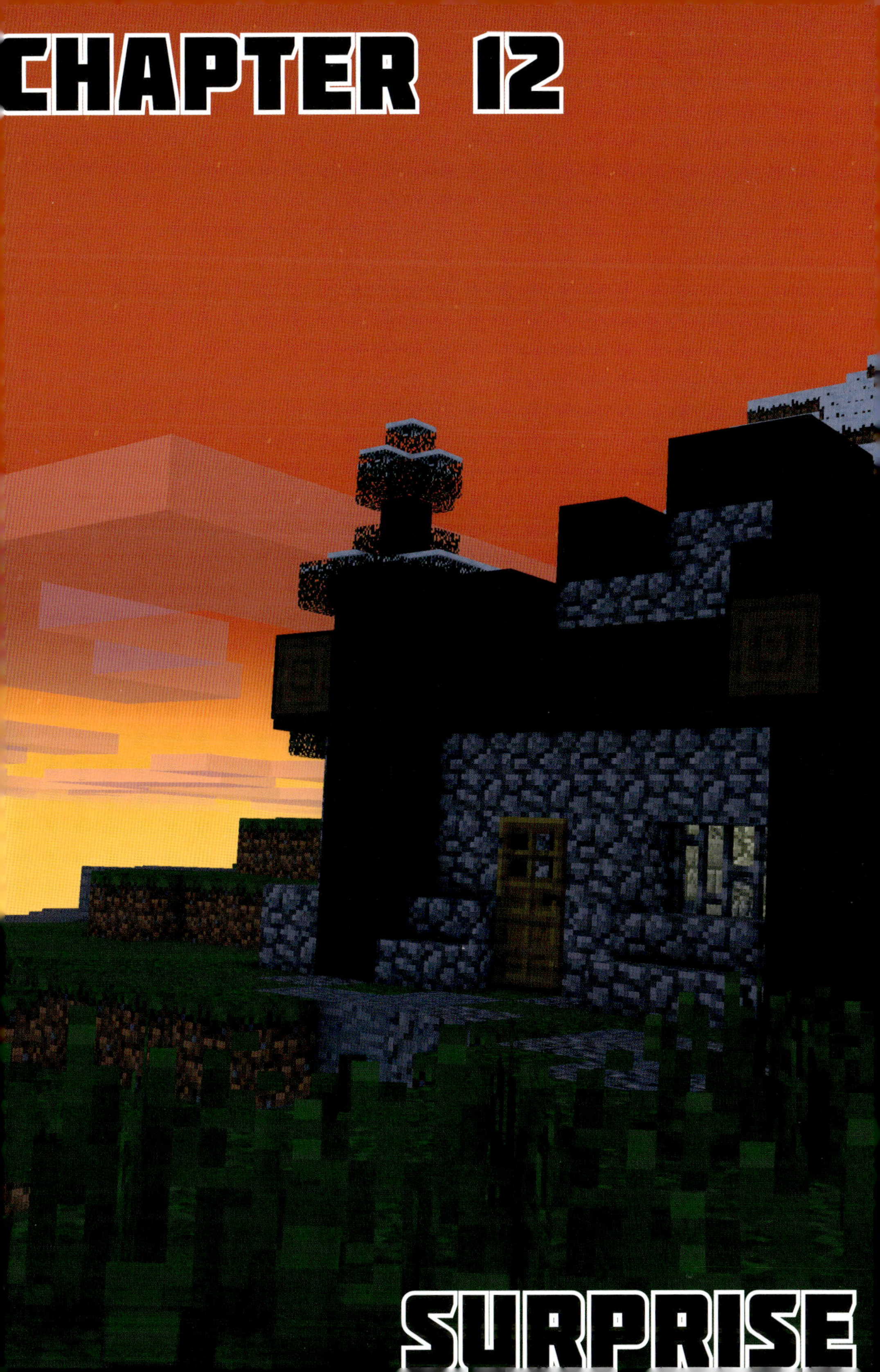

SURPRISE

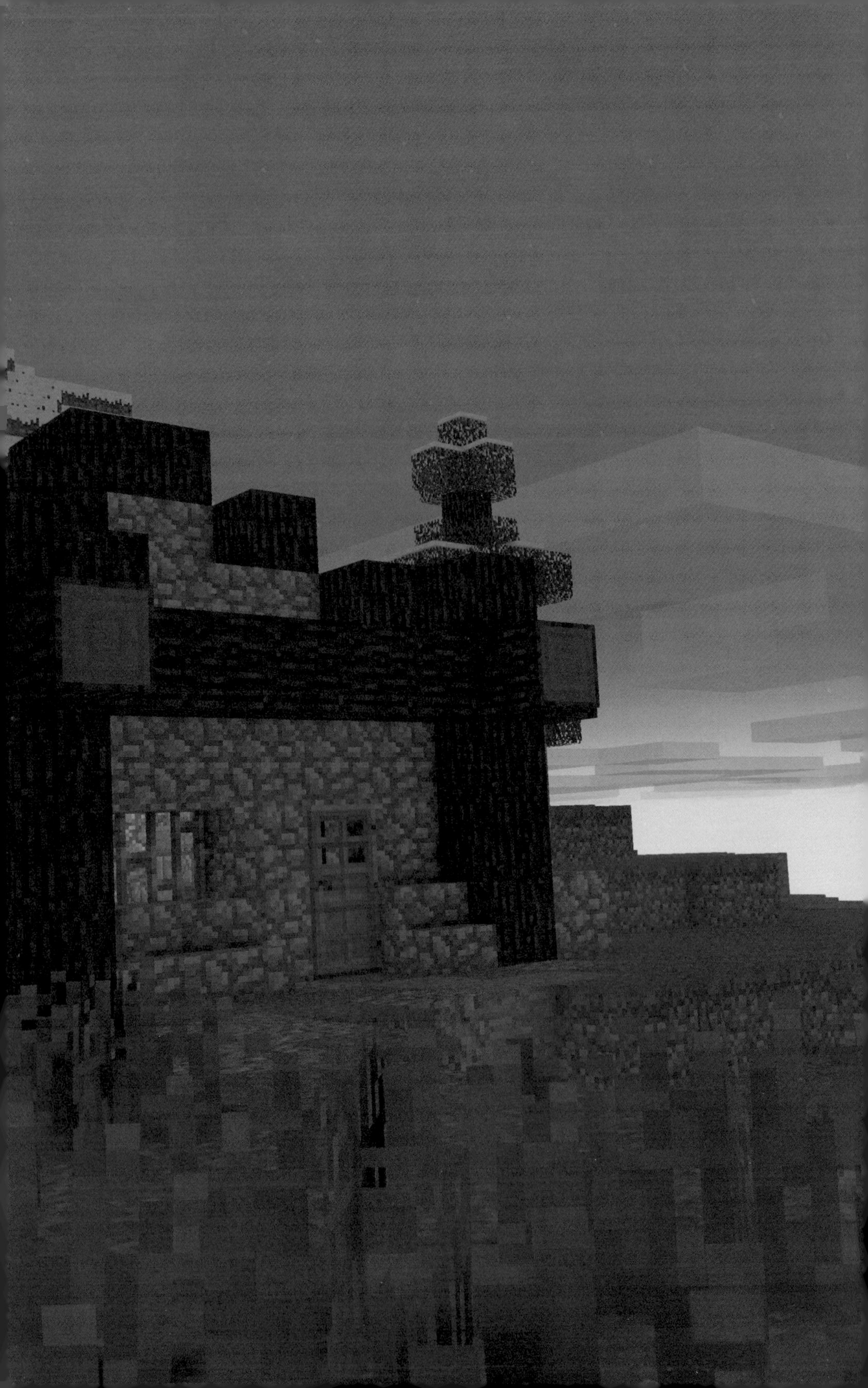

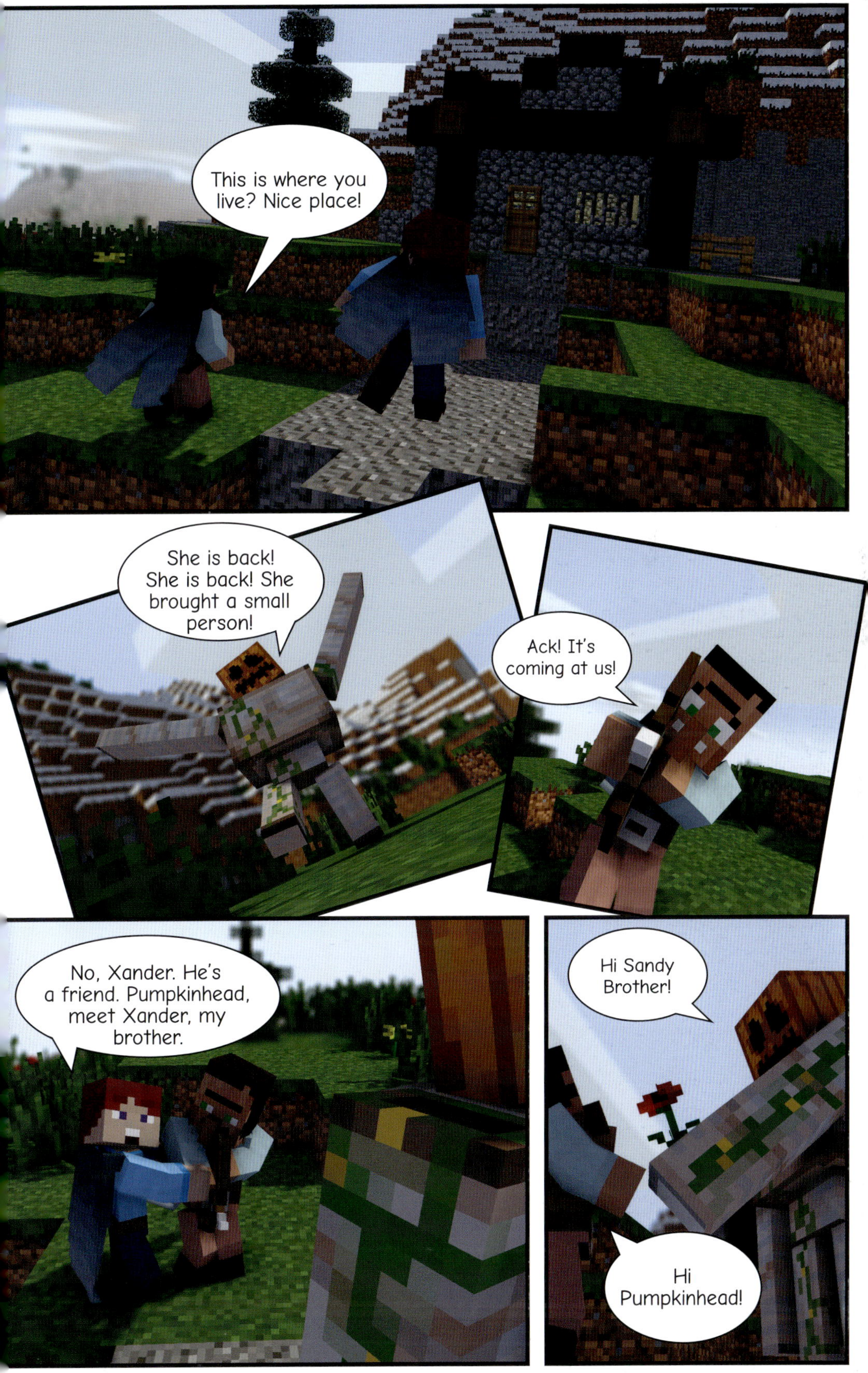
This is where you live? Nice place!
She is back! She is back! She brought a small person!
Ack! It's coming at us!
No, Xander. He's a friend. Pumpkinhead, meet Xander, my brother.
Hi Sandy Brother!
Hi Pumpkinhead!

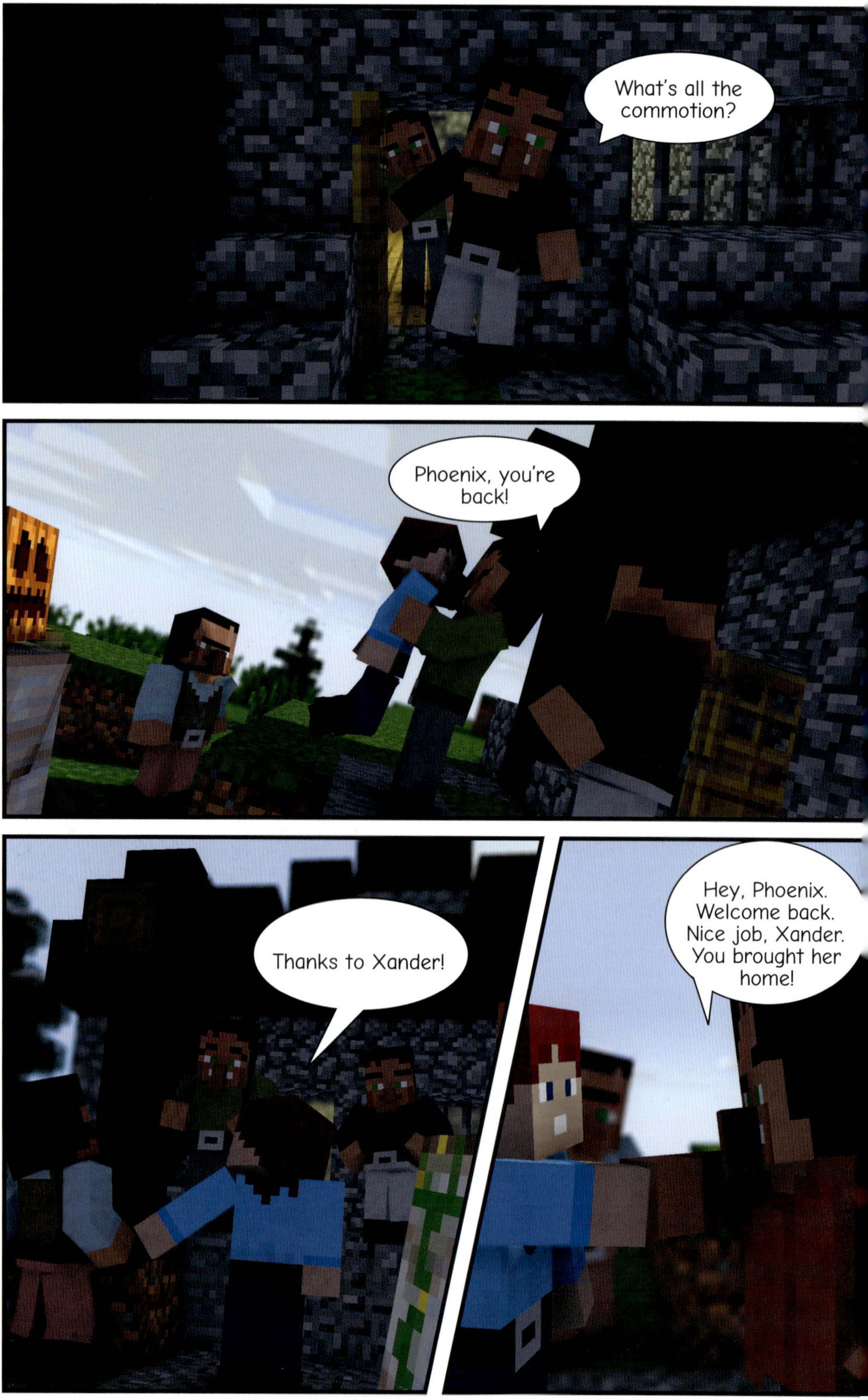
What's all the commotion?
Phoenix, you're back!
Thanks to Xander!
Hey, Phoenix. Welcome back. Nice job, Xander. You brought her home!

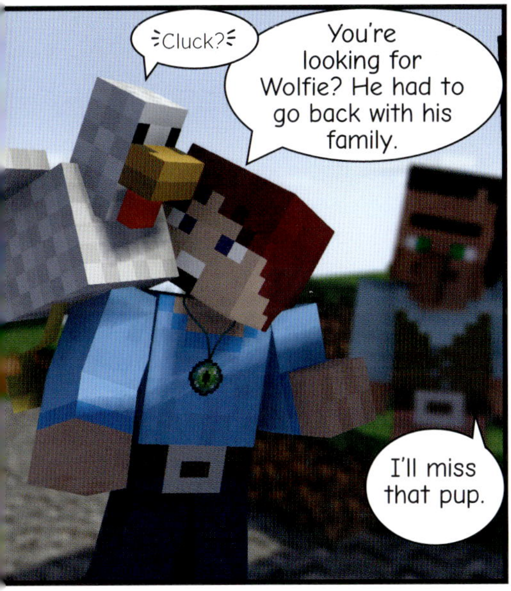
Cluck?
You're looking for Wolfie? He had to go back with his family.
I'll miss that pup.

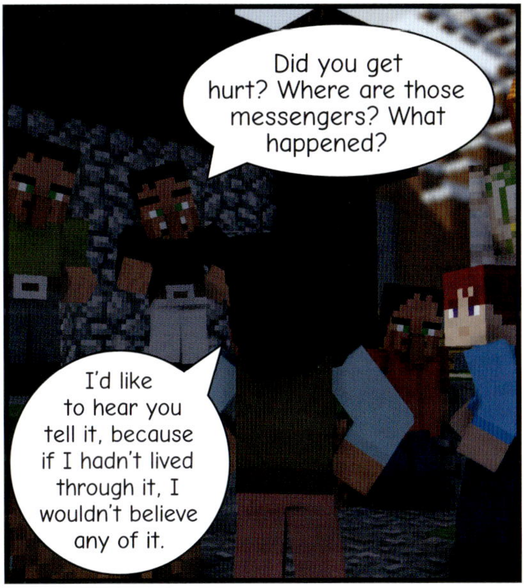
Did you get hurt? Where are those messengers? What happened?
I'd like to hear you tell it, because if I hadn't lived through it, I wouldn't believe any of it.

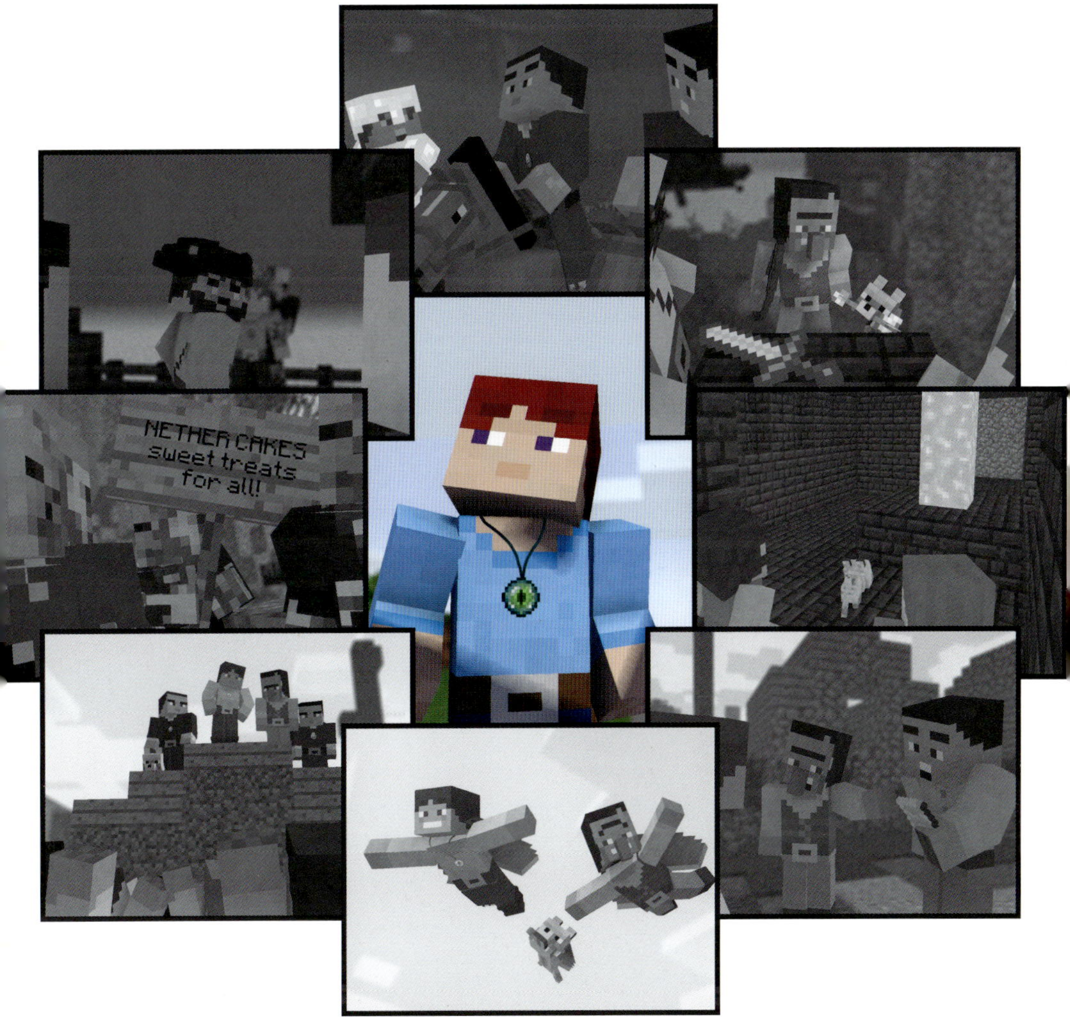
NETHER CAKES
sweet treats
for all!

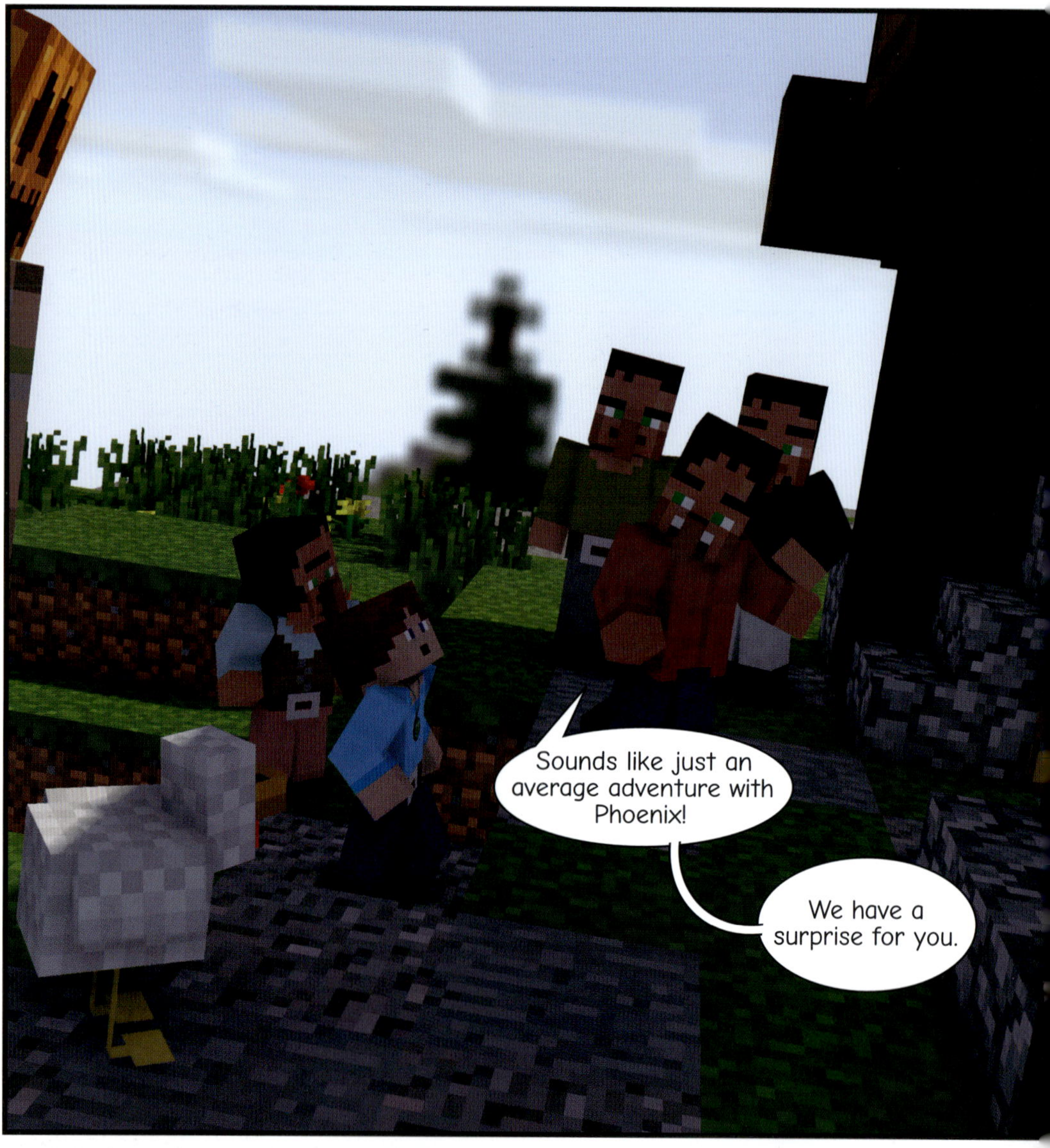
Sounds like just an average adventure with Phoenix!
We have a surprise for you.

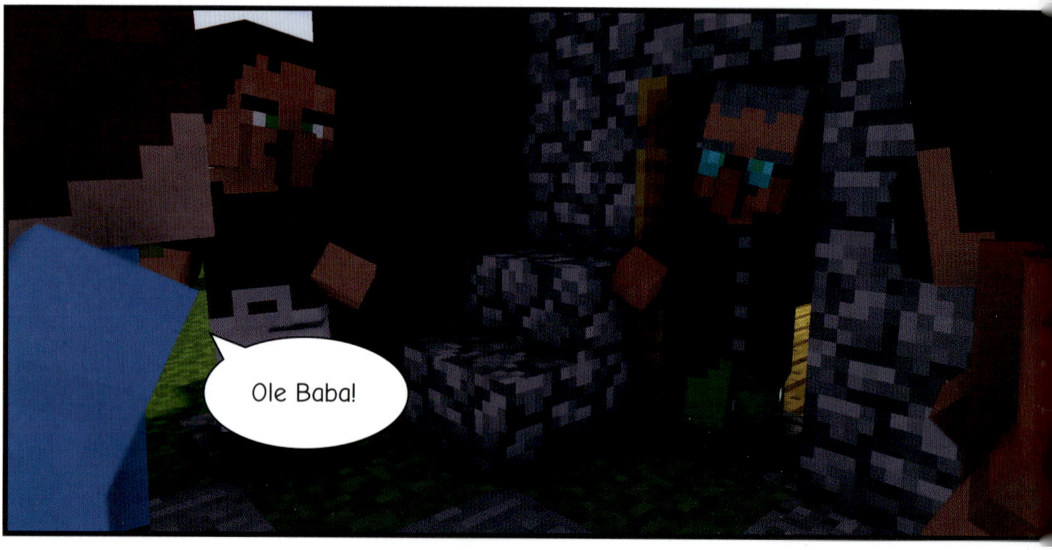
Ole Baba!

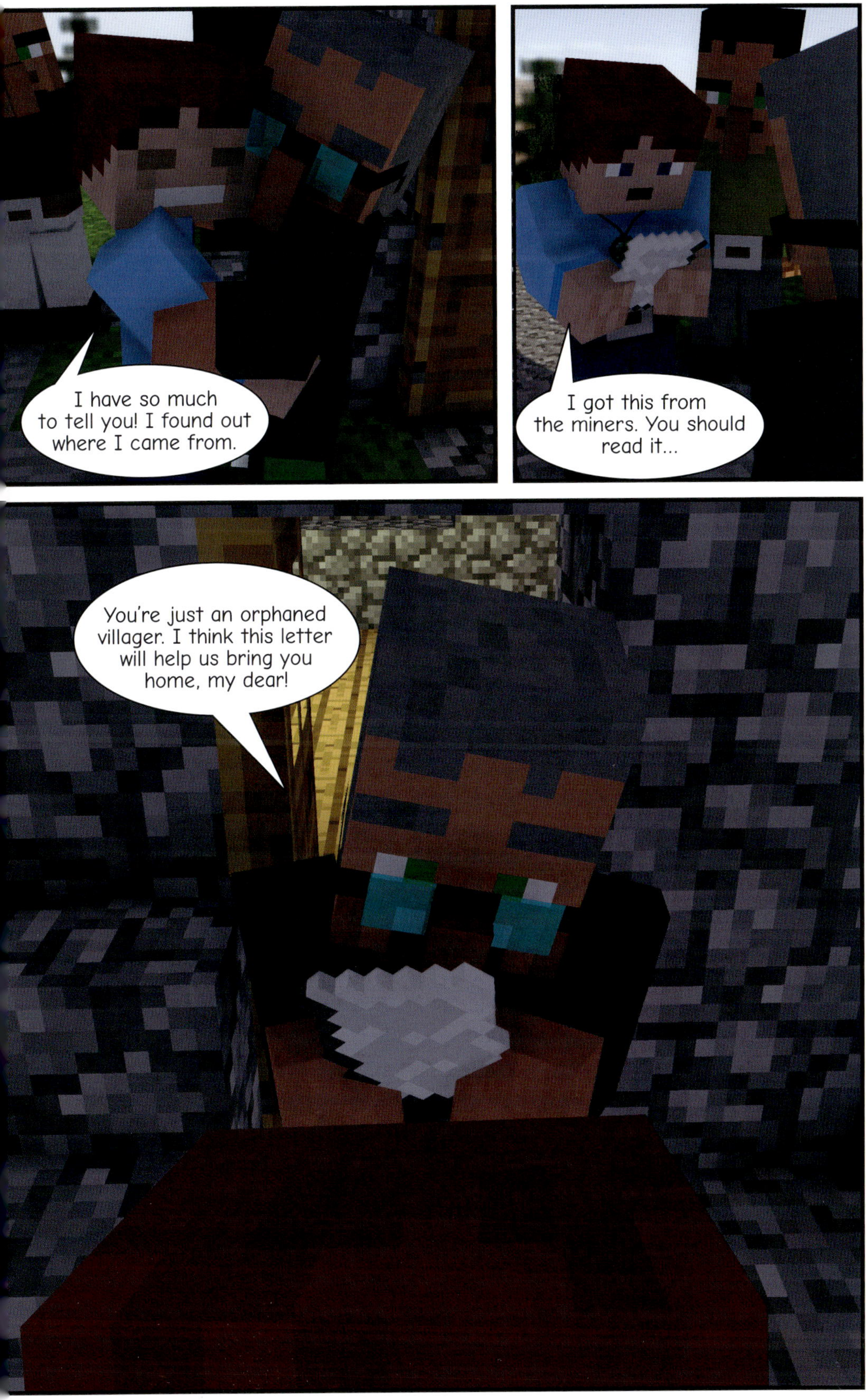
I have so much to tell you! I found out where I came from.
I got this from the miners. You should read it...
You're just an orphaned villager. I think this letter will help us bring you home, my dear!

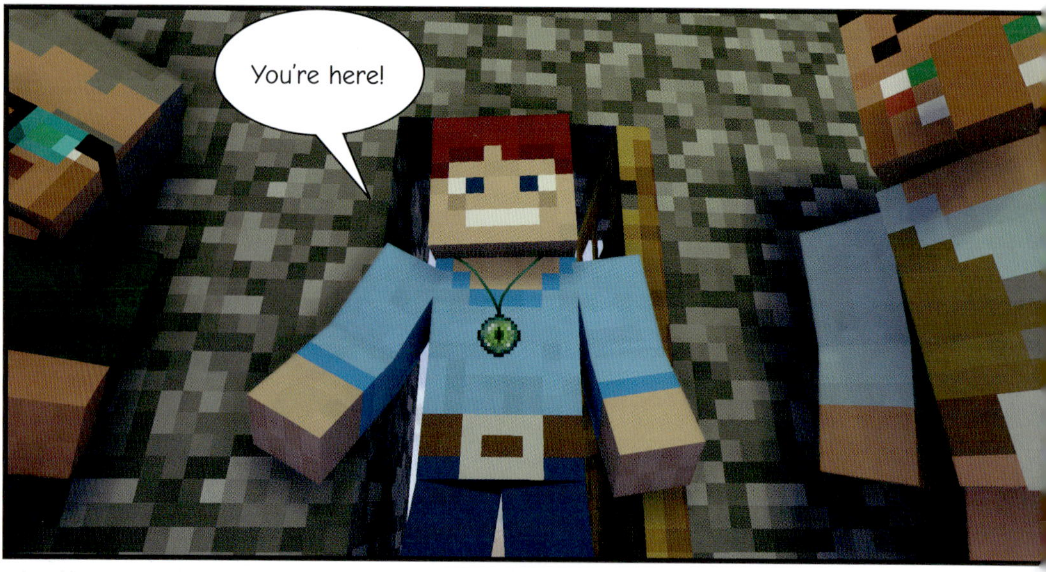
You're here!

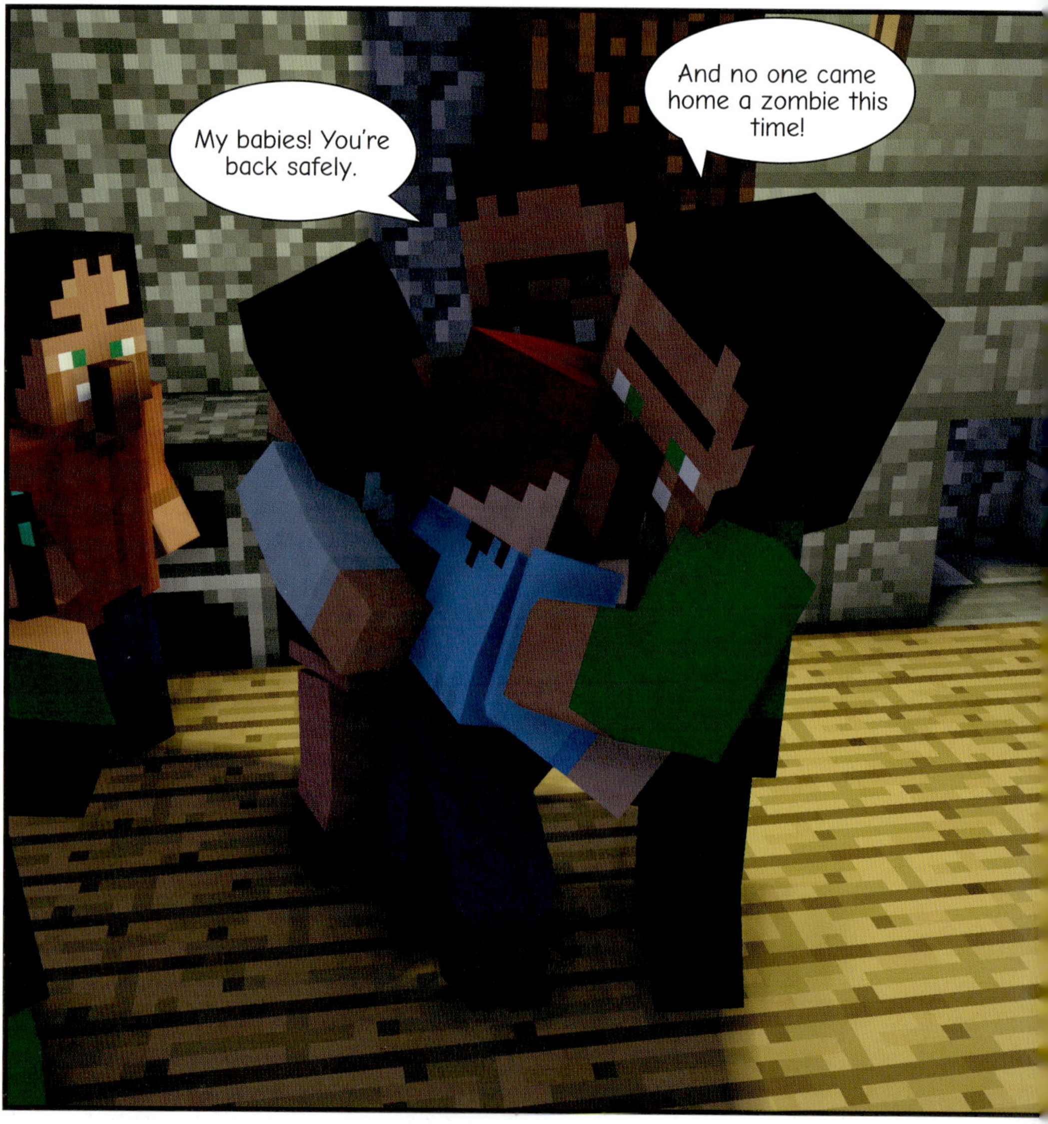
My babies! You're back safely.
And no one came home a zombie this time!

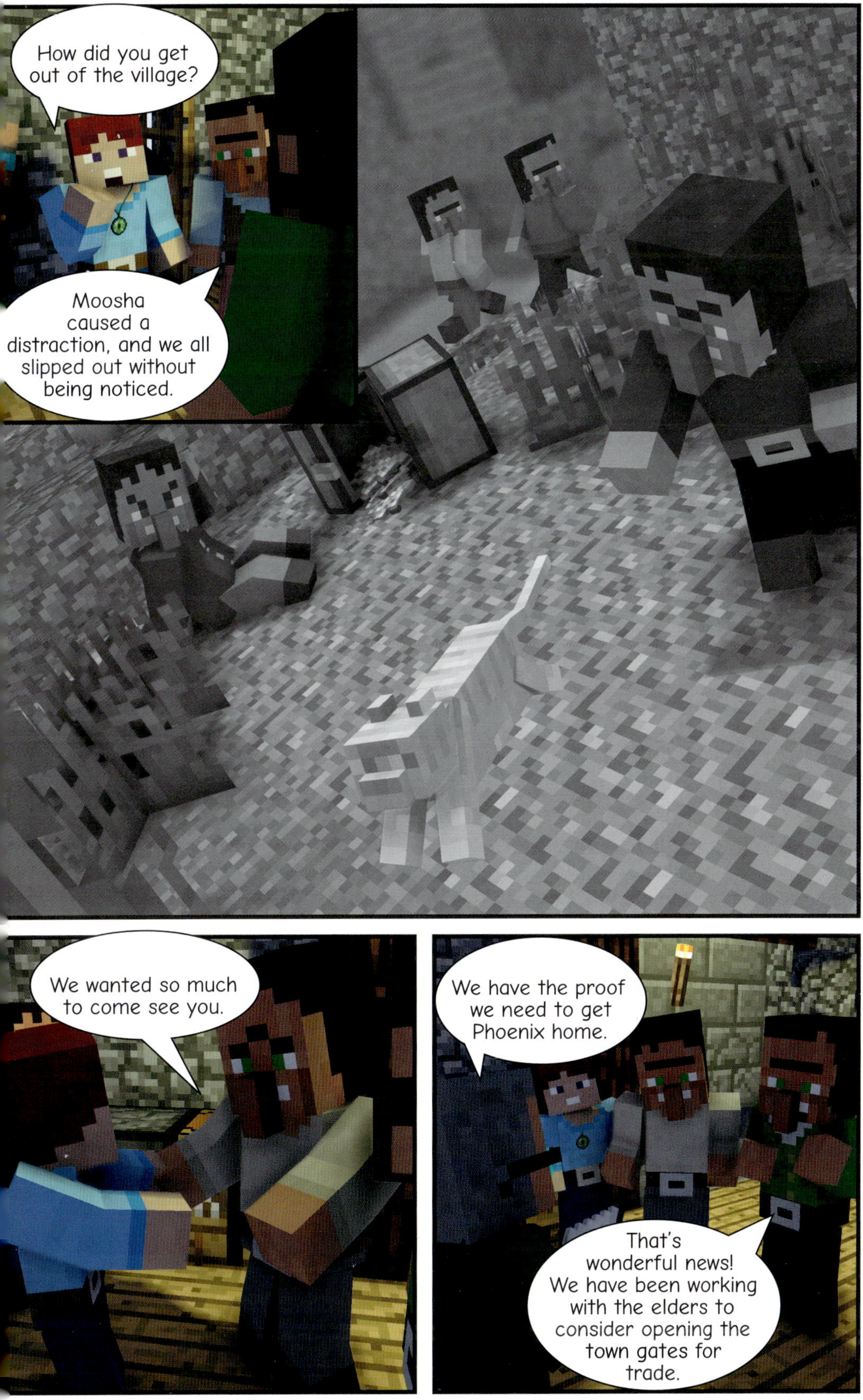
How did you get out of the village?
Moosha caused a distraction, and we all slipped out without being noticed.
We wanted so much to come see you.
We have the proof we need to get Phoenix home.
That's wonderful news! We have been working with the elders to consider opening the town gates for trade.

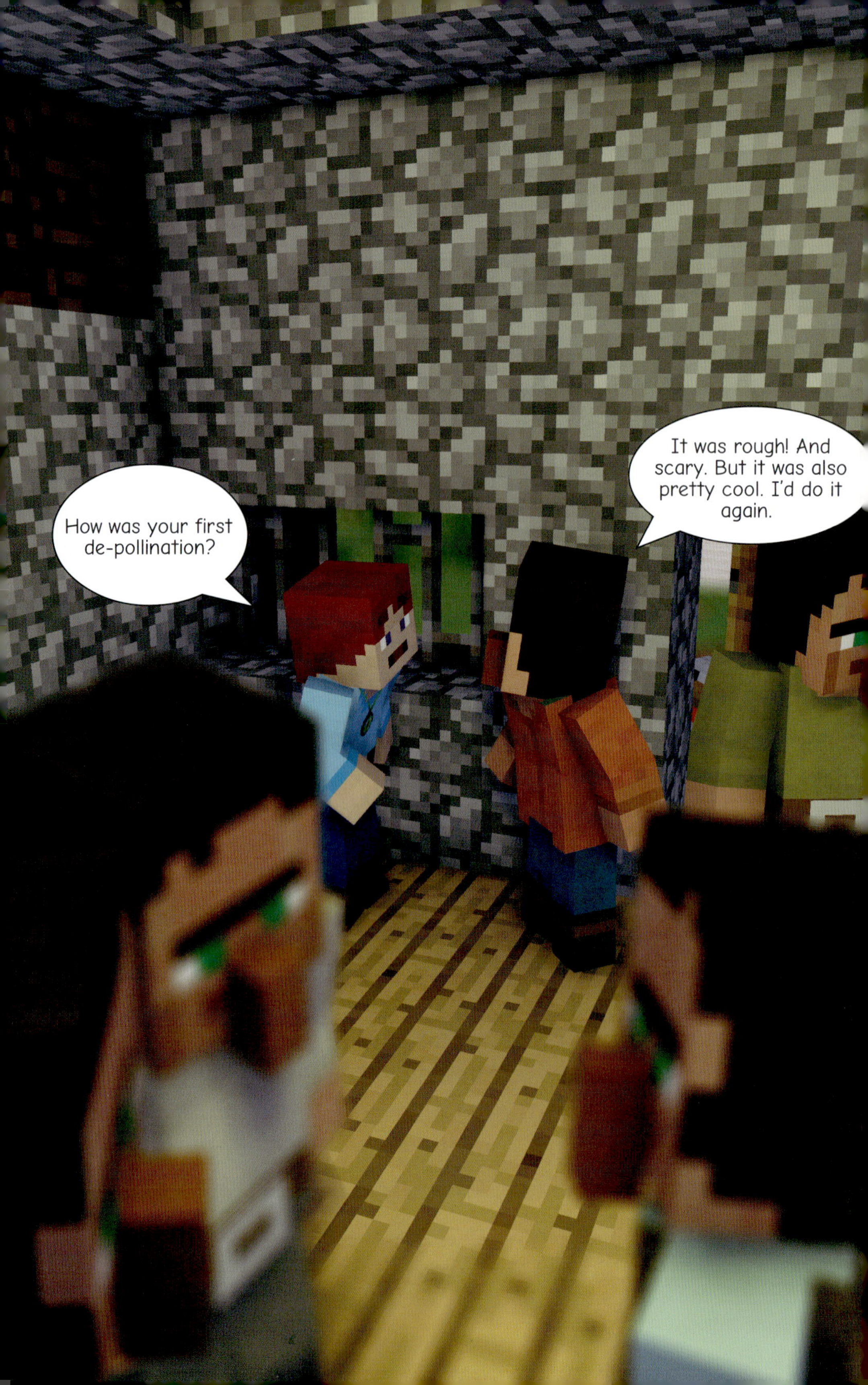
How was your first de-pollination?
It was rough! And scary. But it was also pretty cool. I'd do it again.

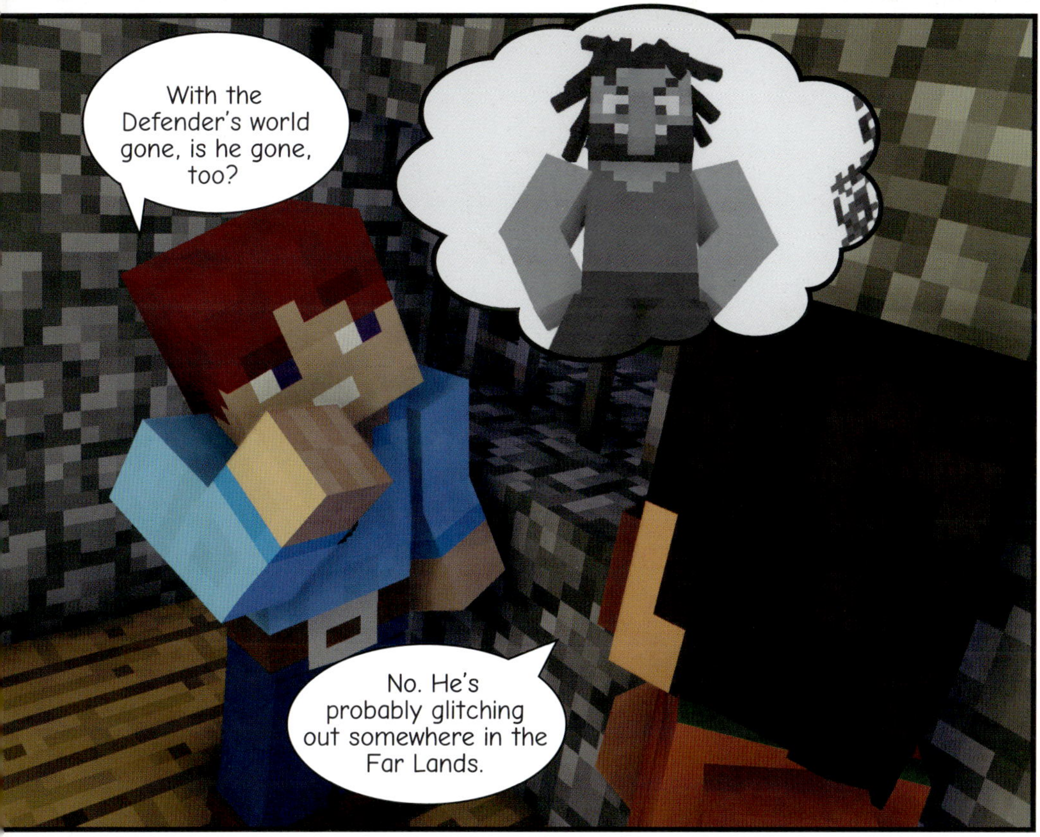
With the Defender's world gone, is he gone, too?
No. He's probably glitching out somewhere in the Far Lands.

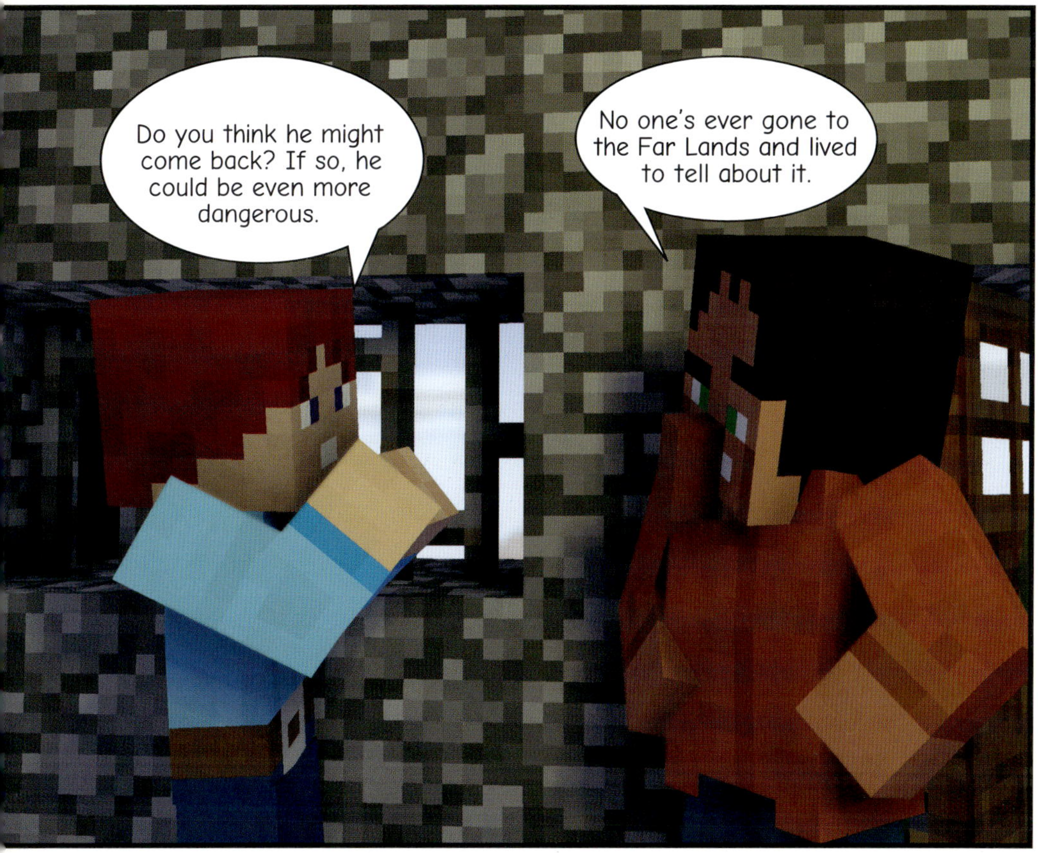
Do you think he might come back? If so, he could be even more dangerous.
No one's ever gone to the Far Lands and lived to tell about it.

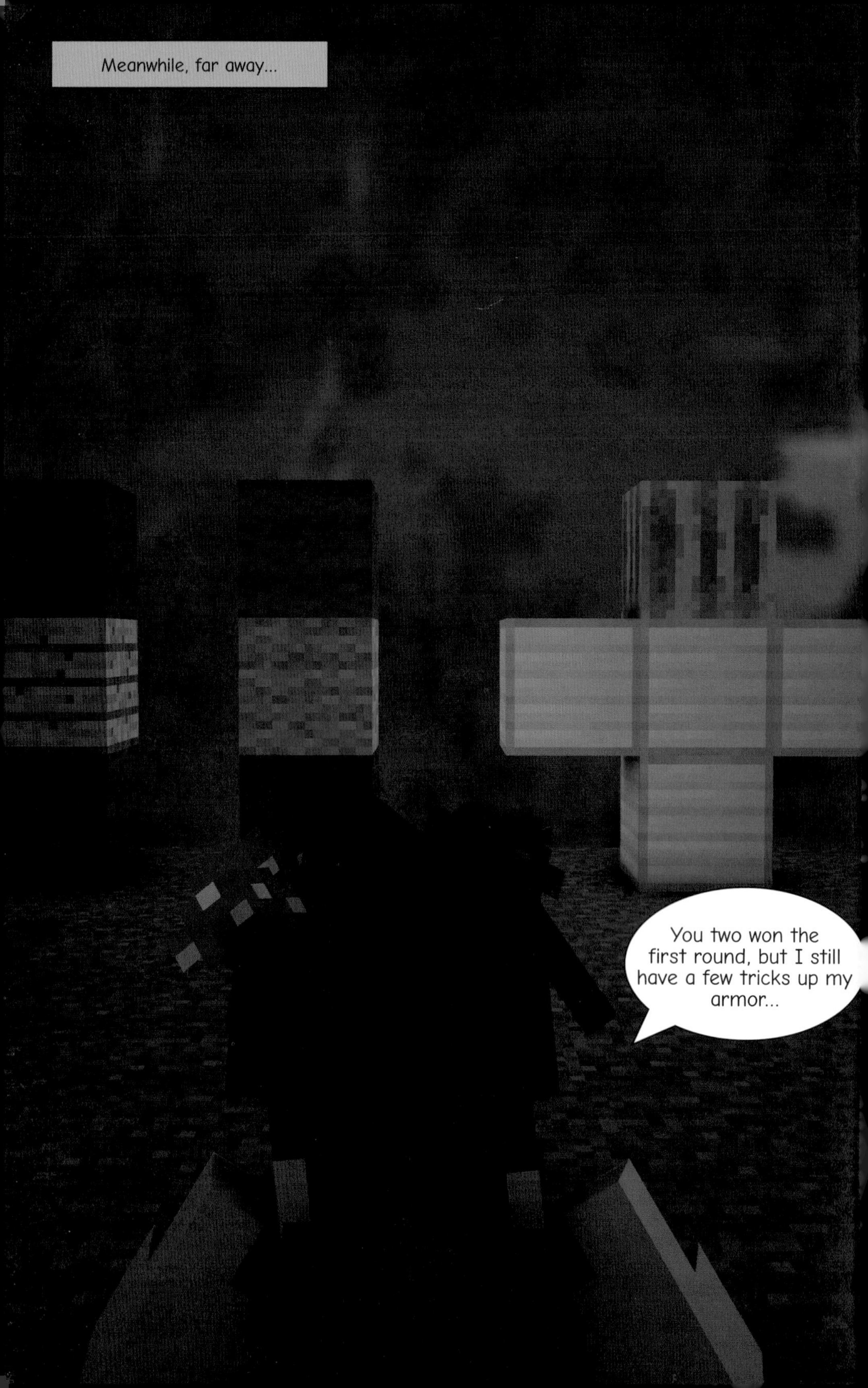
Meanwhile, far away...
You two won the first round, but I still have a few tricks up my armor...

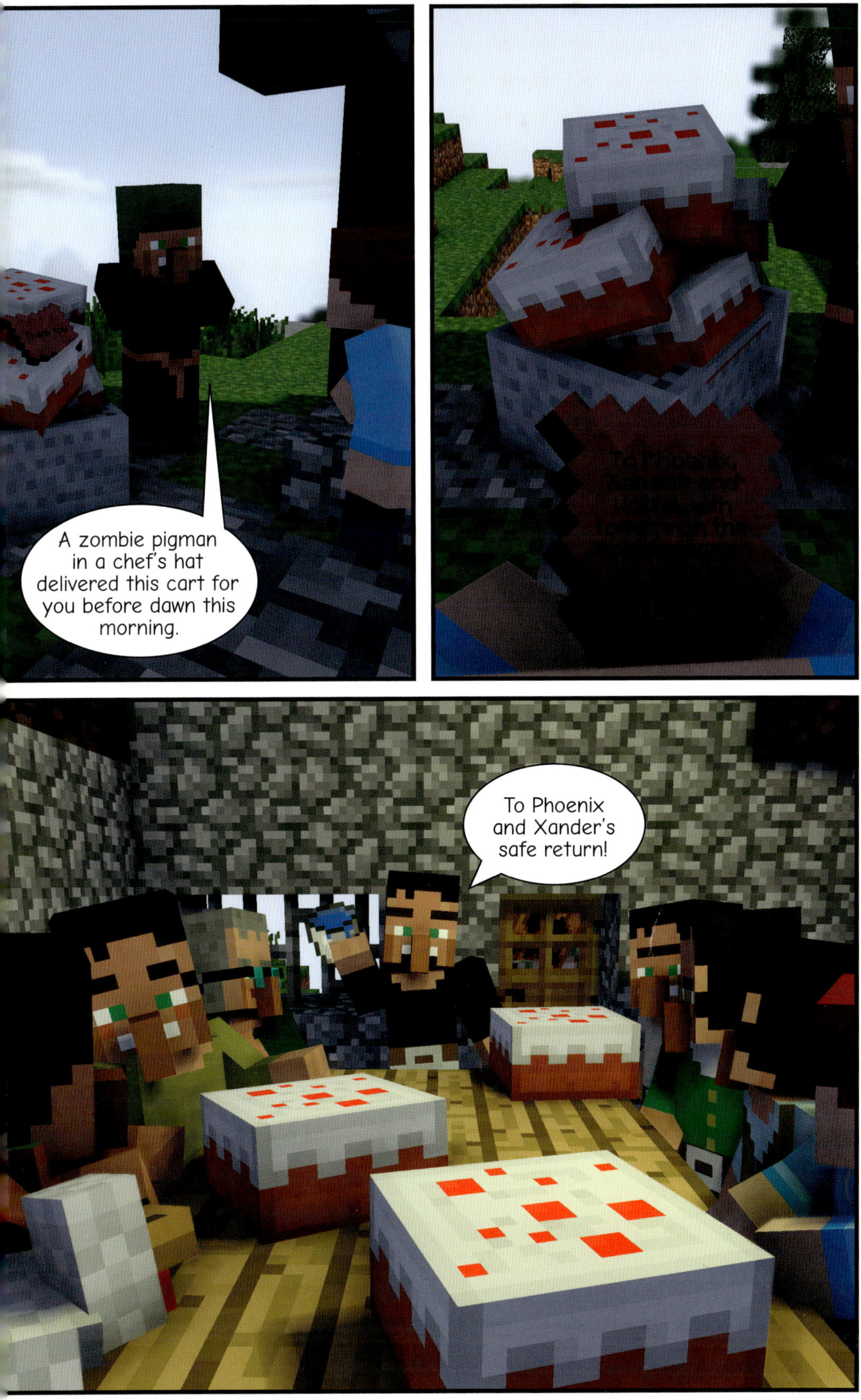
A zombie pigman in a chef's hat delivered this cart for you before dawn this morning.
To Phoenix and Xander's safe return!

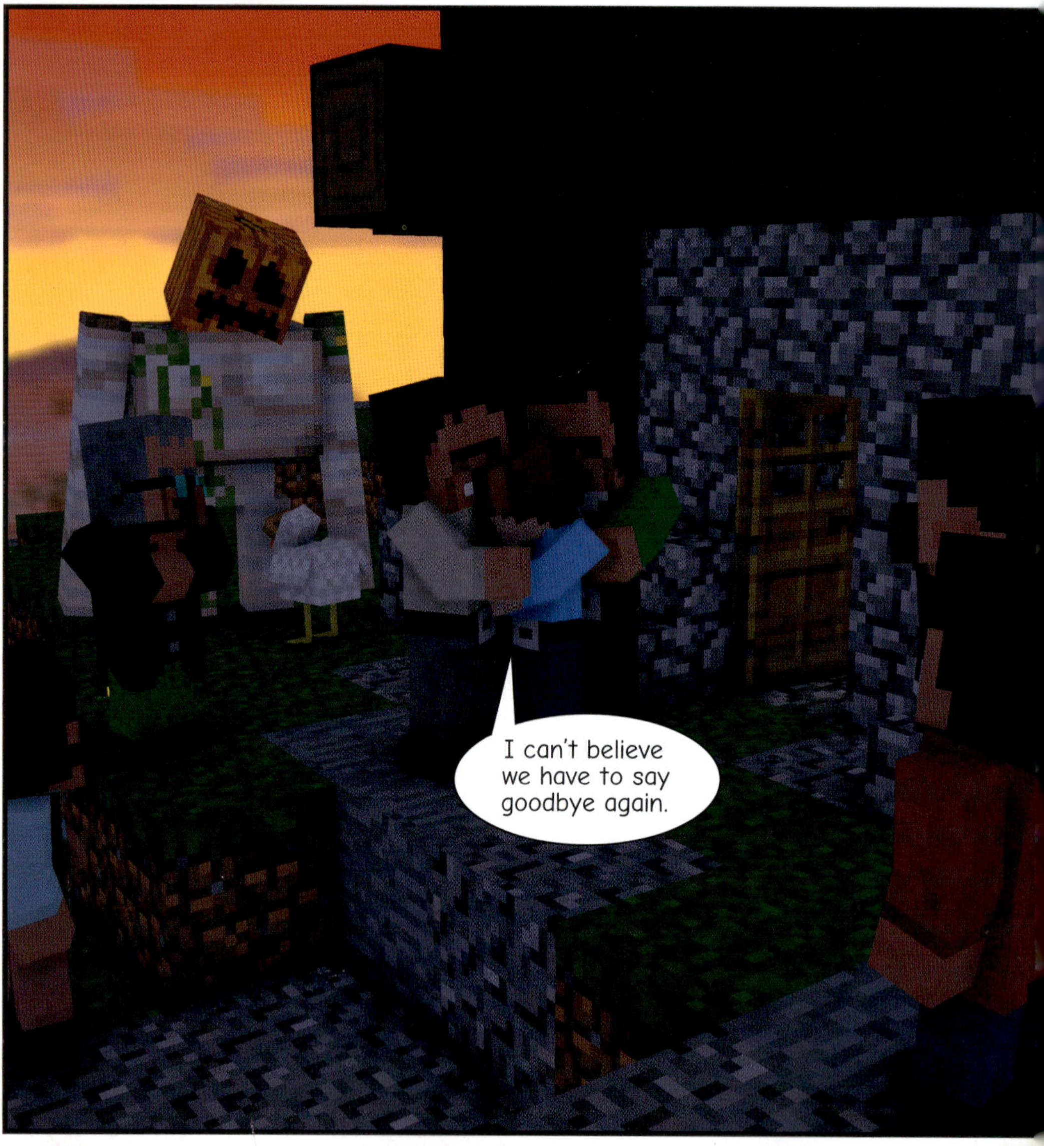
I can't believe we have to say goodbye again.

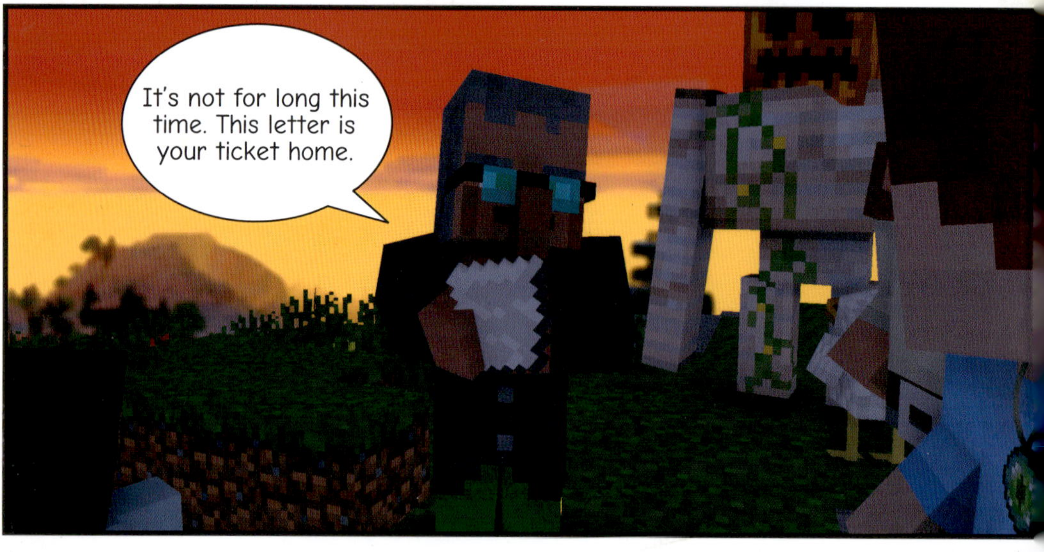
It's not for long this time. This letter is your ticket home.

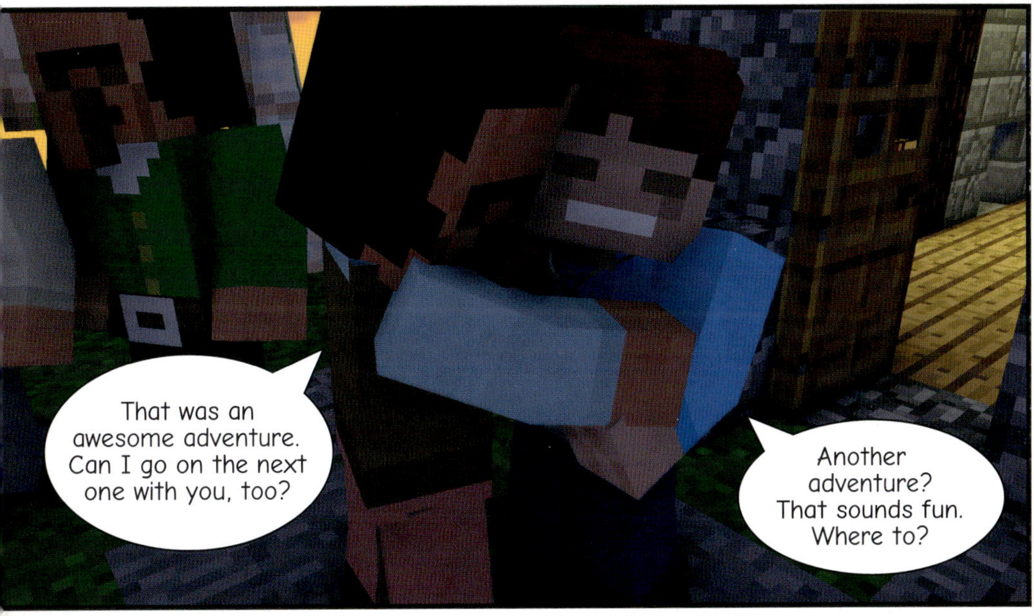
That was an awesome adventure. Can I go on the next one with you, too?
Another adventure? That sounds fun. Where to?

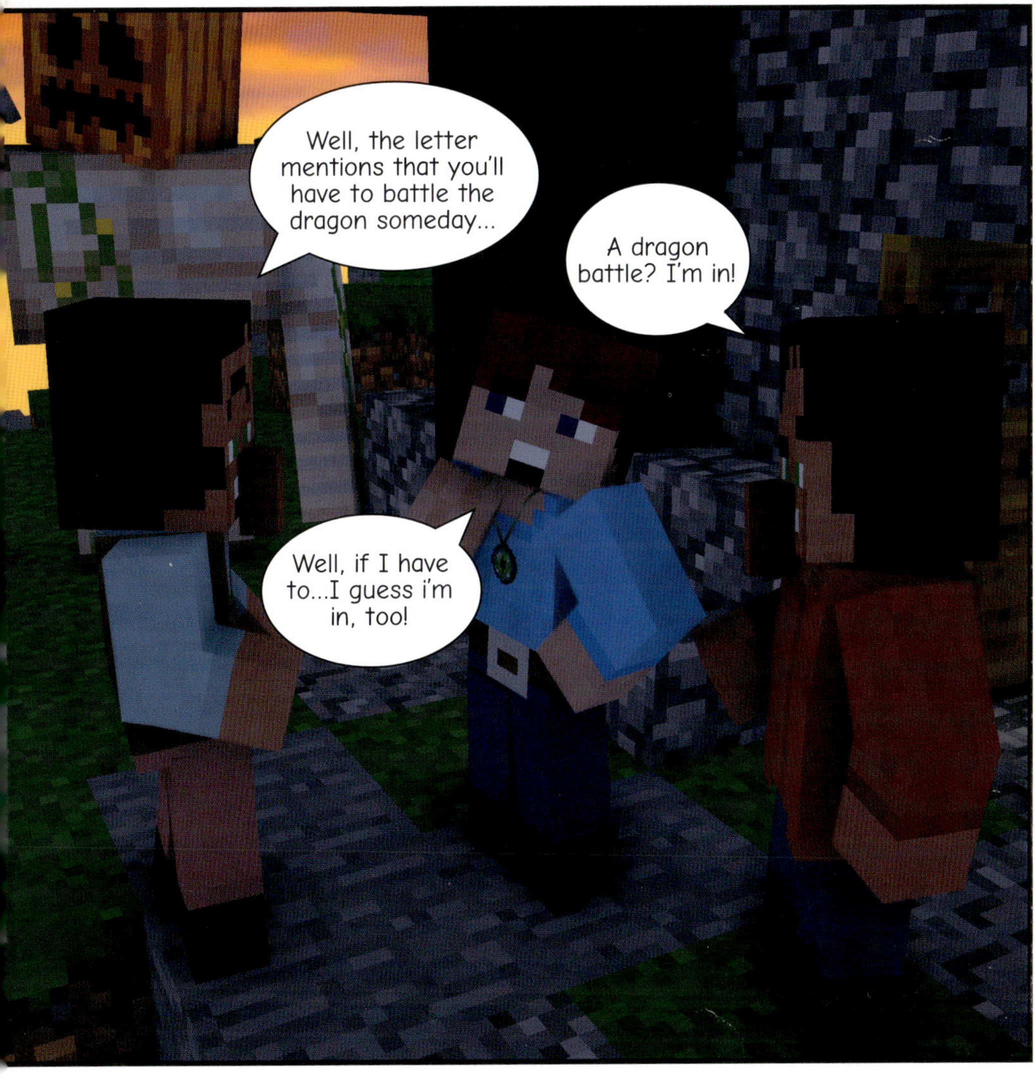
Well, the letter mentions that you'll have to battle the dragon someday...
A dragon battle? I'm in!
Well, if I have to...I guess i'm in, too!

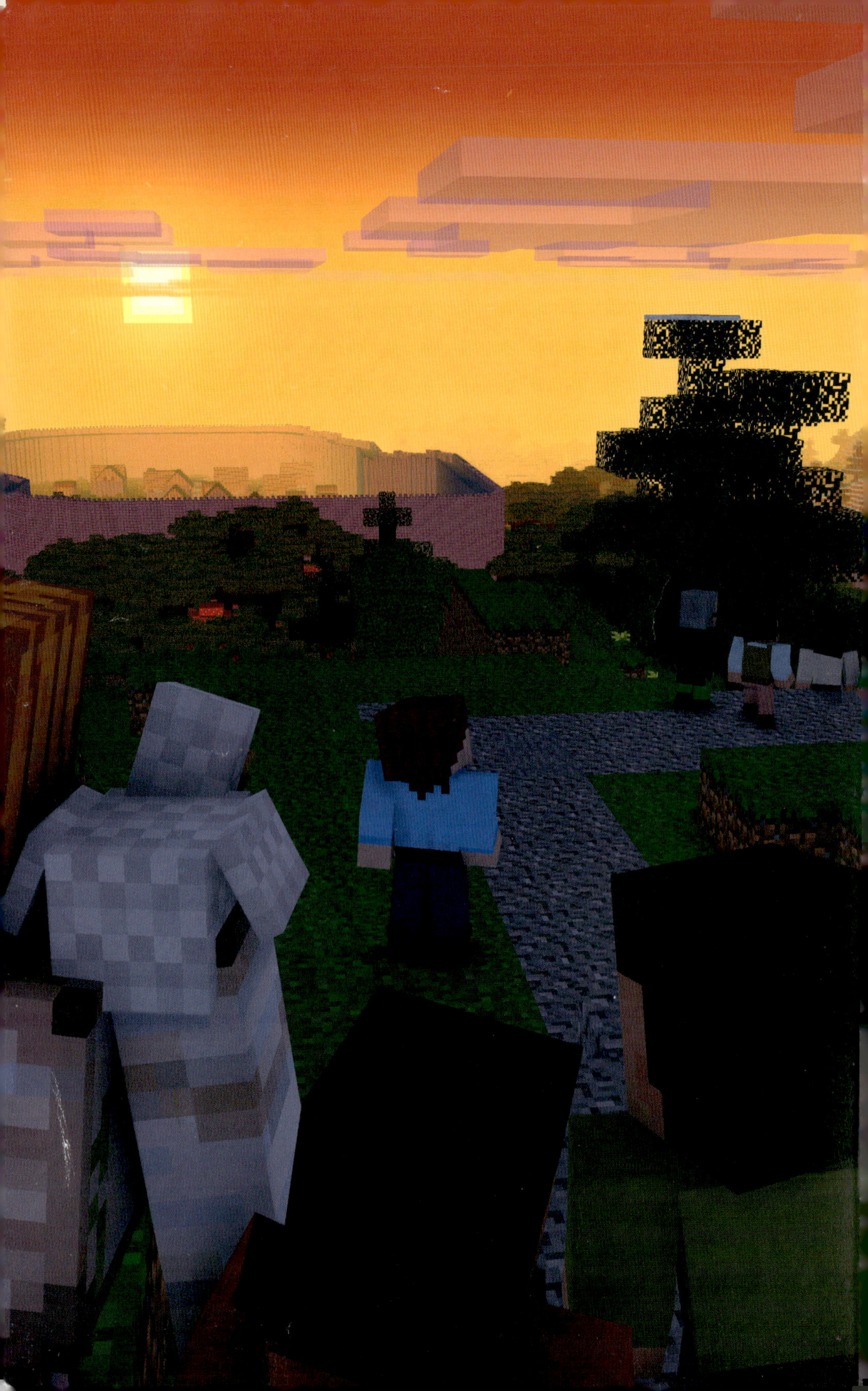